ROOM ONE HUNDRED

A Tinkerer's Tale

ALSO BY CHARLOTTE GEHLE

The Elemental: Rise of the Shade

ROOM ONE HUNDRED

A Tinkerer's Tale

Charlotte Gehle

Copyright © 2017 by Charlotte Gehle Original

Published in the United States by Charlotte Gehle

ISBN 978-0-9888489-3-1

*For my mom and dad, Jeff, Matt, and
Whittney, the family I was born with.*

*For Beth, Laura, Rob, Jack, Connor, Kate, Gavin, Cohen, and
Addison, who filled our family with happiness and smiles.*

*For Dave, Deb, Chris, Logan, Abby, Olivia, Shannon, Kaylie,
and Jenna, the family I was lucky enough to marry into.*

*For the friends I think of as family, Andrea, Abby, and
Todd, who always seem to be there when I need them.*

*And, most especially, for my best friend, my husband
Ben, who makes things better, just by being himself.*

CHAPTER ONE

As far as Zara Turner was concerned, there were two types of people in the world, those who tinkered and those who did not. Zara was a singular-minded sort of a young woman, the sort who focused on her work and forgot that the world around her moved and changed. She forgot that others went out and lived in the world, while she sat inside, tinkering away at her inventions. Her best friends were automatons, cat and dog bots—robots and machines that spoke to her in metallic voices. She found the timbre of their non-human voices soothing, or so her application to the Crow's Nest said.

Zara was in her final semester at the Tinker's Academy, at the top of her class. Other students went out and lived, drank beer at the local taverns, got into mischief and had an overall bang-up good time. Zara Turner did not.

That was what threw him.

Mr. Gilbert Wills, the head of the Crow's Nest listened to the blonde-haired, freckled young woman explain Spy-ders, an invention of hers, patent pending. She very brilliantly created these little spiders made of metal and microchip, then tinkered with them to make them spy worthy. She meant them to be for government use. The Spy-ders went into a room undetected, spun a small web in the corner where, with radio waves and a small gramophone on its ear, it recorded the conversations unnoticed—two hours' worth—packed up its web, then left and returned back to the person who sent it out. That was a brilliant bit of tech, and it was one of five amazing inventions she brought to the table. Bulletproof umbrella with a gun in the handle, pocket watch with a controlled blast good for opening a safe. Coffee pot that heated itself and a refrigeration unit that kept creamer cold, along with a few snacks, marvelous for a stakeout and personal use. Those two were being sold all over, she was making money as they caught on. Not much, but some. She would have a job with the government, no matter where Mr. Wills put her.

But where to put her?

She wanted to work in Room Thirty, with all the other Tinkerers. She was quiet, withdrawn, and never looked anyone in the eye for long. He sighed. She was giving her speech and putting over half the room asleep with her technical jargon. That was not an exaggeration. Mr. Wills actually saw five men asleep, five! She was fairly boring, yet oddly endearing. She was so excited, her pretty face was alive with delight. Several young men she went to school with and the ones, like himself, who had no interest in how the Spy-ders worked, were enchanted. Mr. Wills glanced around and hid a smile. They were completely enamored by her, especially the other tinkerers.

To put it plainly, Zara Turner was lovely and had no idea how beautiful she was. She was freckled, all over her body, arms, neck—every place! They were adorable. She was tall and slender, stood eye to eye with most men, not overly curvy, but distinctly female; her thin hands were small, her voice soft and sweet. She had a mass of very thick, golden hair that was braided over one shoulder. Her eyes were set wide and sky blue, framed with blonde lashes and brows. She had full lips and beautiful teeth, a button nose. Zara was not traditionally beautiful by Jakardian standards, most men favored dark-haired woman with dark eyes and lush curves, but there was just something about her. Even with her dull talk and lack of social skills.

She stood before the room dressed in a simple, knee-length brown skirt with a white shirt—modest with a high neck and a ruffle at the front. She wore short boots that matched the color of her skirt perfectly. They were of the very latest fashion and style, of course, because her mother ran Turner's Fashion Emporium. The woman was a designer clothing empire, and she knew how to dress women of every shape and size—her daughter was no exception. Her mother picked out all of Zara's clothing, she had told Mr. Wills so when he interviewed her and according to her mother, Zara let her automaton maid dress her, creating some kind of a chip for the bot that tracked which pieces went with what. Mrs. Turner told Mr. Wills that Zara had no fashion sense at all, as if it were the greatest offense a woman could make. Mr. Wills thought that it was resourceful of her—to use the bot, given her ineptitude for dressing herself; it impressed him that she would know her weaknesses and use her talents to compensate for them. Not everyone could be a fashion maven like Zara's mother. Regardless of how she came to be wearing what she had on, Miss Turner looked beautiful. He had not expected her to be beautiful.

Her sisters were hideous and her mother marginally attractive, at best!

Both her sisters were older—models for Mrs. Turner at her shop. Caitlyn, two years older than Zara's twenty-two years, reminded Mr. Wills of a lollipop. That was the most polite way to describe her. She had a massive head, just gigantic, and a very tiny, very thin body. She was not unpleasant looking, her features were fine, brown eyes and hair, same as the eldest sister, Temperance. To give credit where it was due, Temperance had a magnificent figure, lush curves, large perfect breasts, along with a huge hooked nose, beady eyes and, bless her, beaver teeth like her mother's that didn't quite fit in her mouth. Mrs. Turner used her eldest daughters on the campaign to sell her clothing. Their pictures were plastered all over the land of Jakarda, especially here in Jakarda City. The general consensus was, if those clothes could make those two very odd and unattractive-looking Turner girls look presentable, imagine what they could do with your attractive daughters?

He came in expecting to see a girl that looked like them. Instead, he saw a graceful, beautiful, freckled girl with intelligent eyes and a charming smile. But what to do with her?

Mr. Wills sighed, fidgeting in the uncomfortable red velvet seat in the presentation theater of the Academy. Zara's father had worked for the Crow's Nest. Hal Turner was an excellent Tinkerer, but he had nothing on his daughter. She beat his test scores by over twenty points. She was the top scorer on the Academy tests since its inception sixty years ago, when Jakarda separated from the Folliesend Empire and became a superpower of its own. She made a tinkerer joke and the other tinkerers laughed. He smiled to be polite, even though he didn't understand the damn joke. It was a good one, because they were laughing delightedly. She went back to being dull, bless her heart. He sighed and watched her, brow furrowed. Where to put her? Room One Hundred as an agent? Or Room Thirty with the tinkerers who stayed inside behind a desk?

His nephew needed to find a tinker that was willing to work with him.

Harrison was troublesome, bless him. Although Mr. Wills loved him dearly, he was just so impulsive, always putting other agents and tinkerers in the line of fire. Usually Harrison managed to come out unscathed, but his tinkerers—less suited to hand to hand combat—were usually pretty banged up when they worked with him. Harrison was charming, handsome, confident, and, a huge pain in the butt. He was reckless and overconfident. He was his best agent admittedly, but he drove off every tinkerer they got in Room One Hundred because his plans were spur of the moment and often completely improvised. The truth was, he normally only considered how only he would get out of sticky situations himself, not the person with him.

Wills' other agents were fine, they knew this about him and adapted to his spur of the moment plans, adjusting with them and keeping themselves safe. The tinkerers, more suited to gadgetry building and working on the sidelines, most often left with a broken bone or a gunshot wound some place being the result of that pairing. Eventually they tired of missions with Harrison, then flatly refused to work with him, asking for a transfer. It suited Harrison just fine, he hated them all, except Dill, who started in Room One Hundred the same day Harrison did. Harrison had taken a shine to Dill. But could this girl be another Dill?

Mr. Wills had five agents in Room One Hundred. Dill was a tinkerer, he went with the agents on cases, but he was no good at the social situations, his workload was too much to handle these days. That might have been why Harrison liked him. He was always mentioning how tinkerers slowed him down, how Dill knew just when to get involved. Harrison knew he needed their expertise, freely admitted to that, he just could not understand why they were so cautious, why they were shaken when guns and blast guns went off, or why they disliked being blown up. That was his nephew for you. He lived for the excitement, thought everyone else should, too. That, perhaps, was his greatest shortcoming.

Mr. Wills needed someone who would be better in the field, kept a cool head when guns were fired and did not run from a fight, some tinkerers left Harrison on his own. He was furious of course—bad form, that. Harrison had chased off five other tinkerers so far. And he had only worked in the department for the past six years! He terrified or injured at least one tinker so many times in a year, they would demand a transfer, leaving poor Dill to fill in. Dill was wonderful and adaptable most of the time, but the lad was not suited to highbrow events. He hated balls and art galas, or anything you had to dress up to go to. He was more of a behind the scenes man. And he was Mr. Wills' best! Dill stuck with his agents, always. Room One Hundred had six agents, himself included. He needed two tinkerers for six agents at a minimum, his boss insisted. Dill was overworked and exhausted, he had asked for help.

Mr. Wills eyed Zara, uncertain if she could manage the job. She was terribly soft spoken and quiet. All he knew was, his nephew was slightly more cautious when a lady was involved. It was his plan to bring in a female tinkerer all along. Harrison had been seeing another agent, FeFe LaMay, for several months. His sister hated her, he didn't blame her. She wasn't the sort of lady you wanted your son to end up with. FeFe enjoyed the company of men, she was polished and sexy, confident, clever, too, but she was a female version of Harrison. Perfect female agent, horrible for his nephew. They let one another act recklessly, never once considering they could be better agents and people if they tried a bit harder to change some bad behaviors, because they both felt they had none to change.

Mr. Wills clapped when Zara finished her presentation with a smile. She was the last to present. A few young men came to speak with her. She smiled at them, chatting softly as she packed up her Spy-ders, answering their questions, hugging her elbows behind her back, her head tilted to the side. She looked as pretty as a picture up there, those freckles suited her. He'd have to speak with her, it was as simple as that.

Mr. Wills walked to the front of the room as the others filtered away. She looked at him as he approached. She was prettier in person, delicate looking. She was more pale than most ladies, and there were those freckles. He found he liked them even more up close. They suited her, made her look adorable, if you asked him. Her father had freckles, too, and she looked like him, but softer, sweeter. He offered her a smile.

"Hello, Miss Turner. I wanted to tell you, I very much enjoyed your presentation," he said.

She smiled warmly at him, "Oh, thank you, Mister…"

"Wills. My name is Gilbert Wills, I'm with the Crow's Nest," he said.

She blinked, then adjusted her clothes a little. "Oh. It's nice to meet you, sir."

Mr. Wills smiled, "And you! I was a friend of your father's."

Her expression softened, "You knew my papa?"

He smiled then because her expression was so wistful, "Yes. Yes, I knew Hal. He worked with me for, oh, twelve years."

In Room One Hundred?" she said.

He arched his brows, "You know, then?"

"That he was a field agent? Of course, I knew. He told me, for starters. He said I was sensible enough to figure it out. I already had at eight, just never asked him. Plus, a normal tinkerer is not blown to bits in a dirigible above Jakarda City on the job. He should never have left his desk, right?" she teased, with a little smile.

"Indeed!" he said with a chuckle. Mr. Wills studied her, then he did something he had never done in his twenty years with the Nest, "Tell me, would you like to be a field agent with the Nest?"

Her eyes widened in disbelief, "An agent? Me?"

"Yes, you, Miss Turner," he said.

Zara studied him, "I applied to work with the other tinkerers. I believe in the work you do there and I have an aptitude for spy gadgetry. I can keep a secret and I'm the best tinkerer this academy has ever seen."

"I agree with that, but not an answer to my question. Care to walk with me?" he said.

She glanced at the people hanging around, mostly young men. She nodded, "Certainly. Can I buy you a cup of coffee at the Tinker-Time Cafe, Mr. Wills?"

He smiled, "I'd love that, Miss Turner."

She picked up her leather bag and a small box full of Spy-ders with a smile and walked beside him. They took their time, making their way to the cafe in silence across the busy street littered with student tinkerers, most of them the rumpled, studious sort. The campus was a mechanical marvel, the students about carrying copper, silver and steel creations, chatting amiably, full of young people hoping to change their city, or even the world.

Jakarda was at the center of modern innovation. Tall skyscrapers, made of brick and metal, burst with people in steam powered cars and carriages driven by automatons on the paved streets that weaved throughout the stores, restaurants, tinkering firms and businesses. People came here to the city to see things grow, and change, because it moved faster here than any other place, and the modern people in it knew it was special. But, it was the Academy that made it great, churning out young people who planned to make it even better, bigger. Mr. Wills knew it to be true. The tinkerers, agents, police officers, business people, chemists, and so on from the Academy, they were the city's future. They were the reason for all this modernness, all this greatness. Which is why he so loved coming here to the Academy's, recruiting.

The cafe was popular with the students, but nearly empty at the moment at three in the afternoon. It was a decent place, clean, but inexpensive to suit the needs of the student population, with pictures of popular tinkerer inventions on the walls and robot servers to take your order at the table. The floors were tiled, trimmed with bits of silver, and covered in scuff marks from the small tires the automatons moved about on. The smell of fried food hung in the air. There was one human in the place—and she ran the cash register. Even the cooks were bots, but he would expect nothing less from tinkerers. Most of them preferred bots to humans. They got a table near the spotless windows. Mr. Wills ordered a coffee and Zara followed suit. He studied her. She sat there quietly, comfortable with his perusal, her expression curious as she studied him in return.

"Why would you want me to be an agent?" she said quietly.

He smiled, "Why wouldn't I?"

"My father told me about the agents with the Crow's Nest. There are a number of reasons I'm not suited for it. For one, female agents are beautiful and lethal. I'm neither of those things," she said.

He studied her. She was sincere. She didn't have any idea how beautiful she was. How could she not know a thing like that? Her hideous sisters believed they were, but she did not. They were about the town often and quick to jump in front of a camera for a picture in the paper, craving the attention as if it were oxygen itself. And hags, both of them.

"You'd be a tinkerer agent. That is different. Most of the time, the tinkerer agents operate near the agent. Stay close by in case they are needed to either talk them through a tinkering situation or step in if needed. You're brilliant and quick under pressure. Your instructors told me they had never seen someone assemble ocular cameras or take apart a bomb so quickly. We could use someone like you in the field," he said.

"What about all the other times?" she said.

"What other times?" he asked.

"You said most of the time, that's what I would do. What about all the other times?" she said.

"All the other times, you'd need to know how to fight. How to be in the field, what to do when attending art galas, balls. Sometimes you'd need to speak to an unsavory sort. You might need to talk with local police, gather information and learn to lie with ease. Your main goal would be your mission, you might have to pretend to be married to our male agents occasionally, one in particular," he said.

She looked terrified, "Oh. I'm a terrible dancer and I've been told I'm boring. I don't date much either, sir."

He was taken aback by her honesty and more taken aback that someone had actually told her she was boring. That was uncalled for, that sort of rudeness.

"Social niceties can be taught," he said.

"I'm not sure any man would want to pretend to be married to me."

Mr. Wills looked at her in shock. She was in earnest! He could see it in her expression.

"Why not?" he said.

"I'm covered in freckles, as tall as a man and I'm a tinkerer. I don't date like other women my age do, nor am I asked to balls or art gala events. I'm not even asked out for coffee or to a pub, Mr. Wills. I don't know that I would be of any kind of use to you in that capacity," she said, looking at him levelly, her brow furrowed.

"Miss Turner, you are a lovely young woman. You would make any man a lovely wife. I have no idea why you don't know how lovely you are, but as a man, believe me when I say, you would do fine. If that is your only reason for saying no, then—"

"It isn't. I'm terrible in social situations," she said.

He chuckled, "Why?"

"You mean besides the fact that I have nothing in common with anyone but other tinkerers?" she said.

Mr. Wills studied her thoughtfully.

"How hard do you try to have something in common? Do you make an effort to find topics of conversation, or drone on and on about tinkering then get upset when the average person disappoints you with their lack of knowledge? You have to know that there are over sixty-thousand people in Jakarda City, maybe five or six hundred of them are tinkerers. You're outnumbered. Logically, it would be best for you to learn to adapt to that statistic."

She laughed then, her eyes dancing, "Logic! You know how to hit me where it hurts by making good sense."

He chuckled, "Of course! Right in the brain. I'm a recruiter. You are not the first tinkerer I've had to convince to come and work for me."

She laughed delightedly, "You are good at it, I'll give you that." Her expression turned to sudden, quiet seriousness. She spoke so softly, he could barely hear her. "There is one other problem, Mr. Wills, my papa died tinkering for the Crow's Nest. I don't wish to suffer his same fate."

Mr. Wills sighed, "Yes. I cannot promise the same won't happen to you."

"I don't expect you to. I just…Mr. Wills, when my papa died, I lost the only person who cared about me at all. You see, I'm nothing like my mother and sisters. They told me they spoke to you, I can't imagine their glowing endorsement of me brought you here. I had two close friends, one of which I dated briefly, loved, then he slept with that other friend of mine, and now I don't even have those two. I'm not well liked, nor am I the social sort. I ramble on and go off topic often, most people find it annoying. I have trouble making female friends, men don't like me because I'm so much smarter than them and the ones who do like me, I'm not attracted to in the slightest. I am not popular at all. My papa was. He was charming and funny, handsome, dashing. People liked him because he was funny and kind. I can see why you would want him to be your recruit or part of your team. I believe in being honest, so I will be straight with you because you were my papa's friend. Why would you want me for anything other than tinkering? What could I possibly bring to you as an agent, Mr. Wills?"

Mr. Wills was uncharacteristically speechless. He had never met someone who thought so little of herself. Not ever. She was being completely honest, he could see it in her face. She genuinely felt she had nothing to offer him or anyone else, but her tinkering. She knew how smart she was, but that seemed to be all she knew. He thought back to all the interviews he'd conducted about her, all those people had said basically the same thing about her. That she had no self-esteem or confidence at all, that she was sad and reserved. They mentioned her lack of social skills, said she veered off topic and often avoided large crowds.

"Because of your father, I suppose. He was my partner most of the time, my tinkerer. Back then, we paired people one on one. Not like now, where we randomly pair tinkerers with agents. We found one supervisor, myself, five agents and two tinkerers per department works out well, as does rotating the lead agent on cases. Miss Turner, I promised your papa I would look out for you if you ever applied for a job at the Crow's Nest. I'm going to tell you the truth, because I think nothing else will work with you. You can decide what you want after that. I came to get a better picture of who you are because of the interviews I conducted. You see, every single person I spoke to described you as lonely," he said gently. Zara looked at her coffee cup and avoided his gaze. "I heard Zara Turner was withdrawn, isolates herself, lacks friends and close contact with others. That she cares more about machines than people and if I'm being honest, the fact that Hal's daughter turned out like that bothered me. He would have hated that you were unhappy, he loved you so. He was such a warm, good man."

She seemed to be struggling not to cry. That's when he knew she wasn't cold, like the machines she worked on. She didn't know how else to be, because she wasn't sure how to change the way she was. His heart constricted. He reached over and rested his hand on hers. She looked at him in surprise.

"Zara, there are two reasons I want you. My supervisor wants you in Room Thirty with the other tinkerers. He told me there was no way you could manage to do what your father did after reading all the reports and such. I don't know if you can be the tinkerer we need in Room One Hundred, I really don't. What I do know is, if you are lonely, this will force you to get outside of yourself. To interact, to change and make friends because doing what we do, you make friends, especially with the members of your team. It makes the most unlikely friendships and couples for that matter. Some of the agents stay, some of them are temporary, but you will get better with people because you have to. In that job, you learn to be social. I'd like to help you, because I liked your papa. He was my friend and I truly believe you are more like him than you realize. I told him if you ever applied there, I'd help you, so I shall give you the job if you want it. It's as simple as that," he said.

She arched her brows, "He liked you, too. He told me about his friend, Mr. Wills. I imagine I would get better with people in that job, I have no place to go but up. What's the other reason for me to try?"

"Reason two is that I have an agent that might benefit from working with a female. He's a notorious womanizer, polished and charming, women throw themselves at him. Do be careful if you take the job, blondes are his preference and he loves blue eyes, but any female he finds appealing will do. He is not choosy in the slightest. At any rate, he has chased off an average of one tinkerer a year since he became an agent. He's demanding, rude and critical and he does not work well with others. He will be slightly more kind to you because you are a female, but only slightly," he said.

Zara laughed, "He sounds marvelous. Why keep him around?"

"He's my best agent, hands down. Closes more cases, does what he has to, gets the job done. He's normally kinder to females, gentler, as I mentioned and I am out of ideas when it comes to him. There are not a hell of a lot of female tinkerers, certainly not pretty ones like you. You're one of four female tinkerers that graduated from the Academy in your class and the others want to make items that are not useful to the Crow's Nest in the slightest. I'm out of ideas with him, to be frank. You are my last hope," he said.

She took a sip of coffee and hugged her mug with two hands, "If I were to take the position, might it be for, say, a two-month trial period? I don't know how I'd be in a crisis and I'd hate to lose the tinkerer job in Room Thirty because of it. I make good gadgetry as a tinkerer, and I do so want to be useful."

He leaned in, "I will guarantee you a spot in Room Thirty if after two months you want it. I can arrange it."

Zara took a deep breath, "Well, then, we have an accord. I'll give being a tinkerer field agent my best effort, Mr. Wills."

She extended her small hand. He smiled and shook it, "Excellent. You start in two days. Don't tell your family."

"I don't speak to them, not to worry. I live alone. I just got an apartment two blocks from the Crow's Nest about six months ago," Zara said.

"In the Green Isle?" he said.

"No, in the Industrial District," she said.

Mr. Wills refrained from wincing. The Industrial District was a bad neighborhood, it was poverty stricken and the streets stunk from all the industry. Only those who were poor normally lived there—desperate. What was she doing in a place like that, given her inventions on the market and her mother's financial success? He knew Amanda was not fond of her youngest, he got that impression in the interview, but he never expected her to send her to live there. She could afford to get her a nice place in the Green Isle, the section of Jakarda City where most young professionals her age lived and worked. Zara finished her coffee in a few gulps.

"I'm sorry, Mr. Wills, but I have to be at a prior engagement. I shall see you in two days' time at the Crow's Nest," she said.

"Excellent! I am your superior if anyone asks. I'll expect you in Room One Hundred. Be there at eight A.M. sharp," he said with a smile.

She smiled back and shook his hand, picking up her leather satchel and box, "I'll look forward to it."

"Miss Turner, if I may ask, what did I say to convince you?" he said.

Her eyes met his briefly, then she looked away, "I don't want to be lonely the rest of my life. You said aloud something that until now, I have ignored. You said it, and it was the truth, although I didn't know until that moment. I am lonely. Perhaps I can learn to be better with people and if I try, make a true friend or two. I'd settle for just one. This might make me more like everyone else. I'd like to be less odd and have friends if I can."

His heart squeezed. He offered her a small smile, "I'm quite certain you can."

She smiled, "Time will tell! I'm off then. Goodbye."

He watched her walk off. He had a terrible ache in his chest, seeing Hal's daughter like that. He meant what he said about her father. They were good friends and he always had liked and admired Hal. He guessed about her loneliness, and he was right. He hated that he was right, but it seemed to do the trick. Something told him she knew he was manipulating her, and she didn't care. What he had said was the right thing if it convinced her to give this a shot. He hoped to God she was less lonely doing this job, he really did. Mr. Wills had not been prepared for the sadness in her big blue eyes. He hadn't been prepared for that at all.

CHAPTER TWO

Harrison Lowell ran a hand through his hair in frustration as he paced the floor of Room One Hundred. It was a large square space they used as an office, a conference area, and a lab. But unlike most other rooms in the building, it was moved often up and down and around the core of the towering Crow's Nest headquarters building. It never sat in the same spot the same time in one week, and the other people in other rooms had grown used to small fires and explosions emanating from it, thanks to their tinker, Dill. He was always working on spy tech for the six agents who worked out of Room One Hundred.

Harrison stopped at the windows and looked out over the city. They were positioned pretty high in the building today. Harrison loved to be at the center of all the tall buildings covered in brick, steel, copper, silver and for the very wealthy, gold. Jakarda was a land that thrived on the latest technologies, from steam powered carriages with flight capabilities, to steam powered bicycles and cars. Innovation was at the city's core and with those innovations, came people who wished to use them for nefarious means. Enter the Crow's Nest, the government agency who strived to stop them. Living in a time where women and men pushed the boundaries of modern ingenuity and science was in itself, a great gift. Harrison loved that he was a part of it. Although he himself could not make a single gadget, he sure as hell liked to use them.

He glanced around the office and felt that sense of purpose, of belonging. This was his home, the place where he fit, even on days like today when he was good and annoyed. To the far right were two massive tinkering tables filled with automatons, mostly birds, wires, gears, copper, silver and gold tinkering things, Harrison didn't know what the hell most of it was. To the left, five desks lined up neatly, his at the back, closest to the door, and in its center, a massive round oak table where he and the rest of the team met to discuss the day's cases. It was spacious, full of modern technology and cozy with its padded chairs and easy, comfortable company. Each morning, the agents of Room One Hundred laughed together, got assignments, sipped coffee and gobbled up pastries here in the Crow's Nest, the governmental building of Jakarda City. They were the sort of team the other agent rooms strived to be like, they got on so well.

Harrison loved that part of the day, when he, FeFe, Simon, Douglas and Marcus traded stories with Dill and Mr. Wills. The seven of them made the perfect team, which was why none of the other tinkerers they brought in ever worked out. They already had a perfect balance in this room, so why the hell was Mr. Wills making them try this again? They had no need for another agent. None whatsoever.

"Another one? Really, Mr. Wills! They just never work out! Harrison is right! We're fine as we are," FeFe said.

Harrison offered her a smile. He and FeFe had had sex in his carriage on the way here this morning. One of the best parts of having a steam powered carriage run by a robot was that he never had to drive, leaving him to screw with ladies in the carriage, and FeFe loved a good screw. He studied the petite dark haired woman with a smile. She had lovely olive skin and a flawless complexion. Dark eyes and ruby red lips—he did love red lipstick. Nothing sexier than a lady with red lips, in his estimation. She enjoyed no strings attached sex, too. She got off on the adventure of the job like he did, they were aggressive and passionate. She felt him watching her. She offered him a sexual smile he returned.

Dill shoved his glasses up his nose. He was a tinkerer, perpetually rumpled, his brown hair always on end. "Mr. Wills, you know

I'm not one to question you, but it does seem a fair assessment. Bringing another chap in is—"

"Lady...I'm bringing in a lady. Best tinkerer the academy has ever seen. She made the Spy-ders you all fought over and the bullet-proof umbrella with the gun in the handle, not to mention the steam powered coffee pot we all adore and the little refrigeration unit for creamer and sandwiches on stake outs we all love. That's a brilliant bit of tinkering! She also invented the ocular camera you went on about Dill, the one we put on the drones; and she figured out how to make the steam powered carriage go faster, worked on the flying conversions too. Oh! And those little controlled bombs you all love, the ones made from a pocket watch that have a blast in a dome that silences the small charge? She made those, patents on all of those things and more. Smart as a whip!"

Harrison smiled a little, "A lady?"

"Yes, indeed! It occurred to me a lady might fit in better than a gent, poor FeFe alone all the time with us fellows. Besides, no matter what all of you say, we have to have another tinkerer. No way around it. My director insists, so we must do this. I like her, thought you all might, too," Mr. Wills said.

A lady might be a welcome addition, Harrison thought, if they had to have another tinkerer. He loved ladies and most female agents tended to be like FeFe. Lush, lethal and intelligent. He loved those qualities in a woman, confidence was sexy. They seemed to enjoy male companionship too, that could be fun. This just might be the answer, the blokes Mr. Wills brought in were unacceptable cowards.

"What's her name?" FeFe snapped.

Harrison smirked. She was clearly jealous. She liked being the only female to be doted on in Room One Hundred. She had been the only woman for the past four years, when she started at the Crow's Nest.

"Turner," he said.

"Turner?" Marcus said in alarm, his blue eyes sharp, "Please, don't tell us she's of the Turner's Fashion Emporium family. Which one is she? The one that looks like a lollipop or the other one, the one with the horse face and the perfect body?"

"I'd take horse face so long as I got to see that body of hers. Beautiful breasts," Harrison said.

The others nodded, agreeing with him.

"Bloody magnificent breasts," Douglas said with a smile, his brown eyes dancing.

"Perfect," Simon said.

"Put a burlap sack on her head and I'm in heaven," Harrison said.

They chortled with laughter. Harrison smirked, relaxing in his cushy red chair.

FeFe, accustomed to their talk rolled her eyes, "Well, which is it? Lollipop or horse face?"

"Neither. They are in possession of a younger sister, she's just graduated from the Academy, her name is Miss Zara Turner," he said.

"There's another one?" Dill said.

Harrison chuckled, because Dill, unlike the rest of them, was a gentleman. He normally didn't say rude things, but even he looked repulsed. The Turner's were the ugliest models he and the rest of Jakarda had ever seen. They were plastered everywhere and socialized often, so their pictures were in the social section of the newspaper several times a week with the caption, "The handsome Turner sisters dressed to impress!" beneath it. That was the kindest way to describe them. They did dress well, their clothing was the height of fashion, they had impeccable taste, like Mrs. Turner herself. That was where the appeal ended.

"Well, at least she's a top notch tinkerer, even if she's ugly," Marcus said sitting back and adjusting his black jacket, his eyes dancing in amusement, "I love those inventions of hers."

"I'll agree with you there. She will be useful, unlike the last tinkerers we had," Harrison said.

"I do love a good gadget. It might be nice to have another woman present. When does this ugly young lady get here?" FeFe asked, touching up her lipstick.

There was a knock on the door. Mr. Wills smiled, his eyes twinkling with mischief. That worried Harrison.

"That will be her now," Mr. Wills said.

Harrison and the others groaned, bracing themselves for the assault that was about to take place on their eyes. They stood up, grumbling and filed in behind Mr. Wills, ready to welcome the new agent because they knew it was expected of them, given the stern look he sent them. Mr. Wills opened the door. They looked with a wince. Harrison's jaw dropped. His heart thumped hard in his chest. Standing at the door was a most beautiful woman. She had on a maroon dress that hugged her narrow shape, slipped across her hips and down a skirt that clung around her thighs and ended just short of her knees in ruffles. She wore tall black boots that were flat and laced up the front. She was very tall and slender, her frame tiny. She had a few curves, and her breasts were small, but inviting. Unlike most ladies, she wore no hat, just a simple clip with some gears and a bit of lace clipped into her thick blonde hair. She had big, sky blue eyes that were lovely. She had on a touch of makeup, berry colored lips and black mascara on her blonde lashes, which brushed her cheeks as she glanced down to step into the room, then curled up into her brows as she looked up at them. Everywhere her skin showed there were freckles all over, everywhere. He'd never seen so many freckles. She smiled warmly at Mr. Wills and Harrison gaped at her. She had a lovely smile, nice white small teeth. They were adorable, she was adorable. She was nothing like FeFe—the sort of woman men fell over themselves to be with because of her sexual prowess and abundance of confidence. FeFe was womanly, sophisticated and polished. This girl was sweet-faced, lovely in a natural way, the sort of woman who was cute, rather than striking, like FeFe.

"Are you lost?" FeFe asked.

She laughed softly, "No. I'm where I'm supposed to be, if this is in fact Room One Hundred."

Her voice was soft too, breathless, quiet. She was the most ladylike woman Harrison had ever met. He grinned broadly and looked at the others. They looked as thrilled as he, except maybe for FeFe. Poor Dill's mouth was hanging open. She was a tinkerer and beautiful to boot. That rarely happened, and he was in a state of shock. Female tinkerers normally looked sloppy, she was impeccably dressed and tidy.

"She belongs here! Welcome, Miss Turner! Right on time!" Harrison said, recovering his composure.

"Am I? I got a flat tire on my motorized bicycle because I used that new product, halonite, to fix it. That product is garbage! Never again will I use it," she said in a huff.

"It's weak and cheap. I won't use it either," Dill said walking towards her with a smile, "I'm Dillbert Polk, Dill, tinkerer like you. We'll be working together pretty often, making gadgets for the team. Might I say, the work you did on the Spy-ders is quite the finest bit of tinkering I have seen in years."

She offered him a dazzling smile, as if she were being paid the highest of compliments, "Thank you! I know who you are, of course. You're a legend at the Academy. I love what you did on the cameras, the ones that can go underwater and take photographs. Brilliant! I have one at home, it's wonderful!"

Dill flushed and smoothed his hair. He was always rumpled, poor Dill. He looked like a tinkerer. His disheveled brown hair and warm brown eyes crinkled at the sides when he smiled. Everything about Dill was warm and kind despite his perpetually rumpled state. Miss Turner didn't seem to mind his wrinkled shirt and vest, nor his mussed slacks a bit, as she offered him a shy smile.

"You two can talk tinkering later. Right now, let me introduce the rest of the team. Zara Turner, meet Simon Rayling," Mr. Wills said.

Simon grinned and she blushed. Harrison felt a rush of annoyance. Simon was successful with women, oozed charm and polish in a way that none of the others could ever seem to manage so well. He laughed often, and he was the chameleon of their group, the one who melted from one situation to the next flawlessly, with such ease, you never even know he was doing it. Harrison was not sure why it irritated him, Simon's polish, but it did in that moment.

"Pleasure to meet you. I like your controlled blast pocket watch. Got me out of a jam once," Simon said.

"Did it? I'd love to hear about it sometime," she said.

"Telling you about it would be my pleasure," Simon said.

He gave her a flirtatious smile that she returned with a shy one and looked at Douglas, who stood eye to eye with her. Douglas was a good chap, the sort that blended in with the lower set here in Jakarda, knew every in and out when it came to the rougher type they sometimes associated with. He'd worked his way up from nothing, clawing to make something of himself, refusing to be a poor Northern farmer like his family, struggling for their next meal. Harrison liked him, he was hardworking, salt of the earth, always had your back if you needed him. Bit of a Rake, but it came in their profession. Women loved male agents, and Douglas, although not quite as handsome as the rest of them, seemed to do better than they did. Perhaps because he was genuinely humble, and kind, even if he was arrogantly confident at times.

"I'm Douglas Fairbanks, pleased to meet you, Zara Turner," Douglas said, his brown eyes dancing.

"And I you, Mr. Fairbanks," Zara said with a polite smile.

"Miss Turner, this is Marcus Brook," Mr. Wills said.

Marcus offered Zara a dazzling smile that seemed to take her aback, because she reddened a bit, staring at him. He was tall, golden haired and looked just like his trust fund, his friend Marcus. He was considered a catch by the upper crust because of his family background and the ladies here loved that a man of good social standing took a low paying government job just because. Marcus was a bit stiff, his manners always intact. He showed little emotion, which many mistook for his being cold, but in truth, Marcus was a good man. He was a product of his upbringing, and often formal, even distant, but he didn't want to be. He tried so hard not to be, Harrison knew he did. He asked Harrison and the others often how to be more like them, fumbling through relating to the average man, endearing himself to anyone who knew him.

"Nice to meet you," Zara said.

"You, as well," he said, sending her an intense, sexy look.

She blushed again, looking away, avoiding his gaze. FeFe rolled her eyes and plastered on a smile.

"I'm FeFe LaMay."

Zara turned to her with a smile, "Hello."

"Hello. Tell me, are you qualified to tinker at a ball? How will you be in a situation like that?" FeFe said.

Zara studied her silently. She had the most intelligent gaze Harrison had ever seen. Zara tilted her head toward FeFe and smirked, "I have two left feet, I am an appallingly bad dancer, possibly worse at making small talk. While we're on the topic of my faults, I have never thrown a punch in my life, nor am I good at physically demanding work. But I am the smartest person to graduate the Tinkerers Academy, and I will learn whatever is taught to me. In time, I'll do fine, Miss LaMay."

FeFe was taken aback by the quiet, calm tone of her voice. There was no challenge in it, simply fact. Harrison found himself smiling broadly. She had guts, he'd give her that.

"I'm Harrison Lowell. Welcome to Room One Hundred," he said.

She looked at him, her soft blue eyes meeting his. His heart went faster. He felt himself falling into her eyes. That blue, so bright—so wide and framed by thick eyelashes—incredible. He offered her a rakish grin. She gave him an amused smile back.

"Nice to meet you, Mr. Lowell," she said.

"Don't worry about the dancing. If you dance with me, I'll make you look good," he said.

She laughed, "Certain of yourself, are you?"

"You bet," he said.

He smiled while she studied him and then was taken back when she turned to look around the room with apparent curiosity. Why the hell didn't she flirt with him? With any of them? She spotted Dill's metal birds. Her face lit up. She looked at Dill with a grin.

"Are those your aviary-bots? I read about them at the Academy in the newsletter!" She said.

"Yes! I can show you, if it's ok, Mr. Wills?" Dill said.

Mr. Wills rolled his eyes, "Five minutes till meeting, short version Dill. No more than five minutes!"

Dill offered her his arm. She took it and they hurried over, Dill telling her something about the birds. She watched him intently, nodding as he explained things Harrison had no chance of ever understanding. He was still looking at her, he couldn't help it.

"This is a damn welcome edition," Douglas said quietly.

"Yes, it sure as hell is," Harrison said, his eyes traveling the length of her.

"She's beautiful," Simon said.

"I like her hair and freckles. I like delicate women, natural ones like her who don't wear too much makeup," Marcus said.

"Adorable," Douglas agreed.

"Honestly! All of you acting like she's the prettiest woman you ever met! Freckles are not fashionable!" FeFe said.

"I don't care. They work on her. I love blondes with blue eyes," Harrison said.

The others agreed with a laugh. They came to sit down for the meeting. Dill pulled a chair out for Zara, who thanked him with a smile. He grinned at her, sitting beside her. Douglas beat Harrison to the chair on the other side of her. Harrison sat across from her instead, that way he could flirt with her, make eye contact, see if she liked him and figure out what sort of person she was.

Harrison had no intention of letting her get too close, nothing like that. He decided long ago, he didn't want to end up like his parents, prattling on about the old days. As far as he could tell, being an agent was the best thing that had ever happened to them, and falling in love, having a family, it robbed them of their only great joy, giving way to an ordinary, dull life. No, he would not end up like his parents, former agents pining for a lost life of happiness. He didn't want anything serious, he would never settle down, but he would gladly bed her if she was willing.

"Miss Turner, can I call you Zara?" Mr. Wills said.

"Of course," Zara said, setting her bag on the ground.

"Excellent. Zara, we pass out pastries and coffee each morning. We discuss cases we're on, what's new with tinkering. We all work together in this office, we have a cooperative and joint effort here," he said. Zara smiled, but refrained from comment, so he went on,

"Our latest case involves the Reform Mechanics. You familiar with them?"

"Of course! They're in the papers all the time. They were always recruiting at the Academy. They approached me often. I had a bad encounter with one man, he broke my arm when I declined his invitation to join the mechanics," she said.

"Broke your arm? I wouldn't have let him close enough to me to do it. How did you get away?" FeFe said.

"I tossed him through a brick wall with this," Zara said. She reached in her bag and took out a gauntlet, "I have a patent pending. It's called a strong glove. If you wear it, you can lift three times your bodyweight. It fuses with the nervous system. You can also shock someone, it knocks them out cold."

"Can I try it?" Harrison asked excitedly.

She looked at his palms and nodded, then took out a small set of tools, "Your hands are massive, you're a very large man. Give me a moment to adjust the width."

They watched her move quickly, tinkering with the glove in under a minute. Dill watched her, his expression almost awed.

"You're incredible, your dexterity and speed—I've never seen the like," he said.

She smiled, "Thank you. Come and try it, Mr. Lowell?"

Harrison sauntered over with a sexy smile, "Call me Harrison."

"If you wish for me to," she said.

Harrison chuckled, amused by how formal she was. She had very good manners, but she was a bit stiff and cold if you asked him. She held up the gauntlet, avoiding his gaze, even though he was standing right in front of her, looking right at her. He sent Mr. Wills a questioning look, who smiled tightly at Harrison, his expression revealed nothing, but something in his eyes made Harrison believe he found her a puzzle as well. Harrison normally read people straight away, but this woman was different. Zara helped him put the glove on, tugging it into place, adjusting the metal arm at the side when it didn't fit. She was fast, efficient, confident.

She didn't meet his eyes once.

She examined it one last time, then nodded, "Squeeze your fist to turn it on, hold for three seconds."

He nodded and felt this tingling sensation travel up his arm. He shook his head when it felt like it hit his brain, "Whoa! That's something."

"That's normal, takes some getting used to. Pick something very heavy up," she said.

He did as she asked and lifted the automaton, Reggie, over his head one handed. He grinned excitedly at her, "This is fantastic!"

"If you want to electrocute something, push the button on the side, the silver one. I wouldn't do that robot, though, he's got a counteractive measure, he'll shock you in return," she said.

Harrison nodded and shocked the cat-bot, Tails, that got the brunt of Dill's tinkering inventions. Zara squeaked, her eyes wide.

"It's just a cat-bot," he said.

"I know. I like them. I'll fix it," she muttered.

Harrison shrugged, ignoring her. He grinned about the fine bit of spy tech on his hand. She did make exceptional gadgets. Zara picked up the cat-bot while the others tried the glove. Even FeFe gushed about it. Zara fixed the cat-bot while they passed the gauntlet around, playing with it and lifting things up. FeFe particularly liked practicing with it. Harrison glanced at Zara sitting alone at the table. Even Dill had gotten up to give it a try, yet, she sat there, by herself, her hands moving rapidly as she tinkered with the cat-bot, never once looking up at them. Harrison watched her with a thoughtful expression.

It bothered him that she didn't smile much for reasons he couldn't understand. She was just so…sad. There was something melancholy about her, something distant and lonely, it felt wrong for her and he realized—he hated it. She looked up at them and smiled a little, then went back to tinkering. He was good at assessing people, his best skill, and Miss Zara Turner, if he wagered a guess, was an unhappy person. He frowned. God, she was beautiful sitting there with all that golden hair. She was as pretty as a picture, her posture straight as she worked. He watched her small, delicate hands. It was puzzling—it had been sometime since Harrison hadn't been able to instantly read someone upon meeting them. He smiled a little. He liked it.

Mr. Wills called them back to the table a big smile on his face. He was getting older, in his early fifties now, and he had just lifted a filing cabinet over his head. He looked like he was thrilled about that. Harrison grinned at his uncle, clapping him on the back. He sat down, and passed around the coffee and pastries.

Mr. Wills addressed each of them as he spoke. "Zara is new, as you all know. She needs to be trained to fight, shoot a weapon, basic field training. She'll need to know what to do in the event of her being needed in the line of duty. Each of you has your strengths. Douglas, hand to hand combat for her. That's up to you. Simon, weapons, teach her all the types and varieties, how to shoot and use them. Marcus, if you could show her the files on the Reform Mechanics and the other big crime players here, that would be wonderful. You're a genius at research—our best. That should do for a start—the rest of you, help her how you can, as will I. Zara, you'll have two hours of training a day, every morning following this meeting. It will all be a crash course at first. But we'll give you the time to catch up and the training you need, not to worry. Have you ever had any experience other than the gauntlet thing at combat?" he asked.

"Ah, I have shot a gun before, well, a gun of sorts—this one," She said taking it from her bag, "It's a blast gun, it uses a massive sound wave to knock people out for several hours. I've also shot this, a grappling hook gun, it's a small one that can be concealed in a lady's garter belt or a gent's sock. The grappling hook is retractable. With a few clicks you can have it out and ready to go. It supports up to two hundred and fifty pounds. If you're light like me, it goes, very, very fast. It's sort of a terrifying sensation, but rather a fun one. I have patents on both, I can make one for everyone if you'd like me to…" She looked up from the gadgets she was demonstrating. "Oh, sorry, I'm side tracked, I do that. No, I've never used a real gun with bullets or fought with anyone enough to know anything more than basic instinctual things. I did pass the physical exams at the Academy. On a side note, I do test most of my experiments before sending them out—" She arched her neck and looked around, "Is there a fire extinguisher in here? Many of my ideas catch fire."

The others laughed then, because she had looked around nervously, her eyes searching for the extinguisher. Harrison found her rambling insecurity oddly adorable, she could change topics in that soft breathless voice of hers three times in under one minute. He chuckled.

"Mine do too," Dill reassured her. "We have extinguishers right next to our desks on the right side, large copper ones. It's ok if that happens, hardly anyone reacts anymore."

She looked at her hands and chuckled softly, "I'm happy it isn't just me catching things on fire."

"No! I do it all the time, job hazard," Dill said with a grin.

Zara laughed aloud, "I've burned off my eyebrows twice now."

"Five times for me. I make a lot of combustibles," Dill said.

She offered him a pretty smile, "I try to avoid those. I'm more of a tech lady, I like a nice weapon, or gadgetry, best."

Dill grinned at her and shoved up his glasses, "Me, too!"

They grinned at each other. Harrison felt a sudden rush of irritation. He crossed his arms and looked at Mr. Wills, "Why am I not teaching her anything?"

"You are being punished for blowing up my last carriage, that was the third and last time, Harrison. You have a lot of paperwork to do, as well you know," he said.

FeFe laughed at Harrison's annoyed expression, "You have to admit, it has been you who wrecks the carriages."

"Mine is messed up!" he replied defensively, "I had to borrow one." He looked at FeFe with a level gaze, "I'm an excellent teacher, I have lots that I can show her."

FeFe met his look, "She seems the innocent sort, Harrison, the things you have to show her are better suited to another sort of woman." She turned to Mr. Wills, "What am I to teach our new recruit? I can show her lots of things a lady specifically needs to know in the field."

Harrison snorted and then and glanced across the table at Zara. She had a tight smile on her face. What was that about, he wondered?

Mr. Wills sighed, "You will eventually, FeFe and Harrison, once you catch up on the paperwork, feel free to pitch in during training sessions, if you wish to. I appreciate everyone being so willing to help with the new person, that does not happen often here, not at all! Zara, the rest of your day will be spent tinkering with Dill. I have to admit, though, I'm curious—do you have any more inventions in that bag?"

Zara nodded and Harrison, along with everyone else leaned forward eagerly. She took out some odd silver triangles, flat on the bottom, pointed at the top. They were covered in wires twisted over the top to make a crisscross pattern. The wires were copper with a solid, silvery tip, about the size of a baseball. She set one in the palm of her hand and covered it with the other.

"I made these little sun powered lights. Dill, perhaps you can help me improve them. They absorb the sun's energy. In turn, they hold onto it with these sun panels at the top, I call these sun lights. Good in dark places. Trouble is, each of them holds the light for different amounts of time. I have no idea why. That doesn't happen to me often. My math is sound, but they continue to disappoint me," she said.

She set the light onto the table. It let off a bright glow in the office, even with the four tall windows at the left. Harrison smiled, those would come in handy due to their small size and the portability factors.

"Brilliant idea," he said with sincerity, his eyes meeting hers.

"Yes, they would be if they worked properly," she said with a sigh.

Harrison studied her, "Something tells me you'll make them work."

She grinned at him then, "Of course, I will. Last thing is this. I'm trying to build a communication device. It's got this small screen for the person's image. I'll show you."

She took out a rectangular copper box with a set of two prongs at the top. There were four buttons and a few openings. She pressed the button and her image popped up in black and white on the front.

"That should be the person I am speaking to, not me. I can't get the camera right, but it works, in theory. You speak into this mini gramophone at the bottom and it records a message, which has to be under a minute. It takes thirty-seconds for the message to get to another person in a transfer." She talked while turning the machine around in her hands, making adjustments. "On a mission, I suppose it could be used for communicating back to Mr. Wills, or another agent, or your tinkerer, or your mother, I suppose. There are probably other things that it could be made to do—like a radio signal or something—It does not work either, not correctly, but I'm nearly there…" She stopped and looked up, "I'm blathering again. I do that."

"We've been working on something like this for ages," Dill said looking at it and examining it. "You're much further then we've been able to get!"

Zara smiled and passed him the device. He immediately began following the circuitry, his expression eager as he muttered to himself about the components she used and wondering aloud at her cleverness.

"Anything else in that bag, honey?" Harrison said.

"Sketches of my designs, personal things and a tin of marshmallows. They're my favorite," she said.

He chuckled, "Marshmallows?"

She nodded, but didn't elaborate. Mr. Wills was looking at the rest of her gadgets, they all were. Harrison sat back, smiled and shook his head. She was brilliant. Her ideas were innovative, and fresh. He watched her take a small bite of cherry danish and sip her coffee. She was so feminine, so quiet. Marcus offered her a sexy smile that she returned with a shy one. She was certainly not a conversationalist. He glanced at FeFe. She was watching him as he studied Zara, and her eyes narrowed. He offered her a half smile that she returned with a come hither one of her own. Harrison rested an elbow on the back of his chair. He didn't know what to make of Miss Zara Turner. He would have to reserve judgment on her.

CHAPTER THREE

Zara had no idea what to say. When she accepted the position, she never imagined that the men she'd be working with would be so handsome. All of them! There were handsome tinkerers, lots of them, but not striking like these men. They were dashing, fit men, not soft handsome ones like she was used to. Simon was tall and lightly muscled, and impeccably dressed. She liked his auburn hair and the smattering of freckles on his nose. He didn't have an abundance of them like she did, just the right amount. He was wearing a three-piece suit in black. He looked rakish, Simon did. Marcus was like a blonde god, and she could hardly speak to him. He was tall, broad shouldered and so attractive, he would never give the likes of her a second look! He was a truly beautiful man. Douglas was not the physical specimen, as the other men were, but there was something about him: his confidence, the mischief in his smile, maybe the twinkle in his eye. His northern Jacardian accent was compelling, too. She thought his charm was as deeply attractive as the others' handsome features were. Dill was good-looking in the way most male tinkerers she met were. He was disheveled, his clothes rumpled and he exuded a kind of uncertainty that comes with sharp intelligence. But she liked his unruly brown hair and bespectacled, kind eyes, and he was far more fit than most tinkerers she met. He had a nice smile. There was nothing at all aggressive about him. He was gentle and personable. She felt comfortable with him.

There was nothing at all gentle about Harrison Lowell. He was not the best looking man in the room, but he somehow was the best looking to her. He was a massive man, very broad shouldered and every movement seemed to accentuate mounds of muscle. His eyes were so dark, they nearly looked black, and his hair matched those eyes. There was a wildness about him, a very masculine aggression that demanded: you will notice me. He flirted with her as if flirting was second nature to him, sending sexy smiles and intense looks her way. He had a stern jaw and dark stubble on his face. His hair was longer than the others, and wavy in spots and he didn't seem to care that it was not in fashion. He was arrogant. So arrogant! He walked around as if he owned the place, his steps confident and sure. He was nothing at all like Zara; and yet, she thought him the most handsome man she had ever laid eyes on. She was fairly certain he knew of his rugged handsomeness and its effect on females.

Zara looked at FeFe. She hated Zara. Zara could tell the moment she had walked into the room. Zara knew she was no beauty, but she was far better looking than her older sisters, and FeFe had expected her to be equally as unappealing as her siblings. They were pleasantly surprised she was not ugly like them, she could tell. Zara knew her sisters were ugly, she had for years, and because they were as ugly on the inside as they were on the outside, she felt it was fine to admit to it. Were they kind to her, she would have defended their homeliness, but since Cait looked like an orange on a toothpick and Tempie had the face of a donkey, she decided it was okay to disparage them, given their hatefulness towards her.

Zara felt oddly at home the moment she walked into Room One Hundred. She had never felt that way before walking into a place. She had grown to feel that way at the Academy, certainly she felt that way at her apartment, but it had taken her months to feel at home there—yet here? She liked it here. She was a little uncomfortable with all these men, but men had generally been kinder to her than women in her lifetime. Her mother and sisters were so cruel. At the Tinkerers Academy, her chums had been men, except Sara. Sara was a nice girl, timid. She worked at the Academy now as a professor's assistant. She and Sara had got on splendidly, getting together for coffee once a week to talk and complain about the boys who were threatened by their intelligence. 'Til Sara met Vince, Zara's second boyfriend, the only one at the Academy, and the two of them had sex. In Zara's bed.

That was difficult to take because she had loved Vince very much, thought she might marry him. She and Vince had worked on the portable coffee pot, had a falling out. She made the damn thing, all of the inner-workings, Vince covered it in copper and made the handle, certainly making it good-looking, but that was all he did. She gave him thirty-percent of the credit for making the shell her invention came in—it was more than generous. He was furious, and to get back at her, had sex with Sara. She walked in on the two of them and he smirked, like the whole thing was amusing. Sara felt badly, she could tell. He had used her, too. Now, the only female friend she had ever made was trying to be her friend again, and Zara refused to consider that.

Zara had thought because Sara was intelligent like Zara she wouldn't be like her mother and sisters, but she was wrong. Sara could be unkind. Her sister Tempie had slept with her boyfriend Mike, to whom Zara had lost her virginity, in secondary school. She had loved him very deeply, too. She hoped to marry him as well, but, he took one look at Tempie's lush figure, found he didn't mind her horse face, and then the two of them became a couple. Tempie loved it, of course. She was always more cruel to Zara than Cait, who was indifferent to her most of the time. Zara shook off those old thoughts and focused on Mr. Wills' current dialogue.

"The Reform Mechanics! We went off on a tangent there, a pleasant one, but back to work. They have been recruiting aggressively, or trying too. They have developed a reputation for extreme behavior in the last year or so, been in all the papers, what with robbing all the balls and galas given by the wealthy this season, they have been making quite a mess for us to clean up. You know how it is—with all the parties this city throws and the coming out balls. Everyone else comes to the city from the country and has a ball at one of the ballrooms. The Gold family, one of the wealthier moguls around—they run the dirigible system, and they are having a ball for their daughter Wanda in three weeks' time," Mr. Wills said.

Zara did not know how it was, having only attended four balls in her lifetime, all of which she hated. During the last one, she spent her time hiding on the balcony after Tempie made fun of how badly she was dancing in front of a bunch of her gentleman friends. As if that were not bad enough, Tempie introduced her as a distant relation while her mother laughed and didn't bother to correct her.

"Oh, I do love a ball!" FeFe said.

"I'm aware you do, however we need someone under cover. Two someone's to pretend to be an engaged couple. I cannot send Dill, he is not suited for balls. I'm going to send Zara as a tinkerer. We need one. Zara, the guests at the ball are being knocked out. All of them, an entire room of them out cold, at these events. Each time, the Reform Mechanics, or whoever is robbing these balls, takes jewels, and baubles off the knocked out guests, then breaks into the safe and steals maps," he said.

"Maps?" Zara asked, her curiosity overtaking the nervousness she felt.

"Yes, maps. From the Grant family, they own the railroads, they took a map of the tracks. From the Maddox family, they took a map of the shipping routes and I assume they want the dirigible paths from the Gold's as well," he said.

Zara's brow furrowed, "But, how are all of those connected?"

"That is the question, isn't it?" he said.

Zara tilted her head to the side then offered a small smile, "Not my area, I'm afraid. I'll leave it to all you clever agents."

Mr. Wills studied her, "I suspect, you might be better at making connections then you think, Zara. I know how smart you are and it is not exclusive to tinkering."

Zara felt an odd rush of affection for him. He was a kind man, complimentary. She found she liked him. She offered him a rare, genuine smile.

"I have my moments, Mr. Wills," she said.

He chuckled, "I'm certain you do."

She laughed, liking him even more. He reminded her of her papa a little. He had a way of seeing there was more to her then everyone thought. She liked that. She took a bite of her pastry, still grinning. She glanced over Harrison was staring at her—his eyes, well, soft. The way he looked at her made her get an odd, fluttery feeling in her chest. The pit of her stomach sort of somersaulted. Her smiled became guarded. She looked away and sipped her coffee. He was frowning at her now. He looked a little annoyed, so she ignored him, assuming she had done something to make him dislike her. She glanced around. Everyone was looking at her. She wiped her mouth with a napkin, worried she had pastry on her face.

"Well, then! Simon, why don't you go to the docks with Douglas and Marcus, see what you can learn from the Reform Mechanic's patch we got off of the gentleman's coat," Mr. Wills said, setting the patch on the table.

Zara looked at the patch and frowned, "Mr. Wills, that's not a Reform Mechanic's patch. There are two gears, yes, but it does not have that lettering at the top or the rose on the bottom like the usual patch does. Reform Mechanics' patches have two gears and R.M. where these strange words are." She stroked a slender finger across the embroidered letters.

He looked at it, his brows arched, "They do?"

"Yes. I remember it because I thought it a tacky symbol when they came to recruit me at the Academy. My mother is always saying brown and gold are ghastly together or I would never have noticed. She mentioned it often because I had a tendency to pair those colors as a girl, not realizing they didn't always look nice together," Zara said.

Harrison picked up the patch. "What language is this?" he asked.

"I don't know, Mr. Lowell," she said.

"Call me Harrison, Zara. We're on a first name basis in this room," he said.

"Harrison, then. I have never seen that language before," she replied.

Douglas extended his hand, "Maybe its Northern Jakarda, the old language. I'm from the Northern part of Jakarda, hence the accent. I know some. May I?"

Mr. Wills handed it to him. Douglas looked at it, then shook his head, "Nah. It's not that."

Zara offered him a smile, "That was an excellent thought."

Douglas grinned at her, "Thanks. I, too, have my moments."

She smiled delightedly, "I'm sure."

He winked at her, and she laughed softly. Harrison reached across the table, taking the patch. He studied it, his brow furrowed, "The men dress in brown coats, those long duster types. They wear scarves to conceal their faces and the hats, like the mechanics. Perhaps this is a new branch of criminals we are meant to think are the Reform Mechanics."

Zara was taken aback, because that made good since. She knew the second she met him, he was the rake Mr. Wills warned her about. She had not expected him to be intelligent, just impulsive and brutish, after how Mr. Wills had described him.

To what end?" Marcus asked.

"To throw us off, I would guess. If we go after our Reform Mechanics leads, it gives them time to do whatever it is they are doing with those maps," FeFe said.

"Exactly. How could we miss a thing like that?" Marcus asked.

Simon shook his head, "We're used to dealing with them. I confess, I didn't look that closely. I'm the one who retrieved it at the last ball when I was knocked out cold from the gas—yanked it off a coat when I fell trying to grab the man in the long duster."

"You were?" Zara asked.

"Yes! I was dancing with FeFe. Harrison was there as well. The gas was expelled, then we were both in a heap, her baubles and my pocket watch missing, a damned horrible headache and a sour stomach to prove it," Simon said.

"They took my favorite pistol. I was not happy," Harrison said.

She got the impression he was very angry that had happened to him at all, he didn't strike her as the sort to be bested by anything. Zara nodded, studying him. He looked right back at her, an amused look on his face. He sat back and gave her a half smile, as if his perusal of him delighted him, completely misunderstanding her interest. She leaned forward. He grinned and followed suit.

"Tell me, did any of you notice any smells before you went down?" she said.

Harrison considered, "Yes. Yes, there was a spicy kind of a smell, it was very strong. Did you smell that FeFe? Simon?"

"I did, now that you mention it. Made my eyes burn and my nose run," Simon said.

"Yes, I thought it was cheap cologne. Do you have a notion as to what it was, tinkerer?" FeFe said.

Zara's mind was racing. She shut her eyes to think, slow her brain down, then opened them, her eyes fixed on the table, "The compound would have to be a derivative of ether, and the distribution...how large was the room? How many people?"

"There were, I'd say, two hundred guests or so," FeFe said.

"How many on the wait staff? Were they automatons or people?" She asked. She took out some paper and searched for a pen, "I can never find my bloody pen!"

Simon grinned and offered her one from his lapel, "Here you are."

"Thank you!" she said.

She looked at Harrison expectantly, "Well? People?"

"Both automatons and human, I'd say, maybe fifteen humans, the rest automatons. Might have been a few more," Harrison said.

Zara nodded and chewed her lip, "And the room size?"

"Maybe one hundred and fifty feet by one hundred, if I had to rough guess," Simon said excitedly, watching her with a smile.

"So that means..." She jotted the equations quickly, her mind moving fast, her equation faster, "Carry the two...ok, I have it. In a room that size. Ah! Wait, Zara...for people who don't understand you. I have trouble talking in terms others understand." All of them, even FeFe were smiling at her then. She looked at the ceiling, struggling to explain in a way they would understand, "Ok. Um, in a room that large, there is so much oxygen we take in as humans and carbon dioxide, that's the natural byproduct of human beings, what we expel breathing among other things, it's the carbon dioxide and the oxygen that matters. I assume the windows were closed to make people pass out the way they did, it's the only way the propulsion system would have worked."

FeFe nodded, "They were closed, now that you mention it. So hot in there, too! Damned uncomfortable."

"Right. I bet someone in that party pretended to be a waiter or butler, I'm not sure what they're called, I don't get out much, hardly matters—I'm babbling, sorry. They would have shut the windows and doors to cut off the fresh air supply, circulation would have thwarted whatever they used to send that noxious gas around the room to knock everyone out. In a room that size, with that many people, they would need some sort of a distribution carrier, a—a way for people to inhale whatever chemical substance that was. Ether has a spicy smell, I know because I have accidentally knocked myself out with it a few times during my early tinkering days. It reminds me of a spice shop and a sweaty man, it's a terrible smell. It's spicy, stings the nostrils and eyes. They are using something within these homes to distribute this stuff, the how and why have me interested, it's very clever, that concoction. I'd like to know so I can use it myself. If I could make a mini gas bomb to be tossed on the enemy, imagine what fun that would be in a fight, boom! Down they all go!" she said.

Zara got lost in thought for a moment, thinking of how she could stun people with a mixture like that. Harrison and the others exchanged amused, but confused glances.

"Good lord! You're worse than Dill! You make no sense at all. What is the point, Zara?" FeFe demanded.

"Oh! I forgot to make it. I do that. I apologize, my brain never stops working. In a room that size, with that many people, someone would not be completely under. A compound like that would be unreliable in its distribution, no way to spread it evenly. Ether is volatile. Too much or too little and it is not as effective. In some cases, ether creates, a—-ah, I don't know what you'd call it, but think of that place between being asleep and awake, when you are aware that things are happening, but your dreams haven't started. With that many people in a room that size, several someone's were in that state. They had to have heard or seen something, maybe they don't even know they did, but they did. Did you speak to the guests?" she said.

"Some of them," Douglas said.

"I'd speak to them all. They can help," Zara said.

"How certain of this are you?" Mr. Wills said.

Zara smiled then, "Mr. Wills, I'm rarely incorrect. My math is sound. Given the number of people, the dimensions of the room and the propulsion needed to distribute a product like that, I guarantee someone was in a sort of groggy, half-awake, half-asleep state. FeFe, Simon and Harrison were out cold, having only smelled whatever it was leaving them vulnerable to robbery, headache and nausea, I'm sorry about that. It's happened to me before, very unpleasant. They were nearest to the distribution point, I would guess if they didn't see anything at all until they woke. I'll make you a portable gas mask, one for everyone to filter out toxins and chemicals should that happen again. The trick with most gas masks is they don't account for the chemicals and down you go. Found that out the hard way too. Gave myself a shiner on the edge of my desk."

"I'll help you make those, I'd like to learn how," Dill said.

She smiled at him, "Marvelous! I can teach you, it's not difficult."

He nodded and offered her a genuine smile that Zara returned. She quite liked Dill. She finished her pastry and looked up. They were all grinning at her. She flushed a little.

"I, ah—say odd—things. Did I do that? I babble. I mentioned—ah, my mind doesn't shut down. Full of ideas, all kinds," she said.

"No! You just helped us out. More than we had to go on before," Simon said with a grin, "How would they get that mixture around?"

She took a sip of coffee and shrugged, "I have no idea, but it's very exciting! It would have to move quickly, the propulsion element would be key in a room so large. Can't have a slow moving domino effect giving people time to rush out in a panic, can you? Fast acting and comprehensive, diabolically clever that is. You three, you didn't see anything did you?"

"Like what?" FeFe asked, her expression intrigued.

She was the only one who seemed irritated by her, but she didn't begrudge Zara her intelligence. She seemed reluctantly impressed. Zara shrugged.

"Anything unusual around, automatons flying above, smoke billowing from some place, I don't know exactly. But, I shall endeavor to find out, preferably not knocking myself out in the process," she said.

FeFe rolled her eyes, "Are we really going to interview two hundred people at the word of the new girl with no field experience who has no idea how it was all done?"

Zara bristled, "I don't need field experience to know this, I assure you. It's mathematics—solid principles of logic and science—all things I'm unparalleled in as a tinkerer. I may lack some skills, but I do not lack here, Miss LaMay. Someone saw something because with that number of people, there is no way to guarantee they were all knocked out cold as you were. Getting them all down at once would have been difficult on its own. Ask them."

Zara said it with such absolute certainty, it seemed to take them all aback. Mr. Wills grinned and sipped his coffee. Harrison was looking at her, his dark eyes intent. She raised her chin a notch and stuck to her theory.

"I think It's worth looking into!" Mr. Wills rose as if to signal an end to the debriefing. "All of you, begin the interviews! Divide them up. Zara and Dill, get to work on those masks to filter out the chemicals and toxins. We'll need those either way since the enemy has this knock out gas. Zara, tomorrow you begin your other training. Today, get acclimated, ask questions, get to know the team. As for looking into these people, I believe I told you to talk to them all anyway, did I not, Room One Hundred?" He looked around the table.

The rest of them looked ashamed then. All except Harrison. He was sitting back, studying Zara thoughtfully. Her eyes met his. He offered her a slow smile, his expression sexual. Zara looked away quickly. Her eyes met Dill's.

"Shall we?" she said.

"Yes! I'm very pleased to be working with you, Zara," he said.

"And I you, Dill," Zara said.

She picked up her gadgets and put them in her bag, drank the last of her coffee and went with him to the tinkering tables. The two of them made a good pair, Zara decided. They worked quietly and passed one another tools without having to be asked. Zara felt comfortable with Dill, but then, she usually did with other tinkerers.

"I understand your mother runs Turner's Fashion Emporium. My mother and sister love the clothes," Dill said.

"Yes. My sisters love working with her, they like modeling and clothing My mother is a shrewd business woman. She knows what looks nice and she's very good at catering to the ladies in all regions of Jakarda. Fashions vary from one region to the next, as I understand it," Zara said.

She was determined to make friends with some people, small talk was not her strong suit, but she wanted to be better. Mr. Wills' comment about her being lonely had hit her hard. She never considered it much because admitting it to herself was difficult. However, hearing him say it out loud triggered something inside her. She wanted to have friends so badly, true friends. This was her chance.

"Turner's a genius!" FeFe said as she walked past the tinkerer's tables. "I get all my clothes and underthings from her. I love her fashions, so bold and sexy. Is what you have on one of hers?" FeFe asked.

Zara looked down at her clothes, "Yes, it is! She makes me special boots with no heel because I'm so terribly tall."

"You're not that tall! You make yourself sound like a giant!" Harrison said from across the room as he rummaged in the drawers for something.

Zara laughed genuinely at his expression, "I do stand eye to eye with some men. You're just very tall and muscled, Harrison. All women have to be smaller than you!"

He laughed, "Got me there. But, you're very small and feminine. You're not big at all."

She blinked at him in surprise, "I'm not?"

He shook his head, "Not in the slightest."

"Oh," she said.

She turned back to her work in confusion. Her mother said she was big. She assumed she had told the truth.

"I didn't realize your mother made such—ah, basic clothing with high necklines," FeFe said, pulling on a pair of lace gloves. She wore a form-fitting dress that showed off her curves, her bosom, and her shapely legs which were wrapped in a sexy set of fishnet stockings.

"Oh! She makes all styles. I have all these horrible freckles to cover," Zara said, bending a piece of silver to help Dill with the mask.

Dill looked at her, "I like your freckles."

"So do I," the other men in the room said, nearly in unison.

Zara made a face and looked at her arms, "I was told they were hideous and I should cover them to make them less noticeable because they're ugly."

"Who the hell told you a stupid thing like that?" Harrison stood up from the drawer.

Zara glanced at him, "My mother."

They exchanged glances. Zara didn't notice, she was tinkering. Dill was looking at her in disbelief. Zara was gently bending some silver, her head cocked to the side. He smiled at her when she handed him the piece he needed. She smiled back, unaware that even FeFe looked shocked.

"Your mother said you were ugly?" Marcus asked.

She glanced at him, "Yes. She also mentioned I was as tall as a man, and that was a bad thing as well. Hardly matters."

She was still working when she realized the room had gone silent.

Zara looked up at them all staring at her. She winced, "I'm attempting to be friendly, did I muck it up by sharing too much or saying something odd?"

Harrison's expression softened, he quietly answered her, "No—no, you did fine. We were just taken aback because your mother seems very nice in those photos of her plastered all over town."

Zara smiled, "Oh! Well, she has fine points. She is very clever, and an excellent business woman."

"Did she ever ask you to be a model for her?" Simon asked with a smile.

Me? No! Why would she ask me to be a model? I'm nothing special. My sisters are more well-suited to that sort of thing. I would hate being plastered all over billboards and posters. I'd rather smash myself over the head with a hammer then do a fashion debut! I don't even like going to watch them. Hours of dresses and frills, and—and—I don't even know what most of it is, to tell you the truth. I'm not the sort to 'ooh!' and 'ahh!' over a handbag or a silly hat," Zara said.

Harrison snorted with laughter, they all did. Zara laughed softly.

"Well, you'd have been a welcome addition to those posters, a lovely one at that," Douglas said.

Zara gave him a quizzical look, then smiled. She shrugged, unsure of what to say. Her reaction had them all exchanging looks. Mr. Wills watched them with a smirk. He patted Zara's shoulder.

"Good work, m'dear. Shouldn't you all be getting to those interviews, divide and conquer!" he said.

They nodded and headed out. The Crow's Nest, aptly named for the massive copper crow's nest at the very top of the building where two dirigibles were anchored, was a tall, silver, copper and gold building with the official Jakardian Government seal centered on the front of the glass entrance. A mechanical hand holding a human hand within a copper, gold and silver circle stood out from the center of the seal. The team traveled through the revolving door, one at a time as they emerged onto the street. The gentleman stopped under a twenty-foot, curved awning of burnished copper, headed towards their steam powered carriages and automobiles to take them to their separate assignments.

FeFe caught a handsome carriage, grumbling to herself about 'added duties' because of the new girl and waved nonchalantly as she took off away from the curb.

Douglas looked at Harrison and the rest of the gents. "She has no clue at all she's beautiful, does she?" he said.

"None!" Marcus said in disbelief.

They looked at Harrison, whom they expected to disprove their theory. Harrison Lowell could read people better than anyone, he always knew their tell. He nodded slowly.

"I agree with you. She has no idea," he said, as if he couldn't believe it, either.

"I like her," Simon said with a smile, "She's odd, to be sure, with all that strange babbling and talking to herself, but she's likable. It's oddly endearing, I find her quite adorable."

"I agree. So lovely and sweet-faced," Marcus said, "I like her long eyelashes and the breathless way she speaks."

Douglas nodded, "Aye, quiet, feminine and unassuming. Nothing at all like our FeFe."

"Not in the slightest!" Marcus laughed.

"Do you like her, Harrison?" Simon asked.

Harrison opened his mouth and closed it. He did, he liked her a great deal. He wasn't sure that he was comfortable with that, just yet. He never liked people at first, he always waited to see what they were hiding. But, Zara? She was fairly open and guileless. He paused, realizing—he did like Zara Turner. A lot. Right from the start, too. Trouble was, she didn't like him. He could tell. But he wasn't going to tell them that.

"I don't dislike her and that's a start. Hated all five of her predecessors, but she has potential. We'll give her a chance to prove herself. Can't deny that she's brilliant! Her inventions blew me away," he said.

They were all in agreement about that. They went to their carriages and steam powered cars to conduct interviews.

Three hours later, Harrison was speaking to Mrs. Silva Templeton. Mrs. Templeton had smelled the spicy scent that he, Simon and FeFe had inhaled, but still saw ten to twelve men in long brown coats, gas masks and scarves, and one woman. One of the men scooped up her favorite pearl necklace and matching ear bobs. She saw them run off with her husband's pocket watch, too. Better than that, Mrs. Templeton saw a smoky substance coming from the steam powered heater coils in the house. Zara was right. That had to be the distribution method, and there was one right where he, Simon and FeFe had been standing. Harrison was thrilled that she was right. Whatever else anyone thought, Zara had earned all that confidence she had when it came to her intelligence and as an added bonus, he realized, she managed to impress him. That had never happened with any of her predecessors.

CHAPTER FOUR

Zara looked at FeFe and grimaced. After a week of training with the gents and tinkering with Dill, Mr. Wills had asked FeFe to teach her about being coy and flirtatious. Zara stood to the side of Douglas' desk as he propped himself on the edge and FeFe leaned into his thigh. She batted her eyes at Douglas who grinned at her. She rubbed his arm with her fingertip and ran it down his forearm and the inside of his leg. She leaned in showing her breasts to him. Douglas followed the line of her cleavage with his eyes and then offered up a bit of the information she was seeking. FeFe giggled encouragement at him and stood up, arching her back slightly. She ran her hand along the side of her breast and smiled over her shoulder as she walked to her desk and opened the third drawer. Douglas didn't move off the edge of his desk for a while. He crossed his ankles and just stared at the floor. Zara watched FeFe walk away.

Harrison was watching the exchange nearby, a smirk on his face as he finished his paperwork. Zara frowned.

"See what I mean?" FeFe said to Zara. She grinned and peeled back the wrapper of a chocolate bar that had been hidden in the drawer. "If you give them a little, men will tell you anything." Her eyes glittered as she bit into the chocolate.

Zara crossed the room to the conference table. She sat down and crossed her arms, "I don't have your assets and I refuse to act as if I'm a fool."

Harrison burst out laughing. FeFe didn't remove her gaze from Zara's face, but her eyebrows moved closely together and her mouth went firm.

"Then you will fail. You cannot be as bad at flirting as this!" FeFe said. She moved back to her desk, "Mr. Wills, it's been two days and she will not take any of my suggestions!"

"FeFe, it's not as if I don't take them into consideration, I'm just…look at you and look at me! We could not be more different. You're a walking, talking, breathing embodiment of what men find attractive. I am not at all what's in fashion and I don't mind at all! I like myself just fine, but how can I be expected to be you when I'm nothing at all like you?" Zara asked.

"She's got a point," Marcus said.

He sat down next to her and took her hand, "Try smiling and looking less suspicious. Pay attention to what people say and try not to let your mind wander. People seem to bore you with their small talk, you have to listen to be a part of the conversation. That's a start."

Zara looked at him and offered a bright smile, "That's excellent advice, Marcus."

Marcus smiled slowly back, "Smile like that. Just like that."

Zara reddened and laughed as she looked away, pulling her hand from his grasp.

"Do that too, that's damned adorable!" Douglas said.

Zara turned redder, "Oh, do stop! I'm making a ninny of myself, blushing as if I were eleven years old again!"

"I have nothing to teach her, Mr. Wills. She is right. We are too different, she's much sweeter and more good than I. Have you ever seduced a man in your life, Zara?" FeFe asked.

Zara considered it, then laughed heartily, "Once. It went all wrong, I tripped over a lamp and gave myself a bloody nose. The end result was kissing, but there was far more laughing involved then I would have liked. It was an exercise in futility, one I never repeated again."

Douglas laughed, his eyes dancing, "Were you trying to be sexy, then?"

"I suppose. I was trying to act like my sister Temperance. She sort of walks with her breasts thrust forward, they're massive, she looks like the prow of a ship. Anyway, I gave it a go and it was ridiculous! The man I was with told me just to be myself, he didn't seem to mind my oddness."

Marcus grinned, "I don't mind it, either."

She laughed and nudged her shoulder to his, "That's kind of you to say. I do try, I simply do not get social things. Discussing the weather is dull, why must one do it?"

Douglas laughed, "No idea! I quite agree with you, Zara."

She shrugged and batted her eyes, "Like that?"

"Dear lord! Not so fast, you look like an insect," FeFe said.

"Hmm! I have more in common with my sister Tempie than I realized," she said.

Even FeFe laughed then, but she tried to cover it. Zara just giggled and went back to her lesson. She felt someone watching her. She glanced over her shoulder. Harrison was watching her with a thoughtful expression. He offered her a sexy smile. She smiled back politely. She wondered if he was capable of having a normal conversation with a woman, one that did not involve flirting or sexual advances. She had seen him talk to FeFe and several other women in the building. She only ever heard him refer to them as honey or sweetheart as he passed out winks all the time. He never talked to any of them normally at all.

She didn't dislike him, she just did not get the chance to know him over her first week. He was standoffish and formal, not like the others, who were trying to make her fit in. FeFe barely put in an effort, but she did try because Mr. Wills asked her. Admittedly, it took her a whole week to feel comfortable enough to talk to them and make jokes. She took a while to warm to people, but she was doing her best to be more involved.

She and Dill tinkered on the masks and made grappling guns for everyone during her first week. He was fun to work with. The team was thrilled about those masks, and thanked her. She was fast, efficient, made two guns to Dill's one.

"We're going to lunch, want to come?" Dill asked.

"Oh, no thank you. I'm not very hungry," she said.

He nodded and they left. Harrison was still working at his desk, determined to finish his paperwork today. Zara took out some nuts and dried fruit. She hadn't enough money to go out to lunch. She rationed her small bag of food, it had to be enough for tomorrow too. She had a large cup of coffee with creamer to fill her up.

"You don't eat much, do you?" Harrison said.

Zara shrugged, "Not really. You seem as if you do, you're very big."

He laughed, "I guess so. You never join us for lunch."

"I don't eat out much. Large crowds of people sometimes make me uncomfortable," she said, lying because she didn't want him to know she was too poor to afford it like the others.

Harrison was frowning at her, as if he knew she lied. He was opening his mouth to say something to her when Mr. Wills came in with the head of the Crow's Nest, Nathan Chapel. Zara stood and shook the man's hand with a smile. She glanced at Harrison. He didn't seem happy she had fibbed.

Harrison watched her closely as she talked quietly to Mr. Chapel, who was complimenting her on the spy tech and asking her to show the other tinkerers the blueprints so they could make similar tools for the agents in room Ninety-Nine, Ninety-Eight and room Ninety, the other field agents. She had lied to him just now, about the crowds. Harrison had no idea why she lied, but she had.

Just when she seemed to be warming up, she shut down on him, made him distrust her again. He watched her today, oddly delighted by the way she mocked FeFe's tutelage. She was intelligent enough to know that sort of flirting would never work for her. That was something in itself. It bothered him she didn't think she was as pretty as FeFe, bothered him more that Douglas, Simon and Marcus flirted with her so aggressively, but he was fairly sure she didn't realize what they were doing. She was dreadful with people, with flirting and with social cues. Marcus and FeFe had been working with her all morning, Douglas jumped in to help as well. The three of them were trying their best, she simply missed things. She was giving it her best, it was very endearing. She wanted to do well.

Mr. Wills left the room with Zara and Mr. Chapel. She looked excited to be making those gadgets for other agents. Harrison strode to his uncle's desk and snatched her file from within the drawer at the bottom. He sat down and began reading, determined to learn what he could about Zara Turner before they got back. He only got through the first page when he felt Room One Hundred moving on its track downwards because they had returned. Harrison stuffed the file back in frustration and returned to his desk. He hadn't learned anything at all, dammit.

He drummed his fingers on his desk, frowning when she walked back inside. She looked at him, smiling a bit. He offered her a sexual look back. She quickly looked away. His ire increased. Why the hell didn't she like him the way she liked the others? Women always liked him! He felt a rush of annoyance. Why did he want her to so badly, and what was she hiding? Harrison was determined to find out. He had to get that damn file. Zara was as perplexing as the case he was on, a puzzle, and he intended to figure both of them out.

In Room Thirty, Zara explained to the other tinkerers how to make her inventions. They nodded and smiled at her. Three of them, all men, walked up and introduced themselves to her. One of them, Rory McVickers, a handsome chap with blonde hair and hazel eyes sent her a level look.

"Listen, Zara. We all used to work in Room One Hundred. We were like you, wanted a taste of the field work. Had we been placed in other rooms with sensible agents, into any one of the other three field agent rooms, we would have loved the job. In fact, two former tinkerers from Room One Hundred have moved on to the other field offices and have loved the experience. You be careful of Harrison Lowell. I got shot because he talked me into one of his idiotic plans. I want to do field work, but not with that guy. He's so arrogant, puts everyone in danger and doesn't care who's hurt!" Rory said angrily.

"He's right. I was electrocuted on a rooftop! He pushed the wire in my hand and I got zapped! Laughed about it after," a plump fellow named Connor said.

"Oh, my! What was the wire for?" Zara asked.

"We were trying to stop some bad men in an elevator from escaping, but that's hardly the point! He cares more about getting the job done then if we die doing it," Connor said.

Zara frowned, because the very definition of a field agent was to do that, stop the bad guys at whatever cost. She wondered if these dolts understood that when they took the job. A little zap seemed worth it to her!

"What else has he done?" she asked curiously.

"He flirts with women shamelessly, you're very attractive. Be careful! He even seduces women on the job to procure information! He will do anything—anything at all to get the job done!" the third visitor, Samuel Sharp, said.

He reminded Zara of a large rat. She studied him silently. He was most likely jealous of Harrison's handsomeness, there was a bitter edge to his voice. If she had to guess, Harrison seduced a woman he fancied and he was envious.

"Did he get you hurt as well, Samuel?" Zara said.

He snorted, "Yes! Dagger in the thigh. Claimed he was pulling me out of the way. Using me as a human shield, is more like it. I have a scar!"

Zara nodded, aggravated by the way they were cutting Harrison down. What did a small scar matter? "I'll keep this in mind. This has been enlightening! Tell me, do you understand the schematics of the blueprints?" They smiled and nodded. Zara returned their smiles, "Well! Any questions, I'm over in Room One Hundred. Easy enough for you to find since the lot of you is familiar with it!"

They laughed and she left Room Thirty with a wave. She stood on the orange and gold marble ground floor of the Crow's Nest considering what she had learned when a man, handsome in a dull and rumpled way, approached her.

"Zara Turner, I presume?" he said.

"Indeed I am! And you are?" she said.

"I'm Charlie Macnamera. I used to be in Room One Hundred," he said.

Zara blinked. Good grief! Were they all seeking her out to warn her?

"Right, you're in Room Ninety now, correct?" she said.

He smiled. He had a very nice smile, "Yes, indeed! I wished to speak to you about Harrison Lowell."

"Of course!" Zara said, feeling annoyed on Harrison's behalf.

"He's a good chap. He loves the work here and the job, but he's the sort that is the job," he said.

"I'm not certain I understand your meaning, Mr. Macnamera."

"Well, he's impulsive, does what he has to in order to get the job done. Some of the others who worked with him, they'll tell you he's a bad guy, put them in the line of danger. That's true, to an extent. It's just that the only thing that matters to him is winning. Solving the case. If you get in his way, he will trounce you and put you in harm's way without a thought to get the job done. You will not matter to him, no one does except the people in that room with him. Understand? I found I couldn't work with someone that had no respect at all for me. He told me I needed to earn his respect, that respect shouldn't be given automatically! Can you believe that?"

Zara blinked, because she actually could believe that. She found herself agreeing with Harrison. Respect was earned. Instead of saying so, she smiled politely.

"Thanks for letting me know."

"Certainly! Oh, yes! Gerald! Come meet Zara Turner," he said.

Gerald, an intelligent-looking man a little older than she sauntered over. He was one of those rare tinkerers that didn't look rumpled. He was clean, well-dressed certainly. He ran a hand through his sandy hair.

"Warned her, have you, Charlie?" Gerald said.

"Yes, I have," Charlie said.

"Good. Miss Turner, that rogue got me shot in the shoulder. Shot! We were on a job facing down the Reform Mechanics. He had this reckless plan and we were in the line of fire running through a building that collapsed all around us, nearly taking us down with it. I was the latest tinker victim of Room One Hundred. I'd hate to see you be the next," he said.

Zara nodded slowly, "Tell me, did you solve your cases with him, catch the bad guys?"

They exchanged looks, then nodded.

"Yes, all of them," Gerald said.

"But at what cost?" Charlie exclaimed, "Sure, Room One Hundred has the best success rate, but not all of us are Dill. He's willing to put his life at risk as a tinkerer, he likes it! Told us it was exciting!"

Gerald nodded, "Chap's insane. You seem like the sensible sort. You should get out while you still can, unscathed, Miss Turner."

Zara smiled at them, "I appreciate the pep talk, but I really must get back to work. This has been illuminating, to say the least, gentleman."

They tipped their hats to her. Zara hurried back to Room One Hundred, waving to Mary, the receptionist at the front desk, who called each room down when someone needed to come in. She looked over at the gents she had just talked to, smiled, then turned away, rolling her eyes. What a pack of jellyfish! No wonder they didn't belong in Room One Hundred. No guts at all. Zara was not sure if she belonged there herself, but she knew one thing, she had more guts then the lot of those men combined. A scar! Stabbed in the leg? It didn't sound pleasant, but none of them died. They had no idea at all what it meant to be an agent. None. Perhaps she had an edge because her papa used to tell her all about what he did in that room, his heroics. She knew what was expected of her and Zara Turner never lost at anything if she set her mind to it. She was far too intelligent for that.

CHAPTER FIVE

Zara mimicked the motion Douglas demonstrated for her. She was getting decent at attacks. She had been practicing with him for two weeks now. He nodded at her in approval. She was happy with the work she had been performing and with her help in the investigation. Harrison, Douglas and Simon had all found people who were in the groggy state at the robbery, per her suggestion. They had seen an odd smoke coming from the pipes, which meant Zara knew how the substance was distributed. That discovery seemed to endear her to all of them except FeFe, who had no chance of ever endearing herself to Zara after their many failed lessons; and for Harrison, who seemed hesitant to trust her at all. It mattered very little to her. She was hesitant of him too, especially after her talks with the former tinkerers of Room One Hundred. She had decided they were idiots, that they did not know what was expected of them on the job, but all of them had said he was reckless. She had been watching him these past weeks and had to agree with them—at least partially.

Harrison was just so—arrogant. She didn't find his arrogance and abundance of charm comfortable. It bothered her, actually, because it made her feel so unsettled, gave her a funny feeling in the pit of her stomach that was not at all unpleasant, but she did not know what to make of it. The way he was always so sure of himself made her simultaneously impressed and annoyed. She hated the way he looked at her, it made her unsettled, causing that strange feeling. He studied her constantly and when she noticed him watching her, and looked at him, he'd send her this sexual smile. She ignored him and looked away, wishing he would just have a normal conversation with her, talk to her as if he valued her input in the room. When she looked away in frustration, he seemed more irritated than before, so he did it more often. He didn't seem to take her hint, that she was not interested in him for sex and she was leery of a friendship with him. She had never met a man like Harrison before, and he quite intimidated Zara.

"You've got it now! Should be able to get away well enough," Douglas said with a smile.

"Thank you! I enjoy this training we do very much! You're a skilled fighter and I like the exercise. It's very fun to learn something new," Zara said.

Douglas smiled, as if she had paid him the best kind of compliment, "Thank you. I've enjoyed our time together. I've got lots more to teach you."

"I'm certain of that," Zara laughed.

He studied her thoughtfully, then tugged on her braid, "Your hair reminds me of gold. I'm a fan of the blonde hair, myself."

Zara smiled, "Are you? I've always liked my hair, too. My papa had blonde hair and the freckles like me. He was handsome, I think. Had a big nose like my sister Temperance, but it looked very good on him, not so beaky as hers. He tugged on my braid as you just did. I always liked that."

She offered him a genuine smile. Douglas sighed and grinned at her, "Aye? I'll do it again sometime if you smile at me like that."

Zara reddened and giggled breathlessly, unsure of what to say. He was kind, a bit rough around the edges, but so much kinder than the other men in the room. He told her all about his upbringing in Northern Jakarda, and how he was very poor growing up. In the North, they faced famine, the farmers struggled to eat, even to live; and his family was still recovering. He was one of eight children, eight! A wealthy uncle helped him come to the city, get an education and a career. She quite admired him. Douglas was a very good man.

Douglas chuckled at her red cheeks and winked at her, "Love it when you blush! Come on then, once more."

Zara did as he asked. They were working on a mat in the center of Room One Hundred. Zara learned on her second day in the building, that the rooms moved all around the center of the Crow's Nest and Mary, the girl at the front desk, called the rooms down as needed. She had explained the process to Zara, while Zara was mending her coffee pot. The rooms were designed to shift levels and changed spots. A numeric code was selected where the door to each room would be dropped, into one of the five slots on either side of the main entrance hall, then moved the agents' offices onto on a series of tracks so all one hundred rooms shuffled along a maze of tracking. Zara loved that Room One Hundred changed location on the left side of the building. Sometimes they were street level, other times they were at the top with no window at all. She liked to go to the glass at the edge of the room and look down the deep corridor to see all the rooms moving about on sturdy rails and wheels, down all those flights to street level and back up to the tip top of the building. She loved and adored the tinker who invented this design—so clever. Sometimes they were on the corner of the tower with windows surrounding the perimeter and she liked that as well, because then she could see the whole of the city—skyscrapers all around, carriages moving up and down, and the people bustling below, so tiny they looked like ants scuttling about. It thrilled her, gave her such a rush to be a part of this world, a part of the Crow's Nest. Her papa, he would have been so proud of her. At first, the moving was hard to get used to, then she found she quite liked it. It was a tinkerer's dream to be in a room that was a tinker in itself.

She went through the moves with Douglas again. He nodded in approval, correcting her kindly and encouragingly as he always did, his soft brown eyes crinkled at the sides from his smiles.

"She's letting her guard down, Douglas," Harrison said.

"We're working on that, hands up, Zara," he said. She did as he asked, her expression determined.

Harrison strode onto the mat with them, "Show me."

He looked angry, for reasons she couldn't fathom. Harrison always seemed irritated with her. She showed him what she was taught. He grabbed her, spun her away from him and slammed her hard on the mat face first. She cried out when her nose connected with the ground, the metallic taste of blood on her lips.

"Oh, shit! I'm sorry, are you ok?" he asked.

An old feeling, one she hadn't felt in some time kicked in. The instinct to protect herself was a familiar one. Zara turned and kicked him in his manly parts as hard as she could. His face turned purple, his knees buckled. He crumpled on the mat with a grunt. She clutched her nose, blood gushing from her fingers and scrambled away from him, her eyes full of anger.

"You brute! I've been doing this for only two weeks! I still have a lot to learn!" she snapped.

"Not all that much. I didn't teach you that. That always works in a pinch, well done," Douglas said, roaring with laughter.

Zara relaxed and offered him a smile. Douglas hurried over with a handkerchief from the cabinet and held it to her nose, then gently probed her nose with her fingers.

"I don't think it's broken," he said.

Zara was struggling not to cry, "Okay."

"I'm—sorry," Harrison gasped, sitting up with a flinch, his eyes locked on her face, "Well done—with the shot to the crotch."

Douglas pushed her hair back from her face and neck and it fell out of its braid, blonde pieces tumbling all over.

Simon dropped to his haunches beside her, "Had that coming, Harrison. You frightened her, she's pale. Why did you do that? You all right, Zara?"

Her lip wobbled and she nodded. She took a deep breath, "It hurts. Are you sure it's not broken, Douglas?"

"I don't think so. Simon, take a look, eh?" he said.

"Let me help you up," Simon said.

She allowed him to help her to her feet. He slid his arm around her and she sat down in a chair nearby. She found Simon endearing because he was kind, and he laughed all the time. He found so many things funny that she missed! She liked sitting with him—he made her laugh with his jokes. Usually he was very jovial, but he wasn't laughing now. Zara was shaking a little, and both he and Douglas looked worried. Harrison watched her closely, his face tight. Zara avoided his gaze. She was a little afraid of him, now. He was bigger, stronger. He could hurt her the same way her mother had, she'd been right to be wary of him. Her eyes met his and she looked away, her head down.

He knew.

He knew that she had been hit before, he could tell. He looked upset, his eyes apologetic. She took a deep breath and smiled in an attempt to cover her shock, at least in front of Douglas and Simon, who assumed she was rattled because she had never been hurt before.

"I'm ok, just took me aback," she said.

Simon checked her nose, gently touching it. She winced a few times. He smiled, "You're ok. Going to be a bit bruised, but fine. You can go and change into your regular clothes and get washed up in the ladies' washroom. We can do our weapons training on the roof. Meet me up there?"

"Ok. Thank you," she said.

Simon winked at her. He and Douglas left her be, shaking their heads at Harrison as they passed by. He had the decency to flush and shrug, as if to say he didn't mean it. Harrison stood to his feet and started toward her. In a sudden rush of fear and uncertainty, she jumped up and hurried away from him, her head down. She left with a muttered apology and went to the ladies room down the hall, her breathing a bit labored.

She stood at the counter and turned on the cold water. Looking at her reflection, she closed her eyes, visions of her mother whipping her with a switch, calling her ugly and useless flashing in her mind. She shook them off and cleaned the blood off her face with shaky hands. Her nose was red and angry, she was very pale, her eyes wide, fearful. She took off the pants and shirt she trained in, stowing them in her locker and pulled on a simple dress with a brown leather vest and a grey and white striped midi skirt with a ruffle at the bottom. She pulled on white stockings and little grey slippers. Her dress had little capped sleeves, which showed her long, milky arms covered in freckles. The pretty outfit was one of her mother's newest creations.

She brushed her hair and braided it over one shoulder. She stepped back from the counter, took a deep breath and looked at herself.

"It's not the same thing. You are not a victim anymore," she said aloud.

"You speaking to me?" someone asked.

Zara turned around to see Mary, the receptionist, emerging from the end stall and shook her head, "No, just talking to myself."

Mary smiled, her blue eyes bright against her olive skin. She wore an abundance of makeup and tight, low cut clothing. The rumor Zara had heard was that she used to be a lady of the night. Zara admired her, if that was the case, securing a job for herself and learning a skill other than ones from the bedroom. Mary was very sweet to her, always said hello, asked her about herself and her time in Room One Hundred. They were stationary, the washrooms, on the main floor near the front desk where Mary worked with the other receptionists. They were alone in the ladies washroom. The toilets were aligned to the left of the entrance; a bank of sinks set into long counters with benches ran down the center of the washroom on either side of a narrow divider; and the small area with lockers for changing was off to the right as you walked in. Each of the wooden lockers was small, with a lock to safely stow a few small things. Zara folded and carefully put her workout clothes away and locked the wooden door. Mary mistook her silence and activity as a slight.

"I'm sorry," Mary said, "You most likely don't wish to talk to the likes of me, fine lady such as yourself." Her eyes were red as if she had been crying.

Zara frowned. She walked over and sat down, "Of course I'll speak to you. I was just hurt in my fight training in Room One Hundred. Harrison Lowell smashed my face to the ground to show me my guard was not up and it quite rattled me. It was all I could do not to cry right then in the room. I reacted and kicked him in his, er, manly parts. I'm just embarrassed, I suppose."

Mary laughed delightedly, "Right in the cock and balls, then?"

Zara reddened at the use of her crass language, but she smiled and nodded, "Very hard, too."

Mary leaned her shoulder into Zara's, "I'd like to have seen that. Rushed to the ladies' to recover, then?"

Zara nodded, "Yes."

Mary smiled her lip wobbling, and fidgeted with her dress, tugging a bit at the hem, as if she wanted to make it longer. It was one of her mother's designs.

"I like your dress. My mother is Mrs. Turner, of Turner's Emporium," Zara said.

Mary grinned, "I love her stuff! Some of the other ladies, they were just disparaging me because I'm not a fine lady, but I liked this dress, the blue matches my eyes. They said it was not appropriate for work—too short and low cut, better for an evening out. I came in here same as you, to gather my wits. Other girls here, they ain't nice to me."

Zara nodded, "I understand. Other ladies, they don't much like me either."

"Why not?" Mary asked.

Zara sighed, "I'm a tinkerer. Top of my class at the Academy. I'm not very good with people Mary, and I find I don't trust other women. My mother and sisters, they were…"

"Cruel types. I think that when I see them in the posters—bitches," Mary said.

Zara flushed, laughing at her colorful use of language, "Yes, they are. The only other woman in my office is FeFe LaMont and she doesn't like me at all."

"That's because Harrison Lowell never takes his eyes off you and they have a carnal relationship with each other," Mary said.

"What?—they do?" Zara said, ignoring the surge of disappointment she felt at learning Harrison and FeFe were intimate.

"Harrison gets around, all the lads in Room One Hundred do. Except Dill, he and I partake in dates and sex on occasion. He's a handsome man, I don't mind he's rumpled and talks in riddles," Mary said.

"I don't mind that about him, either. I like Dill, he and I are the same. Mary, I don't know if you'd care to, but, would you like to have lunch with me today?" Zara asked.

Mary's eyes watered, "Zara, you're real sweet, but you don't want to be seen with me. The other girls, they're never going to warm to you if we have lunch together. You've been kind, fixed my coffee pot for me the other morning when I mentioned it wasn't working, didn't charge me a cent! You talk with me too, like an equal. I like you, but I don't want to ruin your reputation because I used to be a lady of the night."

Zara huffed, "I think what you have done for yourself is remarkable. You were a lady of the night, certainly, but you made something of yourself by securing a good job here at the Crow's Nest. You have good job now, a secretarial background and you are very good at running the show up front. I was very impressed today when you showed me how the Nest works. It doesn't matter to me what you did before. Our past shapes us, it isn't who we are forever. We can change, if we wish to. Be more. You see, I'm odd, Mary. I know I am. The truth is...I live on my own and I have for six months. I moved out of my mother's house because...because she beat me. Until I fought back and struck her same as she did with me. She beat me badly and when I tasted my own blood again today—I came in here to get a hold of myself because I had to remember: this was different, that I'm strong, same as you. Harrison was trying to teach me, not hurt me on purpose as she did, but I have old hurts I sometimes think might never heal. I fought back against my mother and made something of myself, too. We're the same, you and I. We do what we must to survive, to hell with those who would judge us for doing the best we can."

Mary's eyes filled. She leaned in and hugged Zara tightly. It had been some time since Zara had hugged a real person, not just her automaton Annie, who picked out her clothes and did her hair, cooked her meals and kept her apartment cleaned up. Annie had been Zara's only company for years. Her hugs were cold, but Zara loved them. Her papa had made Annie, it was all she had left of him. Mary's hug was nice, kind and much warmer than Annie's. Zara shut her eyes, reveling in how it made her feel to have another person care about her, and her affection for Mary increased in that moment because of the kindness the other woman showed her.

"You and I, we're going to be friends, Zara," Mary said.

Zara smiled at her, "Of course we are."

Mary looked happy then, "You on a fixed budget, too?"

"Yes! I'm in desperate need of funds at the moment. I've been eating nuts, bread and butter for months. I have a patent on that coffee pot you're fond of, but the funds are tied up. I tinker in my building to save a dollar a month for rent. I can hardly meet my expenses on my salary here," Zara said.

"Me too! I live on Elm and Washburn. That apartment complex has ten places. Nice neighbors, good sort. You?" She said.

"I live at Second and Broadway Park, in the Holmes Building," Zara said.

"I'm not far from you, next block! We're practically neighbors, it's a sign. You stick with me. I know all the cheap places. Today, we go for soup at Miggy's Delicatessen, you'll love it!" she said.

Zara smiled, "I'm very excited!"

Mary studied her and smiled, "Me, too. I needed a good chum."

Me, too. I have to go meet Simon. He's teaching me to shoot a gun," Zara said.

"He fancies you, so do Douglas and Marcus. They mention you and your pretty clothes and hair. Douglas wants to ask you to dinner, but they all hold back, I think because Harrison fancies you, too," Mary said.

Zara huffed, "Me? That's nonsense! I really must go now, lots for me to do. See you soon!"

Mary laughed and waved, then went to clean herself up. Zara smiled because she looked as happy as Zara felt. She walked to the elevator leading to the roof. Harrison appeared out of nowhere and took her arm, pulling her to the side into a nook to be alone.

"I'm so sorry I hurt you, Zara, are you ok?" he said.

Zara pulled her arm from him and nodded avoiding his gaze, "I'm fine. You just startled me, that's all. I'm sorry I reacted badly. Are your, er, parts, in order?"

He laughed heartily, "My parts will recover, thank you."

"Good," she said with a small smile and actually looked him in the eyes.

"I know it's none of my business, Zara, but can you tell me who hit you?" Harrison said.

She stilled, flushing. She swallowed hard, "What do you mean?"

Harrison took her hand, his eyes searching her face, "You know what I mean, Zara. Who was it?"

Zara took a deep breath. She couldn't pull her eyes away from his face. He knew; and she had to tell the truth. He was not the sort of man to lie to, he'd know if she tried. Still, she hesitated, afraid to trust him. He offered her a real smile, not the sort he normally tried to offer her. She took a deep breath, "It was my mother. I don't want to discuss the particulars with you, it's over now. Please don't tell anyone. It's in the past."

"I would never do that," his face and voice assured her. "I can keep a secret, part of the job. I know you live alone and you never discuss your family, is that why?"

She nodded, but she didn't elaborate. Harrison surprised her by cupping her cheek. She looked at him, her heart going fast.

"Hey—That wasn't your fault...what she did. It is not your fault," he emphasized the last few words. "You're smart and capable. You impress me and everyone in this office and for the record, she's wrong about you—wrong about your looks. You're very beautiful. You're not too tall and your freckles are adorable. You don't know you are beautiful, but you should. You don't have to be confident about your tinkering exclusively, you are lovely and funny when you open up, sweet too, and kind. She shouldn't have beat you. It was bad, I can tell by how afraid you looked when I took you down. You fought back—good for you. I hope you fought her back, too. Was she ever kind to you?" he asked, stroking her cheek with his thumb.

"When my papa was alive, she mostly left me be. She ignored me and left my care to him, but she was never nice to me. When he died, she didn't bother to hide her dislike and that's when the beatings started," Zara said.

He shut his eyes and Zara realized, he was much more tender-hearted than she had realized. He spoke softly, "I'm so sorry, Zara."

Zara smiled, "I only see her once a month now. I'm not to be pitied. She taught me people can only truly hurt you if you let them. I got out and I'm strong. I have my own place, I got away from her and that hell I was living in, I have a good job here and I love the work. That's fine by me, only seeing her when I must. We're polite and we meet publicly. Sometimes, I panic in those situations like we were in, you and I. That's why I told Mr. Wills I wasn't sure I was suited for this job. The fighting…it brings back more than I would like it to, but I can take care of myself. I just did. I can do this job, I just need practice."

"Of course you can do it, you were amazing," Harrison said.

Zara took a step back and shrugged, "Time will tell. I appreciate your apology. But I have to meet Simon. I'll see you shortly."

Harrison watched her go, a frown on his face. Dammit! Her mother beat her; he suspected it was a relative. He never would have guessed it was her mother, not that charming woman on the posters all over Jakarda. He pegged it as being those sisters of hers. They seemed like viperous little harpies, oozing sweetness and batting their eyes in the phoniest of displays. Shit! He hated being right sometimes. He took a steadying breath and went back into Room One Hundred. He sat down and gazed out the window, resting his elbows on the desk, hands clasped in front of him.

It explained her behavior. It took her a whole week to warm up to them, she was so guarded. FeFe blamed it on her being a tinkerer, said they were odd. She was right, they normally were, but there was something about Zara that told him it wasn't just because she was odd. She looked so pleased when they listened, as if she was unaccustomed to being heard, to being listened to. Every time she was a paid a compliment, any compliment on her tinkering, she flushed and smiled as if she was happy, but when someone said her hair looked pretty or complimented her looks, she got this skeptical look. She always politely thanked whomever complimented her, she had the best manners, but she didn't believe them. Someone had drilled into her head that she was ugly and worthless. And it was her mother. Zara was strong, a fighter. Not one to cry about her bad luck, she just changed it. He admired that.

Harrison had thought it was an act, her odd behavior, but now he realized it wasn't. She had no confidence at all about her looks and no social skills because she isolated herself, afraid to be hurt because her mother was so cruel. She knew how smart she was, her tinkering was no doubt put to good use by her mother and sister, but that was all she knew. She had no friends either, he had finally read her file. He swiped it off Mr. Wills' desk yesterday. There were two interviews with people she went to school with, both of them seemed like assholes. One was an ex-lover, the other a former friend.

He knew how that felt, the betrayal Zara suffered. He'd had a friend of his own do something similar to him—a man he'd grown up with, his best friend, James Carver. James had slept with his girlfriend, a woman Harrison cared deeply for. He was pretty sure it was because Harrison got into the Crow's Nest, and James didn't. Harrison had never thought they would stop being friends over something so stupid—a woman—not after they had known each other since they were children. Sure, they had their ups and downs, competed a bit, but he expected more of James. Yes, Harrison knew exactly how Zara felt, being hurt by friends like that.

Harrison broke the rules reading that file, but he read everyone's. He hadn't been prepared to feel bad for Zara. He had thought she was an icy bitch, a snob who thought she was better than him. He thought that was why she didn't flirt with him and looked away when he tried to get her attention, something he desperately wanted for reasons he couldn't fathom. None of the things that always worked for him with women worked with her, not one! Yet, she had warmed to the others, chatting with them and making jokes. She liked Marcus better than him! No one liked Marcus more than Harrison. He was so stiff. Yet, Zara seemed to admire him, and Harrison hated it, the two of them shared a love of the compu-bot and research, and they sat and talked to one another about it, laughing. Harrison wanted something in common with her very much, because, even though Zara was on the quiet side, to be sure, he just knew she wasn't cold.

She wasn't any of the things he first thought she was.

Harrison had never so badly misjudged someone. Zara was a lonely, brilliant woman struggling to make her way in the world, and he was a jaded asshole for not realizing it. It bothered him, the way she warmed up to everyone but him, so he flirted more aggressively with her in the hope that she would flirt back. When she didn't respond to him, he decided she was a prude or a bitch. He had acted like a prick to her. He was critical and hard on her in every area except tinkering, he had no complaints there. He ran a hand over his face and sighed. She had him all discombobulated!

"What's your issue, Harrison? Is it your cock? Do you need someone to stroke it? I can help with that," FeFe said with a smile.

He chuckled, "Can you?"

"You know I can. Care to go up to the roof for some air?" she said.

"Can't, honey, Simon and Zara are up there," he said.

"Little miss brains is ruining our morning screw," FeFe said.

Harrison felt a rush of irritation, "Don't call her that."

FeFe's brown eyes flashed, "Oh, no...Don't tell me she's won you over, too? After just a few weeks?"

Harrison smiled, lounging back in his chair, "What is your problem with her? Is it because she's so beautiful?"

"That beanpole with all those freckles who dresses like a prude? Hardly," FeFe said.

He had struck a nerve, "It is! I never would have guessed that you would be so intimidated by another woman in Room One Hundred."

FeFe stood angrily and flipped her hair over her shoulder, "Since you like her so much, you can go to her for sex. Of course, you'll have to wait forever. She strikes me as the virginal sort."

Harrison laughed and sent her an I-told-you-so-look. She stomped over to the keypad on the wall and punched the button to take the room down with Harrison still laughing at her. She glared at him and walked out. Marcus sent him a look.

"What did you do to tick her off?" Marcus asked.

"I stood up for Zara. I like her," Harrison said.

Marcus smiled, "Me, too. There is something about her. She's doing good work here as well. She's getting the names of all the major players in the Reform Mechanics. I like working with her. She looks at me and listens to everything I say, as if I'm the most interesting person she ever met. I like that about her very much, it's cute. She asks a lot of questions, seems to like all the intrigue that goes along with the job. She has an aptitude for this sort of work and I like listening to her speak in that soft, breathless voice of hers."

"She's very inciteful, that is nice and she's right most of the time. I like her voice, too. She's so graceful," Harrison agreed, shaking off the irritation he felt when Marcus mentioned his like of her.

"She's wonderful to tinker with. She knows what I need without me having to ask and vice versa. That's never happened to me before," Dill said from across the room, facing them.

"She's a peach! Harrison, I need you to go and check on something for me, I'd like you to take Zara with you, get her used to cases. We had a witness come forward, I'd like you to take her and show her how to do an interview. Her name is Millicent Meriweather," Mr. Wills said.

Harrison nodded, standing. Zara walked into the room with Simon just then, her hand in the crook of his arm, giggling like crazy, "Did I really kill a bird? I didn't mean to!"

Simon laughed heartily, the chap was always laughing, "It was an accident! It's hard to say, it dove down so quick. I told you how I accidentally shot that crow once, it happens to the best of us! Don't fuss over it!"

Zara laughed delightedly, "Poor fellow! I'm not the best shot."

"You're getting there, Zara," Simon said with a warm smile.

Harrison found himself glaring at her hand in the crook of his arm, and at the way they were smiling at one another. Simon was very cheerful, always endearing himself to someone, especially women. It seemed he had done so with Zara, too. He was fun, plain and simple, and Zara had noticed. Harrison stood, walking over to her with a smile.

"Zara, Mr. Wills wants me to take you on a call, to get you used to being in the field," Harrison said.

"Ok. Will we be back in time for lunch? I'm supposed to have lunch with Mary today," she said.

Harrison glanced at the others, who arched their brows. Marcus winced. Harrison studied Zara, wondering if she knew Mary's former vocation, "Mary?"

"Yes! I admire her. She turned her life around. She was in a disreputable profession before, I like her," Zara said, taking her leather bag and pulling the strap over her head. She lifted her braid from under it and pulled on her gloves.

Harrison grinned at the others, who were smiling at each other. Of course she knew, she was too inciteful not to know.

"I will have you back in time for your lunch date," Harrison said.

Zara offered him a smile, "Thank you!"

He nodded, ignoring his rapidly beating heart. He had no idea why she did that to him, but he liked how she made him feel. He offered her his arm. She took it nervously. Harrison smiled and led her to the door. He punched in the code and the room moved downwards. FeFe was standing there, smoothing her dress. Jeff Teagen, a dark haired tinkerer was grinning at her, his glasses askew. She'd obviously just had sex with him to try and make Harrison jealous. He sent her an amused smile. FeFe was predictable if nothing else.

"Shall we, Zara?" he asked.

"Ok," Zara said.

Harrison tipped his hat and left with Zara on his arm, FeFe glaring furiously behind him. Zara glanced at FeFe, then at him. Zara laughed heartily.

"She looked as though she'd just sucked a lemon," she said.

"I have no idea why," he said as straight faced as he could muster.

Zara laughed and gave him a suspicious look. He smiled innocently and she burst into laughter. Harrison found himself chuckling because she was laughing so hard.

"You're a bit of a rake, aren't you?" she said.

"Little bit," he agreed with a chuckle.

"How come you're a rake?" Zara asked.

Harrison arched his brows, "Because I've enjoyed the company of many women?"

"No! I meant, how come so many at once? Can you not enjoy them just one at a time?" she asked, her expression curious.

She struck a nerve, but Harrison didn't show it, offering her another smile, "I suppose so. I just think it's fun, dating more than one lady at once."

Zara was quiet a moment, as if carefully considering his words, "I could see why. You must have been badly hurt by a woman to make you feel that way. A man hurt me like that once, too. I understand not wanting to let someone in."

Harrison's heart squeezed. She was too smart for her own good, she went and figured him out. He smiled charmingly, refraining from comment. Zara had already moved on, she grinned at Mary as they strode past the circular desk at the front of the Crow's Nest, their shoes tapping loudly on the marble floor.

"I'll be back in time for lunch," Zara said, smiling at the woman.

"I'm excited!" Mary said.

Zara smiled, "Me, too!"

Harrison studied Zara, his heart hammering, partly because he was afraid she'd ask which woman hurt him, and partly because she was beautiful to watch. Her shapely mouth curved sweetly when she smiled and made her blue eyes twinkle. In that dress, there hinted that a supple, graceful body existed under it, too, and made something buzz inside him. She had some shapely, long legs. He liked her legs. His thoughts tumbled to her wrapping them around him while he kissed her full lips. He cleared his throat and forced those thoughts from his head. She was just warming up to him, best not to scare her off with flirting. He got the impression that he intimidated her and she wasn't sure how to take him trying to seduce her. He planned to make her more comfortable, treat her better. She deserved it. She had earned his respect, and his admiration. There was more to her than how she looked. He took her to his carriage. It was parked behind the Crow's Nest.

"Take us to Millicent Meriweather's house," Harrison said.

"Very good sir, to Morgan Meateater's," the automaton said.

Zara burst out laughing at Harrison's annoyed expression, "Something is the matter with him."

"He has a short, I can fix it. Give me a boost."

Harrison helped her up to the front, taking advantage of getting a good look at her long slender legs and the garters that held up her stockings. He looked away, trying to hide the fact that he enjoyed the view. He'd grown accustomed to afternoon sex with FeFe. It seemed every little thing turned him on, including a pretty set of legs and a garter belt. Zara opened the panel with tools she got from her bag and had Hank, his driver, set to go in no time.

Harrison put his hands at Zara's waist and lifted her down. She smiled at him.

"He had a short in his voice box and navigation system. It will mess with his ability to take you to the right place, especially if it's not somewhere he's accustomed to going. All set!" she said.

"He's been acting up since we were shot at," he said.

He still had his hands at her waist. She looked up at him, her blue eyes wide, "You were shot at?"

He nodded and took a step back, "Yes. Let's be off."

Zara nodded and got into the carriage.

"Why were you shot at?" she asked.

"A plan went south," Harrison said.

"Job hazard?" Zara asked.

He laughed, "Sometimes."

Harrison's carriage was steam powered and flew like most modern models. However, his had a lean to it of about four degrees. Harrison sighed in annoyance. Zara giggled again.

"I can fix that for you, too. You're off balance. It will only take me a few moments," she laughed.

"Thanks," he said with a chuckle.

They managed to reach their destination. Zara kept laughing, so he found himself laughing. It was a very bumpy, crooked ride in which they were facing one another on the black benches, smashed to the left wall of the covered carriage.

"At least you have a carriage! I'm too poor for a carriage, although I'd love one. I ride one of those steam powered motor bicycles to work. Mine is the little red and black one out front chained to the tree," Zara said.

"That's yours? I always wanted to ride in one!" he said, leading her to the door of a stately home in the nicer part of the city. It was white with a copper roof and shutters with beautiful roses framing the front door.

"You can try out mine. I modified it, it goes forty miles per hour!" she said excitedly.

He grinned, "That sounds fun!"

"It is! I have to tie my skirts in the front when I go that fast or show everyone my underthings, that would be the downside," she said.

He chuckled, "Not to whoever saw them."

She snorted with laughter. Harrison took her hand in his and held it gently, "Can't be as fun as that crooked carriage ride we just had."

"I quite enjoyed that!" she giggled.

He squeezed her hand and laughed, "You have a good sense of humor, Zara."

"You're funny, as well, Harrison," she said with a bright smile.

Harrison's heart went faster. What the hell was happening to him? He felt a little like when he was a teenager and Charlene Mills moved in next door with her lovely blonde hair and blue eyes. His heart had gone fast and he acted like a fool, grinning at her like the green young man he was. He let go of Zara's hand and rapped on the door. Zara looked around.

"I like this house. It's lovely," she said.

"It is. How is your apartment?" he asked.

"It's a hovel," Zara said.

Harrison threw his head back and laughed because she was completely serious, "That's a shame, Zara."

She smiled and shrugged, "Well, it is! It's all I can afford. I don't mind you knowing since you know my history a bit. It's a complete dump."

"I believe you! You're very honest," he said.

"I have heard that before. Just me, I suppose," she said.

A maid bot, all gold plated—the mark of a wealthy person with money to burn—answered the door. She had a fancy uniform, and a more human face, the mark of a well-made bot. She wore a gold maid's uniform, had two distinct legs instead of legs moulded at the bottom of one solid piece like the ones Harrison had in his home. The expensive models looked more fancy, like this one.

"Harrison Lowell and Zara Turner to see Mrs. Merriweather. We're from the Crow's Nest, she contacted us," Harrison said.

"You've been expected. Please come in," the robot said. They followed it down a hallway, it hovered on a small set of tracks flush with the polished wooden floor. The track system was expensive too, top of the line. This woman was quite wealthy.

They were led into a grand sitting room that had blue wallpaper and an abundance of flowers in vases all over, the room was littered with flowered items, as if it were an indoor garden, the effect was overwhelming. An older woman stood, she was very fat, and dressed in a gown too young for her that showed off her thick legs in fishnet stockings. Harrison smiled charmingly as they were introduced by the robot.

"Mrs. Merriweather, how good of you to meet with my associate and I. It's a pleasure to meet you. I hope your ordeal has not been overly taxing," he said.

"Oh, you handsome man! It was, it truly was. When my friend Susan Hempsburg, of the Green Isle Hempsburg's, told me you wished to speak to all those involved in one of those garish robberies, I simply had to come forward," she said.

Harrison nodded, smiling charmingly, "Of course you did. You seem the sort to do her civic duty."

She nodded somberly, "I am. I truly am."

Harrison smiled at Zara, "This is Miss Turner. She has a few questions for you."

Zara seemed to have been struck dumb by his charm and he needed to snap her out of it. She was staring at him, her eyes wide. Zara recovered, smiling as she turned her attention to Mrs. Merriweather.

"Oh, indeed I do! I wish to tell you I'm sorry for all that you suffered. Was anything taken from you?" Zara asked.

Mrs. Merriweather seemed to like the wide-eyed curiosity and full attention Zara was showing her, "Why, yes there was! My favorite brooch. It was my mother's."

"Oh, no! It had sentimental value most of all, then?" Zara said.

"Indeed, young woman. Indeed," she said.

Zara offered her a small smile, "Dreadful. Were you injured? Many of the guests fell and were hurt, as I understand it."

"I was! I have a series of bruises. Lucky for me, I landed on my son, Philbert," she said.

Zara's lips quirked. Harrison fought the urge to laugh as she carefully controlled her expression, "Was he injured, Mrs. Merriweather?"

"Bruised to bits and he sprained a toe!" she said, fanning herself rapidly.

Zara was struggling not to laugh. Harrison's heart went rapid again, she was damn cute. He looked away, and took over for her, "That is terrible. Did you happen to smell or see anything unusual?"

"I smelled something spicy and strongly scented. Made my nose and eyes water. It hit me, I was light headed, then Philbert caught me and we both went down. In the haze of vapor, whitish in color, I saw a man. He was very muscled and handsome, like you, Mr. Lowell. He was wearing a gas mask and a wide brimmed hat. He took my brooch, plucked it from my neck. I remember him distinctly because behind the mask he had one brown eye and one blue. He was dressed like the others, in a duster and scarf, common clothes if you ask me," she sniffed.

Zara glanced at him, her eyes wide. He sent her a cautioning look and she schooled her expressions. She was not good at hiding things, he'd have to work with her. She nearly laughed in the woman's face and now she looked excited.

"Two different colored eyes? Huh. Exactly how tall did he seem?" Zara asked.

"Stand up, Mr. Lowell," Mrs. Merriweather said.

Harrison did as she asked and stood, "Might taller than you, I'd say. An inch or two, but he was muscled like you. Had long hair for a man, dashing in a criminal way."

Harrison nodded and looked at Zara expectantly. She smiled.

"Is there anything else you might tell us?" Zara asked.

Mrs. Merriweather considered, "He had a woman with him. She was busty, dressed in a nice gown. She was handsome, more than beautiful, voluptuous with dark hair. She had on a gas mask, but I could swear she was a guest. She had on a duster, but her shoes! She had on elegant, high-heeled shoes more suited to evening wear and stockings!"

Zara arched her brows, "Really?"

"Just so!" Mrs. Merriweather said.

Zara looked at Harrison, her eyes wide. He was really going to need to work with her. He smiled charmingly and took Mrs. Merriweather's hand. He brought it to his lips and offered her a half smile.

"Well, you have been most helpful. I do appreciate it, Mrs. Merriweather," he said.

She flicked out her tacky, laced fan and shook it at her face, giggling like a schoolgirl, "It was my pleasure, Mr. Lowell."

"We shall see ourselves out, ma'am. Thank you for your time. If we have more questions or you think of anything more, contact us," he said, handing her his business card with a wink.

She giggled and nodded, "Nice to meet you!"

"And you!" Zara said with a smile.

They left. Zara fixed his carriage on her knees in under three minutes while he watched her with a grin. Safely inside, carriage straight, they drove back to the Crow's Nest.

"Was she telling the truth? I don't know how you can tell, but you seem to know when someone tells the truth," Zara said.

"Yes, she was," Harrison said. He smiled because she had noticed that—and that was something in itself. It normally took people a while to read him, but she got that right away, "Or she believes she is. I wonder who this mystery woman could be?"

Zara frowned, "No idea and no way to find out. I rather like this intrigue part of the job. Did I do ok?"

"Yes. You did very well. We need to work on you not showing everything in your expressions. You are an open book. Nice you kept from laughing at her, though," Harrison said with a smirk.

"She's very fat! Her poor son is lucky she didn't sprain more than his toe! I let my imagination get away from me, can you picture it? I saw him as thin as she is fat, scrambling to save his rotund mama, and taking a fall from the gas at the same time," Zara giggled.

He found himself laughing as he pictured just that, "I've gone and made him bald."

Zara snorted with laughter, "Oh, better still! Perhaps he said something like, 'mother, noooo!' upon their descent."

Harrison was laughing so hard he clutched at his sides, "There is an image!"

"I know! I do that sometimes, Harrison, I let my mind jump to conclusions. Helps me in tinkering, makes me laugh in real life situations. Also makes me bad at a ball," Zara said.

"I can see why!" he said.

She studied him with a smile, "We're going to be friends, I think."

Harrison's heart hammered fast. He refrained from winking at her. With a straight look and a slight nod he replied, "Yes. Yes, I believe we are."

CHAPTER SIX

Zara tried to focus on Harrison's lessons on schooling her expressions, but he looked so handsome today, she could hardly think straight. He had on tan slacks with a matching vest and a white shirt with the sleeves rolled up to his elbows in a casual, masculine manner that suited him. It was very hot today, she had her hair pinned up on her head with blonde pieces of it tumbling all about her head. She had on a pair of pants that her mother had designed. They were short pants—only came to the knee—and with a white shirt and a vest, it was a cool, perfect outfit for a hot day. It was terribly hot today. They had all the windows open in Room One Hundred, but at ground level, there was not much of a breeze.

"No, I can still see it in your eyes," Harrison said.

Zara stomped her foot in frustration, "You can? I'm trying so hard. Have I improved at all?"

"Yes, very much so. You're doing fine, Zara. I can just tell, so someone who is skilled at interrogation might be able to, as well," he said.

She huffed and sat back, her expression miserable. She glanced at the others, they were all lounging on the other side of the room, "I'm not good with people."

She said it quietly, so none of the others would hear.

"You are much better than you think," he said, his expression softening as he looked at her and held out his hand to help her up.

She smiled at him and took his hand. She suddenly stood on her tiptoes and kissed his cheek. He tilted his head at her in surprise. "What—?"

"You're patient and kind with me. I thank you for that. But now, I have to meet Mary for lunch. We can resume our torture after that," she grinned.

He laughed softly. His look toward her—his expression almost... tender—made Zara flush and look away. She grabbed her bag and put it over her head, then hurried from the room, not looking back. It had been a few days since they had been to Mrs. Merriweather's. Since that time, they had quickly developed a friendship. Harrison was different with her. He was not as aggressive and flirtatious as he was with other women. He spoke to her like an equal and it was making her heart go faster. He was gentle, and kind, but he pushed her to be better. He had been helping with her fighting too. His willingness to help with the others' training of her was as if he wanted her to be successful. It made her feel necessary, and that just felt incredible.

Zara walked to meet Mary, confusing thoughts about Harrison swimming in her head. She offered Mary a smile. Mary was wearing another low-cut, can-can, dancer-style dress today. This one was red and more suited for a merry evening out. She had the figure for it, but she looked a bit unsuitable for the office. Her hair was piled high on top of her head and she was wearing too much makeup again, but Zara didn't care. She and Mary had eaten lunch together three times now, and Mary was teaching Zara how to flirt.

"What's the matter, Zara? You got a confused look on your face," Mary grabbed her beaded purse, linked her arm with Zara's and waved to Jenny, her lunch replacement.

As Mary predicted, the other girls had stopped speaking to Zara when she and Mary had become chummy, but she didn't care. She just ignored the people looking at them disapprovingly as they were headed out of the building. Mary was worth a hundred times more than any of the others. She was kind and funny, and she didn't care at all that Zara was sometimes quiet or awkward. Mary just filled in the silence for her, making Zara feel completely at ease and accepted. They walked across the marble floor and out onto the busy street.

Steam-powered carriages moved up and down the road, business professionals scuttled in and out of buildings, and couples walked here and there. The city was busy with people enjoying this warm summer's day. The brick, steel, silver, copper and gold skyscrapers of the busy downtown area of Jakarda looked impressive in the afternoon light. Dirigibles flew lazily overhead, flying coaches hummed, and motorized bikes buzzed in the street. It was always so busy, and there was so much movement. Zara loved that about her city.

"Harrison acts differently toward me, now," Zara said.

"How so?" Mary said.

"Well, he's…I have no idea! He doesn't flirt like he was doing before or act arrogant with me. He's trying to be my friend, I suppose. Everyone has noticed! Marcus was teasing him and FeFe, well, she's made more than one rude comment. You know how she is! But he just keeps doing it, laughs them off, he's never embarrassed, and he keeps helping me to be a better agent, encouraging me and making me laugh."

"Ah! Well, that's because he fancies you," she said.

Zara's stomach swooped. She felt a rush of happiness, "No! No, he can't fancy me. He's so handsome and I'm not all that good looking."

Mary gave her an incredulous look, "What are you talking about? I work in the front and a lot of gents, including the ones you work with, talk about 'the lovely Zara Turner' and her long legs and blonde hair. They wax poetic about your blue eyes and perky smile. Don't give me that garbage about the freckles, they like them, too!"

Zara flushed, "I told you what my mother said, Mary. How am I supposed to know if it was true or not? It never occurred to me she might lie. It's hard to fathom why she would tell me I was ugly if I am not."

"And I told you, she was a bully just like my dad, who beat me and attacked me sexually!" she said in a huff.

Zara sighed, "It's hard to believe, me being beautiful."

"Why?" Mary said.

Zara frowned and ignored the question, "My mother sends me boxes of clothing every month from her shop, did I tell you that?"

"No! Lucky you!" she said.

Zara nodded, "I know! I have pretty things, and they're free, but they are all like this. None of it is like your clothes, y'know—alluring. My sisters wear those things, but not me. I guess, I figured it didn't matter, but now, I find myself wanting to look pretty. Men do seem to like me, now that I noticed, but I don't quite know how to be pretty. I want to."

"For Harrison?" she asked, pushing the door open to the dinner on the corner.

Zara reddened, "Well—yes, but mostly for me."

Mary squealed excitedly and led her to their favorite table in the corner of the run down diner. It was clean and the food was delicious. They ordered the soup and bread, as usual. Mary sat back and sipped her coffee.

"The thing is, he sees you like he never saw a girl before. Sees you as a friend," she said.

Zara's face fell. She shrugged then, "Well, I see him as a friend, too. That's ok by me."

Mary laughed, "He sees you as more than a friend too, Zara. He's just never had a friend who's a woman before. He's thrown by it."

"Do you think it's because he knows about my mother, that he pities me? His wanting to be my friend? I will not be pitied!"

"No! I think he feels compassion for you, same as me. You don't pity me for what my dad did, do you?" Mary asked.

"No! I admire you for starting over and getting out," Zara replied.

"There you go! I feel the same about you. That's why he's trying to be your friend. He knows you need one, same as me and he likes you for you."

"Good, I hope so. I have to see my mother tonight. She's helping me choose a dress in her store for the gala and then we are all going to dinner at Dusset's with my sisters."

"Dusset's! Fancy, best you change from your work duds before you go to the shop."

"I have a dress at work to wear. I can change before I go."

"I'll give you a hand with your hair if you'd like. Wake up late again?" Mary smiled.

Zara nodded, "Annie is broken, too. I am never buying halonite again. Everything I've used it on to tinker with has broken down entirely."

"You mentioned it doesn't work worth a shit," Mary said.

Zara laughed at her colorful language and nodded. Their soup came then and they dug into the hearty beef vegetable, grinning at one another.

Zara glanced at the waitress to make sure they were alone, "I had a question for you—about sex."

Mary grinned and leaned in, "Did you now?"

Zara reddened, "Yes, I told you, I've only been with the two men, and it was not as exciting as you told me it should have been. Pleasant, but they liked it far more than I."

"I recall. Shame you didn't have better lovers," Mary said.

Zara got redder still, clearing her throat, "I overheard Simon telling the gents in Room One Hundred about a woman he met who, ah, used her mouth on his…his…"

"Cock? That's called oral sex, Zara. Men love it. See—you trail kisses down the chest and belly to the cock, give lit a few licks and kisses take it in your mouth a few times, making the same move as when you have sex, see? In and out," she said.

Zara nodded, "I get it. And is that done on a lady, the licking and kisses?"

"Yes! Gosh, you had you some shit lovers, huh?" she said.

"Apparently."

"Little different for a lady and some gents don't like doing that, but the good ones do. When they do it right, feels marvelous. Simon like it?" she asked.

"He said it made him, um, rock hard and burst like an over-cooked sausage," Zara whispered, her face and neck very hot.

Mary laughed heartily, slapping the top of the table, "Loved it, then! Dill came to me again last night. I like him."

"He did? Did he take you on a date, again?" Zara asked with a smile.

"He did. We had a proper dinner at the little restaurant he likes, called the Tinker Time Cafe, we took a walk, then back to his place for a bit of fun in the sack. He told me I was beautiful and we kissed for ages, so tender and sweet making love to me the way he does. He's so gentle, Zara. I'm not with any gents but him at the moment. He took me to the picture show over the weekend, saw an exciting film about police officers and robbers. But, you know, he doesn't want anyone at work to know about us," Mary said sadly.

Zara frowned, because she had learned that about Dill first hand. She asked him if he had a nice date with Mary and he got all red and flustered, said she was just a friend he spent time with. Zara was surprised, because Dill seemed like a very good man, but he didn't want anyone to know he dated a former prostitute. Zara made a point to tell him how much she admired Mary, how much she liked her, mentioning what a good person she was, how she was becoming her good friend. He agreed with her wholeheartedly, but he still did not acknowledge their relationship, his eyes darting to FeFe, who stood nearby listening with a sour expression. Zara dropped it, but she found herself disappointed with him.

"Well, he's very private. Maybe he needs time. You said yourself, your affair with him started when I started at the Nest. It's only been a few weeks," Zara said.

"That's true!" Mary said brightening.

Zara felt a twinge of guilt, because she was not certain Dill would ever admit to it. He was so shy, plus he didn't seem to want to tell anyone. Zara had no idea why. She smiled at her friend instead of blabbing like she normally would have. Harrison told her that sometimes it was more kind to give people hope than to dash it with realism, after she shot apart one of Dill's ideas to fix her communication device and hurt his feelings. She apologized to Dill and explained, wringing her hands, that she wasn't good with people. It seemed to endear her to him, because he admitted he wasn't either. She took him to lunch after, they had soup here because she was too poor to afford anything else.

Zara and Mary finished lunch, talking about other things, laughing. They went back to the office. Zara trained with Harrison some more, then worked on tinkering with Dill. They managed to make a large metal bird that worked by flying and snapping pictures. They had it fly out one of the open windows and take photos of the city below. It returned and upon inspection of the results there was a great cheer because it was a brilliant bit of spy tech.

Zara grinned the whole time she raced downstairs to change for her dinner. She pulled on a pretty yellow dress that was fitted to her hips, adorned with little brass buttons, shorter in front and longer in the back where it had three ruffles. She pulled on some stockings and heeled shoes. Mary did her hair for her—styling it down, curling the bottom and pinning it back with a yellow flower that was made by her mother to match the simple dress. Zara put on mascara and pink lipstick then ran back to Room One Hundred to get her bag, her other dress neatly folded in her arms.

When she walked in, she was in such a rush, she didn't notice all of them staring at her. She put her dress in her pack and glanced up. Harrison was smiling at her with that rakish smile of his.

"You…look beautiful. Where you off to?" he asked.

"I'm meeting my mother to choose a dress for the ball at her dress shop. I asked her for help since I am not skilled at dressing myself. Then we're having dinner at Dusset's with my sisters," Zara hastily explained.

"That sounds lovely! You should wear yellow all the time. It suits you," Dill said, reddening a little.

Zara offered him a smile, "Thank you, Dill. Sweet of you to say. You too, Harrison! Mary did my hair for me, thank goodness. I only know how to braid."

"You should wear your hair down more. It's a nice look for you," Harrison said gruffly.

She reddened and shrugged, "Thanks. I have to go. I'll see you all tomorrow."

Simon offered her a bow with a sexy smile that made her get more red. Marcus, who flirted with her all the time smiled and studied her then grinned and winked. Douglas gave her a dreamy smile and sighed. Mr. Wills tipped his hat.

"Oh for heaven's sake! I wear dresses every day, the lot of you are acting like I come to work in a paper bag!" Zara said.

"Your dresses are not so pretty and ladylike as this. They're more the sensible sort, honey. You should wear this kind," Harrison said, his eyes intense.

She looked at it, "I'd ruin it with grease! It's yellow! That's impractical for a tinkerer." She leveled a look at them all, then grinned and flourished her graceful arm, "You get me as I am gents, but I do clean up nicely, I suppose. I'm late now!"

She rushed out the door with a wave. They were grinning at her, laughing at her outburst. She hurried off down the block to her mother's shop, her steps faltering as she got closer. She took a deep breath at the edge of the building and went inside the revolving door, bracing herself for the unkindness to follow. The shop was full of beautiful things. Dresses were displayed on busts, the adornments and options listed in scrolled letters nearby. They were lovely, all of them. Some short, some long, ranging from simple to elaborate. The walls were papered in a simple pink and cream stripe, the carpet was pink as well, two large portraits of her sisters in elaborate gowns hung predominantly on the wall. In the back, in a private salon, was where the underthings could be purchased.

"Zara! My dear, you look quite nice," her mother said, clearly surprised.

Zara ignored her tone and smiled, "Thank you. I love this dress, it's a fun color. I wear a lot of drab colors. Do you think we might choose some more colorful things this time? I still want them to be practical because of my work, but the other girls at the office look so much more put together than I."

Mrs. Turner, a handsome woman with brown hair and eyes, looked at her daughter in surprise, "Of course. Must be a man to impress."

"Lots of them, mother," Zara said with a smile.

Mrs. Turner laughed, "Well then, come with your mother."

Zara smiled. They picked a knee-length, sky blue and navy striped dress with three-quarter sleeves, embellished with navy buttons and a wide collar; and a fitted red vest with black pants and a black shirt. She chose two blue shirts to go with simple vests that matched the blue of her eyes and selected some simple skirts and pants in pretty purples, pinks and yellows, prettier hair adornments and some complementary jewelry. All of it was simple, but it was in bolder colors than plain brown, or black and white as she was used to wearing before.

"Since I have you open to suggestions, how about this dress for your ball," her mother said.

Zara looked at the daring blue dress in satin, a corset at the top and two long ruffles at the bottom. It would show off her cleavage and the bare skin on her arms. Zara took a deep breath and nodded.

"I am going with a handsome gentleman. I would like to look pretty," Zara said.

Her mother smiled, "You will look attractive in this gown, dearest, but you will never look pretty, not with those freckles."

Zara ignored her, recalling the way the gents had looked at her not that long ago, "I think this gown might do just fine, mother. And I will be fine on my own. He just might like me."

Mrs. Turner looked at Zara with eyes wide in shock, especially when Zara chose lacy underthings and sexy stockings to go with her new outfits. She handed them over to Zara, free of charge as usual, and wrapped them to send to Zara's apartment by courier bot. They strolled to dinner after in silence, falling into the familiar pattern of rarely speaking to one another. Dinner was not as horrible as usual. Zara practiced what she had learned, asking them all about what was new, avoiding the tinkering talk, trying to listen, and smiling often.

"Zara!" Cait said flipping her massive head to the side, her eyes wide, "You are almost charming tonight!"

"Thank you! You know, I quite like my job. I've been there three weeks. I have a nice female friend I have lunch with a few times a week and I like working with all the gents in my room. There is one other woman in our department. She's not very nice, but that's ok.

We get on as well as can be expected, we're just different, she and I," Zara said.

Tempie nodded, and smiled. She was the uglier of Zara's sisters, both inside and out, "You are different than most ladies, dear sister."

They waited for her to get mad and storm off, but Zara just laughed, "You know, the gentleman I met, he actually likes that about me. Isn't that marvelous?"

They gaped at her. Cait, who was not overly bright and had to work to be mean, nodded, "It actually is! I'm glad, Zara. Is he handsome?"

"He is. He's quite the most handsome, dashing man I ever met," Zara said.

They smiled at her as if they all had sucked a lemon. Zara had to fight down the urge to laugh. They finished their meal, Zara taking their jabs without anger, controlling her expression. She walked back to the Crow's Nest, her smiles used up from the abuse she took, but her confidence unshaken—she did it. She sighed and unhooked her motorized bicycle.

"How did it go?" Harrison asked.

Zara squeaked and clutched her chest, spinning to look at him, "Harrison!"

He laughed, "Sorry."

"You startled me, I was lost in thought. What are you doing here so late?" she asked.

"Going over the pictures again, want to be sharp for tomorrow night. You never answered me," he said.

Zara rubbed her head, "Well, it was good practice for all the phony things I have to do tomorrow night. I used all the tricks you taught me. Laughed off all the jabs and insults and made it through a meal without storming off. So, I was pleased. I also let my mother choose clothing for me in colors other than brown, black and white, she was thrilled. Normally, I don't let her pick and I'm rude. I confused her entirely."

Harrison didn't laugh like she expected him to. He studied her closely, "Did she hit you?"

Zara shook her head, "I told you. She doesn't do that anymore."

"Forgive me, but if she did it before, she will do it again," he said.

They stood there and looked at one another in silence for a while. Zara nodded finally and sighed, as if she had the weight of that statement looming over her. He took her hand. She rubbed her temple again and shut her eyes.

"Zara?" her mother's voice pierced the moment.

"Mama!" she said, spinning around.

"You forgot your jewelry. I wanted to drop it off to you. Is this the young man escorting you to the ball tomorrow?" she asked.

"Yes. Mama, this is Harrison Lowell. Harrison, my mother, Amanda Turner," Zara said.

Harrison offered her a tight smile, not a charming one. Zara's sisters ran up, gaping at him with their mouths hanging open. He was a very good looking man, they couldn't believe he had asked their sister out.

"You're the man taking her to the ball? Zara Turner, boring tinkerer and boring dresser?" Tempie said.

Zara's face and neck reddened. She looked down, avoiding his gaze. He squeezed her hand and slid his arm around her waist. He kissed her cheek and grinned.

"I like the way she dresses. I love a woman who leaves something to the imagination, a true lady. She's brilliant, she graduated top of her class, highest scores at the academy since its inception. Of course, you're her family, so you know that. I took one look at all this blonde hair and the big blue eyes and found myself smitten. Freckles are adorable if you ask me!" he said, sending her a sexy smile.

Zara schooled her expression and grinned at him, "I like you very much, Harrison."

He smiled then, "Likewise, honey. Did she tell you the ball is at Rhinehold estate? Family friends of mine, nicest people. I'm looking forward to it."

"She can't even dance!" Cait said.

"I can too, just not very well," Zara said.

"I don't care. I don't care at all," Harrison said.

He leaned down and kissed Zara softly. Her heart went so fast, it felt like it might hammer from her chest. She looked at him and blinked once. He smiled at her a little, his eyes soft. He stroked her cheek with his thumb and Zara completely forgot he was acting. He was so handsome and his lips were very soft.

"Here!" Mrs. Turner snapped.

Zara jumped, stepping back in a rush, "Sorry, mama. Thanks for bringing the bag."

"Since you used up all your money this month on a dress, don't expect the groceries. Girls! Let's go!" she said.

They hurried off behind her. Zara shut her eyes.

"Shit!" she said.

"Groceries?" Harrison asked.

"It's nothing. Don't worry yourself. She's just being herself. Thanks for pretending to be my suitor," she said.

"It wasn't hard to pretend I liked you, Zara. I do like you," Harrison said.

She smiled, "I like you, too. I'm tired, so I'm going to go home. We have a big day tomorrow, you and I."

Harrison grinned, "Nervous?"

"Yes, but we'll muddle through," Zara said.

Harrison stood as if he seemed to want her to tease him or crack a joke, but she couldn't manage. She went too far with her mother, and now she wasn't going to have enough food for the next month. She forced a smile toward Harrison and rode her motorized bicycle home. She parked it and chained it on the fence near her place. She walked into the small brick building and climbed to the second floor. She unlocked the door to number twenty-one B and went inside. She smiled at her cat-bot, Hammond, and her dog-bot, Paws. She stroked their metallic heads gently.

Zara's apartment consisted of two very dated sofas, one blue and one brown, procured from her mother's attic, and a red chair that was her papa's. They were situated in front of a fireplace with three framed pictures of her papa and her when she was small, and a pretty picture of flowers Zara drew. On the far wall was her tinkering table.

It was covered in bits of wire, parts, metal, gears, screws, nails and all manner of tinkering bits. She had a very small kitchen, a table with two chairs, and a faded rug that stretched from the kitchen into the living room. She had made her lamps from bits of scrap metal, and even though they were far from pretty, they were functional. Zara walked into her bedroom. Her mother had allowed her to take her bedroom furniture and whatever she could find in the attic. As a result, she had three mismatched sets of dishes, old pots and pans, chipped coffee mugs and a beat up set of utensils. She had an icebox, a sink, a toaster and the coffee pot she made as a prototype for her patent. Her bedroom set was dark wood, but fine and well made. She had the matching chest of drawers and the dresser, as well as the pretty quilt, rug and curtains. The curtains in her living room were a faded blue, and threadbare. Still, this was her home, and she was happier here than she ever was living with her family. There was a knock on her door. An automaton had brought all her clothing. She thanked him and carried it to her room. She hung everything carefully and then started to cry. Zara was not one to cry, but for some reason, this night she sobbed brokenly, and put on her pajamas. She cried herself to sleep. When she woke in the morning, her eyes were red and swollen.

CHAPTER SEVEN

Harrison was nervous. Not because of his mission, but because when he had kissed Zara it was to shut up her family, but it ended up being the best kiss he ever had. She looked at him with those amazing blue eyes and Harrison Lowell fell into the most powerful crush on a woman he ever had before. He never got nervous, but he was nervous to see her this morning. He looked up, his heart giving a thump when the door opened. FeFe walked in. Harrison felt a rush of disappointment and went back to his pastry and coffee.

"Harrison! Ready for your ball with the tinkerer mouse to-night?" FeFe asked.

"FeFe, shut up. Just leave her alone, dammit," he snapped.

Mr. Wills looked at him in surprise, "Yes, FeFe, do shut up. She's been working hard and I'm sure she'll be wonderful. You could try and be kind to her, I know it's difficult for you think of someone besides yourself, but do try. You could have helped her, instead, you let your own jealousy guild you and gave up on her lessons, ignoring my orders and leaving it to your team to help her. You did not think of the team at all, or the fact that she is now part of it. It will reflect in your review, FeFe."

FeFe reddened, "I didn't realize. Of course it does. For the record, I am not jealous. However, she is a member of this team and I will strive to do better."

"I should hope so," Mr. Wills said.

Zara stepped off the elevator and Harrison stood with a smile, smoothing his clothes a little. She smiled. Her eyes were red and a bit puffy. His smile fell. He walked over to her. She looked exhausted or ill. He wasn't sure which.

"Morning! How are you?" he asked softly.

"I'm fine," she said.

He put a hand on her elbow, "You okay?"

"Yes!" she said with a falsely bright smile.

"Don't worry about tonight. I'll take care of you," he said.

She softened, "I know you will. You're a good friend. I had trouble sleeping, that's all. Nerves. I made you something because I was up. I wanted to thank you for being so nice to me yesterday and for all your help and kindness."

She took out something wrapped in paper, carefully opening it.

"Cufflinks?" he said, eyeing the black and gold cufflinks closely.

"The one on the left has a sharp rope in it, should you need to choke someone to death. The other is a tracking device, I have one in my compact. If we're separated, it will track the other person, beep slowly, lead you in their direction, beeps faster and louder the closer you are to them," she said.

Harrison grinned, "That's so amazing! Where did you get the cufflinks?"

"They—were my papa's," she answered in a quiet voice.

He looked at her and smiled, "You want—me? To have them?"

"Yes. Thank you for your help, truly," she said.

"You're welcome."

He put them carefully in his pocket, his heart accelerating. They walked over to the table. Zara reached for a pastry and coffee, then she took a second one. Harrison chuckled and had another pastry, sitting beside her. Zara gobbled them up, then had another. The others came in and sat down. He watched Zara eat four pastries and a coffee with a smirk. He winked at her.

"Hungry?" he said.

She nodded and had two cups of coffee.

The day moved by at a crawl. Zara left work an hour early to get ready for the ball. Harrison left for home shortly after her departure. He found he was nervous. He showered and put on his best tuxedo with the cufflinks she made him. He looked at himself in the bedroom mirror. He looked dashing, handsome, his dark hair styled for once, a closer shave then he normally bothered with. He turned from the mirror and walked out. His room was tasteful, done in blue and grey, masculine. His townhouse was nicely decorated, too. He lived in a brownstone in the nicer part of the city. He walked downstairs to his office and picked up his gun, strapping it to his calf in a holster. He put the small gas mask Zara made him in his pocket. Harrison looked into his living room at the simple brown leather furniture and the lamps. He had a Victrola, Harrison liked music, and two book shelves full of books. His kitchen was neatly decorated all in black and white, with a new floor. He had a chef-bot and a maid-bot that didn't run on tracks, instead their wheels led them about wherever they were needed. Even though he lived alone, he had a simple bedroom set in the spare room upstairs just in case he had guests.

Harrison walked to his carriage shed, excited to pick up Zara and got into his black carriage. He rode to her building. He blinked at it in disbelief as the carriage pulled up to the curb. She lived in a less than nice part of the city, in the industrial section. This couldn't be right! He told her doorman he'd be back, that he was fetching Zara. The automaton promised to keep an eye on his carriage. He would need the bot to pay close attention in this neighborhood.

The elevator was broken, so he walked up to her apartment. The building was worse on the inside. The tile flooring was chipped, the paint was blistered and peeling in spots. There was a large crack in the wall next to her apartment door. Harrison knocked on the door. Zara opened it with a smile and Harrison forgot every thought he had harbored about her living space.

She was a vision, a goddess, wearing a floor length gown in the bluest satin. The bodice was styled as a corset and rounded the tops of her breasts perfectly under the curve of her collar bones. Her hair hung golden and gleaming, cascading in curls down one shoulder.

She smiled at him with eyelashes adorned with mascara and lush, red lipstick—his preference.

"Hi!" she said.

"Hello, there. You look truly beautiful," Harrison said.

"Do I? I'm too nervous to tell," she said.

She grabbed her purse, but not before he caught a glimpse of her apartment. His lips parted. It was worse than he had thought while coming in the building. She had three mismatched pieces of furniture, her curtains had holes in them and the rug was threadbare. He smiled at her and pretended not to notice her hovel. A maid bot came out carrying a blue wrap that matched her dress. She smiled.

"Oh, right! Thanks, Annie," she said.

"Of course, Miss Zara. Will you introduce me to your friend?" the bot mechanically replied.

"Oh, sure! Harrison, this is Annie. I built her with my papa, she's a real help to me. She dresses me, does my hair and cooks for me. She's been with me since I was eight," Zara said.

Harrison's heart squeezed a little, "Nice to meet you Annie."

"And you, sir," she said in her metallic robot voice.

A dog and a cat bot came running up. Zara patted their heads and put on her wrap. Harrison walked out with her. She locked three locks on her door. Harrison watched her with a smile. She didn't seem to think there was anything wrong with this place. She had so little, he really was an ass for being so suspicious of her. She walked towards the elevator.

"That isn't working," he said.

"Again? I just fixed it! I get a dollar off my rent for doing tinkering and maintenance for the tenants. I just fixed that two days ago. I keep telling the owner to stop buying halonite pieces, if she would just spring for steel, copper or silver, it would cost more up front, but the thing would work long term!"

As if on cue, a woman came out and yelled at Zara, said her tinkering wasn't good and that was the reason the elevator didn't work.

"Madam, you do realize you have the top graduate of the Tinkerer's Academy living in your building, right? She works for the

Jakarda Government and when I say top, I mean she is the top in the history of the academy. If she tells you to buy steel, copper or silver parts, you should trust her," Harrison said with a charming smile.

The woman looked at Zara, "Well, she does fix all the other things no problem. I'll get new parts tomorrow. I didn't realize, hon," she said.

Zara smiled, "That's okay, Mrs. Brombauer. I'm grateful to you for letting me do the work here."

"You do a good job, except that damn elevator. Tomorrow you fix that and the heat in Mr. Billings place again," she said.

Zara nodded, "I'm on it!"

The older woman patted her cheek and went inside. Zara reddened a little, "Sorry."

"That's ok. You, ah, do all the maintenance here?" he said.

"Yes, and I clean the bathrooms and the lobby two times a week," she said.

Harrison had never felt like a bigger ass for doubting her. As if the horrible family was not enough, her mother beating her and being verbally abusive, she was a janitor and tinkerer in her building to pay for the rent and she lived in a shit hole.

"That's very industrious of you," he said.

"Thanks! I do what I must. I don't mind hard work, not a bit! I have those patents for the coffee pot and the mini fridge. I'm still waiting on my checks, the papers were misfiled, or some nonsense. I've been tinkering on an at-home bread cooker, Annie helped me get the measurements right, you know with the flour and things. Bread is normally bought at stores, so this would be a way for the home cook to save money. I have made two successful loaves of bread now, I plan to get the patent and get local stores to sell them with my coffee pot and mini refrigeration unit," she said with a smile.

Harrison helped her into the carriage and studied her excited expression, "I misjudged you when we met. I'm sorry."

She tilted her head, "You did?"

"Yes. I thought you were….it doesn't really matter. I was very wrong. I'm sorry," he said.

"Oh, that's ok! I wasn't sure I liked you, either," she said.

"Why the hell not?" he said.

"You're so different than me. You're confident and intelligent in a way that I'm not smart at all. Your smart with cases and especially with people. I thought, how could someone like me ever be friends with him? But look at us! We have formed a friendship, you and I, and an unlikely one at that. I just hope after all my training and work, I don't screw this up. I know I mentioned my lack of skill when it comes to dancing. I'm terrible!"

"Why is that?" he asked, feeling oddly happy she thought he was smart.

"I have two left feet."

He chuckled, "You're very graceful and delicate, I find that hard to believe."

"I lose count. There are just so many people and I have so many ideas," she said with a frown.

"I'll help you out. Remember, we're engaged, you and I," he said.

"I did. I had Mary teach me about being affectionate," she said.

He arched his brows, "You had Mary teach you?"

"Yes! I was curious about many things between couples," she said.

"You, ah, you have been with a man, though?" he said.

"Of course I have! I'm twenty-two years old! I was just unaware of some of the, ah, logistics and courting requirements."

He found himself grinning, "Courting requirements?"

She laughed, "I don't know what they're called! You see now why I needed Mary? FeFe was supposed to help me, but I was too embarrassed to ask her. She was always laughing at me. Mary cleared things up."

"Such as?" he said, his curiosity getting the better of him.

"She said if we're to pretend to be a couple, it's all right if I hold your hand, or arm, or kiss your cheek."

"You didn't know that?" Harrison asked.

"No. To be honest, I never pay attention to what couples do. She said cuddling up to you was good, but not in a sexual, loose-woman way. I doubt that will be a problem for me. I'm not the sexual sort of lady," Zara said making a face that made him laugh.

"You're better at it then you realize. Just be yourself, smile at me often and look like you like me. Hold my hand, kiss my cheek. School your expressions and try not to talk tinker too often," he said.

"I got it! I won't let you down," she said nervously.

He smiled and took her hand, "I know you won't."

She smiled then and fidgeted and looked down at her chest, tugging at her dress, "This dress is so tight. I feel like I could explode out of it."

He chuckled, "It looks marvelous on you. Matches your eyes. And, just if you wanted to know—I love red lipstick."

"Mary recommended it. She picked it out for me, and the mascara, the sort I use is not covering my blonde lashes enough. I had no idea. I was worried because I think she wears a touch too much makeup," Zara said.

"She's toned it down, if you can imagine," Harrison said.

"Really? Oh, my," Zara muttered.

He laughed heartily, "I know!"

Zara's stomach growled. She rested her hand on it, "I was too nervous to eat."

"They'll have appetizers. We can have some," he said.

They pulled in front of a large house that stood three stories tall. The white stone house had every window alight and glowing with beautiful golden lights. The main floor held the grand ballroom. Harrison had been here before on occasion for the Crow's Nest. Zara could not help but to gape as they exited the carriage.

"Shut your mouth, honey," he said.

She snapped it shut and schooled her expression, "I've never been to a place like this."

"What about your coming out?" he said.

"I never had one. My mother said it was a waste of money for someone who looked like me. I didn't care, I didn't want one anyway," she said.

He fought the urge to swear. He forced a smile, "Too busy studying?"

"Yes! That was the year I invented, Spy-ders, I think," Zara said.

He smiled and handed their invitation to the solid gold butler at the door, "Welcome, Harrison Lowell and Zara Turner."

"Thank you," Zara said.

He smiled because she always answered bots as if they were people. He found that adorable. They were to her, he supposed. They walked inside and made a left toward the ballroom. He led Zara to the food table. She made herself a plate, and he followed suit. She took more than was fashionable, but he didn't correct her. She ate it slowly, with excellent manners even though he kept hearing her growling stomach. She sipped her champagne and made a face.

He laughed, "Don't like it?"

"No. I've never tried it before," she said.

He smiled at her again. She wasn't kidding when she said she lacked social skills, she looked curiously at everything and sent him questioning looks about clothes and people. He found himself quietly explaining trends and wait staff while she listened intently. Still, she ate her food and sipped her champagne like a lady, smiling at others who nodded to them. When she was finished eating, he asked her to dance. She was a worse dancer than he could have imagined. He found himself laughing. She counted, and looked at her feet. It was the most adorable thing he ever saw. A few times, she trounced on his foot, winced, and apologized, her face red.

He grinned and kissed her, "I couldn't care less, honey."

She laughed and shrugged. He led her, his hand in hers to get some punch after they finished.

"Harrison Lowell! Might have known," a man said.

Harrison winced, and plastered on a charming smile, "James Crane. How are you?"

"Fine. Who's this?" he said turning to Zara.

"This is my fiancéé, Zara Turner. Zara, this is James Crane, an acquaintance of mine from my childhood," he said.

"Oh! How lovely! It's nice to meet you! What do you do?" she asked.

"I'm a police officer," he said.

"How nice! I'm happy you're here! Do you think they'll be another robbery like the other ballrooms that were hit?" she asked.

Harrison smiled at how she managed to make her eyes wide, and full of worry. His lessons were paying off, even he believed her. James, pompous fool, puffed up his chest.

"Not on my watch, Miss Turner. I have fifteen of my men inside and out, checking for anything suspicious," he said.

Zara relaxed, "Oh, good! Isn't that a relief, darling?"

"Yes," he agreed with eyebrows raised.

She offered him a smitten, adoring look that caught him off guard and made his pulse hammer, "Not that I need to be protected with you around, my love."

She kissed him then, her hand at his face. Harrison lost his head and crushed his mouth to hers. His kiss was demanding and inappropriate for a public place. He pulled back when he realized his mistake. Zara's eyes fluttered open.

"You're an excellent kisser," she breathed.

Harrison grinned, "So are you, honey."

James chuckled, "Well, you are smitten, Harrison! Never thought I'd see the day a ladies man like you was taken by just one woman."

Harrison shrugged, "What can I say? You meet the right one and you fall hard."

He realized with a jolt that he was in danger of doing just that from the moment he said it. He felt an acute sense of panic. He couldn't let that happen, risk his freedom, his career for anyone. Harrison sternly told himself to calm down. She was his friend! Nothing had happened, he was acting irrational. He glanced at Zara. She smiled at him, then looked at James.

"Mr. Crane, were you present at any of the robberies before? I heard some people were hurt."

James softened at her worried expression, "Now, now, Miss Turner. No need to worry your pretty head! It's going to be just fine! I have men on every floor and in the basement!"

Zara stilled, then smiled, "That's good news!"

She was onto something, Harrison cued in on her reaction, and was struggling to keep it quiet. When James wandered off, they walked onto the balcony. Zara pulled him to the side. He moved in like he was kissing her and pressed his cheek towards her ear. She smelled lovely, like lemon juice. It was a fresh smell, suited her.

"Well?" he said.

"He spilled his guts to me! Men on every floor. I think the system I need to check is in the basement. He's watching your every move, so I'll have to slip down to check."

"We can't separate! This is your first mission!" Harrison said.

"Well, one of us has to distract that buffoon. Here he is watching us now, good grief!" she said.

She turned her head and kissed him, pressing the full length of her body to his. Harrison kissed her back with a moan. He tangled his hands in her hair, it was even softer than he expected. He touched his tongue to hers. He felt her nipples harden against his chest, his anatomy followed suit. He rubbed himself against her. She moaned and he kissed his way down her neck. She put her hand in his hair, her breath coming out fast.

He was about to reach for the bottom of her skirt, when she pulled back, breathing hard, "Ok. I-I think I can get past him now."

Harrison blinked and took a step back, "Right. Be careful. If you're not back in twenty minutes, I'm coming for you."

She nodded and slipped back into the party, making her way to the other side of the ballroom. He watched her, rubbing the back of his neck. What the hell happened to him? He lost his head completely! He never did that, especially not on a job. He wasn't sure what made him more angry, the fact that he lost his head, or that she didn't. She kissed him like she had, but, she also had the ability to pull back, to stop. He found he wanted her to like it as much as he had.

"You're a fool," he muttered to himself.

He took a deep breath and went in after her. He helped himself to a glass of champagne that he drank in two gulps, then took another. This was going to be a long night.

Zara felt shaky, but whether it was from the lack of food she'd eaten all day or the kiss, she couldn't be sure. She lost her head completely, kissing Harrison. Worse than that, she loved it. She liked to be in control, to keep a level head, to tinker and that was it. But in the back of her mind, even though she knew he was acting, that kiss was the best of her life. He was a marvelous actor, she almost believed he wanted her. She could swear she felt how hard he got, but Mary said it was like that for a man. They could be turned on even when they didn't care about a woman, if she was willing. That's what she assumed had happened with Harrison. After all, she had pressed her breasts to his chest and behaved like a loose woman, moaning and kissing him like a fool. She had never been so embarrassed in her life! What must he think of her?

Zara made her way through the ballroom towards the basement stairwell. In most houses along this district, they would be found near the right of the entrance. She spotted a man standing near the front foyer. Judging from his inexpensive tuxedo, she assumed he was one of the police officers. She was trying to work out a plan to get past him without him getting suspicious, when he collapsed. Zara caught the whiff of something spicy and got dizzy. She hurriedly held her breath and pulled on her small copper mask. Holding it over her nose and mouth, she hooked the two leather straps around her ears. She stepped over the man and peered down the basement stairs.

Great cabbage hat!

It was so dark, she couldn't see very well inside. Hugging the wall, she slowly descended to the sub floor. She crouched down and crawled against the cool concrete to get a better look in the dim surroundings. In the hazy darkness, eyes watering, she spotted two men in brown dusters wearing gas masks and head lamps. They carried copper tubs of something. Her eyes burned from whatever it was in the air, thank god for the mask filtering out toxins or she'd be out cold. Zara's heart pounded. The steam powered heating system for the house needed a water source, and they were dumping the mixture of it directly into the water that was in turn heated by coals in the power cylinder beneath it. That was a brilliant move, they must have found a way to get the ether compound just right so it combined with the water to—

"Stop it, Zara! Figure that out later, you fool," she muttered to herself.

She reached in her bag and took out her lipstick. She clicked the top two times and shot a dart at one of the men. It hit him in the neck. His hand shot up to grab it, then he crumbled in a heap dropping his copper container. His companion turned to see what was going on when Zara shot him too, sending the substance spilling all over the floor. Uh-oh, that was a problem. Zara ran over to them and set the container on its side. A pair of arms grabbed her from behind. She screamed and elbowed the man in the ribs hard. He dropped her and she crawled away. She fumbled for the gun in her garter, but he beat her to his own weapon. A shot rang out. It struck her in the arm. She screamed inside her mask and reached for her self-targeting gun that she'd invented and strapped to the other leg. A blast of blue light shot from her gun, striking the man in the chest. He flew back and crashed into the copper container that held the water, leaving a massive dent in the copper basin. Zara was breathing hard, fairly certain she had killed him, his neck was at an odd angle. Of course, she reasoned, he had shot her, so she did what she had to do.

"Focus!" she spoke muffled into her mask.

Zara yanked off the men's masks so they wouldn't wake up. She tossed them to the side into the corner where they wouldn't see them if they came to. She pulled on their gloves and carefully put samples of each substance into little vials she carried in her bag at all times. You never know when a sample would be needed, she reasoned, as she put cork stoppers onto four good samples. She worked steadily, hardly noticing her arm, until she realized she had blood streaming in a hot river down her arm. Adrenaline, most likely, she thought. She tied a handkerchief around her arms with her good hand and whimpered while pulling it taut with her teeth. She looked at the copper barrels lying on the floor. She had to get them out of here. How the deuce had they gotten them in?

She glanced around, her mind racing. She spotted two filthy windows, about two feet tall. They were open. Of course! She raced over and looked out. Her eyes traveled the landscape in search of more thugs, but the coast was clear She hoisted the first container out the window with some difficulty and a lot of swearing on her part. She did the same with second, it was much lighter, as so much of it spilled when she shot the man who fell with it. She looked at the spillage on the floor and considered what to do. The fumes from the ether were so strong, her eyes ran streaks of mascara down her face and around the gas mask. She walked over to the valve on the wall and opened it. Water spewed all over the floor, soaking her dress in the process. She shut the water off, turning the crank with all her might. She hoped that would dilute the spill enough that breathing normally again would be okay, and not knock out more guests as it was intended to do.

Turning, she looked at the huge boiler. What about what they put into the heating system? She shrugged and picked up a wrench that was on one man's belt. She smashed the pipes so it stopped pumping the noxious chemical into the ballroom, then shut off the system and opened the vents so the water would eventually evaporate. The substance would filter out, as long as she left the windows open. She could go now. Zara crawled out the window, panting with pain and the effort and looked around. She smashed the glass windows for good measure, then dragged the copper tub to the woods at the edge of the property. She nervously dumped the first barrel, her eyes darting about for attackers, then ran back, soaking wet skirt in hand, and grabbed the second. She was nearly finished with the second barrel when another shot rang out. It struck her in the same arm, except this time it did not graze her. She felt it rip through her flesh and exit the back, leaving a hot, burning sensation in its stead and more fresh, red blood. She fell on her backside with a scream. She grabbed her gun from her garter and pointed it away from her, looking for a target. She grimaced as she saw a man coming towards her, preparing to shoot again. She shot him in the chest, her gun set to stun. He fell face down in front of her, skidding towards her out-stretched leg. She scrambled back, breathing hard. She stared at him for a moment. He was a massive man, he could have done serious harm to her. She took a good look at his face and committed it to memory like she had the others. She stood up on shaky legs. She tore off a ruffle from the bottom of her gown and pressed it to her arm, whimpering as she did. It was bad, that wound, it was very bad, and it hurt like the devil.

She had to find Harrison. There were too many of these men, more than they had realized given the testimony of those robbed at past parties. She considered what to do next. It would be easy to run, to hide. She thought about Harrison and swore. She had to help him, she couldn't leave him, after all, they were partners. She stumbled back to the house, ignoring the pain in her arm. She grabbed the wrench as a weapon and limping around the outside of the ballroom, started yanking open all the doors and windows she could reach, smashing the glass when she couldn't find the strength to push open the windows. Inside the room, four men in trench coats and gas masks moved among the sleeping guests. People began stirring inside. The men, startled and swirling where they stood, tried to see who was breaking windows.

"What do we do? They're waking up and she hasn't gotten it yet!" one said in a panic.

Zara knew they'd see her, but she yanked open the doors to the patio anyway.

"Someone stop her!" one of them shouted pointing at her. Zara didn't stick around to see who it was. She smashed two more windows with the wrench and ran to the next set of doors just as three of the men ran out brandishing guns. One let out a shot in her direction. She yelped and circled the corner of the building. At least she managed to open most of the doors, the damage was done. The people would be up soon and if the perpetrators didn't leave, they'd be caught. She was running along the garden side of the house when she heard the sound of shattering glass. She yelped as two men came flying out the window, rolling about like animals. Harrison! She recognized his gas mask, it was him! The other man got the upper hand and had him pinned down. With extreme effort, Zara rushed over and conked the man over the head with the wrench. Harrison shoved his limp body off and looked back down the yard at the three men barreling into the fight. He jumped up and knocked the first man's gun out of his hand and punched him hard. Another one came at Zara. She hit him with the wrench, but her hit wasn't hard enough to deter him from punching her hard in the stomach. She crumbled in a heap. He loomed over her taking aim, when Harrison tackled him, having somehow managed to beat the other man to a pulp, too. Zara grabbed her blaster, and shot one of the men who was starting to recover. She yanked off their gas masks and chucked them as far as she could throw into the trees then took a stack of folded papers from the jacket of the one who fell out the window. She clutched them in her bloodied arm and looked at Harrison, who had managed to knock the last man out. He spun around, saw her sitting there, bleeding all over the documents. He raced over and yanked her up.

"We have to get the hell out of here, come on," he said.

She nodded and ran beside him, her heart going wild. They approached the front of the house. Two men were walking toward them. Harrison grabbed her hand and jerked her in another direction. They ran toward a side drive where the carriages had been positioned. She spotted Harrison's carriage buried among all the others.

"Oh, no! What now?" she said.

They had been seen. Shots zipped past them. One caught Harrison in the side of the leg, grazing him. He swore and kept moving, his hand tightening in hers. They ran into the stables. Harrison spotted a lone horse and grabbed its brown mane, leading him out of the stables in a rush. He mounted the animal, settled himself on its bare back and pulled her up in front of himself seconds after. Zara stifled a scream of pain, and felt more blood rushing down her arm. She bunched her dress around her hips as she sat astride and tried to grip its neck with her knees. "Sorry, honey. Let's go!" he said, kicking the horse.

They burst from the barn at a gallop. Zara managed to remover her pistol from her leg holster and shoot towards two of the men. Thankfully, none of their bullets connected with either them or the horse. Harrison aimed the horse into the woods. They moved at a breakneck pace through the trees, Zara trying to see if they were being followed. She was shaking badly. She still had the documents clutched in her bloody hand at her chest. She yanked off her gas mask, and shoved it into her little wrist purse. She gasped for air, her chest heaving.

Harrison slowed the horse, pulling his gas mask off and handing it to Zara who shook as she put it away. He looked behind them. "I think it's ok, now," he panted, "We're safe for now, they can't catch us. You did good. That was quick thinking, getting the papers." She nodded rapidly. Harrison turned the horse toward where the woods would run along the main part of town. His arm tightened around her midsection.

"Breathe slower, Zara. Try to calm down," he said. "Can you tell me what happened after you left? Talk slow, honey, relax."

She explained what she happened step by step. He kept looking at her and smiling, "That was quick thinking! You were incredible."

Zara nodded, "I did my best. What happened to you?"

"I was in the ballroom. I smelled that spicy smell and put on the mask, then pretended to fall like the rest of the people, face down to hide it. Had to wait till none of them were looking, then I snuck off. I knew from the information we gathered that the safe and all the valuables were on the third floor, that's where all the private bedrooms are, guest rooms are on the second floor. I snuck up there, had to fight a few guys on the way, think I killed some, like you. I was fighting someone when the man, the one with the documents went zipping past us, so I went after him. He had a dark haired woman with him, she was all covered up like the rest of them, shouting orders. We struggled and went flying out the window, he was tall, but strong. That's when I ran into you. What happened to your arm?" he asked.

"I was shot twice," she leaned against him, trying to focus. "The first grazed me, second was bad, went through one side and out the back. I'm—I'm feeling dizzy and sick to my stomach, is that usual?" Her voice was thick.

Harrison looked at her sharply, his expression worried. Zara's vision blurred. Her eyes rolled back in her head. Everything went black.

CHAPTER EIGHT

Harrison watched people fall in heaps as the gas filtered from the radiators. Zara was right about the distribution system. She was so damn smart. He pulled on his mask with a final gulp of air, then crumbled like the others feigning a knock-out from the heaven knows what spewing into the room in a cloud of smoke. He watched covertly as a group of people, maybe ten or so, started yanking jewels and other baubles from the heaps of people strewn about the ballroom floor.

They were dressed like the Reform Mechanics, someone wanted them to believe the Mechanics were behind the attack, just like they suspected. Harrison crawled across the floor pausing each time one of the thieves turned his direction. When he had moved close enough to the hall passage, he got to his feet, sneaking out of the room and past the ruffians behind this attack. Creeping down the long hallway to a corridor full of rooms, listened hard for voices.

"It's this way," someone said, "What we need is over here."

Harrison, not one to see if a situation was safe or not, followed after three men, keeping a short distance from them, crouching down a bit to stay hidden. There were so many blasted doors upstairs, he had to duck into a few to keep from being discovered.

"Here it is, in the office like she said," one of them said.

"Got them?" the other asked.

"Yep," a third voice replied.

Harrison waited for just a moment, then rushed into the room, and tackled the nearest man who was holding a stack of papers. They rolled about on the floor, punching each other hard. The other two hurried over to them. One of them grabbed Harrison from behind. Harrison forced him backwards, slamming him into the wall, then lowered his shoulder and tackled the third man. Unfortunately, this particular enemy was enormous and strong. The large man grabbed Harrison, throwing them off balance. He and Harrison went flying out the window with a crash, bits of glass and wood cutting them up in the process. They fought fiercely until the bigger fellow pinned him to the ground. He swung his fists to no avail when the great man suddenly grunted. Someone had conked him over the head with a wrench. Harrison adjusted his mask, looking to see who came to his aid.

Zara.

In that moment, Harrison had never seen a more perfect woman. He could have kissed her, but now wasn't the time. The other two men came tumbling out the broken window after them, and one went straight at Zara, who was curled in a ball on the ground. Harrison tackled him with a roar, punching him until he stopped moving, then went after the second fellow. He had every intention of beating the third, when Zara shot him with a blaster.

He looked at her, the blood rushing in his ears. She really was perfect. She was sitting on the ground, panting hard, papers clutched in her arms. Harrison yanked her to her feet, leading her away. He tried one direction, then rerouted her to another. When the carriages were not available, he got a horse from the barn, yanked her up, and rode like hell. All he could think of was keeping her safe. He didn't even know if they got what they needed, wasn't sure he cared. All he knew, was that she hadn't left him, and his admiration for her, his affection seemed to expand.

He asked her what happened and as she explained how brilliant, how clever she'd been, he found himself smiling. She was brilliant, and much better at this than he would have guessed. She had gone and surprised him again. Harrison thought he could get used to her surprises.

Until she fainted.

Harrison swore and held Zara tightly. She was too limp, her head flopped to one side. He kicked the horse back into a run and rode as fast as he could towards the Crow's Nest. They couldn't go to a hospital, too many questions. He tried to take an assessment of her. She was chalky white, even her lips. He ran his fingers along her neck, felt for a pulse. His heart hammered. Her arm was soaked with blood, so was the side of her dress and part of his jacket. She must have been bleeding for a long time. She had tried to use something to stop the bleeding, but he couldn't tell what. She was intelligent and resourceful in the field. She acted, she didn't hide like his past tinkerers, and then she came back to find him. To help him, when she could have just as easily left him behind. She had the opportunity to go, but she stayed because of him. He set his jaw and hoped the Crow's Nest medics were on call.

The horse's hooves pounded on the pavement.

She had come back.

No way he could have managed all those men alone. She was doing better than he expected at the ball. She was sweet and charming. A few times she talked tinker too much with the other guests, but he just squeezed her hand or kissed her cheek, and she knew their signal to step back. She changed the subject back to mundane talk, looking so damn beautiful he lost his head and stared at her because he thought she was the most beautiful woman he had ever met in his life.

Her apartment. Shit, he had not expected that. She had so little, the walls were cracked in spots. It was a hovel, he realized, she was poor. He remembered when he started at the Nest, he didn't make much either. Tinkerers made more because of their patents, but not a hell of a lot more. You didn't go into government work for the money, that was for sure. She mentioned her mother gave her free clothes every few weeks, that had to help. She always dressed so nicely, he assumed she was fine financially. Shit, even her automaton was ancient. That was one of the earliest models. The newer ones were more sleek looking, less boxy and one solid color, not a mismatched bunch of parts worked together like that. Annie was a relic, but Zara loved her. He could tell.

He stopped in front of the Crow's Nest. It was well past midnight and he had just ridden a horse down the cobblestone streets of the city with a bloodied, unconscious woman clutched to his chest. Nothing conspicuous there! Harrison leaned her forward and dismounted, then carefully lifted Zara down. She weighed much lighter than he expected, he could feel her ribs through her dress. She was too thin. He cradled her to his chest, limping from the spot where the bullet had grazed his leg. He punched in the night code awkwardly and walked through the revolving door. It locked behind him with a clang.

At just that moment, Dill came walking out of Room One Hundred which had been moved to the ground floor, along with the other rooms remaining that held agents working after hours, in case their departments needed them. He looked up from the papers he held and rushed over.

"Zara! What happened?" he gasped.

"She was shot twice. Dry West in the hospital room?" he said.

"Yes! He's on call tonight, I can call the room up. Is that a horse on the sidewalk?" Dill asked.

"Had to improvise," Harrison shrugged.

Dill chuckled, but his expression reflected his worry. Harrison knew he often slept in Room One Hundred, if he slept at all. Dill was always tinkering and the poor guy had no social life to speak of. There was a night desk girl, too, Harrison was fairly sure Dill was having sex with her and Mary, as well as FeFe. He tended to make friends with women before he slept with them. Even though he had never been great with women, and hid in the office a lot. He told Harrison once that he preferred to have sex with a woman he knew and cared about, and that one night stands were not his first choice. Harrison was determined to help out this poor, misguided soul and made a point to invite Dill when he and the other guys went for a beer after that. The one night stand was a male agents area of expertise. They picked woman up in the pubs, but Dill never did, no matter how they tried to coach him. He usually got embarrassed and left early. Funny, he took Mary and the night girl on nice dates before having sex with them, he couldn't bring himself to simply have sex with woman without knowing who she was first—even if the dame was willing. He was even friends with FeFe, they had been for years. FeFe liked Dill, she told Harrison so. She saw them talking all the time, laughing. He thought Dill liked Mary as more than just a friend, but he was too embarrassed to say so. He had no idea why, she was a good woman. Harrison didn't think it mattered if she used to be a lady of the night. She had some tough breaks to overcome, and Zara liked her. If Zara liked her, there must be real value there.

Room Twenty glided into place on the lobby level and Harrison limped across the floor. Dill rushed ahead of them and held the door while Harrison tried to hurry with Zara into the sterile, white room with hospital beds down the wall opposite the door. Dr. West was there. He was a very short man with warm, brown eyes and was the best doctor Harrison had ever met. He rushed to help Harrison lay Zara onto one of the beds. She still had the bloodied documents clutched to her chest. He took them from her gently and removed her wrist pouch, which was far heavier than it looked. It was stuffed with things because Zara's bags were always stuffed with things. He thought that was yet another of her adorable quirks.

"Doc, she was shot twice in the arm," he said.

"I can see that," Dr. West's hands were deft checking over Zara's body. He glanced at Harrison's leg, "So were you, I see."

"It was just a graze, I'm ok," Harrison shrugged.

"Sit down over there," he said, "Yvette, stitch him up." He nodded at Harrison.

Yvette Hemmings, a young doctor in training, came over and proceeded to cut the leg of his pants off. She cleaned the wound, numbed the area and started stitching him up. Harrison watched her start to work. She was a pretty woman with blue eyes and brown, wavy hair. Harrison had never seen her wear a dress. She said that she wore pants to work every day because it was more practical. He could understand why, now that he saw her at work, straddling the rolling stool and maneuvering the supplies laden cart. She was already a good doctor, nearly as good as Doc West.

He looked across Yvette's bent head to where Dr. West was examining Zara. He'd already gotten her out of her dress and into an exam gown. An I-V line ran into her left wrist. "Will she be ok?" Harrison asked.

"Yes, I think so," he replied while tying off a stitch. "I don't like the color of her skin though, why is she starving?"

Harrison's heart skipped a beat, "What? I've seen her down four pastries in less than five minutes. She can't be starving herself."

"Look how thin she is, her bones stick out. She's naturally tall and thin, but she's underweight by at least fifteen pounds. Her fingers are gaunt and her skin, when it's pressed on, looks yellow. That's the mark of jaundice and malnutrition," he said.

Harrison shut his eyes. Her apartment! "She lives alone. I saw her place today, she hardly has anything. I don't think she has much money."

"But, when I asked her about skipping lunch, she told me she forgets to eat, said she wasn't hungry," Dill said, looking upset. He still stood near the door to the room.

"She always eats the pastries every morning. At least two, sometimes three and she told me her and Mary get discounted soup and day old bread three days a week when they go to lunch. She ate at the ball tonight, a big plate of food. Oh, my god. How did I miss it?" He turned to look at Dill. "Whenever someone brings in something free, she eats her fill, Dill," Harrison said.

Dill paled and swallowed hard, "I asked her to lunch—as friends—a few times, but she always said she was busy. I didn't know she couldn't afford lunch. I would have paid for her to eat—I didn't know."

Harrison nodded. "She wouldn't have let you pay for her. How could you have known?" He propped his elbows and leaned back on the bed. "God dammit! She's doing her best...I'm such an idiot. I should have noticed sooner Will she be ok?" he asked the doctor.

"She's anemic. She most likely rarely eats meat, since it's more expensive. She needs more fruits and vegetables too, she's lacking the vitamins she needs to function. I'm certain she's been having dizzy spells—ignoring them most likely," he replied.

Harrison tried to swallow, but the lump in his throat wouldn't budge. "Dammit."

Harrison sat up, swinging his legs over the edge of the table with a nod to Yvette and looked at Zara, his brow furrowed. Dill had moved to the chair near her bed, and sat with his elbows on his knees.

"She didn't want us to know. What should we do?" Dill said.

"No idea," Harrison said, rubbing his face.

Dr. West checked the wound on her arm and adjusted the I-V line, "See that she has food to eat here, of course. Things higher in fat and richer in protein, like dairy and meat, fruit if you can manage, even dried fruit or nuts. I'm sure she's eating a little every day. As I said, she is naturally thin, but this—? This is too thin. The bullet went clean through. I need to keep her here overnight. Dr. Hemmings, can you help me move her to a clean bed and get her into a fresh gown? I've stitched her up and cleaned her wound, but she needs a quick sponge bath. Gentlemen, step behind the screen for a moment."

Harrison and Dill did as they were told, and stood there, exchanging glances with one another.

"Can we buy her food, or is that too pushy?" Harrison asked.

"Too pushy. Maybe we can sneak things in, nuts and fruit, dried meat and cheese like the doc said so she'll eat at least the pastries for breakfast and that for lunch," Dill suggested.

"Two meals are better than one," Harrison said.

Dill nodded and cleaned his glasses on his shirt, "I like her. I like her more than I expected to. I was intimidated when she came to the office. She scored higher than me on the tests. I was jealous, I admit to that. What I didn't expect was to like her as much as I do. She's kind to me. Other people tell me I'm odd, but I'm still a fairly well-adjusted tinkerer, considering. She laughs at my jokes and compliments me. She told me I looked handsome the other day. I don't hear that much."

"Mary tells you that all the time, you fool," Harrison chided.

Dill reddened, "But she's a, a…"

"A good woman, a tough one who turned her life around, Dill. She likes you," he said.

Dill reddened, "I know. I like her, too."

Harrison chuckled, "Then tell her."

"I just like someone else more."

Harrison was pretty sure he meant Zara, and he found that he hated the idea. He gave him a sideways look and Dill flushed apologetically.

"Okay, I think we're done here," Dry West said as he pulled back the curtain. Zara lay on two pillows, the blankets folded under her arms. The bed was tilted to a reclining position. But she was awake!

Harrison rushed over to Zara. He smiled down at her in relief.

"Did I faint?" she asked.

"Yes," he said.

She frowned, "Well, I'm not one of those ladies who does that. I'm very disappointed in myself."

"You were shot twice. I think it's ok this once," he said.

She huffed. Harrison laughed. He stroked her hair gently. It was so damn soft—like silk—and thick, too. She looked at him with her big blue eyes and his heart gave a thump. He smiled at her.

"You ok, partner?" he said.

"I'm fine," she said in a rush.

He grinned, "Of course you are. You're very tough. You can handle yourself just fine."

He was still stroking her hair. It occurred to him he should stop, but she was very sedated and looking at him with a little smile on those perfect lips. It was all he could do not to kiss her. He stared at those perfect lips. He could just kiss— The door banged open. Harrison jerked back and looked up. Mr. Wills was striding into the room, looking rumpled.

"Why did I get a courier bot from the local police department saying they suspected it was two of my agents who rode off on a horse after a group of men tried to rob people at the ball? Why is it that I didn't get a courier from my own agents? How is it that I was not made aware of the situation?" he stormed furiously. Dill had jumped up against the wall. Harrison looked at him, then back at Mr. Wills.

"Because Zara was shot twice," he spoke evenly.

Mr. Wills paused, his eyebrows raised at Harrison. Harrison pursed his lips and gave a stiff nod. Mr. Wills let out a long breath and nodded back. He strode to Zara's bedside and looked down at her. She was very pale. "Are you ok?" he asked.

"I'm fine," she smiled.

She didn't look fine, she looked terrible, and nearly as white as the sheet neatly folded under her arm. She still had dark streaks of mascara under her eyes and on her face. Her eyes were bloodshot and glazed from the medication. Harrison refrained from stroking her hair. He put his hands behind his back and clasped them together.

"Well, obviously, a quick get-away was necessary if she was shot. Tell me what happened," Mr. Wills said.

Harrison explained the whole debacle. Mr. Wills listened closely, his eyes sharp. He arched his brows and smiled when Harrison told him what Zara did, looking impressed.

"Well, Miss Turner! You have surprised me," he said.

"There are samples of that stuff in my purse," Zara said.

"We got these, too," Harrison said.

Mr. Wills opened the blood-stained stack of papers and studied them, "More maps! What the deuce are these people up to?"

"I don't know, but I think they robbed the guests to throw everyone off. The maps were the real targets. They're trying to find something, but what, I don't know," Harrison said.

Mr. Wills nodded, "Zara, you rest now. Harrison, a word if you please."

"Yes, sir," he said looking back at Zara. Her eyes were already shut. He let out a sigh and stiffly stood to follow Mr. Wills.

Harrison was hesitant to leave her, but as he began to move away from her side, Dr. West and Dr. Hemmings were already checking the machines and marking her chart. He knew she was in good hands. He walked with his uncle and Dill across the hall. They sat at the conference table. Mr. Wills spread out the maps. They studied them all, debating about what they could be using them for until dawn. When FeFe, Simon, Marcus and Douglas showed up, they were guzzling coffee and eating day old pastries, still trying to understand the damn maps.

"What the hell happened to you?" FeFe said, eyeing him.

"The ball went a little sideways," he said.

He didn't elaborate, he was too tired.

"Where's Zara?" Simon asked.

"She was shot twice in the arm, she's ok. Resting in the hospital room," he said.

The other gents turned and strode from the room, exchanging worried glances. Harrison jumped up and followed them, annoyed.

"Why are you coming?" Simon asked, glaring at him, "I'm going to check on her. None of you need to come."

"I'm coming! I like her, she's a good person. Does great work here and she was shot. She's my friend, same as yours," Douglas said.

"I like her, too," Marcus snapped.

"Oh, for heaven's sake," FeFe said.

She sighed and came along, too. They walked into the hospital wing to find an empty room.

"Where the hell is Zara?" Harrison asked.

Dr. West glanced over, "I made her eat a hearty breakfast, take some vitamins, which I sent home with her after a stern talk about healthy eating, then she said something about having jobs to do today, and insisted she had to fix an elevator. I tried to stop her, but she said she had to. I cannot make a grown woman stay, not one as determined as she is."

Harrison swore, "I'll check on her. I know where she is."

"She went to fix an elevator with two gunshot wounds? I think I might love her," Douglas said with a grin.

Harrison fought the urge to punch him. He could barely contain his fury. His eyes narrowed and he glared at Douglas. Simon snorted with laughter, eyeing Harrison's stony expression.

"Harrison, seems you like her a little more than most of the girls you know. But that can't be, because you never truly like any lady. Unlike the rest of us, 'never date just one woman' is your motto, if I recall," Marcus said.

Harrison flushed, "I do like her. She's my friend and she did a hell of a job last night. She—" he hesitated only a moment. Most of the agents didn't even catch it, "—she came back for me when things got dicey, I wouldn't have made it out without her. Dill's the only tinkerer with the guts to help me like that before…she's got courage."

Douglas grinned, eyeing him up and down, "Well, I'll be! Do you have an actual crush on her? That sounded like a compliment to me, even admiration if I were to analyze your voice correctly. Are you in love?"

"No, dammit! I like her," he snapped.

"Aye, of course," Douglas said with a twinkle in his eye.

Harrison turned on his heel and stormed out. He heard them all laughing, and caught a glimpse of a furious looking FeFe as that laughter followed him out the revolving door. He didn't have his own ride, so he hailed a Hansom Carriage and rode it to the estate where he'd left his carriage during the escape. There were several still at the estate, all of which he searched just in case. Then, he took his to the market where he bought food under the pretense of feeding her lunch. He got more than he needed, but enough to keep from looking suspicious. He took his carriage to Zara's apartment building. He had to leave it parked on the street in that seedy neighborhood she lived in. He asked Marvin, the automaton at the door, to keep an eye on it.

Harrison carried in a paper sack of groceries. He was about to climb the steps when he heard Zara.

"Great cabbage hat! Come on!" she said angrily.

He chuckled, walking over to the open elevator, "Great cabbage hat?"

She jumped, smiling at him, "My mother made this hat once. It was supposed to be a rose. She asked what I thought of it, and I said, 'Great cabbage hat, mama!' enthusiastically. My papa laughed himself silly and we started saying it when our tinkering went south. She was deeply offended."

He chuckled, "That's funny."

She shrugged, wiping her pale face. She smeared grease all over it. She had on black pants and a grey shirt, very baggy on her with sleeves rolled up at the bottoms because they were too long. She was filthy, her arm in a sling. She looked white as can be, ill and pasty. Her hair was pulled back in a ponytail. She looked perfect as far as he was concerned, she was adorable, even when not at her best.

"How's the arm?" he asked.

"It's killing me. I can't get this, my landlady is going to up my rent if I don't fix it this time. She spent a fortune on parts at your suggestion, I got a courier bot in the hospital room this morning demanding I get here, so I had to rush home ," Zara said.

"I can help. I bet it's hard to do one-handed. Tell me what to do," Harrison said. He set down the bag and rolled up his sleeves.

"What's that?" Zara asked.

"I brought you lunch. I wasn't sure what you liked, so I got you a bit of everything," he said.

Zara smiled, "Really?"

Harrison chuffed her under the chin, "You bet. You saved my life last night. Least I could do."

"That's sweet of you!" she said with a bright smile.

Harrison stared at her, his heart going fast, "Not a problem."

"I'm nearly finished. See those wires there?" she said.

"The copper or the silver?" he said.

"Both. Connect the copper to the copper, silver to the silver by twisting them and putting this little cap on one, then the other," she said. He did as she said, "Good job! Now, this is where I had trouble. Turn this crank five times to move us up and expose the next set of wires."

He did it easily, "Like that?"

"Perfect. Now this part…I think your hands are too big," she said.

He looked at his hands and chuckled, "Possibly."

"Can you hold this fuse for me? I can secure it. I have to bypass the old fuses, they keep shorting out," she said.

"Ok," he said.

He held the part up. She stood in front of him, her back on his chest. He smelled her head, lemons again. He found he loved that fresh smell of hers. She put the new fuse in. They repeated this process three more times, until they were on the top floor. He helped her put a few new bars and panels on, it was actually sort of fun. When they finished, they rode the elevator up and down. He found himself smiling, oddly proud he was able to fix something, since he'd never tried before. His father was a tinkerer, he helped him a few times as a kid, but his sister Emily was more interested in the technical things than him. He liked more exciting things and being outside, like getting into mischief. Come to think of it, he still did, but he found he appreciated this part of tinkering, that satisfaction when something worked. This was fun for a change of pace. He and Zara rode the elevator to the bottom. She took down the out of order sign, then rode it to her apartment. She grabbed a bag of her tools. He took it from her and picked up the groceries.

"You're bleeding. I'll look at it. You might have torn your stitches," he said.

She nodded, looking exhausted, "I had to fix the heat upstairs first, middle of summer, but he wants his heat fixed. I washed the restrooms down, too, had a complaint about that, then the elevator. My arm hurts so badly. I think I have something for the pain."

Harrison's lips thinned from worry, she looked so pale. She went to her apartment and unlocked the door. He set her tools on her tinkering table, then walked to the kitchen, telling himself not to stare. In the daylight, her place was worse than he had noticed last night. The cracks in the walls were deep, the curtains full of even more holes then he realized. Her furniture was so worn and faded, you could nearly see the stuffing in spots. He set the bag down and smiled at her when she peeked in. He put a fresh bandage on her quickly, the tear wasn't bad, then they went in for the food.

"I got a little of everything. I wasn't sure what you liked. We've never had lunch together before," he said.

"I like most everything. Grapes! I love those! Oranges too? I can never afford fresh fruit, well, I do get apples in the discount bin if they're not to bruised up, apricots of I'm lucky or cherries. I love fruit," she said.

He smiled, his heart squeezing, "Good! I got some almonds, two kinds of dried meat, crackers, bread and three types of cheese, too. You like this?"

She nodded eagerly, "Yes! I like all this."

She got out some mismatched plates and glasses that were two different sizes. She took out a jug of lemonade.

"Do you like lemonade? Annie made it," she said.

"I love it," Harrison nodded.

He helped her set the table, then he cut the meat and cheese on a cutting board, then set the fruit out for them on yet another patterned plate. The cups had chips in them, so did the plates. Zara winced.

"I-I'm sorry I don't have nicer things. I had to take what was in the attic at my mother's—her old things she didn't want anymore," she said.

He shrugged, "I didn't even notice."

She sent him a look, "Of course you did. You notice everything, you're the most observant person I've ever met. You're just being too kind to say anything rude. I don't have nice things. But then, I really have never cared that much."

"Much?" he said.

"Except when people come over, like you. Then I wish I had at least one matching set of dishes, free of chips. You want hear what's funny?" she said, eating a grape.

"What?" Harrison asked, making a sandwich for himself.

Zara followed suit, "I like it better here, even with all this shabbiness. I was always on edge in my mother's house. I hid all the time, tried to stay out of sight. They all hate me and I was forever being backhanded or beaten with a switch. My sisters didn't hit, but they said the most horrible things to me, mostly Tempie. I love this place. I don't care of it's shabby or in a bad neighborhood. The things I had living with my mother, they were nice. I always had new parts to tinker with, the best of everything, great food and even though she was mean, I had what I needed, piles of what I needed, more than what I need. But I was miserable. I'm happy here. I love my job and I have friends. This is the first real home I've had since my papa died. Those other things don't matter. I find I like shabby."

She smiled at Harrison. He took in her grease smudged face, crooked ponytail, and sincere expression. His eyes softened, and his heart quickened. How had he missed how remarkable she was? How had he been so very stupid?

"You're the most amazing person I have ever met, Zara," he said.

Her eyes locked with his. She grinned happily, her eyes twinkling.

"Thank you, Harrison. I feel that way about you, too," she said softly.

Their shared looked hung comfortably on the silence. An urge to lean closer grew inside Harrison and leaned slightly toward her to kiss her when she took a big bite of her sandwich.

She closed her eyes around the bite with a pleasant moan. "It's been a long time since I had good bread. I had a lot of terrible loaves with Annie and my machine. Burned mostly, so I ate out the middle. I didn't want to waste anything, but some of it was so vile!"

He laughed heartily, "I can imagine. You started that fire the other day at work, you're pretty good at burning things."

"That was Dill, I swear! The wires went up. But…I helped, I suppose," she said with a giggle.

He grinned, winking at her. They ate in silence for a while. Zara ate an orange, some grapes, a sandwich and cheese. Harrison was relieved. There was enough food remaining to get her through the weekend. He wished he'd gotten more, or maybe eaten less, but he didn't want her be suspicious. He helped Zara put the rest of the food in her ice box, then they walked into the living room. Zara gestured to the couch. He sat beside her with a smile.

"Do you have to go back to the Nest?" she said.

He nodded, "Yes. I'm going to look through the files for some of the men I saw, see if I can make a connection."

"Ok. I have to rest, but I can do the same when I get back. I tried to record their images in my mind, but the evening was sort of a frazzled blur. Thanks for lunch. I won't keep you. I should rest, I'm very tired and my arm hurts badly," she said.

"Ok," Harrison said.

He took a deep breath and stood with a smile.

"Thanks for stopping by," she said.

"Of course! Let me know if you need anything, send a courier bot," he said.

"Ok. I will, thank you," she said.

He leaned in and kissed her before he thought about what he was doing. She blinked in surprise. He flushed and offered her a half smile. She laughed and hugged him around the middle, resting her cheek on his shoulder, holding him tightly with one arm. He smiled and held her gently, careful not to hurt her. They stood there for a long time, until she pulled back. He felt confused by these feelings she causing. She needed him, and it felt better to be needed than he imagined. She stepped in, kissing his cheek very close to his lips. His heart thumped. She smiled at him and he offered her a small smile back. He felt a rush of fear, of terror looking at her. He was in trouble, sinking into something he didn't want, something that could potentially cost him his freedom, his happiness. He pulled away this time.

"I have to go, honey. I'll see you later, ok? I'll come and check on you after work, before I go home," he said, schooling his expression into a friendly one.

"Ok. That'd be great... Thank you."

He tugged on his vest, then left with a smile. On the way back to the Nest, it occurred to him, he might be falling for her. Until now, he had not admitted that to himself, insisting he was just being a good friend. It scared the hell out of him. Instead of coming back later, he went straight home and made a point to not think about her for the rest of the weekend.

CHAPTER NINE

Zara was getting too interested in Harrison. She had wanted him to kiss her so badly when he was at her place. He was kind enough to bring her lunch on Friday, and to help her fix the elevator. She was managing to keep up with all the tinkering for her building, and her arm was feeling a tad better each day. She had made a new friend too, a young girl named Trixie who liked to tinker as well. She was about eight. She and her mother lived on the floor above her. Zara liked her, she was bright. She had big blue eyes and fiery red hair. Her uncle was a tinkerer, a nice man in his fifties. He worked at the motorized bicycle factory. She met them after her apartment was broken into, all her food stolen and some of her jewelry, including a necklace her papa gave her. She didn't care about the other things, just that necklace. They saw her crying when James Crane, Harrison's friend, yelled at her for acting foolish. Trixie's father called him a brute and asked him to leave.

Zara started her bike and put on her goggles. She drove to work and got off. She had on the pretty navy and blue striped dress, her hair pinned up in a large knot above her head, and a bow pinned at the top. She stowed her goggles in her leather bag and went inside.

Mary smiled, "Zara! Blue is your color, you look like an angel. I like your makeup too, that berry colored lipstick and mascara is perfect on you. How's your arm?"

Zara smiled, "It's aching today, but I'm fine. Thanks for coming to see me yesterday."

"You're my best friend, course I did! Sorry, again, your place was torn up like that, shame you lost that necklace. Today's a new day, fresh start, I like to say. I got something to show you!" Mary said. She held up a large vase of flowers with a happy smile, "Dill got me flowers! Is that not the most romantic gesture? FeFe was envious!"

Zara grinned, "It's very romantic! How lovely!"

Mary giggled, setting them down, a dreamy smile on her face, "He asked me out again tonight, right in front of a bunch of the other ladies."

Zara smiled, "He's a very good man. I'm happy for you, Mary."

"See you at lunch, then?" she said.

Zara nodded and waved. She walked to the room, her smile fading. She fiddled with her ear bobs. They were little blue gears. She had on the matching necklace. She waited for Room One Hundred, looking at the ground.

"Why the frown when you look so pretty?" Marcus asked.

Zara smiled at him, "Thanks. My arm is hurting a little."

He took a step towards her, his blue eyes full of worry, "I heard what happened. How do you feel?"

"Not bad, just aches a bit. On top of that, someone broke into my apartment yesterday," Zara said.

Marcus took her hand and held it tightly. Zara noticed he was a bit stiff at times, but he was such a warm man, once you got to know him. He was very intelligent, he could have easily been a tinkerer. He followed a lot of what Dill and she said, "You call the police?"

"Yes. They took a necklace my papa got me. It was a little gold hammer. I loved that, I have so little from him. They trashed up some of my things, smashed my poor dog-bot. I had to put him back together. I'm a bit down, I suppose, because of all my bad luck lately."

Marcus offered her a smile, his handsome face kind, "Come on, then. I'll cheer you up. How about a pastry and some coffee?"

Zara agreed. He put his arm around her and they walked inside. He kissed her head and she hugged him around the middle, finding she needed human contact more than she used to these days. She glanced up to see Harrison watching them, his brow furrowed, his eyes darting between them.

"Morning, all! Zara's having a tough go of it. Her apartment was broken into this weekend," Marcus said, rubbing her back.

Harrison crossed the room and took her hands, "What did they take?"

"I don't have much, just a gold necklace my papa gave me. They smashed my dog bot and trashed everything, made a huge mess! They broke my bread maker and smashed all my tinkering supplies," she said, struggling not to cry.

Harrison made a pained noise, swearing, "I'm sorry."

Zara took a steadying breath, "It's ok. Nothing to be done about it, now. Does anyone have pain medication. They smashed my bottle."

"I have some," Dill said.

She smiled at him and walked to the table. She sat down in a huff.

Mr. Wills looked at her, "Was the bread making machine the one you hoped to patent?"

"Yes, my new prototype to present to the committee. Now I have to rebuild and postpone my appointment," she said.

Mr. Wills nodded sympathetically and passed her some pastry. Zara sighed angrily. She got herself coffee with shaky hands, she had not felt well since she was shot. She frowned at her plate.

"I don't know how they got in! I have three locks on my door, I always double check the locks and wiggle the door handle. It was like I left them open so they could walk right in. Then they only took a few things and smashed the rest. Thank goodness for Annie. She alerted the police with the her internal telegraph. I know it's a dated method, but she's old and they came straight away. For some reason, they didn't smash her," Zara said.

"Why didn't you contact me?" Harrison said.

"It was late last night, especially after the police left and what could anyone do? I was out for the evening," she said.

"Did you have a date?" FeFe asked.

Zara laughed, "No. I never have dates, I'm not like you, FeFe. You have scads of men lined up to date you. I was in my building down the hall with my neighbors. We didn't hear a thing! I was with this little girl I like, Trixie Goshian, and her parents, John and Amy, her uncle was there too. I was fixing Trixie's bird-bot. She made it herself, but she bought those halonite pieces and he fell apart. She's only eight, she loves it. I found her crying in the hall, so I took her some of my parts and showed her how to work with them. Neither of her parents are tinkerers, nice people though. They had me for dinner—cabbage soup. I'm not a fan of cabbage, but it was all right and so sweet of them to include me. I think the uncle might fancy me, he's very old, I don't like him like that, but he is a tinkerer, fun to talk to. I'm doing it again, losing track, babbling on like I do. Sorry! I came home after an excellent night, my door was wide open and everything all torn apart! They took some of my clothes! I had to call my mother and have her send me more, she was furious with me, called me, well, it hardly matters."

"Why would she be mad if you were robbed?" Douglas said.

"She's insane, I have no idea," rolling her eyes in an uncharacteristically annoyed gesture.

They laughed heartily and Zara chuckled. She looked at her pastry and picked at it.

"I'll call the police and see what I can do to help," Mr. Wills said.

"James Crane was the officer, Harrison. That went how you'd expect now that he knows I work here and I'm a tinkerer and a friend of yours," she said.

Harrison winced, "He's an ass. Was he horrible?"

"He made me cry. He called me an idiot and said I deserved it!" she said forlornly.

Harrison looked livid, "He made you cry?"

"That's uncalled for!" Marcus said.

"That guy's an asshole, Zara. Pay him no mind," Douglas said.

Zara shrugged, "It did look like I left the door unlocked. He said I was stupid to do it in a neighborhood like that. Maybe I did, I could have. I haven't felt very good since I was shot, maybe it's my fault."

Mr. Wills studied her, "I want you to go see Dr. West after breakfast."

"I'm not hungry. I'll go now," she said.

She stood. For some reason. Harrison and Dill exchanged glances. Dill jumped up.

"You might feel better if you eat!" Dill said.

Zara shook her head, "No thanks, I'm ok. Just tired from all the excitement."

Zara went to see Dr. West. He checked her out and took some blood. He gave her an antibiotic for the gunshot wound, as it had become infected, and she was running a fever. Zara was sweaty and irritable. She went back to the room, assuring them she was fine and sat at the desk with Dill to tinker. She worked on a small camera that could take fifteen pictures. It was so tiny, it could be concealed in a pocket. It looked like a thin box, except that the camera was inside and if you pressed the top, it snapped the picture. She tried it out a few times, then developed the pictures.

"That's a good invention, useful," Dill said.

Zara smiled and wiped at her head. She was sweating profusely, "Thank you."

"I have some sausages and a cheese tray my mother brought over this weekend. I live alone, and there was lots of food so I brought it in to share with everyone. Would you like some?" he said.

Zara shook her head, "No thanks. If I feel better later, I will take some. I think that medicine Dr. West gave me made my stomach sour."

"Ok," he said with a frown, "You skipped breakfast."

"I'm fine! Just not myself," she said.

She went back to tinkering. As the day went on, she felt worse and worse. Zara stood to get a piece she needed an hour later and crumbled in a heap to the echoing sound of Dill calling out her name.

•   •   •

Harrison paced the floor of Room One Hundred. Zara had part of a bullet in her arm. It had embedded itself in her bone, causing a nasty infection of some kind. Dr. West was in surgery with her now. Harrison was scared to death. He was nuts about her. He'd known her nearly a month, and she meant more to him then he realized. When he saw her fall, he felt like he couldn't breathe, like he was hurt himself. He had never been more afraid. He thought she had died. She looked dead, she was so pale and thin. She was in trouble, and he couldn't help her. Harrison had a bad feeling about that robbery in her apartment too, there was something off about that.

He walked over to his uncle and crossed his arms, "Her apartment, it—"

"Was no accident. I know. I think they left a mess, trashed it and took that necklace because they were looking for this map she recovered. She's a beautiful lady, distinctive. It's possible one of our enemies discovered who she is," Mr. Wills said.

"So, whoever is doing those robberies is after her?" Douglas said.

"It's possible. Dill, I want you to go to her apartment and install that marvelous unbreakable lock of yours for her when she is ready to go home. We'll have a sentinel bird or two circle her place and I will alert the local police. They agree with me, say it wasn't random. I called Crane this morning, spoke to him myself. She has nothing of value and they were more bent on destruction. You'll be happy to know I yelled at Mr. Crane for making her cry. He said she sobbed and said she only had three of her papa's things left, and they took one of them. Mentioned he felt quite bad," Mr. Wills said.

Harrison swore, "Bastards."

"Where does she live?" Simon asked.

"She lives in the industrial section of town in that old red building across from the new halonite plant. Her place is rough, she doesn't have much," Harrison said.

"Why does she live there? Her mother is wealthy!" FeFe said distastefully.

"Because unlike you, she doesn't take handouts from her parents, FeFe. She lives on her own and pays for everything herself. She god-damn fixes things in the building for a break on rent and cleans the toilets. She is still waiting on her damn patent checks!" Harrison said.

Dill's eyebrows met in the middle, a deep frown on his face, "She should have gotten those in a month! Especially with how her coffee pots are selling, she should be making quite a bit of money."

Harrison frowned, "Really?"

Dill nodded, "She should be making piles of money, too. She told me she shared that patent with her ex-boyfriend, Vincent, she went to school with him. He was to get thirty percent for designing the outside covering. It is handsome, but I think he deserved more like twenty. He took her to court over it, can you believe that? Judge ruled in her favor when he couldn't explain the internal workings at all. Vince sounds like a complete cad to me, one of those men who tries to pass of your ideas as their own. I've met a few of those in my time."

Harrison felt a rush of anger, "Mr. Wills, what's his last name?"

"You get the feeling he's been cashing her checks, too?" Mr. Wills said.

"I sure as hell do, dammit!" he said.

"Take someone with you so you don't kill him," Mr. Wills said, fishing out his address.

"I'll come," Douglas said.

Douglas was a scrapper, he loved boxing, and he looked angry. Harrison was glad to have him. They took the address and walked down the street. It was a block and a half over, he had a nice shop, this Vince.

"You think he's stealing from her?" Douglas said.

"No idea. But if he is and she's living in a dump because of it, he will regret it," Harrison said.

Douglas nodded, "He sure as hell will."

They walked to Vincent's tinkering shop called "Home Fixes Fast." It was one of those high end shops with a shiny silver sign and a nice window display of all sorts of modern home contraptions, including a coffee pot and portable fridge made by Zara. Harrison and

Douglas exchanged angry glances. Harrison pushed open the door. A plump man with brown hair and blue eyes smiled at him.

"Hello! Can I help you?" he said.

"Yes! I'm looking for Vincent Waters," he said.

"You found him!" he said with a smile.

Harrison frowned. This was him? This fat, average looking man dated Zara? He and Douglas exchanged surprised looks.

Harrison flashed him a smile, "Hello. My name is Harrison Lowell. This is my associate, Douglas Fairbanks. We work with Zara Turner at the Crow's Nest."

He looked momentarily stricken, then smiled, "Zara! She's a wonderful woman. How is she?"

"She's fine, except that she hasn't received a penny from that royalty check for the coffee pot she made in your front window, and as I understand it, she was the one who made the inner workings, while all you did, was make the cover. You seem to have a lot of them in your in your shop here, big sellers, aye?" Douglas asked, cracking his knuckles.

Vincent's eyes darted to the door, "Ah, yes. Our best, actually, besides that fridge she made. People like to picnic and travel with both. The mobility, it was a brilliant idea on her part. However, making that outside look so sleek was not easy! She did not deserve eighty percent!"

"You got more than you deserve at thirty percent! You covered her brilliance in a shiny coating and tried to act like it was your damn idea! Listen to me, you asshole. She deserves that money! She's smarter than you, all you made was the damn cover and a court of law in Jakarda City voted in her favor. A court, so if you have her money, you are breaking the law and I am not happy about it," Harrison snarled, taking a step towards him.

Vincent took a step back, his hands up in a gesture of surrender, "Please! There have only been three checks so far!"

"You god damned better not have taken her money, Vincent. She's a friend of ours, we don't take kindly to people who hurt our friends," Douglas said, taking a menacing step forward.

"I didn't! I have the checks here! I have been getting them by accident! They didn't have her address, I would never have cashed them! I just wanted her to sweat a little because of what happened in court!" he said.

"Sweat a little? You are lucky I don't kill you. If you ever try to do anything to hurt her in any way again, I will find you and you will be sorry. Where are the checks?" Harrison said, his chest heaving.

"Here! They're here!" Vincent squeaked.

He opened a drawer and handed him three checks, all of which had enough money to keep her from being hungry for quite a while. Douglas and Harrison looked at them, they exchanged angry looks with one another at the sight of the sizable amount.

"You're a real bastard, you know that? You're going to call the office and see that she gets those checks from the company producing her products on a mass scale, or we will be back and next time, you'll pay, aye?" Douglas said.

Vincent nodded, sending his jowls bouncing, "Of course. Yes! I understand!"

"We catch a whiff of anything unsavory here and you will be arrested. I'll have you thrown into a cell with no hope of getting out," Harrison said.

Vincent swallowed hard, his jowell's wobbling a bit, "I understand."

Harrison stormed out, furious with him. Douglas grinned at him walking up beside him, his brown eyes dancing.

"Normally you're the charming sort, telling the bad guys your friend will bust them up with a smirk. We were both tough guys then, nice change of pace. Never saw you lose your head like that," Douglas said.

"You should see that shit hole she lives in, Douglas. There are cracks in the walls, holes in the rug and curtains, all her things are second hand and shitty. She is barely making it and that pudgy asshole is hiding her money because he's jealous she's smarter than him. He's going to shit himself when that bread cooker she made comes out!" he said.

Douglas laughed heartily, "Dill let it slip to me about her being anemic and starving. Made me sick. I see her eating scraps at lunch, I thought she was a small eater. I felt terrible knowing I'm off having a hearty meal while she's hardly got a thing at all. I know how it feels to go hungry. As a lad, sometimes my stomach hurt so bad, my whole body ached with it, and there my poor folks sat passing their food to us. Aye, I know how she feels, Harrison. She's proud, same as I was. I knew there was no way she'd accept my charity, it's why I brought in those apples for the office."

Harrison winced, because he knew she wouldn't want them to know that, "Did you tell anyone?"

"No. No, and I told Dill to keep his fat trap shut. She's proud, and I don't know what went on, but she has no relationship with her family. She doesn't talk about anyone but her papa and the only thing she ever says about her mother is she's a good business woman. That's no glowing endorsement. I may not have your powers of observation, but I'm not an idiot. I knew her home life was a bad one."

"Yeah. It's not good, her family situation," Harrison said.

"She told you about it, then?" Douglas said.

"Yes," Harrison said, refusing to betray her trust.

Douglas studied him, "I'm going to say this as your friend, Harrison. We've worked together since we started here, went to The Crow's Nest training. I've known you since we were eighteen, nine years now, nearly ten. In that time I have always thought you were an arrogant prick at times, but a hell of an agent."

Harrison laughed, "What's your point?"

"My point is, that in nine years, I have never seen you care about a woman. Not really care. You've only ever tried to get in the ladies' pants. I know how you said you don't want a family, just the job. You don't date women long like the rest of us. I like to date a lady three or four times at minimum before I hop in the sack with her. Look, Zara, she's a nice woman, a good one. She's not like FeFe, who has had sex with all of us because she sees it as a challenge and she doesn't give a shit what anyone thinks about her. Zara is special. She's wild about you. We've all seen it, she looks up to you as a teacher and a friend. You like her, too. I'm not getting in your business, but she's the sort of woman you get serious about, Harrison. If you can't do that with her, don't lead her on. I get the feeling she's been hurt enough. For the record, I think you could be good together. You see, she makes you a hell of a lot less arrogant. She teases you and laughs at you when you act like a pompous ass, then you laugh because she is right. You care about her, I know you do, try not to hurt her or just be her friend if it's all you can give her. Don't break her heart. She's so sweet and kind, I honestly wish she saw me like she sees you, but I'm her chum. As her friend, I'm asking you to be kind to her, aye?" Douglas said.

Harrison nodded, taking Douglas's suggestion to heart. They went inside the Crow's Nest, but Harrison didn't comment about his friend's wise words. He knew he was right and he wasn't sure what he could give Zara. What he did know, was that he didn't think he could stop himself from being with her. He liked her too much to stay away, and that scared him more than anything he had ever felt before. She scared him.

Harrison looked at Mary when they walked in the Nest, "She ok?"

"Still in surgery. You get her checks?" Mary said. He nodded and she grinned, "I'm happy about that! She's my best friend, I brought her dinner on Sunday night. Poor thing, she cried so much about that necklace, I stayed for two hours 'til I knew she was ok. Zara is not the sort to cry, but there she is so pale with a big bandage on her arm, her home smashed apart and I found myself crying to. She and I we got bad families, we look out for one another."

"Your family is bad, too?" Douglas said.

Mary smiled sadly, nodding at him, "Yeah. My father's a bastard of the worst kind."

Douglas sent her a sympathetic smile, "Sorry, Mary. You turned out great of you ask me."

She laughed and offered him a smile, "Thanks, Douglas. I like you, too. I like it here at the Nest, good people, kind ones, especially Zara. She sees good in people with her quiet ways and her cleverness. Saw it in me when I really needed someone to. I'll be grateful to her for the rest of my life for that."

Douglas tipped his hat to Mary with a grin. Harrison glanced down the hall, "Will she be ok?"

"Don't know. She's still in surgery. Doc ran into a complication of some kind. He's still at it, I'm guzzling coffee over here, my nerves are shot," Mary said.

"What kind of a complication?" Harrison said.

"Not certain. The nurse came out, said something about a weird substance in her blood. Dr. West is good. He was on it, had Dr. Hemmings with him. She's top notch, too," Mary said.

Harrison agreed, striding down the hall. He went back to Room One Hundred. He took out all the maps and looked at them. Hours later, when he was about to pull out his hair from worrying, Dr. West came in.

Harrison rushed over with the others, even FeFe looked worried.

"Is she ok?" FeFe asked.

"She's going to be fine. There wasn't a bullet in her bone like I thought, it was this liquid substance, it kept moving within her blood. I think the bullet was dipped in it. The good news is—the bone wasn't cracked like I feared. She was full of the stuff, I have it here. We're lucky it didn't travel to her heart. I had to use a magnetic device to pull it out. I have it all for you to analyze, it's mixed with blood. Dill, I'd like to know what it is. If it's getting into our agents, then we need to know how to combat it," Dr. West said.

"Can I see her?" Harrison asked.

"I'm running a scan with a drone over her. I kept finding little bits, I'm double checking to see that we got it all, just to be safe. It was poisoning her, causing that infection. She needs to rest this time, and she will stay here with me and Dr. Hemmings for several days. I am going to keep scanning, just in case. I have the nurses on board to watch her, no tinkering for the next few days," he said.

"We'll make sure she stays. I'll speak with her myself," Mr. Wills said.

"Give me about twenty minutes, then she can see you all. Should her family be notified?" Dr. West asked.

Harrison's heart squeezed, "No. No, I don't think they'd come."

Dr. West nodded and left Room One Hundred. Harrison watched the room move slowly back up to the tenth floor, then click into place. He walked over to the window, thinking about the substance.

"I think it's halonite," Dill said, walking up beside him, his hands on his hips.

Harrison turned to look at him in surprise, "Halonite?"

"In a liquid form. Halonite is not silver, it's a silver nitrate like material, but I was told at the factory it only came in solid from," Dill said.

"Why would they make bullets from Halonite?" FeFe asked.

"I don't think they did. I think they dipped them in the Halonite like Dr. West said. Maybe because they knew what it would do when it reached the warm temperature of the blood. I've separated some from Zara's blood and it hardened, then shattered in seconds," Dill said.

"What does that mean?" FeFe said, her brow furrowed.

"It means, that someone wanted to poison the person they shot. They knew exactly what it would do when it hit the bloodstream," Mr. Wills said, looking at the samples on Dill's desk, "I need to visit a friend. Don't bombard poor Zara when she's able to receive visitors."

He punched in the code and left. They were on the ground floor after that. Lots of moving today, Mary must have shifted them to a lower level to keep them moving about. Harrison looked at the maps and swore. The others gathered around him.

"I think these maps and the robbery at Zara's might be connected, but how and why, I can't guess," Harrison said.

"Could be they are. We just have to wait and think. I know I'm missing something," Marcus said.

"Me too," Harrison said.

"Well! While you chaps take a look, I'm going to get some air. I'm afraid all this has me very shaken," FeFe said.

"Are you alright?" Dill asked, his expression worried.

FeFe smiled at him, "Would you walk me to the rooftop, Dill?"

Dill, ever the gentleman, agreed. Harrison shook his head. FeFe had sex with Dill sometimes, him being her last choice because of his sloppiness. She was the sort of woman who tired of men easily, and didn't much care who she was with, as long as there was a challenge involved. Dill fancied Mary, so he was a challenge now and worthy of her attention. Plus, the moment he set eyes on FeFe, Dill looked at her like she was a goddess, he told Harrison once he'd never seen a more beautiful women. FeFe loved that, ate up that attention. He escorted her from the room. Harrison was left with Marcus, Simon and Douglas, who decided to check the book of photos for suspects. Harrison looked, too, for something to do. None of the Reform Mechanics were involved as they originally thought. Who the deuce were these people?

CHAPTER TEN

>Zara opened her eyes to a searing pain in her arm hours later. Everyone came to see her, but she was heavily sedated and groggy. She couldn't speak, or even follow conversations. Little did she know, she had spent three days in that state because Mr. Wills and Dr. West thought it best to keep her like that, for fear that she would try and get up and tinker. They fed her vitamins and made her eat large meals high in protein to help with the anemia and malnutrition. Mr. Wills contacted her building supervisor to tell her Zara was very ill, and had been injured on the job. He paid her rent and showed her the royalties checks. Mary brought her things, but the Dr.'s made her stay in bed for the rest of the week, then let her go home Friday night. Harrison took her home with Mary.

Mary and Dill were no longer dating. Mary found him having sex with FeFe on the roof. Dill was overwrought about it, said FeFe threw herself at him and he never meant to hurt Mary, but he had feelings for FeFe and he always had. Zara was in a drug hazed fog, so she didn't have much to say to her friend, other than she was sorry. She fell asleep in Harrison's carriage, her head on his shoulder. She was so pleased to be home—until she saw her apartment trashed and ripped apart for a second time.

Zara looked at it and started to sob brokenly.

Mary hugged her, "Shh! Come on now! It's ok, Zara!"

"N-no! Someone is doing this on purpose! My home! My things! Annie!" she said.

She ran into her room and found her maid-bot, broken. She sat on her bed and wept, "I m-made that with my papa! It's all I have left of him!"

Harrison knelt in front of her, "You can fix it, ok, honey? You're the best tinkerer there is! Dill's going to come and put in all new locks, same ones we have at the Crow's Nest. You're coming to stay with me for a while. I'm calling Dill and Mr. Wills to take care of your place. Get your things. Mary, can you help her?"

"Of course!" Mary said.

Zara got shakily to her feet and packed some clothes and pajamas, "You have a guest room?"

"I have three, one's empty, but I'll get to it eventually," he said.

Zara nodded. She looked at Annie, her expression anguished and touched her copper face, her lip wobbling, "What did I do to make someone so angry?"

Harrison looked furious, "I'll find out who did this. I promise, Zara."

He went and ordered a courier bot. He asked Mr. Wills to come with Dill and a full team to search for evidence because Zara's apartment was broken into again. He mentioned she was heartbroken about Annie, said they were taking her to his place with her bots. He loaded her into the carriage. Zara brought a beat up suitcase with her things in it, carrying her ruined cat and dog bots, her lip wobbling.

"I m-made the cat-bot when I was ten!" she said.

Mary smiled kindly, "I salvaged the smashed pictures of you and your papa, I'll get you new frames. Not to worry!"

Harrison got an odd feeling, "It seems like everything you cared about was destroyed, including your tinkering table."

"Yes. They didn't take anything this time as far as I can tell." She was staring at the pieces in her hands. She had worked with her papa on the cat bot, too, "I don't have anything left that I did with my papa, now. Nothing. They even took my necklace."

Harrison was looking at her with a hopeless look on his face. Zara had stopped crying, but she felt like she didn't have it in her to fight at the moment. Tomorrow would be better, it usually was, but right now, she let herself feel good and bad. She'd been shot, poisoned by halonite in her blood, her house was smashed to bits and the things she loved most dearly destroyed. She shut her eyes and sat back with a sigh.

"Perhaps I shouldn't have taken this job at the Crow's Nest after all. I was recruited at these big firms that paid a lot of money. Maybe I ought to do that instead," she muttered.

"No! It's just a rough patch. You're excellent at this job, you can't quit! It will get better," Harrison said.

She looked at him. He did not excel at making her feel better. She learned years ago to do that for herself, but today was one of those days it wasn't working. Mary tisked and sent him a look.

"Hey, now! You listen here. You still have the memories, can't nobody take those from you, Zara. No one. Don't you let them! You fix those contraptions and they'll be good as new, and they will still be the things you made with your papa because they managed to stay a part of you against the odds, see? Someday when you meet a handsome gent, you'll marry and move them in with you two and tell the story about how you managed to keep those alive against the odds, even when your luck got bad," Mary said.

Zara gave her a watery smile and nodded, "Thank you. Both of you, for being good friends. I'm not so flim-flam normally. I'm acting like a great cabbage hat, feeling sorry for myself. I apologize. I'm just so tired and I don't feel very well."

"It's ok. You're doing fine. Mary is right! You need to rest and feel safe, ok? I got all your tinkering things. You have a few days with me, then you can go back home when Dill takes care of it. You know what a genius he is at locks and security," Harrison said.

"He's amazing. Better than me, and I don't say that much. I'm more for gadgets, he's skilled with making things a fortress, very good at blowing things up. I'm glad he's helping me. Glad you all are," Zara said.

Zara glanced out the window of the stylish carriage Harrison owned. They pulled in the drive of a large brownstone that was two stories. It was a handsome home, with neatly trimmed hedges and a pristine lawn. It was classic and elegant, like the man who owned it. They carried Zara's things into a large sitting room with an impressive brown brick fireplace, manly leather sofas and dark wood tables. He had proper lamps, the sort with stained glass shades. On the walls were paintings of the Crow's Nest, a dirigible and a steam powered carriage in the streets of Jakarda City, all masculine and neat. To the right, was an office, with scads of books to read, a polished dark wood desk and two cozy chairs, and more of those paintings of the city. Zara spotted a kitchen and a dining room off of each of the front rooms, but didn't get a good look at them. They were spacious and fine like the rest of the place. Harrison lead them up a wooden staircase, polished to a shine, past two more two paintings, one of a steam powered car, the other a picturesque oceanside cottage. He had all modern gas lamps in his house, Zara like that. When they reached the top of the steps, Mary and Zara exchanged impressed glances. There were four bedrooms, the largest, at the back of the house, obviously Harrison's, was done in blue and grey. It was a handsome room. Zara spotted a closet full of suits, he wore a variety at the Nest. He led Zara to the room beside his. It was very large, with a massive bed centered on the wall opposite the door. The walls were a green and cream stripe, not overly masculine, with matching curtains at the windows, a dresser, an armoire and a small couch to sit on beside the large window that overlooked the backyard. In this room, there was no painting of the city Harrison loved and protected, there were three black and white photos. One of a man and a woman, the man looked like Harrison, a relation. The next was of a young boy and that man, the last one was of the woman in front of the brownstone. He had more gas lamps of the stained glass variety and a vase with fake flowers on the dresser. It was simple, but Zara found it cozy. She liked things orderly, except when she tinkered.

"Is this room ok? I have two others if you don't like it," he said.

"No! I like it a lot. It's very nice," Zara said.

"Ok! Then make yourself at home. You cannot go back to your apartment until we figure this out, and we will! No need to worry. You're safe here," Harrison said.

He set Annie gently on the ground near the closet. Zara looked at her dented gold head plate made to look like hair and fought the urge to cry. Harrison strode over to her, his expression determined, and hugged her tightly.

"Come on, now! You're going to be fine," he said.

She let herself hold him for a while, her eyes closed while he rubbed her back and kissed her head a few times. Zara nodded and took a step back. Mary came in to hug her.

"You get to stay in this grand house, too!" she said.

Zara laughed, "Yes. My mama's house is fancy like this."

"My grandpa left me this house when he died. It took me ages to redo the rooms, he never changed much after my grandmother passed. My mother helped me do one room a year, I have to reign her in on the budget. As you well know, we don't make a fortune doing what we do. I had most of the furniture reupholstered, he had good pieces, just dated coverings. I'm lucky because he also left me some money and I'm good at investing. I put money into some sportsman's clubs in the city, the dirigible business and the railways. I didn't have much, but I made enough to pay the house off, buy a carriage and my salary maintains it. Don't let it fool you. I just had a good family looking out for me. I own the tiny plot in the back and I have two horses and a hired stableman and his son working for me, Ernie and Walter Bishop. I have a chef-bot who also answers my door. I don't want a butler, I can dress myself!" Harrison said.

Zara laughed, "Annie does my hair and tells me what matches. I'm sure I'll look bad without her to help me. I don't need more than Annie, I'm practical, too."

Harrison smiled, "You could never look bad, honey, no chance. Guest bath is right next to your room when you walk out on the right. Mary can help you get settled, I'm going to tell Mr. Bishop and Ernie you're staying with us, ok?"

"Ok. Thanks again," Zara said.

Harrison offered her a half smile, "Not a problem."

Mary sent her a look when he was gone, "He's in love with you, I think."

Zara's stomach swooped. She shook her head, "No chance."

"Oh, please!" Mary said with a roll of her eyes, "I can see you're not up for debating because you got yourself in a good funk. Let's unpack. It might be a week or so you're here, glad we got your clothes. Funny, none of them were destroyed! I'm going to draw you a nice hot bath. You are going to take it, put on these beautiful blue pajamas and get into bed for a good rest, you look dead tired. Sleeping in a hospital bed the way you did, getting no rest at all."

Zara nodded and Mary hurried to the bathroom. She heard the water go on. Zara unpacked her things tiredly. Mary helped her bathe and washed her hair in a beautiful blue and white tiled bathroom with a fancy claw footed tub. Zara's little bathroom had a very old ancient stand up basin shower, not at all cozy like this tub, but functional. This was a bath for bubbles, and Zara loved bubble baths. Marry added some lemon scented soap to it and helped her wash her hair, jabbering away as she helped Zara. She pulled on pretty silk pajamas that belted at the waist. She added a matching robe and slippers. Mary brushed her hair and dried it with a steam powered hair dryer invented at the academy by Phoebe Dubois, a top tinkerer in Jakarda. It was on the heavy side, but it worked well. Mary said she wanted one and Zara told her they were now for sale in home stores all over. Zara was practically asleep, it felt so nice, Mary doing her hair like that. She crawled into bed. Mary tucked her in and promised to come see her tomorrow. Zara felt safe, knowing Harrison was nearby. Funny, it took her a month to sleep well in her new apartment, every noise woke her. But here, in this fluffy soft bed in Harrison's house, she fell asleep in no time at all.

Someone was knocking on the door sometime later. She opened her eyes groggily, "Come in."

Harrison opened the door with a smile, "Hi. I didn't mean to wake you, but dinner is ready. You missed lunch, are you hungry?"

Zara nodded and crawled out of bed. She winced a little, then pulled on her robe and put on her slippers. She offered Harrison a smile he returned.

"I hope you like roast chicken, potatoes and peas," he said.

"I love roast chicken! I haven't had it in so long," Zara said.

Harrison offered her his arm. She took it with a smile. They walked down his staircase into the sitting room. She looked around. He had some family photos on a table, near some stylish lamps and ornate rugs on the wood floors. It was the home of an adult, an established one. The home of a man who brought ladies over, and wanted to impress them. It worked, Zara was impressed. Compared to her humble living space, the was practically a palace. She sat down with him at a large, ten person table. The chef bot brought out a feast. Zara's mouth watered. She helped herself to food, including fresh rolls with butter, still warm. She grinned at Harrison. He chuckled and winked at her.

"I think bread may be my most favorite food, especially with butter," Zara said.

Harrison laughed, "I like it, too. With jam as well, I love a jam sandwich with peanut butter."

"Me too! My favorite are jam cookies and marshmallows, especially marshmallows. I like them dipped in chocolate, Annie makes them for me like that," Zara said.

"She will again," he said.

"Yes, she will. I just hope they didn't smash her memory chip. I don't think they did, it's far inside. See, she has recordings of my papa's voice. I listen to them when I miss him. She also tucks me into bed at night and strokes my hair. I know most people think the automatons and robots are cold, but, I only had Annie to do that for me. I think she can't love me back, but I love her," Zara said.

"That's ok," Harrison said gruffly.

"The cat and dog-bot are an easy fix, thank goodness!" Zara said.

"That's good news, honey. You were sleeping pretty good in there," Harrison said.

"They woke me up so much in the hospital room. I'm very exhausted! My arm aches and I think part of the problem was the painkillers they gave me. I got so foggy and disconnected," Zara said.

"Yes, they told me what they gave you was strong. I wondered if you knew any of us were there when we visited," Harrison said.

Zara laughed, "Sometimes. Other times I was so confused, you blended together."

"Well, you can get some proper rest here then, we got your things," he said.

"Harrison, is someone trying to kill me because of the papers I took at the ball?" Zara asked.

Harrison sat back with his fork in his hand, then smiled slowly, his eyes twinkling. Her heart went faster. He looked so handsome in his grey pants and vest, his hair tousled.

"I don't know. It does seem like you're being singled out for some reason," he said.

"But, you were there, too! Why would they come for me and not you?" she said.

His dark eyes met hers, "Because I'm a man and I don't stand out, whereas you are a tall, leggy blonde with pretty freckles and big blue eyes. People tend to notice when a beautiful blonde shoots them with a stun gun or runs off with their maps and bests them in a fight, especially one that looks like you."

Zara rolled her eyes, "I'm not beautiful, I—"

"You are, actually. One of the reasons is—because you don't know you are. But, that's not the only reason for you to be targeted. I live in the ritzy part of town, the local police come by often. I have a former spy as my stableman and guardians, the metal birds tucked around outside, were made by Dill. Mr. Wills lives a block over, and the head of the Crow's Nest—he's across the street. My neighbors are old acquaintances of my grandpa, too, also former law enforcement or agents. Only a fool would attack me at home when the seven blocks around me are filled with people who pay high taxes and run the businesses of Jakarda that keep the city going. Not the super wealthy, just that solid upper middle class that make up a top percentage of some of the city's most respected citizens. I lucked out getting this house, my parents are over in the Green Isle with most of the middle class, the other nice, very large and safe portion of Jakarda City. You live in the, ah, more accessible spot," he said.

Zara laughed and sent him a look, "I live in a hovel. That building is falling apart, it's so old! It was one of the first built in Jakarda City. It was nice once, I think. The stink from the halonite plant is terrible, my neighbors are kind enough, but not the sort to get involved if ruffians are about. I get your point. My mother's house is in the Green Isle, too, she hasn't quite graduated to this area, she complains about it often, but the houses hardly come up for sale. She has a house on Young Drive, that very wealthy street near here that considers themselves a part of this section of town, but really is not. Still very respectable, I don't see what the difference is myself, but my mother always hated that she couldn't quite make it in here. How did they find me?"

"Could have followed you home after work. The criminals are aware of where the Crow's Nest is and you look adorable on the motorized bike wearing your goggles and a pretty dress every day," Harrison said.

Zara frowned, "I take the same route, too. I'm a creature of habit."

She sighed and ate some of her food, her thoughts tumbling over themselves. Harrison watched her with a frown.

"You need to eat more to get your strength back. You're so pale, I'm worried about you," he said.

"I'm ok. Don't worry yourself. I took my vitamins, Dr. West said it might be a few days before my appetite comes back. Did you find out what connects all the maps?" she said.

He shook his head, "Not yet. We haven't quite got that. I keep checking all the photos for any sign of those men, it's like they came out of nowhere and decided to be criminals!"

"Maybe they did, Harrison. Maybe they were not before, and now they are because of whatever those maps are for. What would make a person turn from a good citizen to a bad one?" Zara asked.

"Money or the need for it is the main reason," Harrison said.

"So, we find out who needed money and we go from there. By the way, do I have those royalties checks because of you?" Zara said.

Harrison smiled slowly, his eyes locked with hers. Her heart hammered at the mischief in that smile. She had never been more grateful to him or cared for him more.

"Douglas helped. I had a hunch that ex of yours, Vincent, was holding out on you," he said.

"I'm glad one of us did. I kept asking him and he said he didn't get them, either. Thank you," Zara said.

Harrison nodded and went back to his meal. They ate in silence for a while.

"H-How long did you date him? Vincent?" Harrison asked.

"Oh! Um, let's see, eight months, I guess. He was sweet to me at first. I had several classes with him and we were paired up for a project. I thought he was handsome from the get go, gentle. My papa was a gentle sort of a man, so I think that's why I gave him a shot. He was so kind to me. He brought me flowers and candies, told me I looked pretty, complimented me on my tinkering. I fell in love with him pretty quickly. He was the second man I loved. The first was in secondary school. My sister Temperance lured him away with her massive breasts and loose morals!" Zara said.

Harrison burst out laughing, "She did, huh?"

"Yes! I caught them having sex in my mother's sitting room, he had his hands on her, ah, you get my meaning. Then the same thing happened with Vincent and my former friend, Sara. They had sex in my bed in my apartment. I was letting Sara stay with me for the weekend. She hated living with her parents, loved the city. She came from Brookdale every day by train. It wasn't a long train ride, she never minded it, but she was shopping for cheap apartments in the city. One was open in my building and I said I'd put a good word in for her. She did not get my recommendation after that," Zara said.

"I would hope not," Harrison said.

"Have you been with a lot of women?" Zara asked.

He arched his brows and smirked, "I do all right."

Zara giggled, "No! I mean relationships where you're in love. Have you ever had one of those?"

Harrison hesitated, then nodded, "One. I was twenty and at the Crow's Nest Academy. She was a nice girl, or so I thought. I wanted to marry her and I loved her very much. She was sleeping around with a lot of men, a lot. I trusted her, and she very deeply hurt me. I went to school with Douglas, Marcus and Simon, we're the same age. She came onto Marcus, and in an upstanding way, he told me. I didn't believe him, and we got into a fight about her, the fist fight sort. He is not the sort of man to go after another man's woman. I assumed it was him because he's so good looking. But I was wrong. I caught her in bed with James Carver, my childhood friend and roommate. Marcus and I have since come to be friends, but I nearly ruined that because of my stupidity. That's when I learned to read people, to pay attention to their tells so I would not make that mistake again. Love can be dangerous, get you hurt if you're not careful."

"Yes, it certainly can. I should learn that too, people's expressions. I am very bad at reading people, deplorable. I'm very wrong about them most of the time. They seem a good sort to me, then they turn out to be anything but. It's why I'm hesitant to let people in. I'm sure that's why you are, too, after that woman hurt you. I understand, Harrison," Zara said.

"You have this way of seeing more of me than anyone else," Harrison said.

"Do I? Well, you're the same with me! I think it's what makes us good friends. We have a lot in common," she said.

"Suppose we do," Harrison said with a half-smile.

"Romance now, as well! Except for the part where you're a ladies man, I am not like that with the gents. The woman in the offices that do the filing and the paperwork talk, you get around," Zara said.

"I never claimed to be a nice man," Harrison said with a devilish glint in his eyes.

Zara laughed, "You're a very nice man, you just don't want anyone to know."

He seemed taken aback and more than a little flattered, "Well, I've never had a female friend before. You're the first. I didn't trust women for a while, but you're not like other ladies I know."

Zara smiled, her heart squeezing painfully. His words made her feel as if she were an oddity, a freak. She hated that she was so different in that moment. She wished she was prettier, less freckled, better with people. If she were more like Mary or FeFe, he might like her as more than just a friend and she so badly wanted him to. She took a few more bites of her food, then rested a hand on her stomach.

"I'm sorry, I'm still not feeling well. My stomach, it hurts. Do you mind if I go back to bed?" she said.

"No, of course not. Want me to walk you upstairs?" Harrison said, his brow furrowed with worry.

"No, you finish your dinner. I think it's this medication. It doesn't agree with me," she said.

"I can sent a courier-bot to Dr. West, maybe he can give you something else," he said.

"I only have two more days of it. I'm sure I can manage, but thank you for being so kind, and for dinner. It was delicious," Zara said.

Harrison looked at her half-eaten plate with a frown, "Not a problem. In the morning, I'll have my chef-bot make eggs, toast and jam and bacon."

"That sounds wonderful," Zara said with a smile.

Harrison gave her a half smile, "If you need me, I'm in my room next door, ok?"

"Ok," Zara said.

She stood and went upstairs to the guest room. She took one of her pills and got into bed with the lights off. She looked up at the ceiling with a sigh. Her eyes watered.

She loved him.

Harrison was the best man she had ever met, a friend to her this past month and she had fallen for him completely. She loved him more than she ever loved those other men she was with because he was so unlike them. They had been like her, a tinkerer. She loved how Harrison surprised her and taught her things she didn't know. He considered her a friend. She knew he did, and that was ok, because he was the best friend she ever had, besides Mary. It just broke her heart that he found her so odd, so different than other women he felt the need to mention it all the time. She supposed if she were like FeFe, he might consider her. It didn't matter. She had a case to solve, tinkering to do and an apartment to get back to once it was safe. Having two friends was more than she ever had before, and she wasn't about to muck it up by wishing for more with him. Zara rolled on her side and went to sleep, determined to feel better in the morning.

Harrison woke to find Zara at his kitchen table with a plate of food in front of her, parts of her cat or dog bot, he couldn't tell which, sitting on one of his towels, neatly arranged. She had a piece of paper and a pen beside it, she was making notes of some kind. The sight of her tinkering in his house made his heart hammer. Her color was better today, she was a touch less pale. She had on a shirt with capped sleeves, a massive bandage on her arm. She had on a purple vest and pants trimmed with black velvet. Her hair was in a long braid over her shoulder, he got the impression that was the only way she knew how to do her hair. It didn't matter, he loved it like that.

"Morning!" she said with a smile.

"Morning, honey. You look pretty today," he said.

"Oh, thank you! This is new, from my mother. I like these little pants, they're so comfy. I feel a lot better, and I woke hungry! It's been a week since that happened to me," she said.

Harrison smiled and tried to keep from looking relieved. Yesterday she was down, unhappy and broken. She cried. Zara was not the sort to cry. He hated it. The fact that someone had the nerve to make her cry infuriated him more than anything. He never wanted her to do that again. Whoever was doing this to her was going to pay, and he was going to make them. He offered her a smile that she returned. He came to the table and his chef-bot came to bring him food.

"You should name him," she said.

"Who?" Harrison said taking a generous portion of eggs.

"Your chef bot! You should name him something!" Zara said

"Like what?" Harrison said with a chuckle.

She studied the silver bot with a metal mustache and a shiny bald head, her head tilted to the side. She did that when she was thinking, Harrison got a kick out of that. Like most home robots, the chef bot moved on a flat track about the house, he was the affordable, yet stylish model. The track was recessed in the floor so no one would trip on it, seamless, unlike the older homes in Jakarda and the bot moved on the two thin tracks silently. His track ran upstairs and down, but his bot stayed on the lower floor.

"Bernard. He looked like a Bernard to me," Zara said.

He chuckled, "Ok. Bernard then."

Zara smiled at the chef-bot, "From now on Harrison will refer to you as Bernard. You've been given a human name because you're accepted as a member of this household. What has that unlocked?"

"I can make forty more recipes now, and converse with guests when they enter the house. I like the name Bernard, thank you for choosing it for me," Bernard said in a metallic voice.

He rolled off. Harrison looked at Zara in disbelief, "What just happened?"

"Bots are given chips that progress, think of them as children, but with different agendas. When they work to become a part of the household, earning a name means they have achieved the first level and it unlocks more gifts. He'll make you desserts now and specialty dishes based on your current tastes! If you were to marry or live with a woman, it unlocks another level and more recipes suited for your lady's taste, level three skills. Same if you have children, or take on a roommate or house guest, that unlocks more as well. My being here will unlock a second level if I stay for a week or more. Bots are task oriented and progress once they become more acclimated to their surroundings and their owners. If you can help them complete the tasks, they become a more useful machine and cement themselves as a necessity in your household," Zara said.

"What a clever bit of technology! Who invented that?" Harrison said.

"Me. At the Academy when I was eighteen, fresh out the gate, before the Spy-ders. I invented the chip that is sold in all models for the past four years, I do not make much on it, it's only a chip, I didn't make the full model. I made one for Annie. They store information too, he'll recall your favorite foods without having to be told, if you want beef every Friday, he'll remember to make it for you, that sort of thing. Bots are marvelous, but what makes them so useful is the way they never forget a detail like humans do. They, they…"

Her lips parted. She stared at the plate in front of her.

"Zara?"

"Harrison! I know what those maps have in common! We need to get to the Crow's Nest right now!" she said.

He felt a rush of excitement, "Finish eating, then we'll go."

Zara nodded and shoveled in the remaining food on her plate, he did the same. He was happy to see her finish, then grab a muffin for the road.

"Do you know what connection it is?" he said as they raced out the door.

He took her hand and they ran to the carriage, "No! Not exactly, but I think they mean something together!"

He nodded and they rode in silence to the Crow's Nest, each lost in their own thoughts, Zara eating her muffin. Upon their arrival, they ran in, hand in hand, unaware that they had reached for one another at the same time. They waved to Mary, who beamed at them as they hurried back. It was Sunday, so Room One Hundred was empty. Most of the Crow's Nest took Sunday off, but sometimes they came in for a few hours. Harrison got out all the maps and set them down.

"Set them on top of one another," Zara said.

He did as she asked. She smiled excitedly, "Look! Look at these four spots! See how they're all connected by these lines? Each of the maps seems to sort of fill in the missing parts of the others, as if there was no completed map and all of these were needed to create a puzzle! I don't know what they are, but I noticed them all on the maps before, I knew I was missing something!"

"The tunnels! Zara, those are the old tunnels under the city—they're caves. There are four separate ones in all and each of these only show partials of the old tunnels, you're right! Why would they want to get into these tunnels? Nothing at all in them, condemned," Harrison said.

"Look how they all show different branches within the four tunnels! Each of them is a bit different and they form a series of interconnected paths under Jakarda City. They didn't have a complete map for whatever it is they're doing," Zara said.

"Good point. I see what you mean. These maps are all really old. I'm going to check it out. I'll drop you back at my house," he said.

"What? No! No, I'm coming with you. You need a tinkerer and I feel much better," she said.

Harrison opened his mouth to protest, but she raised her chin stubbornly and glared at him. He chuckled.

"Ok, you can come too," he said.

She smiled then and walked to the desk. She handed him a small gun covered in copper parts with a tube on the top.

"I made this for you, don't tell the others. I haven't gotten to theirs yet because of my bad luck. You've been so good to me, I wanted to make you something special. It's a gun that seeks its target without you having to aim, I have one, too. If you're occupied in another direction, hold out your arm and it will zip to the target and shoot them with big blast," she said.

Harrison smiled broadly, "That's brilliant!"

Zara laughed, "Thank you. This is for you, too. It's one of those shock gloves of your own, the patent came through. I made it for you last week. Don't tell the others that, either. I didn't do theirs yet."

His eyes twinkled as he pulled it on, "You're going to make me think you like me best."

She giggled, "I just might."

His heart went fast again. He sent her a rakish grin. She blushed. He never saw her do that before, not from his flirting. He loved it. Her face and neck were very red, it was adorable.

"Come on, partner. Let's go," he said.

She nodded eagerly, grabbing her bag. She put a few things in it and took his hand. Harrison smiled, because it felt so right to him, her little hand in his. He wanted to hold her hand, it made him feel fantastic. He looked at the maps.

"This one is closest, the one right outside the city. We can walk there. We're going to have to check them all. They are not overly safe, they closed them out last year. They used to do tours in there, I went in as a teenager with my class at secondary school," he said.

"I didn't, but I'm five or so years younger than you," she said.

"Yes, they stopped doing the tours the year after I went, two children died in the caves when there was a collapse," he said.

"Great cabbage hat!" she said.

He laughed at her shocked expression, squeezing her hand. They hurried out, hand in hand, walking towards the caves down the busy city street. Harrison felt that familiar rush he always felt when he cracked a clue on a case. He loved his job when it was like this, exciting. They walked along at a quick pace.

"Zara?" someone said.

She stopped so Harrison followed suit. A man was looking at her in disbelief. He was good looking, tall, and he was staring at her like he thought she was beautiful. Harrison hated him on the spot.

"Mike Gaskill! How are you?" Zara asked with a smile.

"I'm good! You look so beautiful, all grown up," he said.

She flushed, "You look very handsome. Harrison, this is Mike Gaskill, he lived next door to me growing up. He taught me how to climb trees and sneak sweets from the kitchen."

Harrison shook his hand, "Nice to meet you."

"You, too. Zara, we should get together, discuss old times," he said.

Zara had a funny look on her face, "Ok. That would be nice."

"Want to meet me for lunch tomorrow at the Tinkerer-Time Cafe like we have a few times? Noon?" he said.

"Sure, that sounds fun," she said.

His eyes traveled over her in a way that made Harrison want to choke the life out of him, "You really look beautiful, Zara. I can't wait."

She turned red and laughed breathlessly, "Me, either."

Harrison was furious. What the hell was she doing having lunch with another man, dammit? Mike tipped his hat, then left with a wave. Harrison grabbed her hand and yanked her down the street.

"Ouch! Harrison, what's the matter?"

"We have a job to do. Come on!" he said.

"I'm sorry, he's very sweet. He knew my mother....well, he patched me up after she got rough. Tried to get me to turn her in, of course I wouldn't. He's a very kind person," she said.

Harrison felt even more irritated, "I'm glad he was nice to you, but we don't have time for social niceties, Zara."

She reddened, "You're right. I'm sorry."

He felt slightly ashamed of himself for being so hard on her. She looked upset, and he hated it. He sighed.

"I'm sorry, you did nothing wrong. I'm anxious about the mission," he said.

"I know, it's not that. I don't like seeing him. He was there this time my mother hit me so hard in the face I had a black eye and a fat lip. I was so embarrassed, told him I fell. He tried to help, called the police when I was sixteen. I insisted it was self-inflicted, except they knew it wasn't. I stopped talking to him after that, there were other reasons, too, but I was unkind to him after he had been friendly to me all my life. I feel bad, because he was right about my mother. He told me he couldn't be my friend because he didn't want to see me die. It was because of him that I fought back at all. I knew he was right, but I was too stubborn to tell him so and I wasn't ready to fight back against my mother then," Zara said.

Harrison squeezed her hand, "Then I'm glad you knew him."

"Me, too. Except I don't want to have lunch with him. I've seen him a few times, and every time I'm ashamed of how I treated him, of what happened to me. Worse than that, I relive the whole experience."

"Then don't go," Harrison said, leading her past tall buildings and into the park on the edge of town.

"I have to. I said I would," she said.

Harrison felt that rush of annoyance again, but refrained from comment. He would never understand women. You would never see a man doing something he didn't want to with someone, it never happened, unless it was work related. She was meeting him to be polite! That was a waste of time. They hurried over to the cave nearby. It had a massive lock on it. Zara took out her tools from her bag and picked the lock easily. He grinned at her because she did it so fast and without hesitation, like he always did himself. They went inside. She took out a triangular shaped light.

"The sun lights! I've been working on them," she said.

It gave off a soft glow from the palm of her hand. Harrison got out his gun. They walked down the cave for a while. He looked down.

"Someone's been here. These footprints are fresh," he said.

"Good observation. I didn't notice that. I think you're very intelligent," she said.

He winked at her. The cave got very damp as they walked on, and oppressively humid. Harrison was sweating badly. The walls dripped with moisture, there was a metallic stink to the place. Zara had a tiny camera, about the size of a box of matches. She was snapping a few pictures here and there, clever idea. Zara looked at the walls, moving more closely towards the moisture, her eyes intent on it.

"Harrison, this is not water dripping over these walls. It's something else," she said.

She lifted a test tube to the wall she had dug from her bag and let the liquid drip inside. It was a silvery color. She studied it with a frown. There were pipes all over collecting whatever it was, and large basins to gather it below. There were these other pipes, too, they were larger, he wasn't sure of their purpose. She touched one and jerked her hand back.

"It's hot, steam," she said.

"I'm sweating damn bad. God, it's warm. The pipes are making it hot in here?" he said.

"I think so, but why?" Zara said.

"No idea, but whoever did this has been gathering this substance for a while. Look at the size of those bins," Harrison said.

"Right again. I think this is halonite," she said.

"That would make sense. If it is in these caves, then that would explain the maps and the desire to know where they are. The four of these in the city could all have this, and there are a lot of hooks and paths down here given the different routes we saw when we combined the maps. The person who knows that would have access to a wealth of halonite," Harrison said.

"Exactly, but why try to hide it? Why not tell people this is where they found it?" Zara said.

"Because this is public land, then anyone could have access to the halonite. Someone is trying to hide their operation and make money on this stuff without everyone knowing," Harrison said.

Zara snapped a few more pictures and stowed the camera in her bag, rummaging for something else, "Public land, that was a clever way to keep it hidden, convincing everyone the tunnels were unsafe, too. What if that was a lie as well?"

"It would have given them time to learn how to harvest the halonite," Harrison said.

"Very astute!" a man said.

Harrison turned around, pushing Zara behind him. Five men stood there, all of them wearing long dusters, goggles and scarves to conceal their faces. The men from the party, the ones pretending to be Reform Mechanics.

"We don't want to share the wealth," he said.

"Who are you?" Zara asked.

"That is an excellent question, Miss Turner. You and Mr. Lowell are both agents of the Crow's Nest and we are the Robotic Patriots. You killed four of my men," the tallest man said.

"They broke the law, so did you. That's not our problem. If you didn't want anyone to die, you shouldn't have done something so stupid," Harrison said.

The man chuckled, "Perhaps I should say the same to you, Mr. Lowell. Right now, you and your lovely partner are the ones about to die."

Zara grabbed Harrison's arm from behind. He tensed. The men charged him. He powered up his glove and shocked one of them as the gun in his hand found a target and wounded another. He punched a third in the face as he connected solidly with his abdomen. Harrison grunted. He hit the man in the face a second time, but he was massive strong, and he could take a hit. Zara screamed. Momentarily distracted, he looked over at her in a panic. Something connected solidly with his skull, then everything went black.

CHAPTER ELEVEN

Zara tugged Harrison along the cave corridor that she recognized from one of their maps because she had stolen that map at the ball. Her arm screamed in pain, blood running freely from the wound she had torn open. Her face was throbbing worse than her blasted arm. She was terrified, her heart hammering as she dragged him in blackness close to the wall, touching it from time to time to make sure she was going in the right direction. She panted, the gas mask over her face making her breath hot and humid. She checked to make sure Harrison's was still in place. She had a sample of one of the vials of the ether compound in her purse from the party that she had planned to test. She grabbed it after Harrison was knocked out and the man she struggled with punched her in the face. She held her breath, smashed it on the ground, pulled on her mask then watched them all fall in a heap. She put a spare gas mask on Harrison and dragged him to safety after tossing all their weapons in the liquid halonite gathering in the basins on the floor.

She had been pulling Harrison for almost thirty minutes down one of the tunnels that branched off. It indicated an exit on that tunnel on the map. She hoped to god she was right and there was one. If her calculations were correct, they would reach the exit soon. She had to pull Harrison through a very small opening to get them in here, it wasn't easy. Harrison groaned. Zara felt a rush of relief. She was terrified he was dead when he went down. He tried to get to her, fighting and punching, his expression panicked when she screamed.

Zara didn't mean to scream, but that man hit her so hard, her face felt as if it was ripped apart. Her mother used to hit her, but never like that. That was something else altogether. Harrison looked terrified, he wanted to help her. Then the big fellow had thumped him over the head with the butt of a rifle.

"Zara?" Harrison said, his voice muffled by the mask.

"Harrison, shh! We're still in the tunnel. I got us away from those men. I think the exit is close," she said.

"How did you get us away?" he asked.

"I threw a vial of the knock out gas they used on us at the ball, got masks on us and pulled you away. We're in one of the tunnels that was on the maps we got from the ball, they don't know about it, but they may hear us if we're too loud. They hit you hard, I thought you were dead," Zara said, her voice breaking.

"It's ok, honey. I'm ok," he said.

"Yeah," she said, crying a little.

"Help me stand," he said.

Zara helped him up, sliding her arm around his waist. He leaned on her heavily. She helped him along, struggling under his weight, he was a very large man and she was not overly strong. They walked along at a slow pace until they came to a ladder. Zara was immensely relieved to be there.

"Can you manage to get up?" Zara asked.

"I can manage. Let me go first, there's a cover on it I have to get off," he said.

Zara nodded and Harrison slowly made his way up the tall ladder. When he got the grate off the top, he climbed up and motioned for her to follow. She scrambled up the ladder, ignoring the pain in her arm. She got out and pushed the cover back on. Harrison helped her out then grabbed the mask from his face, breathing hard. He glanced at her face.

"Shit! Who hit you?" he said.

"One of those men. Is it bad?" she said.

He nodded, "Honey, can you see out of either eye? Your face is so swollen."

"Sort of. It's ok. We have to get out of here. We're two miles from the city if my math is correct," she said.

"Then we're two miles out. I have an idea of how we can get back," he said.

He reached in his pocket and took out a small button. He pushed it and extended his hand. Zara took it, then helped him walk back towards Jakarda City.

"What is that?" she said.

"It's a tracking button Dill gave me. It alerts him when I'm in trouble, we all have one," he said.

Zara smiled, "That's clever."

"Yes, it is. Honey, your arm," he said.

"I tore it carrying you. It's fine," she said.

They walked for ten minutes until Dill showed up in a carriage with Mr. Wills. He helped them into a seat and Zara explained what they had found.

"I took two vials of it, but I think it's halonite," she said.

"If it's under the city, you're right. It is public domain and anyone could take it. Those tunnels never had it before, why now?" Mr. Wills said.

"I couldn't determine that," Zara said.

Harrison's head flopped forward, having succumbed to the knock to the head he suffered from. She put her arm around him, his head rested on her shoulder. She sighed in frustration. It was her fault he was hurt, she felt terrible.

"He was conked over the head very hard," she said stroking his hair and gently probing the back of his head, "That's a very large knot."

"You're not in the best shape, yourself," Mr. Wills said.

"I suppose not," she said.

"I had hoped you would slow him down, make him more cautious," he said.

Zara frowned, "I insisted on coming. If he'd gone alone, they would have killed him."

"I suppose that's something," Mr. Wills said.

Harrison sighed and rested his head on her breast, his arm wrapping around her waist tightly. She smiled a little and laughed softly. She continued to stroke his hair. She looked up to find Mr. Wills grinning happily and Dill watching her with a curious, yet highly amused, look. She smiled.

"He's my friend. We make a good team," she said in a rush.

"I quite agree, Miss Turner," Mr. Wills said.

Zara cleared her throat, "Um, where are we headed?"

"Crow's Nest. You need a doctor. Then I believe you can go back to Harrison's, as long as the doctor says it's all right," Mr. Wills said.

Zara agreed, then she and Dill helped Harrison inside when the carriage rolled to a stop. Dr. West checked them over, scolding Zara for opening her wound when it had started to heal. Harrison was all right, he just needed to rest. Dr. West gave him something for the pain and they went back to his townhouse. Zara made him sit on the bed. She took off his shirt and vest, then his shoes and socks. Harrison watched her with a smile. She reached for his pants. Harrison's hand shot out to stop her.

"What are you doing?" he said.

"I'm taking your pants off. You do have underwear on?" she said.

"Yes," he said.

"I've seen men in their underwear before. You need help. You wobble on your feet like a drunkard," she said.

She reached for his pants and took them off. Harrison sat up a little so she could pull them off. She told herself to be all business, that he was her friend, but he looked very good in nothing but his boxer shorts. She slipped off his socks. She turned down the bed and tucked him in, fussing over him. He grabbed her hand. Her eyes met his.

"I'm fine. I just need rest," he said.

Zara smiled, "Ok. It's been some time since I had anyone at all to fuss over that wasn't a robot. Are you hungry? I can get you some food."

"No, I'm ok. Later, maybe. Can I get a glass of whisky? It's on the dresser in the decanter," he said.

"Ok."

She walked over and poured him a large glass, then handed it to him. He drank it down in four gulps and set the glass on the nightstand.

"Thanks," he said.

"Of course! I'm going to rest in the other room. I'll leave the door open. Call me if you need me, I'm a light sleeper."

"Ok," he said with a half-smile.

Zara hesitated, then bent down and kissed him softly on the cheek, "I'm so happy you're ok."

He smiled and touched her swollen face, "You too."

She nodded then hurried out, resisting the urge to crawl into bed with him. The sight of his muscular chest was enticing, perfect. She kept thinking about the kiss they shared at the ball. She loved him like she never loved anyone before, not even her papa. She pulled on her pajamas, washed her face in the bathroom with difficulty, and got into bed. She laid there, worry making her feel sick to her stomach. She got up and went downstairs. She repaired her dog and cat bot in the dining room. It took her a few hours, they were very torn apart. The tinkering made her feel better, it always did.

Zara cleaned up and went back to the guest room. She worked on Annie for several hours and checked on Harrison, who was snoring loudly, one hand thrown over his head. She tucked the blankets more tightly around him, kissing his head, and went back to her room. She sat on the couch and looked outside. His view was better than hers was at the apartment, the pine trees in his yard were beautiful, he liked the little stables at the back and the cozy house beside it. Her first time she rode a horse was with Harrison and she was passed out for part of it. The view in her mother's house was like this, like a picture. He had rose bushes at the back and a large oak tree with a rope swing. That looked like fun. Her papa used to sit with her before bed, and read to her in a spot like this. She sighed and rested her chin on the back of the velvet sofa, gazing out at the stars.

"Zara?" Harrison said, pulling her from her thoughts.

She turned to find him shirtless in his pajama pants. Her heart gave a thump. He was so handsome with all that dark hair and those amazing eyes of his. His chest was firm, his olive skin suited him. He was so muscular! She liked that chest hair, too. She liked that a lot. Her fingers itched to touch it, to touch him.

"Are you ok?" she said.

"I'm fine. Are you in pain? I came to check on you," Harrison said.

"Oh! It should be the other way around, me checking on you. I'm sore, but it's not bad. I couldn't sleep so I fixed my cat and dog bot, and worked on Annie for a while," Zara said.

"So I see."

She tore her eyes from his perfect chest and smiled, fiddling with her pajamas, "Are you ok? Do you need anything?"

"No, thanks. My head hurts so damn bad, I took another one of those pain pills. I saw the lamp on in here. What you looking at?" he said.

"Your yard. You live in a pretty place. I was thinking how I did once, too. I had a big window like this in my room. My papa and I used to sit together and talk about tinkering, or he'd read to me. I hadn't thought about it in a long time," she said.

Harrison smiled, sauntering over. He sat beside her and rested his elbows on his knees. Zara watched the muscles in his back ripple. He had fantastic olive colored skin, much darker than her pale skin. She wanted to touch him, but she refrained, offering him a small smile, then wincing because it hurt.

"I stayed in this room when I stayed with my grandparents, that's their pictures over there on the wall and me with them as a boy. My grandma, she died when I was twelve. I was concerned about my grandpa being alone, so I spent a lot of time over here. He called this my room. This is the sofa that was in here when I was a kid, I had it reupholstered to match the new decor. This room was green when I used it too, my mom wanted me to pick another color, but it had to be green. I sit in here sometimes and remember the spy stories he told me. He told the most sensational stories," Harrison said with a smile.

"Was he the reason you wanted to work for the Crow's Nest?" she said.

"Yes. His stories were the reason. My mom worked for them too, did I tell you?" he said.

"No! She did?"

"Yes. She was an agent for five years, then she met my father, who was also an agent. They were paired up, he's a tinkerer. Not like you, you're amazing, but a good one, good man, too. My mom's brothers are agents, too. Well, Mr. Wills is one, he's my uncle, but I told you that. My other Uncle, Morris, he runs a restaurant. He was an agent, too," he said.

"Wow! Really was in the family for you. My papa was the only one I know of in my family that was a tinkerer at the Crow's Nest. My mama, she's an excellent business person. Her parents were, too. She went to the technical academy, for only a year. She dropped out when she met my papa, fell head over heels for him. You said you have sisters like me, how many?" she said.

"Three, all of them are older than me," he said.

"Oh, my! Always around women, no wonder you're so good with them. I bet you charmed them all," she said.

He laughed, "They do whatever I ask them, even now. I just grin at them and they do what I want. Joanne, the oldest is unmarried. She works for a big tinkering firm, on the business side. She's a tremendous businesswoman, she does incredible work. She refuses to marry, says she won't unless she meets the right man. My parents fell in love at first sight. They told us when you meet the one for you, you know right away. That they become everything to you and change everything for you. All that nonsense made my other sisters, Emily and Kelly, marry the first men they fell for. Emily has a cheater husband she's currently divorcing, she has a son. Kelly married an idiot. Nice man, so stupid and he can't hold down a job, so she's working two jobs to try and support her baby and her lazy husband. Needless to say, my parents regret telling all of us to marry the love at first sight person in their lives. My mother mentioned she is glad Joanne and I have better sense then Kelly and Emily."

Zara laughed, then clutched her cheek, "I don't believe in love at first sight. I believe that's lust. That's how I lost my virginity."

Harrison threw his head back and laughed at her matter-of-fact way of speaking, "It is?"

"Yes! I was seventeen and I knew a boy who could talk tinkering with me, and he understood me. He was so kind to me too, sweet in a way no one had been before, I'd known him a while, he was a good friend. That never happened to me before then, that lust you feel, that attraction. I was one of the smart kids and if you can imagine, more socially inept then I am today. You've helped me this past month, you know how I ramble. I'm doing it now. Sorry!" she said.

Harrison chuckled, "It's ok. I don't mind when you ramble. Go on."

"Oh! He had reading glasses when he read and all these dark curls. I like men with dark hair. I just realized that. Anyway! I thought he was handsome. We had a class assignment together. He was talking about rerouting a power source and it got me all excited. I kissed him and we had sex on the floor in my mother's sitting room!" she said.

He grinned, "How was it?"

"Better for him than me, but I liked it," she said.

"Oh, no! Did he make it up to you later?" he said.

"No, he did not. We had sex several times, I decided I'm not good at it. I can't stop thinking! I run an internal conversation to myself of what we're doing and of what I could be doing instead. It was like that with Vince, too," Zara said.

Harrison stilled, "Have you ever, ah, enjoyed it?"

"Had an orgasm? No. I pretended to a few times with Vincent, I felt bad, he was trying very hard to please me, he was frustrated. I felt very defective," she said.

Harrison groaned, "That's tough for him and that other guy. First few women I was with didn't have them. That's a learned technique. I'm very good at it, now."

He winked at Zara. She laughed, "I'm certain of that!"

They gazed at one another until Zara looked outside, "I miss my papa. I miss him so much I can't sleep some nights. He would have liked that I got a job at the Crow's Nest, that I made some friends. He would have loved that. I never had any friends in school."

"None?" he said.

"No. I was strange, but I didn't realize it until later. I didn't care until I was older, either. You see at the Nest how I speak out loud to myself when I tinker, Dill does it too, so no one notices, or they're too polite to say so. Most kids are not that polite. The other children were mean to me, called me Zara-bizara. I ignored them, as I mentioned, being the smartest person in the room has its advantages. It was lonely though, but I had my tinkering. I love to tinker, it makes me feel whole, normal. I know it's odd to be more comfortable with machines than people, but, I think it's ok to be like that. I don't think machines are cold, I think people are."

"Shit, Zara. That's not true honey, not at all," Harrison said.

"Great cabbage hat! Don't pity me, I'm happy as I am, truly. I just wanted to have people to speak to from time to time. Machines are reliable, consistent and steady. When they break, I fix them. They give me a purpose and I can count on them. If I didn't have that, can you imagine what I would be like? I rely on them, and they rely on me, I like that relationship," she said.

"Honey, people are the same way. Today, we relied on one another. I was hurt and you did your job, helping me. People can look out for one another, love another, be friends. People are good Zara, they're complicated, not cold. Don't mistake the two. They're flawed, sometimes they say and do shit things, but that doesn't mean you write them off for good. If they want to make it up to you, you give them a chance to, if they deserve it, and they surprise you most of the time. That's been my experience. It's the same as when one of your machines is broken, you fix it. People just want the chance to fix when they stop working right, at least the good ones," Harrison said.

She studied him and nodded, "I believe you're right. I appreciate the way you help me understand people better. You're the best person I ever met, Harrison."

Harrison blinked in surprise, "I know some people who would disagree with you."

"I met your ex-tinkerers. All five of them warned me about you, said you were a loose cannon and I should ask to never go on a mission with you. All of them cornered me to tell me about you. In the same day! The ladies in the office room that do all the filing also warned me to stay away from you, said you were a womanizer who, and this is a direct quote, tossed up more dresses in this department alone then most men toss up in a lifetime," she said with a laugh.

Harrison grinned wickedly, "Well, I do like ladies."

"So what? You're a very handsome man! I don't listen to gossip. People talk about me all the time! I'm an oddball, so I thought I would get to know you myself. Look what you did for me! Let me come and stay with you because my home is unsafe, teaching me about social niceties and such. I think those people never bothered to see the real you," Zara said.

"I appreciate that, but, I can be a cad and an ass, Zara. Don't put me on a pedestal," he said.

She rolled her eyes, "I'm not! I'm not waxing poetic about you, I'm stating fact as I see it. I know you have flaws, we all do. You're very arrogant and pig-headed and impulsive. You're also very convincing, I find myself agreeing to things and ignoring my apprehension because you're so over confident. My trust in your abilities as an agent is very high because of that inflated confidence. You are a flawed individual Harrison, but I find your flaws oddly endearing. What I'm telling you is, you're a great deal better than you give yourself credit for."

Harrison smiled slowly, "Thank you."

Zara nodded, "I wanted you to know, I see you."

Harrison smiled and stood, "I appreciate that, Zara. You should rest. You are not healed yet, your face is in a state."

"I will, now that I know my friend is well," she said.

He smiled again, then left the room, closing the door. Zara sighed and looked out that window. She may as well have told him she loved him. She was such a ninny. She would distance herself from him. She had to, she was falling for him more with each passing day. He could never love her back anyway. Why would he?

•   •   •

Harrison took a deep breath and went to his room. He had never had such a candid conversation with a woman before. Well, a woman he wasn't related to. It was so easy to talk to Zara, he found himself telling her things he never told anyone. She was his best friend, too. He said that to her before to be nice, but he realized it was true just now. She was so sweet and sincere in her matter-of-fact way of talking. He liked that she simply stated how things were. Some women wanted you to guess. Who the hell could get that right? Zara just told him. She admired him and showed him respect and he found himself doing the same for her because no one deserved it more than she did.

When he saw her sitting there, her blonde hair all down in her blue silk pajamas, he looked at her a long time before he walked in. She was so beautiful, so perfect, even with her face all bruised and swollen. His heart hammered in his chest at the sight of her. He hadn't meant to go in her room, but he called out to her anyway.

Harrison had a glass of whisky from the decanter on the dresser, rubbing his eyes. He cared about her more than he ever cared about anyone before. She checked on him earlier, tucked him in and kissed his head. He pretended to be sleeping, but it made his heart beat faster. He loved how she took care of him, fumbled a bit at it, yet somehow managed to do it better than anyone he'd ever known before. Perhaps because she fumbled.

"Oh, shit," he muttered, shutting his eyes.

He had gone and fallen in love with her. He'd never been in love before, not like this, he looked at his parents and never wanted that. He was terrified of losing this job that meant so much to him, he avoided getting close to anyone. His mother had made his father retire from the Crow's Nest, they both had after his second sister was born. They took office jobs, left the job Harrison loved behind. His dad was a tinkerer at a firm now, a very good one and his mother worked as a manager in a marketing firm. They liked their jobs just fine, made good friends. But, whenever they got together as a family, all they did was talk about the glory days as agents, those being the best times of their lives. He wanted to do this job forever, not get married and have to give it up someday. He wanted to be like his uncle, managing a team and going out once in a while. That was his dream.

He'd have to push her away, it was as simple as that. He could do it. She would be here a week or two at most. He'd just keep it friendly, that was all. He could do that. He poured himself another glass of whisky and downed it in two gulps. He got into bed and went to sleep.

The following morning, he got up to find Zara was not at the table and her room was empty. That surprised him, he expected her to be about.

"Bernard, was Zara down for breakfast?" Harrison asked, as he was served pancakes and sausage for breakfast with coffee and juice.

"She left early this morning, sir," Bernard said.

"Do you know where she went?" he asked.

"She said something about cracking the case. She asked me to tell you she would see you at the Nest," he said.

Harrison felt a rush of fear, "Did she say where she was going?"

"No, sir. I apologize," he said.

Harrison drank down his coffee and grabbed his pancakes and sausage. He raced out the door and took his carriage to the Nest, eating the food on the way. What the hell had she done? If she figured something out, she should have told him! Maybe she just went to tinker on something at the Nest. He strode from his carriage to the revolving door and walked in.

"Mary! Do you know where Zara is?" he asked.

"She should be with you! She hasn't been in yet," Mary said.

Harrison swore, "Ok. I'm sure it's nothing."

Mary nodded, her eyes full of worry. Harrison strode past her and went into Room One Hundred, hoping Zara was in there. She wasn't. She wouldn't do anything stupid, would she?

CHAPTER TWELVE

Zara looked at the woman at the desk of the halonite factory and smiled. She had come in to get some products to test a theory, and find as much out as she could about halonite itself. The trouble was, she was not as good at getting information as Harrison. She was struggling to figure out just what to say so it wasn't obvious she was trying to extract information.

"You know, this used to be a motorized bicycle plant. I live nearby, friends of mine made them here, fine products! I love mine," Zara said.

"I have one, too! I love them, so affordable. You know, they say steam powered cars are the new future, but we'll see in time. I love that idea. The carriages just seem to offer a bit more privacy if you ask me. Jakarda is so modern, much better than the little cities nearby. I used to live in Gorren, they are near the bay there, I hated it! They still use horse drawn carriages, whole town smells of poop! I like the city much better. We took over the lease here, oh, six or seven months ago," the woman said, tapping a pink nail on the halonite desk.

Zara smiled, "That's wonderful! I'm a tinkerer, I love using halonite. Tell me, however did the owners get so darn much? It came around out of nowhere with this fine product."

"Oh, they have their ways. This facility is owned by a brother and sister, Mr. Walkerwall and Miss Walkerwall. They are so nice, good to work for! I love working here," the girl said.

"I can see why! This is a very nice store and the facility does seem top notch. Tell me, do you have any information for large orders, or a business proposal? My employer might be interested in a large order," Zara said.

"Of course! Let me gather some things for you," she said.

Zara smiled and the girl procured the necessary documents. The front of the halonite factory had a desk and a small store full of parts. It had halonite floors, a dull silvery color painted with a coating of some kind, the walls were painted blue. Zara wanted to see the factory, but she was pushing it being here. She took the information and her supplies, stuffing them in her bag and put on her goggles with a wave to the helpful receptionist. She rode to the Nest and went in with a satisfied smile. Not too bad, she got the information, after all!

Mary was at the desk. She glared at her, "Zara! Harrison came in over an hour ago, asking where you were! You're supposed to be careful!"

"I had an idea and I had to get my motorized bicycle so he doesn't have to drive me around. I got some more of my things in this bag, too!" she said.

"Your face is a mess!" Mary said.

"I know, I'm ok. I'm telling people I fell down the steps at my apartment. I'm having lunch with an old friend today, I have it covered," she said.

Mary rolled her eyes, "Ok. Harrison might be mad at you."

Zara rolled her eyes. She hurried back to Room One Hundred and walked inside. Harrison spotted her and strode over, his expression murderous.

"Where the hell were you, dammit?" he said, his dark eyes flashing.

"I went to get my motorized bicycle so you don't have to drive me all around, and then to the halonite factory to get some parts. I have an idea as to how they get the liquid halonite into a solid form.

I want to test it by melting some down and I needed more since I tossed my supply," Zara said.

"Why didn't you wake me to come with you? It's dangerous for you to be at your apartment!" he said.

"You were asleep with a head injury and I didn't want to wake you. Besides, I was very careful and I think clever in procuring the information I needed. I know you're letting me stay with you and I'm grateful to you, but I really can take care of myself," Zara said.

Harrison's eyes flashed angrily as he studied her battered face, "Yes. You're doing a bang up job."

"No need for you to insult me, Harrison. I have work to do and lunch plans, I am not going to argue with you if you're going to be rude!" Zara said, stomping over to the tinkerer's desk.

Harrison followed her, "What's your damn theory that was so important?" Zara huffed and glared at him. He sighed and looked at the ceiling, "I'm sorry. I was worried about you. Tell me the theory."

Zara smiled excitedly, "Well, I was thinking about how we found it, all wet like that. In the cave, it was so humid, sticky, remember? I was so hot and nauseous."

"Of course, I complained about it a few times. It felt like a hot shower in there," he said.

"Precisely! I think the added moisture and the heat combine to make the halonite melt from a solid form into those pipes somehow. Mr. Wills, I was wondering if there is some place here at the Nest that has a geological database of the area, or if there is some way for us to find out what's in the ground in that cave. If I knew what it was, maybe I could better identify the properties," Zara said.

Mr. Wills nodded, "Marcus, you have that friend in room fifty-four or whatever number it is. Can you check with her?"

"Deborah Fish? Of course," Marcus said.

"We need to check the other caves, too," Harrison said.

"You should do that with FeFe, Douglas or Simon. I'm going to do this bit of tinkering. I'm a little soured on field work at the moment. My face hurts and I have lunch plans," Zara said.

Harrison flashed her a smile, "Ok. See you later then."

She nodded, "Ok."

She got to work with Dill's help while the others decided what to do with the caves. She was dying to go with them, she didn't want to miss out on finding something significant, but she planned to stick to her decision to avoid Harrison if she could manage it. She grabbed some test tubes and handed them to the others.

"Take samples of dirt or anything unusual for me, please," she said.

They agreed. Harrison frowned.

"Are you certain you don't want to come?" Harrison said.

Her hand fluttered to her face, "I'll sit this one out, if you don't mind. I have had my fill of being beaten and shot at the moment."

His expression softened, "Ok."

"I want everyone in pairs, so I'll be joining you this time, Harrison," Mr. Wills said, "I'll go with you. FeFe and Simon, Douglas, you and Marcus go together when he gets back. Harrison and I will take the tunnel that runs under the city. FeFe and Simon, on the West side and Douglas and Marcus will take the one near the Barneck Ocean that runs beside the docks. Take stun guns and the necessary equipment."

Zara handed them each a sun light and told them how to use them, as well as a stun-glove. She had been working on them since yesterday morning, feeling guilty that she had made one for Harrison and not the others. She set the one for Marcus on the table. The others put theirs on excitedly. Dill gave them each a tracker. Marcus came in with a print-out and handed it to Zara taking his glove with a grin. She read it carefully while the others left. She glanced at Harrison and smiled.

"Be careful," she said.

He grinned excitedly as he dashed out. She sat with Dill and showed him the paper.

"Are you familiar with these things?" she said.

"No. I can go and ask Deborah to explain it if you like," he said.

Zara nodded eagerly and Dill ran out. They were on the ground floor today, good thing too. Lots of in and out. Zara made a neat list of all the tests she wanted to perform on the halonite. She melted it first, but it turned to solid again. She was trying to cool it rapidly when Dill came in, and the halonite shattered. She swore.

"I have it! The ground has traces of a substance they couldn't identify there. A derivative of silver nitrate," Dill said.

Zara considered, "Dill, what if the combination of heat and moisture melts the silver from the soil and rock, then they collect it in those pipes I found."

"It's possible, but to what end? Everyone is starting to learn that halonite is a garbage product. Their sales are down, there was an article in the paper about it a few days ago," Dill said.

"Can I see it?" she said.

Dill nodded and handed her a battered newspaper.

She scanned the article, "Ok…people are finding halonite does not hold up worth a damn. The product snaps, frays and causes nothing but problems for anyone foolish enough to use it. The products declining sales have no place to go but down even more."

Zara considered this, "Huh. Well, we must be missing something. We must. Come on! Let's try the next test."

Dill grinned and agreed. They tried all of her tests, and a few Dill suggested. Not a single one worked. By the time she went to meet Mike for lunch, Zara was good and frustrated. She shook the feeling off and went to the Tinker-Time Cafe, the very one she had met with Mr. Wills in over a month ago. It seemed a happy place to her now, one that changed her life. She felt a rush of nostalgia as she walked in and saw all the automatons mixed in with the patrons.

"Hi, Mike!" Zara said.

Mike looked stricken, "Zara, I thought you'd moved out of your mother's."

"Oh! I did! I actually did misstep on the stairs and fall, for real this time. I live in a very old building, and I lost my footing on a cracked step. I was trying to tinker and walk at the same time, I do the repairs there," she said.

Mike laughed in relief, "I'm glad. I've thought about you often over the years. What do you do now?"

"I work for the Crow's Nest, like my papa tinkerer."

"That's amazing, Zara! You always wanted to do that. Like it?" he said.

"I love it! The people are nice, I have good friends. Enjoy the work! It's exciting and fresh, the items I make, they make a difference. Pay is terrible, but I find I don't care. How about you?" she asked.

"I'm a banker, like my dad. I love my job, I was always good at finance, tinkering is just a hobby for me. Not like you," Mike said.

"You're brilliant with figures, always helped me with the math in my tinkering. Great job, Mike. How's your family?" she asked.

"My folks are good, so is my sister Corina. How's your mom and sisters?" he asked.

"Ok, I suppose. I don't see them much, once a month maybe. My mother sends me the latest fashions as she makes them, we have dinner or lunch and that's that. Sometimes Tempie and Cait come, not often. I'm happy now. I have a terrible, junky apartment in an old building, but I'm happy," she said.

"That's great, Zara, truly. I'm so happy you got away from them," he said.

"As am I. I should have left a long time ago," she said.

They ordered and talked easily, laughing and chatting. At the end of the meal, Mike took her hand.

"I have a favor to ask. My carriage is steam powered, like everyone's these days, but I had a flight package put in. Can you help me with it by any chance? It's not working right," he said.

"Of course! I always wanted to ride in a carriage with flight capabilities. They say they're the new trend, and soon everyone will have one capable of flight," Zara said.

"I heard that, too! I appreciate your taking a look, I can't seem to get it, but I was never the tinkerer you were," he said.

He insisted on paying for the meal, then led her outside to her carriage. She bent down to look at in underneath, when his hand shot out. He covered her mouth with a rag soaked in some spicy smelling concoction that burned her nose and mouth.

Ether.

"I'm sorry about this Zara, truly. But he needs to speak to you," Mike said.

Her eyes rolled in her head, her body went limp. Her last thought was how she never should have agreed to this lunch in the first place.

Harrison returned with his uncle, soaking wet from the cave. Their particular cave, was flooded at one end and they had to trudge through a foot of water to get to the exit. He was freezing, angry, and in possession of a vicious headache when he got back. His Uncle was not in a good mood either, grumbling about how he was glad he didn't do this sort of field work often. Harrison got a spare set of clothes from his carriage and changed in the men's washroom, then returned to Room One Hundred. Dill was tinkering away, glaring at the list Zara made.

"Any luck?" he asked.

"No. Zara and I did all these tests earlier, I did two more since she's been gone. No luck at all," he said.

"Is she having lunch with Mary?" Harrison asked.

"No, a chap named Mike," he said.

Harrison felt a rush of jealousy, "Oh. Yes, I forgot."

"She mentioned they dated in high school until something happened," Dill said.

Harrison flushed angrily, his lips thinning. That was the boy she lost her virginity to? The one that never gave her an orgasm and slept with her sister? Dammit! She never mentioned that to him. He ran a hand through his hair in frustration. Why the hell was she out with him? He had been good looking too, not like the fat chap, Vince, from the kitchen store. Should he be worried? He shook himself mentally. Here he was acting like a fool over her again when he just gave himself that talk last night about distancing himself. It was good she was out with this fellow, very good, even if it felt like his heart was ripped out.

FeFe and Simon came in filthy and sweaty, both of them looking angry. Their search was a bust too, all they had were samples, same as Harrison and Mr. Wills. Douglas and Marcus came in later, having left a bit after them, no worse for the wear, but empty handed. Their cave was not as bad as the rest, they didn't seem to mind. The only cave to have the halonite was the one Harrison and Zara visited. It was clever she tried out that little camera and got all those pictures. Harrison listened to everyone complain as they tried to piece together what was going on. Harrison kept looking at his pocket watch, hoping Zara would return soon. He wasn't concerned after one hour, nor after two. When four hours passed, he was terrified. They all were. Terrified enough to call James Crane at the local police to help find her.

Zara opened her eyes, blinking lethargically. She was floating, there was a large red balloon and clouds overhead. It was like something out of a strange dream. She sort of bobbed up and down, as if she were on a cloud too, but it couldn't be, because she was on a hard bit of wood. It wasn't soft like she imagined a cloud to be. She looked around, trying to get her bearings. She was on the deck of a dirigible. The base was a boat, a beautiful boat with an ornate mermaid carving on the prow. The balloon was large and maroon, secured with dozens of ropes to the ship itself. There were several men and women in long leather jackets. They had emblems on their sleeves, two gears and the letters "RM." Good lord, she was in one of the Reform Mechanics dirigibles. Mike must work for them! That rat. She looked around, her expression furious as she searched for him.

"Ah! Awake at last! Forgive me for tying you up. We have to take precautions," a man said.

She turned to look at the man in question and grew still. He was tall, and broad shouldered with bright green eyes and brown hair. He smiled charmingly. He had on a top hat with goggles on it and he was wearing a set of brown gloves. He looked to be in his late forties, early fifties. He made a dashing picture, he was so handsome.

"What am I doing here?" Zara said.

"You're here, Miss Zara Turner, because you work for the Crow's Nest and you're a tinkerer of such extraordinary talent, that I had to meet you. When Mike mentioned you were an old childhood chum and he could arrange the meeting, I took him up on his offer. He walked up and down the street in front of the Crow's Nest for a week before you showed up! He was dedicated, and I appreciate that. My manners! My name is Bodie Polk," he said, bowing.

He sent her a sexy smile. Zara rolled her eyes, "That's fascinating, but you didn't tell me why I'm here."

He laughed, studying her, "Mike said you were beautiful in a freckled way. He was right. At any rate! You're here, because I need your help."

Zara scoffed indignantly, "I will not help you. You're the member of a group opposed to the government, which I work for. Why the hell should I help you?"

"Because I was there the day your papa died. I know things," he said.

Zara laughed, "Oh, boy! I don't care how he died. I'm a tinkerer. The details of his death are inconsequential, the end result being, he's dead. You'll have to do better than that."

"Very well!" he said angrily.

He strode over to her, and smacked her in the face on the side where she had been hit before. She was taken aback by the cruel gesture, unprepared and let her guard down momentarily. She screamed in agony, and blood ran from her mouth. Fear bubbled up inside her, making her shake in terror as images of her mother coming toward her with a switch replayed in her mind. He kicked her hard in the ribs twice, his expression as fierce and unforgiving as her mother's when she let that same sort of rage get the better of her. She flashed between the present and the past, recalling vividly those beatings she tried so hard to forget.

Zara knew what sort of person struck another, but Bodie didn't seem the type for her, she hadn't readied herself for it. The pain was worse than she remembered, because he was stronger, wailing on her, sending blow after blow on her person as she struggled to get away from this monster, scrambling on ropes that tied her to the hull of the dirigible, left her nowhere to go. The urge to cower was as strong as it ever was. The emotional torment from her flashbacks, that was what she remembered most. Her mother taunting her, calling her silly tinkerer while she twisted her arm back, kicked her in the ribs, yanked on her hair by the fistful. The smell of her flowered perfume, a sickening sweet smell that turned her from any scent with a flower forever. The verbal abuse: ugly girl, waste of clothing. The loathing-filled looks that made her wonder why she was hated so. Zara remembered mama saying she was small, and weak as she sat, cowering on the floor, begging her mama to stop as she looked into her cold, unforgiving gaze as she gripped the switch she kept above the ice box.

She'd be damned if she took it from this man like she did with her mother, once was more than enough.

Zara crawled away from him and put her hands up to cover her head, anticipating the next blow, but refusing to cry as she bled freely, except he didn't strike her again. He knelt beside her, grabbing her wrist, his face tight, as if he didn't want to do what he was doing but had steeled himself to the task of beating an unarmed woman.

"Zara, Mike told me what your mother did to you. Mike told me all about those terrible beatings you endured, the black eyes and bruises. I'll do worse to you if you don't help me," he said.

Zara felt a rush of anger, her eyes meeting his, "He wasn't there for the part when I fought back. I'm no victim anymore, sir. You go ahead and beat me. I can take it. I took it for years, endured much worse from a bully like you. You have nothing on my mother, you fool. I've been taking that since I was ten years old and it hasn't killed me yet. I have no intention of dying here on this deck with a ruffian like you trying to frighten me because of what my mother did like a coward; and you can be damn sure if I do die, I'll find a way to take you with me."

He seemed taken aback by the fierceness in her expression, then he smiled slowly, his eyes full of admiration, "Yes. Yes, I believe you will. I love a strong woman. I'll try the direct approach."

"Might have tried that in the beginning instead of this tactic! What exactly is it you want?" Zara snapped, clutching her ribs.

"I want to know if you think the Reform Mechanics are behind these attacks," he said.

Zara studied him, then laughed, "That's it? No, we don't. We think It's a bunch of people pretending to be you. The patches on their jackets are not that of a Reform Mechanics, but were made to look similar to throw everyone off so they would think it was you. Your attacks are more well-thought, more well-organized and up until recently, less violent. These people were sloppy and stupid, not good fighters. Will you tell me what you know about them now?"

He blinked in surprise, then smiled. He gently helped Zara sit up. She tensely allowed him to, her heart hammering, but her face showed none of her fear, thanks to Harrison's lessons.

"I apologize. I should have guessed since you're a tinkerer, I didn't need to use brute force like I do a field agent," he said.

"If your questions are reasonable, I'll answer them, if not, I won't. Logically, I must, what choice do I have? You have me up in this great big dirigible in the sky! As long as I'm not betraying my government, I will tell you what I'm able to."

He smiled and studied her, "I can see that. Forgive me?"

"Don't push it," she snapped.

He threw his head back and laughed, "Ok. We know that this group is tied to halonite, and whoever owns the supply of the halonite. The odd part is, all the shops that sell it throughout Jakarda, and I'm not talking about simply in Jakarda City, in all of Jakarda, are individual shop owners that have money. They have purchased tons of the stuff from the person who's gathering it. We can't figure out who that person is, they are clever, whoever they are."

Zara considered this and nodded, "I suspected as much."

He smiled slowly, "I bet you have. Mike didn't mention I was going to meet an equal. We tried to recruit you—top scores ever, at the Academy. You see, I held the distinction before you, and you beat me by fifteen points."

Everyone said she beat them by fifteen points. She got the impression it was more, but the men she beat were embarrassed to say so. She could not have beat all of them by fifteen points, those odds would be astronomical!

"Does that make you feel threatened?" Zara asked.

He grinned, "No. No, It makes me curious. Tell me, why did you join the government? They hide things from the public, things we deserve to know."

"Oh, please! You're intelligent—if what you say is true about your scores. People like you and I look at the world with logic. Telling them would create mass panic and chaos. The average person is as dimwitted as we are smart. The work I do at the Crow's Nest matters, I protect the general public from criminals like you by using my tinkering for good. What does the average person need with a grappling gun or a bomb? That's absurd! I believe in that work and in the reasons why the average person does not need my gadgetry," she said.

He sent her a highly amused, yet very impressed look, "Your father said nearly the same thing to me on more than one occasion. He tried to get me to change sides. Will you do that next?"

"No. No, I think part of the reason you like the Reform Mechanics is because of the theatrics and the rush it gives you to reveal so called government plots, tinkers and conspiracies. You like the wildness of it, how you get to play the part of the rebel. I get it, I do. You just assaulted me, a government agent, you'd never make it in a government position. I'm sure some of what you do here is good, has good intentions. It's your methods, and the fact that you just beat me to get me to talk, that I don't agree with. You preyed on something very personal and horrifying to me just now, cementing my choice in joining the Crow's Nest because, for all their faults, they follow the proper channels and don't beat confessions out of people or use their past to manipulate them. At least not right out of the gate. It was brutish and unnecessary, a ham-fisted cowardliness I don't possess and never could. So it looks like I made the right choice in jobs," she said.

He looked uncomfortable, studying her, "It's necessary."

"Yes, you keep telling yourself that. Beating a woman to get what you want, my mother did the same. It didn't work out for her, either. Eventually, I got away from her, as I will from you," Zara said.

He flushed a little, "Point taken! Monty! Lower the dirigible outside the city! We're dropping her off. In exchange for the beating, I'll tell you what I know. The group calls themselves the Robotic Patriots . Believe it or not, they are worse than us. The bombings we've been accused of in recent years, the Robotic Patriots have been behind them, not the Reform Mechanics. Take a look at the one in that apartment complex downtown, the Statler. That was the one that started them all. It was pinned on us, but we didn't do that. We're not in the habit of blowing up homes full of women and children. We do have our standards. All we want is to educate the public, not to hurt them. I got rough with you just now—maybe I shouldn't have. I expected you to be unreasonable like most agents. We've been accused of being militant, but we're not. We only use difficult means when we have to, Zara. When we have to because our options are taken from us! Look at those bombings, please. There were four in total in the past year. It's all connected. I don't know how, but it is. It seems to me you are the person to make the connections."

Zara studied him, "Why are you telling me this?"

He sighed, "Because your father was a friend, of sorts. I'm hoping we can be friends, too."

Zara laughed and glared at him, "Why would my papa be your friend?"

"The simplest answer is, we grew up together and went to tinkering school at the same time. Ask your mother about me, she remembers me, I'm sure," he said.

"I will. Can I ask you something now?" she said.

"Why not?" he said with a grin.

"Is it you who broke into my apartment twice now?" she said.

His eyes widened, "Someone broke into your home? No. No, Zara, I promise, that was not us. Was anything taken?"

"I don't have anything, I'm very poor. Mostly they smashed up things only I would care about," she said.

"Huh! Interesting," he said, studying her thoughtfully.

Zara refrained from comment. The dirigible went down. Zara hurried off the dirigible and watched them fly away. She was hurting, worse than before, and she had no idea where she was. Still, she had learned something, so that was good. At least this wasn't a complete waste of time. Night was falling. She looked at the inky blue sky littered with stars. She was in the woods outside the city. She could see the soft glow of it in the distance. She walked slowly towards it, hoping she didn't pass out and die before she got there.

Bodie Polk watched her go with a smile. She was beautiful, Miss Zara Turner, brave too. She stood up to him, her blue eyes flashing. He didn't want to hurt her, but it was necessary to keep his informant in line. He admired Zara, she was strong, much stronger than her papa ever was. He had been easy to manipulate because of their friendship and his desire to reach Bodie, but she wouldn't be. He'd have to find a new tactic, a way to get her to trust him. He found he didn't want to manipulate her, not after he watched her cower when he hit her. He'd never do it again, it was like watching her father get hurt, and he had been his friend. Plus, she was the same age as his middle daughter. That bothered him most of all. She never should have had to suffer like that at the hands of a parent. A parent, hmm. Something odd in that, if you asked him.

"Contact our friend at the Crow's Nest with a courier bot. Tell them, her acquaintance is off the dirigible. Let them know what we did to Zara is a warning for what's going to happen, too, should they try to come clean with their involvement in all this," Bodie said.

"Aye, sir," Mike said.

Bodie studied the younger man, he looked upset.

"I'm sorry I had to hurt her. I felt bad, she was afraid."

"Her mother is an evil bitch, Bodie," Mike said.

"I realize that. I thought a good beating was the way to get information, expected her to be a victim, but she's a survivor. I miscalculated," Bodie said.

"I told you she wasn't a victim. Zara's sweet and kind, I admit that, but she was always so intelligent and strong. I never should have let her go, she's the sort of woman you hold on to. Her sister has a great body and at sixteen, you think with your cock, not your head. She showed me her breasts and I could think of nothing else," Mike said.

Bodie laughed, "That's a very true statement. At sixteen, breasts are what drives a young man."

"She'll never speak to me again, now," Mike said miserably.

Bodie winced, because the young man had loved her when he was young and had told him as much, "I'm sorry. It was for the cause."

"I know! I know, sir. Just a bit sad. She's gotten more beautiful than I ever imagined she'd be. She's better around people, now. I couldn't believe how she was at lunch, she talked easily, asked me questions and listened. She was a different Zara, still liked to talk tinker, but more normal and approachable. She always looked at the floor when I knew her. My heart went out to her. I wanted to protect her, save her. Turns out, she didn't need me to. She needed to do that herself and gain a little confidence. That mother of hers is evil," Mike said.

"She never hit the sisters?" he said.

"No, sir. Not once, just Zara. You met her papa, she looks just like him, tall with the blonde hair and freckles. I always figured it was that resemblance and the bitterness of his leaving her alone with three daughters to raise that did it. Funny, she doesn't look a thing like her mother or her sisters," he said.

"No! She doesn't at all, all three of them are not lookers. She looks more like Hal and…" Bodie's lips parted.

He laughed mirthlessly, shaking his head. Could it be that was the connection? Hal, poor sap. He never should have married Amanda, not when he loved another woman so much. It would explain why Amanda hated Zara with such passion, and lashed out against her. It was a possibility.

"Mike, you're my best researcher. I want you to look into something for me. Well, two things, actually. The first is those break-in's at Zara's apartment. See if you can discover who did that. The second is Zara's birth," he said.

"Her birth? Why would I do that?" he said.

Bodie smiled, "Because, I think I know why Mrs. Turner is so cruel to her youngest daughter. We're going to help Zara Turner because of my old friend, Hal."

"But, why are we going to help her?" Mike asked.

Bodie smiled, "Because even though we picked different sides, Hal was my best friend. I didn't expect her to be so like him just now. Hal was strong and loyal, I felt like I was seeing my friend again in some ways. I miss him. See, Mike, life can be complicated sometimes. I took one path, Hal took another, but we always helped one another over the years. He died, saving me and ten other people on this very dirigible, including my wife and daughters. Least I can do is look out for his girl when she turned out like him."

Mike smiled, "Yeah. I'm glad we can help her. She deserves to be happy, Bodie."

He studied the young man, "I agree. But if she gets in our way, we have to stop her."

He laughed, "She will."

"She's Hal's daughter. Of that, I have no doubt."

CHAPTER THIRTEEN

Harrison was frantic. Zara had been missing for nearly two days. He and the whole Crow's Nest had been searching for her all over. He hadn't slept since she had gone.

He loved her.

He'd fallen in love with her and now, all he could think, was that he had never told her and now, he might never get the chance. Sure, he didn't know her long, but he didn't give a shit. He loved Zara and he wanted to marry her, to move her out of that shit hole apartment and in with him because facing the rest of his life alone was not an option any longer. He tried to fool himself the other night, to say he could avoid being with her. He was wrong. It only took him one night worrying about her to figure it out. Harrison would tell her about how he wanted to stay working for the Crow's Nest as a life career because he loved it, and he was pretty sure she'd want him to. Hell, he was sure she'd be there with him. She loved it, too. And if she didn't—well, for her—he'd give it up. He understood now why his parents had left it. This job was amazing, but it wasn't everything. Loving someone was more. He and Zara, they'd figure it out as they went.

He shut his eyes tightly, squashing the fear he felt, "Where the hell is she, Dill?"

"I don't know. Mary is so upset. She keeps crying and wringing her hands," he said.

"Everyone is upset," Mr. Wills said.

He looked as bad as Harrison felt. All of them did. They had looked everywhere, but Zara had vanished. There was a knock on the door. Harrison stood and strode over to it. Mary stood there, her eyes wide.

"Harrison! A postal bot came with a missive for Room One Hundred!" Mary said.

She wrung her hands nervously. Harrison grabbed it from her and yanked it open. He read the letter, his heart hammering.

"She's at Jakarda general hospital. She was picked up. She told them she was an agent—they wonder if we want her transferred here to see Dr. West. She's very badly injured and she's suffering from exposure," he read.

"Mary, have her transferred here, quick now!" Mr. Wills said.

Mary nodded and raced off to send the courier bot. Harrison looked around at everyone and rubbed his head. FeFe looked pale, as if she was stricken by what happened. She could be shallow, but she had come to appreciate Zara. After Zara had surprised her with a lipstick that shot knock out darts, FeFe was delighted, then Zara had made for her what FeFe called, lady gadgets, or a camera hidden in a compact. FeFe loved that. He tried to think of something to say to make everyone feel better, and failed. He walked out of the room, the others right behind him, and paced the lobby with his arms crossed instead. The others followed suit, all of them loitering nervously around the perimeter.

Zara was carried in by two men on a stretcher ten minutes later. Harrison's lips parted, his heart squeezed. Her poor face was more beaten and swollen than before. Her arm was in a sling. They had covered her in a thick blanket. She was shivering, sweat was pouring from her head. She was pale, so pale. He shut his eyes. Mary took his hand, her eyes watery.

"Harrison, they beat her," she said.

"I know, Mary. I know," he said.

They followed her into the hospital room. Dr. West asked a lot of questions, the nurses fussed over her and got her settled as Dr. West read what had happened to her. He nodded curtly and got to work. Harrison stayed, watching over her as the doctors spent hours repairing her, running procedures and tests. He did everything he could to comfort her and encourage her through the process. He never left and no one asked him to. It wasn't until the following morning when she opened her eyes with a moan, that he felt a slight relief. Harrison jumped up and ran over to her.

"Honey?" he said.

"Harrison?" she replied.

"Yeah, I've been here all night. How are you feeling? You've been through a lot," he said. His eyes watered and a few tears leaked out. Harrison was not a man who cried, but he'd never been so relieved, "Zara, honey, I have something to tell you."

"Harrison, It has to wait, I can hardly stay awake. Listen to me. I was taken by the leader of the Reform Mechanics. He said he was my papa's friend. His name was Bodie Polk. They were not a part of the attacks, he said it was a group called The Robotic Patriots. I suspected the people who sold halonite had been tricked into buying large quantities of a shoddy product. I think that's the secret, Harrison. You guys need to visit the factories all around Jakarda. I think they might have bought into it thinking they would be rich, but whoever sold them the halonite is the one making the money. If we find out who that is, we find out who is behind all of this," she said, her voice barely a whisper.

"Did Bodie Polk do this to you?" he snarled.

"Yes."

"How the hell can you trust what he said?" Harrison demanded.

"Gut feeling. He never intended to kill me, he let me go. Why would he do that? He just wanted to know if we suspected the Reform Mechanics," she said.

"What did you tell him?" Harrison asked.

"The truth. That they are a deplorable group, I didn't agree with their methods, but in this instance, I didn't think it was them," she said.

He laughed and gently stroked her hair, "I think you're amazing, Zara."

She smiled a slight smile and blinked her eyes lethargically, "He said they didn't trash my apartment either. That means it's really not safe for me."

"You can stay with me, honey. Don't worry about it, ok?"

"Ok. Thank you," she sank back into her pillow, "Harrison, he said to check into the bombings over the past year, the ones the Reform Mechanics were blamed for. He said it was the Robotic Patriots, that's the group's name."

Her eyes drifted shut and she was out cold again. Harrison wiped his eyes and kissed her lips softly. He lingered there, his heart hammering, then stoked her hair some more.

"I love you, Zara Turner. I love you so much," he said quietly.

He stood and walked from the room, his expression mutinous, "Mary, Room One Hundred!"

"I'm keeping it on the ground floor, Harrison. Right next door to the hospital room for now," she said.

Harrison nodded and stormed away. He angrily relayed the message Zara gave him, "Son of a bitch beat her! Claimed to be her papa's friend, then he beat her."

"He was his best friend, actually. He and Hal, they had an arrangement. They would meet and disclose certain bits of information on a neutral ground that was beneficial for both organizations, a necessary evil. Hal found out that his partner at the time was going to blow up the dirigible the Reform Mechanics were on, said they all deserved to die, even the women and children. Hal stopped him, died saving Bodie and his family because they were his friends. Hal Turner was a good man, a very kind one. I admit, in hiring Zara, I hoped for that to be a possibility again, knowing what Hal did for Bodie. Bodie sees things we sometimes do not," Mr. Wills said grudgingly.

"No! No way, dammit. She is not going to be put into the line of fire like that. Look what that bastard did to her to get our attention!" Harrison snarled.

He knew he looked insane, furious. They were gaping at him, all of them. He didn't give a shit.

"That is for her to decide, Harrison. Not you. I know you care about her, we all do. It didn't take her long to fit into our little group, she's like that. Strikes a chord with you. I understand how you feel. What happened to her is terrible, but she will be ok. We will do our jobs, and we will get to the bottom of this. Keep a cool head," Mr. Wills said.

Harrison rubbed his face and sighed, "Sorry. Her face is…she's such a mess. Dr. West was able to counteract the exposure, and make her fingers work. She kept crying and asking how she was going to tinker. I hated it. All I could think last night was that I might have to tell her she couldn't tinker any longer if his methods didn't work. She loves it so much, it would break her heart. Thank god he reversed it. He used the medi-bot she designed on her too, it took away the swelling and mended the gashes, she's looking better after only twenty-four hours. Those are going to be essential in the med kit for agents, they'll save lives. She and Dr. West made the patent. I'm just worried about her."

"I know. We all are. Come on, best way to help her is to do our jobs," he said.

Harrison nodded and got to work. He and Simon left the Crow's Nest for the halonite plant to get answers. He was not in a negotiating mood, either. He strode directly to the girl at the counter and smiled.

"My name is Harrison Lowell. This is my associate, Simon Hempsworth. We are with the Crow's Nest. We're investigating a case. We need to speak to Mr. and Miss Walkerwall right now. You need to make that happen or I'll have you and everyone in this place hauled into jail," he said.

Her eyes widened. She nodded and hurried off. Simon chuckled.

"You must be good and angry. You only get like this when someone has pushed you too far," Simon said.

"You saw what they did to her!" he snapped.

"Yes, I did," Simon smiled and studied him, "You love her. Does that have something to do with it?"

Harrison winced and sent him a guilty look. Simon laughed heartily and clapped him on the shoulder, "We all know it. Even

FeFe. She wanted you to love her, hence her jealousy. She's been having sex with everyone she can open her legs for to make you jealous. She and Dill are at it all the time. Poor chap can't help it, he's liked her for ages. He's going to lose Mary if he's not careful. As for you, I knew you loved her that first week she started. You didn't want to like her, but you had this grudging admiration. You never take your eyes off her now, watch her like she's the most amazing person you ever met. It was all downhill after that first week."

"Shit. Does everyone know?" he muttered.

"Yes, we do! Bets were made as to when you were going to realize. I lost, it seems. Mr. Wills was closest. Unfair advantage, him being your uncle and all. Still, I'm happy for you. She's a hell of a woman. I have a sizable crush on her," he said.

Harrison glared at him, "What?"

"I can't help it. She's so smart and fearless, so matter-of-fact. I like how she sometimes babbles about things and loses track of the conversation because she's so smart her mind can't stop, it's adorable. Then she catches herself and apologizes, it makes me laugh. She's lovely too, damn beautiful. You're a lucky man. You know me, I have crushes on ladies all the time. I'm the romantic sort. I've been in love on numerous occasions. I love to woo and romance, and then I fall out of love, and begin again," he said.

Harrison chuckled, "Yes, I know. I have never been in love. I have these feelings. I'm confused and damn annoyed by them. But they're wonderful too, she's wonderful."

"She's it, then?" Simon said.

"If she'll have me," Harrison said.

"She will. She loves you too, she can't hide it like you do," Simon said.

Harrison felt a rush of happiness, "You think so?"

"Yes. We all do," he said.

Harrison chuckled, "Of course you do."

Simon laughed, "It's ok, Harrison. We're your friends and she is a catch. I kept hoping she might like me, but she took a shine to you from the beginning. Know what I like best about her?"

"What?"

"She's not aware of how wonderful she is. She's so modest and completely clueless she's wonderful. She's just, Zara, and she likes who she is, even if no one else does. I like that confidence in a lady."

Harrison smiled a little, "Yeah. Yeah, I like that, too."

"We're going to hurt that bastard who did that to her, Harrison," Simon assured him.

"We sure as hell are," he said.

The woman at the desk came rushing out, her blue eyes wide, "They'll see you now!"

Harrison offered her a charming smile, "Thank you."

She led them into a factory. There were sheets of halonite being cut into smaller sheets by a dozen men and women. It was a big factory, and they didn't have many employees. What they did have, was a lot of halonite. A hell of a lot. Harrison walked into the office with Simon. A man stood. He seemed around their age, and wore a beard. He had on an expensive-looking suit. The woman he was with was younger, with brown hair, cut to her shoulders. Her eyes were blue. He thought of Zara, his heart squeezing. He hoped she wouldn't wake up when he was gone. He wanted to be there when she did in case she was worried about tinkering again. She needed him.

"Hello! Jane couldn't recall your names, she was to worried about the threat that she might be tossed in jail," Mr. Walkerwall said.

Harrison smiled smoothly, "Well, that threat stands for you and your sister, Mr. Walkerwall. I'm Harrison Lowell, this is my associate, Simon Hepsworth. We are from the Crow's Nest. We're investigating a crime, and we think you might be tied to it. A serious crime that's left one of our agents badly injured and us quite angry about it. So, you're going to talk to us, help us, or we are going to make life difficult for you."

"You dare threaten me?" Mr. Walkerwall said.

"Oh, shut up, Matthew! Forgive my brother. We are already having a miserable life, look out there on the plant floor! Halonite is not the product we were lead to believe it was. We are the victims in this!" Miss Walkerwall said.

She gestured to the wooden table. Harrison sat, Simon sat beside him.

"How so?" Simon asked.

She sighed and sat down, "Sit down, Matt. My brother and I, we inherited money from our parents, they were killed in a steam powered automobile crash. They had a lot of business dealings, all on the up and up, feel free to look into them. We will give you what you want. Matt here is upset because we were bamboozled."

"Can you give us more details?" Harrison asked.

Matt sighed and sat down, rubbing his face, "About six months ago, a company, calling itself Global Technology Incorporated came to us. Said they could get us in on the ground floor, said halonite was strong, durable, perfect for tinkering. Said it would put us on the map. My father, he never had dealings with them before, but one of the men, Greg Bowser, was a friend of his. He had invested in the halonite, too. He has a factory like this that cuts the sheets down and sells it directly to companies and tinkerers directly. He said he was making a fortune. Greg has been very successful, his plant is in Brookdale right outside the city. It's not as big as Jakarda City, and he was making a fortune selling it to local businesses and tinkerers. He said it was a sure thing. Jemma and I combined our cash and bought this factory at a slightly higher price than they were asking, snatched it right out from under the Brother's Kensington Motorized Bicycle Company. They were furious with us, but we needed the space to cut the sheets of halonite and this is the perfect spot."

"Yes, but the catch is, you have to by all the halonite up front. All you think you might need. So, Matt and I bought all we could afford, fifty-thousand dollars' worth, using the reminder of our inheritance. So, we have everything we own invested in this company. Everything. Now, we find that this product is weak and easily broken. That article in the paper that came out last week, it's killing us. Our sales have dropped forty percent over the past week and we are stuck with a product no one wants to use," Jemma concluded.

Simon winced, "Well, that is a shame, but we want the name of the people you dealt with at Global Technology, anything you know about them. We think they obtained the material illegally."

"Oh, shit! Will we go to jail for selling it?" Matt asked.

"Not if you two had no knowledge of it and you were in fact victims of Global Technology. You can expect that we'll be looking into it," Harrison said.

"We'll give you everything we have. We only ever met with a woman, pretty, dark hair and blue eyes. She brought us the documents to be signed, never gave a name. Then these containers of halonite were delivered on unmarked trucks. I guess we should have thought that was suspicious, but we didn't," Jemma said.

Simon offered her a smile, "That's understandable. Did you ever meet anyone but this woman from Global Technology?"

"Never," Matt said.

Harrison and Simon exchanged glances, both thinking the same thing. Find this woman, find Global Technologies. First, they needed to speak to the other owners of the halonite factories to see if their stories meshed. There was more to this than anyone realized.

CHAPTER FOURTEEN

One week later, Zara was up and moving. She went back to Harrison's to shower and change, moving slowly. Her face was no longer swollen, but it was a patchwork of blue, yellow and red bruises, and she had two black eyes. He was waiting for her downstairs. She was finally going back to work today. She had to promise to tinker and tell him if she was tired. She had fixed Annie, who was moving around upstairs with her cat and dog bots. Harrison had collected a bunch of her things, she felt oddly at home here at his place the longer she stayed here.

She looked at herself in the mirror and winced. Blood had gathered in her right eye. At least the feeling had returned to her toes and fingers. She was worried about that. She cried twice in front of Harrison, terrified she wouldn't be able to tinker again. He was so sweet, kissing her numb hands and telling her she'd be fine. He cared for her, letting her stay with him and taking care of her when she was such a mess. When he was at the Crow's Nest, he had the nurse from the office come stay with her each he was gone this past week, then helped her around at night. She spent most of her day sleeping, her recovery slow and Harrison kept her company.

Zara adored him.

She adored him because he was so kind and handsome. He read to her at night from his favorite book, a spy story. Zara loved it, hung on his every word. He paced and gestured when he read, he was an excellent story teller. He stroked her hair until she fell asleep. Zara loved that. He kissed her cheek and looked at her tenderly, she liked that perhaps most of all.

Annie dried her hair and styled it for her. She braided the front and down the side, then joined it with another braid over one shoulder. Zara's mother had sent over new clothes, prettier ones than she used to, at Zara's insistence. She had on a beautiful skirt today, mid-thigh, chocolate brown, a simple A-line with three buttons on either side. She wore a brown and white striped shirt with a matching button at the throat and little ruffles down the front. Zara pulled taut the tall, thigh-high socks with bows on the sides and stepped into short suede ankle boots. She looked pretty and stylish, despite the beaten face. She put on some simple ear bobs made of buttons like the ones on the outfit and her hat and stood, clutching her ribs. They were sore, but mending. Her clothes were not overly tight, so the tight bandage on her ribs didn't show.

"Thanks, Annie," she said.

"Of course, Zara. See you when you return," she said.

She hugged Annie and went carefully down the steps holding her leather bag in her hand. She walked into the dining room with a smile. Harrison grinned at her, eyeing her legs.

"I like those," he said.

"A new fashion called thigh high stockings. Some ladies need a garter belt, but they seem to stay up on me because I'm filling out a little."

"You have amazing legs, and you have put weight on. You look healthy. That's an excellent look for you, honey," he said.

Zara laughed, "Thank you."

"How are you feeling?" he asked, his expression worried.

"Better! I slept very well last night, my ribs hurt less and I can breathe normally now that my face isn't as swollen. It looks much better, I think. I can see clearly out of both eyes, now," she said.

Harrison laughed softly, "Yeah, I noticed. You look pretty."

"Thank you."

Zara's heart thumped away. He was looking at her almost tenderly. He'd been doing that since she was hurt. She found it hard to keep her distance. She sat down gingerly then sighed when her fanny contacted with the chair so she could relax.

"Blasted ribs," she muttered.

Harrison laughed. He was still looking at her, a half smile on his handsome face. She reddened a little and scooted back on her seat, "What did you uncover in Brookdale and Kent?"

"Same as we did with the other companies. They invested a small fortune, had to buy the halonite in bulk, poured all their money into it and now the product is shit. A man approached them about the purchase, or the woman that was mentioned to Simon and I, then the man came to close the deal and deliver all the halonite in an unmarked truck."

Zara winced, "I feel so bad for them, those people who bought that up. I keep thinking there must be something we can do with it, some use for it. I think I can come up with something. I read the files, three of the investors have small children. They'll live in poverty if this fails. Many of them had to work so long to get that money. I'd like to help them if I can."

He reached over and interlocked their fingers, "You're the sweetest person I ever met, Zara."

She offered him a smile and shrugged, her face hot. He grinned at her red face, that sexy half smile of his aimed at her.

"You are getting embarrassed a lot today."

"Well, stop saying sweet things to me to make me blush!" she said.

He grinned, "Never. I like it when you blush."

"My neck and face get red as an apple!" she said.

"I like it. It's cute," he said.

"Oh, for heaven's sake!" she muttered.

Harrison laughed delightedly. There was a knock on the door. Zara helped herself to pancakes, toast and sausage. Dr. West had told her she was too thin, so this past week she had done nothing but eat. She'd put on four pounds in a week. She could hardly eat at first with her face so swollen. But she'd been eating solid food since the day before yesterday, scads of it. She had looked forward to solid food, she was sick to death of porridge, soup and applesauce. She ate a lot of marshmallows too, they were soft, but she loved those so it wasn't a trouble. She shared them with Harrison who gobbled them up, too, especially the ones covered in chocolate.

"Master Harrison, your mother and father are here to see you," Bernard said.

"Oh, shit," Harrison muttered.

"We heard that!" someone, presumably his mother, said.

A beautiful woman walked into the room with a bright smile. She had on one of her mother's outfits, Zara recognized it. She had nut brown hair streaked with grey. Harrison had her smile and teeth, he had a wonderful smile. She had her hair piled in a style to the side, a hat atop her head. She was average height, lovely in the way FeFe was. Her husband looked just like Harrison. Tall, broad shouldered with silvery black hair and the same dark eyes Zara loved about Harrison. He had that same dashing air of arrogance about him. They were staring at her with happy smiles. Zara struggled to her feet to shake their hands.

"Honey, don't get up! She can hardly walk, she's got three broken ribs," he said, clearly worried.

"I can manage fine, no need to fuss," she said.

She smiled and extended her hand, "I'm Zara Turner. I work with Harrison at the Crow's Nest. He's been kind enough to allow me to stay with him until I'm well."

"So we heard! You poor dear, my goodness! Someone beat you badly," Mrs. Lowell said shaking her hand.

"Yes, they certainly did," Zara said.

She extended her hand to his father. He turned it and kissed it with a charming smile. Zara laughed.

"Like father, like son, I see," she said.

He studied her, "Exactly that! Blonde and freckled. I quite like that."

He sent Harrison a look. He flushed a little. Zara didn't know what was going on. She wrapped her arm around her ribs with a smile.

"Oh, you poor dear! Sit down! We'll join you for breakfast. Are these blueberry pancakes? Our bot doesn't make those!" Mrs. Lowell said.

"You have to name him to unlock the new recipes. Zara taught me. There are stages of progress. Zara helped create the chip, giving them an identity makes them more useful to your household, like a part of the family. I get the best food now! Last night we had steak with blue cheese, loaded baked potatoes and creamed spinach," Harrison said.

"That was excellent. I love blue cheese," Zara said.

Harrison winked at her, "I know, honey. You like it stuffed in figs that were the appetizer. You ate a bunch of those, that was damn cute."

She laughed, "So did you!"

"Yes, but I eat a lot of everything."

"That's true. Eat all Annie's marshmallows."

Harrison laughed heartily, his eyes dancing, "I said I was sorry! She made more, they're my favorite now, too. I didn't mean to eat the whole plate!"

Zara laughed, "They're like that, marshmallows."

"I thought cookies were your favorite," Mrs. Lowell said casually.

"They used to be," Harrison said, winking at Zara.

She smiled at him and took a bite of her pancakes. She moved slowly, her eyes on her fork so she didn't spill. She couldn't eat quickly. If she had been paying attention, she would have seen the thrilled looks on Mr. and Mrs. Lowell's faces. Harrison didn't notice, either. He was too busy watching Zara eat, a worried look on his face because she moved so slow. Bernard came out with a plate of mini quiche. Zara grinned and took three.

"I love these! Thanks, Bernard," she said.

"You're very welcome, Zara. I observed you enjoyed them yesterday morning and took it upon myself to make them again today. Blue cheese and walnut," he said.

"Oh, yummy!" Zara said, popping one in her mouth, "Harrison you have to try these! I wish Annie wasn't so old, I could teach her to make them. Her memory is at capacity, I need to come up with something new for her."

He did as she urged and ate one, "Oh, wow! Annie has her uses. Last night she played all that music for us. That was amazing, she has it all stored in her memory. I liked that."

"Thank you!"

"You're welcome," Harrison said.

They smiled at one another for a moment. Zara realized his parents were looking at them. She smiled, unaware they were seeing things she had no idea they saw.

"What brings you over so early?" Zara asked.

"My brother told me a woman was living with my son, so we wanted to meet you," Mrs. Lowell said, eating her pancakes.

"Jeanette! Honestly, we just wanted to introduce ourselves to our son's first female friend," Mr. Lowell said, his eyes dancing.

Zara looked between them, "Oh. This only temporary, I'm not a sponge. Your son has been nothing but a gentleman, I assure you. I was unable to care for myself, this is only my second day of solid food. I have been eating a lot of soft marshmallows."

"Ignore them, they do this sort of thing to butt in. You're fine," Harrison said.

"Oh, Harrison! I had to come by, I do worry. After all, we spoke to Joanne last night," Mrs. Lowell said, taking a bite of quiche.

Harrison turned bright red. His father laughed openly and slapped him on the shoulder, shaking with mirth. Harrison gave him a dirty look. Zara was clearly missing something. That happened to her sometimes, so she thought nothing of it. She went back to her meal. She ate quietly while they talked, thinking about the halonite. Dill had found how to turn it back to a liquid form. She wondered if they could use it as a coating or in some other way. It kept shattering, that was the trouble. She needed a way to make it stronger. Maybe if she bonded it with something else? She glared at her food.

"Honey?" Harrison said.

"Oh! I'm sorry, I do that. I'm a tinkerer, I get lost in thought quite a bit, I was thinking about a case we're working on. I hate when I have something to fix and I can't figure out how to fix it. My mind wanders. What?" Zara said.

"Not to worry! I'm a tinkerer, too, I do it sometimes myself. I asked if you liked working at the Crow's Nest," Mr. Lowell asked.

"Very much! I applied for a desk position with Mr. Wills. He came to me and asked me to be an agent," Zara said.

"He did?" Harrison asked in surprise.

Zara nodded and took a bite of her food. She chewed carefully, "Yes. He came to see my final project. I am fairly sure I put half the audience to sleep going on and on about the applications and the technical elements. I saw five people snoozing away, I'm not making that up. I'm an appealingly bad public speaker."

Harrison erupted into laughter, "Five?"

Zara giggled, "Yes! You can ask Mr. Wills, he noticed them, too. He notices everything. I know I bore people, I can't help it. I love tinkering and I could go on about it for hours. Anyway, he came up to me after the presentation, I was the last one to speak. He introduced himself and he convinced me to be an agent over a very cheap cup of coffee I bought for him."

"How did he do that?" Harrison asked.

She glanced at his parents and then at him, then decided if they were anything like Harrison, they would appreciate an honest answer, "Well, to be frank, he told me I was lonely. He was right. It was one of those moments in your life when someone says something to you and the second they say it, you realize they sized you up in moments, and you had missed it for years. See, it's very hard to be as intelligent as I am. I have trouble speaking to people and my situation with my mother and sisters, well—we're not close. I have not been as fortunate as some people with family and friends, my papa and I were close but he died working for the Crow's Nest in the line of duty. I was eleven at the time. I think I felt like I had no one to talk to from the second he left me. No one that understood me. I'm not a bit like my mother and sisters, odd man out, I suppose. They were always close, but I have nothing in common with them, they're very silly and shallow. I had never considered I was lonely before Mr. Wills said so. He promised if I tried to be an agent, I might get better with people, make some friends, have excellent co-workers and he was right. I don't think I'll ever be like Harrison, everyone likes him. It takes people some time to be used to my blunt way of speaking and yammering on. But that's ok, I have friends, now, and I've been with the Crow's Nest a month and a half. That's all it took! I make an effort to pay attention even though my mind wanders and races all the time. I guess I try to, I don't know, be like everyone else and I have had help learning to be more social. Excellent teachers make a difference, your son, for one, and Mary at the front desk. She's a former lady of the night, but you would not believe the things she knows!" Zara said with a laugh. Harrison snorted with laughter. Zara went on, "The other fellows in Room One Hundred are wonderful to me, I learn so much every day. Mr. Wills gave me a two month trial, said if I hated it in two months I could go to the tinkerers room and hide in my comfort zone. But, I don't wish to. I was terrified that first day because I know some people find me odd. But, I went anyway and I'm glad I did, even if I keep getting beaten up. I think I need to learn to fight better, can you teach me Harrison?"

Harrison was watching her with that look on his face. The one he wore so often now. It made her heart beat faster. He nodded.

"Sure, honey. Anything," he said gruffly.

Mrs. Lowell reached over and squeezed her hand, "I think you're a remarkable young woman and much better with people than you realize."

Mr. Lowell sighed, "Me, too. I think I might have a small crush on you, now."

Zara laughed, "Do you?"

"Yes," he said.

"Really, Edward! He's such a flirt. Only tinkerer I ever met who flirts as well as an agent. I love that about him. We are on the way to see your sister Emily, Harrison. She's finally gotten the divorce, thank goodness! Her husband is a cheat and a layabout!" Mrs. Lowell said.

Zara winced, "I'm sorry to hear that."

"Emily makes poor choices. Not like Harrison or Joanne, his older sister," Mr. Lowell said.

Zara smiled and ate some more of her food.

"Is she ok?" Harrison asked.

Mrs. Lowell sighed, "Hard to say with Em. She's taking good care of Miles, that's what counts."

Harrison nodded, "They staying with you for a time?"

"Yes," Mr. Lowell said miserably.

Zara tried to choke back a chuckle, but she couldn't contain it. Mr. Lowell winked at her, looking very much like his son.

"I'd like to be alone with my lovely wife so I can kiss her whenever she wants me to, which is all the time. She's nuts about me. Company puts a damper on that," he said.

Zara giggled, "I'm sure."

He laughed and Mrs. Lowell giggled. Mr. Lowell sent her a rakish grin, which she returned with a coy one of her own. Harrison rolled his eyes.

"Let me know what I can do to help Emily and Miles," Harrison said.

"You can come to dinner with Zara tomorrow night! Whole family is meeting at Dickerson's Restaurant," Mrs. Lowell said.

Harrison glanced at Zara, "We can, but only if Zara feels ok and she wants to. Today is her first day back to work. Plus, we're on a case, we might not have time."

"Of course!" Mrs. Lowell said.

They finished eating. Zara forced herself to listen, to not let her mind wander as it so often did, laughing and interjecting occasionally. She thanked Bernard for the meal, they all did, then she walked slowly to her motorized bicycle, waving to Harrison's parents, who looked oddly delighted to be picking up their daughter and grandson from a divorce when they said goodbye to Harrison.

"Zara! Honey, with those broken ribs, you should ride in the carriage," he said.

"You do not have to drive me all over in your carriage! I can take care of myself," she said.

"I know you can, but I don't want you to hit a dip in the road and hurt yourself worse," he said.

Zara sighed, "Very well."

She walked over to the carriage and got in, grumbling to herself, "I feel like I can't do anything on my own. I hate it! I can't even live in my apartment because some lunatics are out to get me!"

Harrison gave her a half smile, "Is living with me so bad?"

"No! Of course not, but I feel like I'm taking advantage of a friend. Now your parents come over to make sure we're not, ah, I don't know the term, but they wanted to make sure I didn't have loose morals. I'm sorry."

"Zara, my parents are nosey. That's why they came over. I talk about you all the time, I see them weekly. They know we're friends, I've told them all about you. They wanted to meet you," he said.

"Oh! I hope they liked me. I make a bad first impression," she said.

"No, honey. You make a very good one. They liked you a lot, so do I, so that's all that matters," he said.

She smiled at him, ignoring her hammering heart. He looked so handsome today in black pants, red vest with two sets of buttons down the front, a white shirt and a black bowler hat, the pocket watch she had made him tucked into his pocket on a chain, ready to use if need be. He also had on his gun belt, his blast gun strapped to his hip as always. He noticed her studying him and grinned.

"What you looking at, honey?" he said.

She laughed, "You look very handsome today. Red is nice on you with your dark hair and eyes. Do you ever wear a suit coat?"

"In the colder months. I get too hot in the summer," he said.

He was smiling, his eyes intense, as if he was thrilled she told him he looked handsome. He leaned across the carriage and took her hand in one of his, his eyes locked with hers. Zara's heart went fast. What was he doing? He reached up with the other hand and tugged on her braid.

"I love your hair in a braid. You have the most gorgeous blonde hair. You know, some ladies use a dye on their hair these days to try to get their hair this color," he said.

"They do?" she said breathlessly.

Harrison grinned as if he could tell he excited her. He kissed her with a moan. Zara was taken aback. She blinked in shock, then her eyes fluttered shut. She kissed him back eagerly. He groaned and touched his tongue to hers. Zara forgot herself completely. She lost her brain in that kiss, his lips were so perfect, so demanding, and he was so good at kissing. She reached for him, then inhaled sharply and jerked back.

"Ouch! My ribs," she said.

"You ok?" he asked.

Zara reddened, "Yes. I-I'm sorry. I messed that up. I'm not good at this, I-I-"

"Honey, you didn't mess anything up. Don't worry. The truth is, I like you. I like you more than I should since we work together, and there are a million reasons I shouldn't, but I like you one hell of a lot. As more than a friend should and I'm tired of not showing you. I have wanted to kiss you for weeks, and I still want to. The question is, do you want me to?" he said.

Zara looked at him, her eyes wide. She nodded slowly having misplaced her vocabulary again. He grinned and kissed her some more, his hand on her cheek. They kissed for a long time, even when the carriage stopped and neither of them noticed, they kept kissing, their tongues tangled together, Harrison's hand on the back of her head. Harrison pulled back. It was a good thing too, Zara's brain had stopped working again. She looked at him and smiled. He grinned back, his dark eyes dancing.

"I have a crush on you, Miss Turner. It's a new experience for me. Ladies normally have those on me," he said.

Zara laughed, "I have one on you, too."

He sent her a thrilled look that made her laugh heartily, then clutch her side. She froze and looked at him.

"Harrison! I have it! The halonite! I know what we can do with it!" she said excitedly.

He groaned and kissed her, "I love when you do that. Get a random idea out of nowhere. It's so cute."

He crushed his lips to hers. That delayed them a while longer. They went in ten minutes later, hand in hand. Mary grinned at Zara and rushed over to her. She hugged her tightly. Zara winced from the hug, but didn't say anything. Mary had been so good to her, it was worth a painful hug from her best chum.

"You look much better today, Zara!" she said.

"Thank you. I'm feeling better, ribs hurt, but at least I can see out of both eyes," she said.

"That has improved! Hate to say this, but your mother is waiting for you in the ladies waiting room. I didn't know where else to send her. Your mother tried to drop off your new clothes, the landlady said you were staying with a man. She's good and furious, called you a tramp and a few other nasty things," Mary said.

"I can speak to her with you, if you like," Harrison offered.

Zara sighed, "No. No, I'll be fine. Thank you."

Harrison did not look convinced. He glanced at Mary who sent him a look like she didn't believe Zara would be fine either. Zara walked slowly to the ladies waiting room adjacent to the washroom. She opened the door and went inside.

Mrs. Turner saw Zara. Her lips parted in shock, "What happened?"

"I was hurt on the job, I-"

"What happened to the brown and creme colored thigh high stockings that are meant for that outfit?" she said.

Zara sighed. She should have known, "These were the only ones you sent, mama."

"I'll send the correct ones straight away. Those clash. Your face is a mess. What did you do to yourself this time?" she asked.

"Working a case," she said.

"Happened to your blasted papa all the time, too. Foolish choice, working here. You could have been making piles of money at one of those firms that hire tinkerers. Leave it to you to pick a low paying government job, you cannot be as brilliant as everyone says. You look horrible. I hear you've shacked up with a man. Zara, I am not often in your business these days, but you cannot live with a man unmarried! It isn't done. I know you're odd, but I have to put my foot down about living in sin with a man like that. It's just so tacky and what happens when he tires of you? They always tire of you, trust me," she said.

"Mama, my apartment was broken into twice, my possessions smashed and stolen. I was attacked and hurt on the job, quite badly and I needed help. The man is a co-worker, a friend. He was kind enough to take me in for a time until I am well enough to return home, that's all. I'm not shacking up with him, I'm in his spare room," Zara said.

"Oh! I should have guessed. Who would want you? Of course, that's it!" she said.

Zara flinched as if she hit her. She shook the insult off and forced back the tears that threatened to surface. She was forever doing that, her mama, trying to make her feel small. Each time, there was a split second she believed what her mother said, then Zara quickly realized she was a mean, spiteful woman, a stupid one that Zara didn't have to listen to any longer. Her opinion about Zara being intelligent and beautiful was incorrect. Mrs. Turner showed one face to the public, the face that was her best. She was the charming Mrs. Turner, the head of an empire who dressed impeccably and charmed everyone at parties. She was a different Mrs. Turner behind closed doors, a bully of the worst kind, and she was wrong about Zara. There was nothing at all the matter with her, Mrs. Turner simply didn't like her daughter for reasons unknown. Harrison had just kissed her not long ago, he and the other gents in Room One Hundred told her she looked beautiful often. Zara was not about to mention the kisses she and Harrison shared in the carriage, that would make her mother angry. She'd never believe her, anyway.

"Precisely," Zara said to shut her up.

"Whatever happened with that handsome Mr. Lowell?" she asked.

Zara thought about the kiss they just shared, bursting with happiness at the mention of his name. She made her expression sad instead, she was better at hiding things now. She had not realized her emotions showed in every expression. Her mother liked to see her hurt, never again would she see her like that. Zara's time at the Crow's Nest had paid off. She could make her mother think she was miserable and she would be left alone because it seemed, Mrs. Turner was only truly happy when her daughter was miserable.

She smiled, "It didn't work out."

"He was far too good for you anyway. I knew you'd mess it up!" she said.

Mrs. Turner smiled happily and handed Zara three huge bags of clothes, "These are for you, all the latest in prettier colors and styles. I think you'll love it all. I got you the jewelry and hair pieces, too. I like how Annie did your hair today, I'm going to use that on your sisters. Tempie would look so much better in that style than you do. She's far more lovely."

"Good idea. Mama, I have a question for you. Did Papa ever mention a man called Bodie Polk?" she said.

Mrs. Turner nodded, "Of course! They grew up next door to one another, best friends. Bodie ended up with the Reform Mechanics, your papa at the Crow's Nest. They went separate ways. Your papa, he held out hope for Bodie. That he would come to the right side, as he put it, but Bodie was wild, dashing. He fancied me, you know. I picked your papa. Should have picked Bodie, your papa died and left me with three daughters and an empire to build. Anyway, they faced off constantly here at the Nest. Your papa was always upset after he saw him. He used to come home and tinker for hours, looking sad. He had you join him, remember? You brought him comfort, but I was never allowed to."

Zara ignored the bitter edge in her voice, "I do recall that now, mama. I had forgotten."

Mrs. Turner shrugged, "Bodie Polk. If you see him, tell him I'd love a chance to bed him now that your papa is gone. Your groceries are coming. You look thinner than usual. I think you need them!"

Zara watched her walk out. She was four pounds heavier than she was before, leave it to her mother to notice she was too thin after she was getting healthy again. She sighed and picked up the three bags of clothing. She carried them to Room One Hundred slowly. Mary rushed over to help her.

"How did it go?" she asked.

"Like it always does, but at least I have new clothes and groceries coming. She is always so rude to me," she said.

"Zara, haven't you noticed? The more forlorn you are, the more she delights in giving you things. She knows you hate the handouts. She likes when you need them, makes her feel good for you to take things from her because you have to," she said.

Zara considered her friend's words. She had come to the conclusion herself recently, but Harrison told her it was sometimes nicer to let someone else think they helped you, so she just nodded, "You're right."

Mary smiled and put her arm around her shoulders, "Good news is, won't see her for another month."

Zara laughed, "Very good news!"

Mary helped her carry in the bags and set them near her tinkering desk. Harrison smiled at them, thinking her mother had done something nice. She didn't have the heart to tell him, it was in her papa's will that she feed and clothe Zara until she married. She had to provide the clothes for the duration of her life, the food until she was someone else's burden. It would just upset him because her papa had to put it deliberately into the will, as if he expected trouble. Still, she did tell her about Bodie Polk. That was helpful. Bodie Polk hadn't been lying.

At that very moment, Bodie Polk was looking over the files he sent Mike to retrieve for him about Zara Turner. They were as he suspected. Zara was not Amanda Turner's daughter. Poor Hal. He had been in love with Jessica Ventura for years. She loved him, too, she was just the independent sort. Hal wanted to marry, have children.

Jessie, she was more concerned with a career. She was a smart woman, Jessie. She tinkered on kitchen appliances, made a steam powered toaster they still used today. She died in childbirth, leaving Zara to Hal. Mike did some digging, he had a test done and it showed that Zara was Jessie's daughter He always suspected the two of them had carried on an affair. Damn shame they didn't just live in sin together, but Hal was old fashioned and stupid. They had a fight and he stubbornly refused to be with her after that fight, marrying someone else. Jessie was just as bad, always talking about being an independent woman who doesn't need to marry. Bodie had always thought no one needed to marry, of course they didn't, but if you loved someone very deeply and you wanted to be with them forever, why not marry? He never thought he was the marrying sort, then he met his wife and all he could think of was marrying her. Love changes a person in the best ways if you let it, Jesse was a fool to not know that, and now, because the two of them acted so stupidly, their daughter suffered. Hal married Amanda because she loved him, thinking it would be enough to give him the life he always wanted. It wasn't. Bodie tried to talk him out of it. How he managed to get Zara in that household after his indiscretion, that was a mystery. However, it seemed Amanda had agreed with stipulations. Poor Amanda! She always did love Hal to pieces. It explained the cruelty and the beatings. Bodie shut his eyes tightly, thinking of that poor girl, "Hal, you damned fool."

"Papa, who you talking to?" Bodie's daughter Ellen said.

She was the youngest of his three girls, all around the same age as Zara. She was pretty with brown hair and blue eyes like him. Funny, they had that in common, too, having three daughters. Bodie just went a step further and had a son for his fourth child.

He hugged Ellen, kissing her head. They were in the large family suite in the dirigible. It was decorated simply but beautiful by his wife, a tinkering table at the side, large comfortable blue sofas all around, "Oh, I was just thinking of my old friend, Hal Turner."

"The good one who worked for the Crow's Nest? The one who saved us?"

"That's the one, poppet! His daughter, she's a lot like him. She's a very strong, intelligent and kind woman. He would have been proud of her, I think. She works for the Crow's Nest now, too," he said.

Ellen nodded and studied him, "Why do you look so sad to know that? Shouldn't you be happy she's like the man you cared about and respected, papa?"

"I am! But, she's a very good person like him, and I know something about her that will change her life. She might not want to know. I don't know if I should tell her," he said.

"Of course you should. Courage papa. We are Reform Mechanics. We tell the truth because secrets are poison and it's our job to reveal the secrets, even when it's difficult," Ellen said.

He grinned, "Of course we do! So I shall, poppet! I love you."

"I love you too, papa," she said.

He hugged her tightly. He couldn't help but wonder if Zara Turner had anyone to tell her they loved her since her papa died. The thought made him hold his little girl tighter than usual. Hal would have been heartbroken if he knew how horrible Amanda was to her. Mike had told him things he heard and saw. Zara came to school covered in cuts and bruises, and refused to tell anyone that her mother did the things she did. It made his chest ache, knowing that. He felt sick that he tried to abuse her himself to get a point across to his informant at the nest. He vowed to never do that again. Bodie was going to tell Zara, he had to. But how? She wasn't going to trust Mike again. He'd have to do it himself, if she would ever see him again, that was.

CHAPTER FIFTEEN

Harrison watched Zara walk into the room after seeing her mother. She looked pale and tense. He wanted to strangle the life out of that woman, all she ever did was upset Zara. She set down three massive bags of clothing, at least she did that. That was a nice gesture. He offered her a smile which she returned and sat gingerly beside Dill on a stool. Harrison looked away before everyone noticed him staring at her. He glanced around. Simon and Douglas sent him an amused look. Marcus just smirked. FeFe looked furious. She stomped over to Dill, a challenging look on her pretty face She whispered something in his ear. He reddened, then nodded. She dragged him off for sex. Harrison rolled his eyes. Poor Dill was going to lose Mary if he kept this up, she was bound to find out he was having sex with FeFe, too. Why was he so eager to go with FeFe if he cared about Mary? Women made even the most sensible man act like a fool.

Zara watched them go with a curious look. Her eyes widened when she realized what was happening. She looked at Harrison questioningly. He smirked and wiggled his eyebrows. Her jaw dropped. He chuckled at her expression. She reddened and turned around, muttering something about being the last to know everything which set everyone laughing. Simon rubbed her back.

"You're catching on, though. Not long ago, you wouldn't have noticed at all," he said.

"Noticed what?" Mr. Wills said.

Harrison laughed delightedly, "Nothing, uncle."

"Ok! Harrison, when FeFe gets back I want you two to drive the hour to Dove Town and check on that last halonite factory. I know what the result is likely to be, but to be sure, we need to check," Mr. Wills said.

"Yes, sir!" he said with a happy smile.

Mr. Wills grinned, "You seem chipper this morning."

"Well, I'm having an excellent morning," Harrison said.

Mr. Wills chuckled, "I can see that."

Twenty minutes later FeFe came in adjusting her dress. Dill looked even more rumpled, which was saying something because it was only ten in the morning. He didn't normally look that rumpled till mid-afternoon. He was smiling happily, a dreamy look on his face. Zara glared at him, and he turned red. She went back to tinkering, muttering to herself about him being an idiot. Harrison laughed. Zara's eyes met his. She huffed, clearly annoyed. Her face was such a mess. He still thought her the most beautiful woman he'd ever seen.

She and Dill were conducting some experiments on halonite. Zara offered him a small smile.

"I think we can make paint from this, paint that crackles when you mix it with another color and it cools. I'm hoping we can start a trend in homes, although I am no trend setter. I'd like to help those fools who dumped their money into halonite. I cannot imagine investing in a product on the slick, polished words of another person without testing it first, can you?" she asked.

Harrison snorted with laughter, "I'm guessing Dill's answer is no, birds of a feather, you two are. The rest of us may have fallen for those slick polished words."

"Here, here! I know I would have," Marcus said with a delighted laugh.

"Back a single day and you're already teasing me. It should be a lesson as to common sense! I never take the word of anyone on a tinkering product, it's idiotic!" Zara said, making them laugh harder.

"Here, here!" Dill said with a chuckle, "Proof is in the usage."

He and the others exchanged amused glances. Harrison looked at FeFe and grinned.

"We have to drive to Dove Town to check out the last Halonite factory in all of Jakarda," he told her.

"Forgot to mention, I had the local police do a raid on the cave, the one you and Zara found the halonite in. Jurisdictional nightmare, no one knows whose territory it is, or what to do since it's underground. Zara's pictures proved the stuff was there, but nearly every bit of what they were doing was cleaned out. They found some traces of the halonite in the dirt and on the walls they sent on to us. Nothing left but pipes and a few hardened bins of the stuff. Followed that cave to the end. Seems you and Zara tipped them off and they moved their operation, leaving everything that was useless and no clues to follow," he said.

Harrison swore. The others groaned, exchanging frustrated looks.

"They left because the supply was gone, too," Zara said reading a printout on the desk.

Harrison walked over and rested his hand on her shoulder. He read the paper she had and made a face.

"Yeah, you translate, ok?" he said.

"I asked for the geological readings. Dill spoke to Elizabeth about them, she's in room whatever, I can't keep them all straight. The geology one. Anyway, she said that the rock and soil samples contained Arrogote and Theilan. They are a type of rock when combined, forms halonite. I learned that in the literature we got at the halonite factory, the papers you let me read at home," she said.

He nodded, "I know, I read it too, when we had marshmallows and music. So?"

"So, I think halonite is manmade, possibly an accident. That steam in the tunnels—everything is steam powered these days. Look at some of these pictures, I think they were testing something down there, maybe a weapon, and this was a byproduct they could make money on—this Global Technology—to fund their operations as these Reform Patriots. I wouldn't be at all surprised if we find they're one in the same. See, there's these other traces in the soil, gunpowder, saltpeter, sulfur and charcoal, bombs are made with that. All of that was on the rocks and cave walls in mass quantities. I think Global Technologies needed money for whatever it is they are really working on. They made halonite, and decided to dupe people into investing in it to fund their seedy operations," she said.

"Why do you think that?" Harrison asked.

"Because there was something else in my samples, something I missed when I got the results back the first time. There were traces of sawdust and nitroglycerin, the same things found in dynamite. In old caves like that, they used explosive materials to hollow them out, using controlled blasts, and then they put up the support beams we saw. I assumed that's what it was for when I took the samples, that they had just opened up the tunnels years ago, it wouldn't be unusual for the traces to linger. That cave, it runs towards the docks, we came out pretty close to the water because I took one of the hidden side tunnels. It goes straight to the water according to the maps. What if these people have something they wanted smuggled into Jakarda and that tunnel was blocked. Or, the other option is, they used them to get around to do something within the city they did not want to be seen doing and maybe the tunnels were blocked. Perhaps they needed them open to carry out this plan of theirs. That is option two for that tunnel, these are only theories, mind you. The bombings Bodie Polk mentioned, did you look into them?" Zara asked.

"Yes, I did. They were all blamed on the Reform Mechanics, like he said. In each instance, it could have been the other group he mentioned, the Robotic Patriots , they did start a year ago if what he told you is true," he said.

"So, Zara's theory that Global Technologies and the Robotic Patriots are one in the same is sound. I hate to admit it, but Mr. Polk has never been the sort to kill people. There were women and children hurt, I thought it seemed out of character for him, whole families. He's more of the, "I'll redo this bit of spy tech and tweak it, get a new patent and offer it up to the public" sort. Or he has those protests on products he feels are inferior and takes down companies that he thinks have bad tinkerers who make products to hurt the public. My fear is the halonite makers could be one of those companies he dislikes and he's made up the whole thing. Or, option two is—those people were targeted by these Patriots, but why? What's the connection?" Mr. Wills said.

"I don't know, but I believe Bodie. I know he beat the snot out of me, but, I think he did it because he thought it was the only way to get through to me. When I showed him I was reasonable, he stopped. When I called him out on his methods, he let me go. We talked calmly, and he was a gentleman. This sounds odd, but I think he feels the reputation of the Reform Mechanics is tarnished and he wants the record set straight," Zara said.

"Some reputation!" Douglas said with a roll of his eyes.

The others nodded. Harrison still had his arm around Zara. He didn't bother to move it.

He gently rubbed her shoulder, considering, "Ok. So, let's say Zara is right about one of these theories of hers, the weapon or using the caves to transport something or get somewhere, possibly to do those bombings. Why blow up those locations? Are the groups one and the same? What is the purpose of them, the link that ties them all together? How do we find out which is the right theory?"

"First things first, you and FeFe check on the last halonite place, to be sure we have the same story. We have to start with what we know first, and we know we need to do that. The rest of us will come up with another plan," Mr. Wills said.

Harrison nodded. He bent down and kissed Zara's cheek before he realized what he was doing. The others grinned at him. He flushed. God love Zara, she just smiled at him and went back to tinkering, oblivious to what he did because she was already lost in thought. He found himself grinning. He loved that about her.

He offered FeFe his arm. She took it with a smile and together, they walked to his carriage. Harrison tipped his hat to Mary who gave him a look, unhappy to see him with FeFe as they strode onto the busy sidewalk together. He opened the carriage door. FeFe sat down and crossed her legs, her fishnet stockings suited her. She looked pretty today in blue, her short but stylish dress neatly pressed as usual. She studied him as he sat down.

"I never would have guessed a mousy tinkerer covered in freckles would do it for you, Harrison. She's not at all your type," FeFe said.

Harrison laughed, "What type is that? You, I suppose? You have seen the plethora of women I dated in the office, you know my tastes are very widely suited to all sorts of ladies. As for her being mousey, she is anything but. She's beautiful and I love those freckles of hers. I think Zara Turner is perfect."

"Oh, my god. You love her!" FeFe said, her eyes wide.

Harrison smiled, "What can I say? I'm more like my parents than I thought. Love at first sight."

"She doesn't know? She's oblivious," FeFe said.

"No, she doesn't, and out of friendship, I'd appreciate it if you let me tell her," he said.

FeFe studied him, then nodded. She sighed, looking out the window, "Very well. I love you Harrison. I have for years. I don't suppose that matters to you."

He winced, "FeFe, I told you years ago, I don't feel that way about you. I'm sorry."

She smiled and shrugged as if she didn't care when he knew damn well she did, "I know. But I can't seem to tell my damn heart not to love you, no matter how badly I want to."

"Why are you leading poor Dill on? He's in love with Mary," he said.

She laughed, her dark eyes meeting his, "Dill doesn't love Mary, you idiot! You're as bad as your tinkerer when it comes to matters of the heart. He's in love with me. He told me so. Mary loves him, no doubt about that, and Dill wishes he loved her. He wants to, he's tried to. But like me, he can't seem to help himself. You see, I started out having sex with him to make you jealous, then I found I liked hearing him tell me how much he loved me when we do. He looks at me like I'm perfect and I, god help me, need it. The man worships me and looks at me like no one ever has in my life. I love it, it makes me feel so incredible. So, he and I have been carrying on an affair for over a month now, he's always been my friend. I like Dill, he's so easy to talk to, sweet and handsome in a rumpled sort of a way.

I have never met a kinder man. Since Zara showed up, he's made me happy. He confessed he's loved me for years, told me he always hoped I'd notice him. He is oddly sweet, Dill. He's wonderful, handsome, thoughtful and gentle. I know he's scattered, but I could do a lot worse than to have a man that worships the very ground I walk on who tells me he loves me."

"Yes, you could. He's a good man. I'm sorry if I hurt you," Harrison said gruffly.

She smiled then and took his hand, "You were honest with me from the beginning. That first time I seduced you three years ago in this very carriage. You told me you would gladly have sex with me, but you'd never love me. I didn't love you at the time, foolishly took it as a challenge. I wish I had never done it now. I think I might have loved Dill, if I hadn't."

"Why can't you love Dill, now? It sounds like you care for him deeply and you don't want to admit it to yourself for reasons I don't understand. Take it from me, loving someone, it just happens. Zara is not at all the sort of woman I imagined I'd love, I assumed it would be someone more like you, if it ever did happen. I think we pick the person who balances us out, FeFe. Dill might do that for you. I think you did love me once and I cared for you, but mostly you and I, we were convenient, and I think you know that. I tried to hide from Zara because I didn't want to be in love, but then I realized if I deny myself that, I'm only hurting myself. Why do that, FeFe?" Harrison asked.

She smiled, but she didn't look like she really had an answer. She looked out the window, as if she were considering his words, her brow furrowed. She seemed to realize what he said made sense. FeFe was the sort that was all about appearances, and Dill was not in the slightest. That was her main gripe about him, but if that was all, it was the wrong reason not to love the man. Harrison smiled and shook his head. Women. They talked about being better than men, but in the end, everyone could be judgmental. He was thrilled Zara was more sensible than FeFe.

•   •   •

Zara went in search of Mary. She had been agitated for an entire week, ever since Zara had returned to the nest. Today, she called in sick. Mr. Wills told Zara she never called in sick. The team was working long hours, she and Harrison were like two ships passing in the night. They were never home at the same time. They managed to steal a few kisses, but that was all. It was a shame too, because her ribs were feeling better than ever and her face looked much better. She thought about their conversations, how reading together and eating chocolate covered marshmallows made her want to have sex with him. Thinking about what lay under his fine clothes, and the touch of his hands started a burn deep inside her that rose to a strong ache and would make her actually moan aloud. She wanted him. She wanted him to be the first to give her that climax she had never managed before. She had an intuition that he could do something about that with no trouble at all—if those kisses were any indication. Zara walked up the cheaply tiled steps leading to Mary's apartment. She knocked on door five. It creeped open at her touch. Zara stalled, suddenly alert. Her heart felt as though it had leapt into her throat. Her legs felt as heavy as lead, as if they weighed too much for her to lift. She swallowed hard and pushed open the door slowly.

"Mary?" she called.

She waited, but no one answered. Zara forced her feet to move, a heavy, sick feeling settling in her tummy. She walked forward, her hands in fists. She looked around Mary's tidy apartment. It was covered in doilies, all over. Mary loved to knit doilies. She said her mother taught her. She had flower patterned furniture and an abundance of knick-knacks. Zara checked the little kitchen with its mismatched table and chairs, it was empty. She walked down the hall passing the purple bathroom. She stepped into the bright pink bedroom, also flowered and layered in doilies. It was empty. She relaxed momentarily, taking a few steps in to look around in an attempt to see if anything was missing, it all seemed in order. She wondered if Mary's door had been broken by the same people that broke into her apartment? Of course, nothing was smashed. Zara's eyes traveled over the room. She spotted something. Something red all over the floor and comforter, dots and streaks splashed all over the walls and drapes. Her heartbeat accelerated, it felt like it was coming out of her throat.

"Mary?" she whispered.

She swallowed hard and walked further in the room. She froze, her eyes wide. She noticed a pair of legs in stylish stockings, a seam up the back. Mary always joked they were her favorite because they made her feel sexy. Zara swallowed hard. She made her feet move forward. She felt like she was not really there, as if this were a dream. She looked down. Her breath came out in shallow pants. Mary's dead eyes looked up at the ceiling, there was blood at her throat where someone had silt it. God, there was so much blood! On the walls, the bedding, the curtains, but mostly, on her friend's neck and her favorite red can-can dress. Zara gasped and backed up. She had to get away from this. God! She crashed into the wall, her hand still at her chest. A loose board was knocked free on the wall. She made a move to shove it back into place, panting, her head spinning in fear. She spotted something and frowned. Distracted momentarily, as she always seemed to be, she tugged the board back and reached inside. She pulled out what was inside with a frown.

"Files?" she said.

She opened them curiously and read a few lines, her brow furrowed. Her lips parted. There was a picture of her and a list of things she had told Mary in confidence in the top one. Her abusive past, her papa's death, her lack of sexual knowledge. She had listed every single thing they ever talked about, including all of Zara's favorite foods. She was keeping tabs on her, on everything she did! Zara read it rapidly, feeling sick to her stomach. She moved onto the next one in a rush. There was one for Dill, Harrison and the rest of the team. There was one for other people, too, men Mary told her she'd had affairs with at the Crow's Nest, secrets told to her in confidence. There were over twenty in that loose board, all about the people she met at the Crow's Nest. Zara read them in a rush, scanning them. She came to Harrison's and read it, it wasn't all that thick. She felt sick when she got to the things he'd said about her. Oh, god. He felt sorry for her? She read the others, they felt the same about her, said she was odd, cold. She struggled not to cry. They came round after a month of working with her, all of them did come to like her, but they helped her out of pity and none of them liked her at all at first, they mentioned it to Mary. Worse than that was—Mary didn't like her, either. She called her strange, boring and oblivious. Zara felt sick to her stomach.

"Get a grip. You are not the bigger issue, Zara! Mary was a traitor, but to whom?" she muttered.

She needed to get out of here before someone got the wrong idea. Zara hurriedly secured the board and took the files. She took one last look at Mary, her eyes watering, and stuffed them in her bag. She took a steadying breath.

She raced to the hallway, "Help! Someone help!"

Mrs. Jankowski from across the hall came running out. Zara started to cry.

"What is it, Zara?" she said.

She looked into the woman's kind, aged face, "Mary! Someone killed Mary!"

Mrs. Jankowski's hand fluttered to her chest, "I'll send a courier bot to the police."

Zara sobbed then…because her friend was dead, and because she wondered if she had ever been her friend at all. The things she had written about Zara were told to her in confidence, and she planned to use them against her or give them to someone for god knows what purpose. She had thought she found a true friend at last…she was wrong.

Mr. Wills looked at the files, then at Zara in disbelief. He and Mary had occasionally had sex. He was a man and she was very skilled in the bedroom, particularly with oral sex. She serviced a lot of the single men like himself that were older at the Crow's Nest, who were tied to the job. It was one of the reasons his boss and friend Nathan Cross hired her. She knew that was part of her job and why she got such a high salary, but it was also up to her to choose who she wanted. He had no idea when they laid together in his bed and he told her all the cases he was working on, that she was keeping track of it all. None. She had been so eager, excited, smiling at him all cuddled up, he told her more then he should have, but he assumed she could be trusted. Mr. Wills prided himself as being a good judge of character, but now he wasn't so sure. She had manipulated him completely, using her body to gain access to what he knew. Him and any willing man that had a very high up position in the Crow's Nest. Her files on his team were large because of Dill. She had loved him, drew hearts all over his file with her name and his inside, went on and on about how handsome and kind he was, what a gentleman he was.

He looked at Zara and winced. Her file on Zara contained information Zara shared with Mary because she considered her a friend. Zara had seen it, he knew she had. At first, Mary was mocking of her lack of social skills and oddness, then Mary did grow to genuinely like her. Zara noticed, Mr. Wills knew she did, but he could see that she felt like a fool. He could see it in her expression. Zara was sitting in Room One Hundred. She hadn't spoken in hours. Harrison had her hand. She was just looking out the window. Everyone kept looking at her, even FeFe, and she wasn't the sort to feel compassion for anyone.

"Zara, you had no way of knowing what she was doing," Mr. Wills said.

Zara nodded, but didn't comment. She seemed to be struggling with something. She looked at her hand in Harrison's and pulled it free. She looked at Mr. Wills.

"Mr. Wills, I seem to have made in error in judgment in coming to Room One Hundred. We made a deal when I took this job. You said I could move to the tinkerers office if I felt I didn't like this job. I find I'm not suited for it, after all," Zara said.

Harrison looked up in shock, "Zara, honey, that's not true. Mary turned out to be a traitor, that wasn't your fault."

"I know. I'm just a hindrance for the rest of you, a poor judge of character. If I can't tell a friend from a foe, what use am I to Room One Hundred? Mr. Wills, if you cannot sent me to the tinkerer's room, I wish to resign from the Crow's Nest," she said.

He looked at the determined set of her chin and sighed, "Maybe you could give it a few more days. We need you to help finish this case. You've had a shock. You need time to think."

She shook her head, "I don't need time to think. People are worse than I imagined. I always knew, my mother...I like machines much better. They don't hurt you."

She turned, grabbed her bag and marched to the door. Mr. Wills' heart squeezed. He shut his eyes, sighing in resignation. Harrison rushed after her and took her hand.

"Zara! What about me? I'm your friend," he said.

Zara looked at him and shook her head, "No, Harrison. See, I read her file on you, too. You told her you felt sorry for me because I was so awkward. Called me an icy bitch. All the files from the people in here, even Dill's said...do any of you deny that you became my friends out of pity?"

They were silent. She nodded and looked away, her face raw with hurt. Mr. Wills had never felt like a bigger cad than he did in that moment.

"I said that before I knew you, we all did," Harrison rushed to assure her, "We did feel sorry for you because you seemed so sad, but now we just like you. Friendships take time, they're formed over weeks, months, sometimes even years. We all came to like you, I like you. Please don't go, honey. We need you here, you make a difference. I won't hurt you like Mary did, I promise."

"I'm sorry, Harrison. I just can't do this, it's hard enough for me to trust people—and then I take a chance and...I'm not suited for Room One Hundred," she said.

Mr. Wills stood, "Miss Turner, the job in the tinkerer's office is yours. However, should you wish to rejoin the team, the door is always open. Perhaps in a few weeks, you might change your mind."

Zara nodded, and walked out. He sighed.

"I like her! I said those things at first because it took me a week to have a normal conversation with her, one not about tinkering. She was so quiet and withdrawn," Dill said.

FeFe sighed and took his hand, surprising everyone, "Don't worry about it, Dill. I was the worst to her. I was intimidated because

I liked the attention all of you used to pay me. She's very sweet, and I don't do sweet. She's beautiful, too, I was cruel to her. I feel terrible. She made us a better team. I did come to like her, very much. She told me I deserved lady gadgets, told me I was an excellent agent even when I was unkind. Her inventions are marvelous, but it was more than that. She's so clever, sees things the way none of us see things, she's brilliant."

"Mary asked me what I thought of her, I said she was odd, but smart as can be and she made cool gadgets. It's in there, verbatim," Marcus said.

"She had remarkable recall," Mr. Wills said.

"Hell, yes, she did! Got around, too," Douglas said looking at the large stack of files on lovers.

Mr. Wills looked at Harrison. He was standing there, his back to them, just looking at the door.

He stood up and walked over to his nephew. He rested a hand on his shoulder. Harrison looked at Mr. Wills, his eyes awash with tears. Mr. Wills did something only an uncle would do then. He hugged him tightly.

"Come on, now!" he said, holding his nephew tightly and slapping his back, "You'll be fine!"

"I love her," Harrison mumbled thickly. "I love her and I lost her. I said horrible things about her and she knows now. I didn't mean them, I was mad that she didn't fall for me like other women and I couldn't figure her out at first, that's all. I said those things because I was frustrated she was warming to everyone but me." He tried to clear his throat. "She hates me now."

"Ballocks! She's not dead, she's hurt and she'll come around. She's been disappointed so much, poor thing. Her family life has been horrible," Mr. Wills tried to sound encouraging.

"Jesus!" Simon's voice exploded onto their consciousness, "Jesus, her mother beat her? That's why she lives on her own?"

Harrison wiped at his eyes and walked over. He ripped the file from Simon's hands, "That's none of your damn business, Simon. You don't pity her. She's perfect. She's strong and smart and kinder than anyone I ever met, despite what that woman did to her. She doesn't want anyone's god damned pity! She never feels sorry for herself! She was withdrawn because of what happened, but she's perfect as she is. She's strong and fearless. You heard what she just said, stop that damn pity."

Simon looked at his friend and nodded, "Of course. I just didn't know. Harrison, she's my friend, too. I told you, I like her. I have a crush on her, remember?"

"So do I," Marcus and Douglas said.

"I don't. I'm in love with FeFe," Dill said with a grin, "But I like Zara a lot. I consider her a friend and a twin soul of sorts, we're the same, her and I. And if her mother hurt her, it explains so much and I am ashamed of the things I said about her even more than before."

"If you love FeFe, why did you have sex with Mary?" Douglas asked.

"Because Mary let me date her and FeFe is embarrassed by my rumpled clothes and tinkering. She won't let me take her on a proper date, I hate it," Dill said.

FeFe sighed, "Oh, Dill! It's grown on me, your rumpled clothes! You know I'm shallow, you said it doesn't bother you."

He grinned at her, then planted one on her. Mr. Wills chuckled because FeFe practically melted into him. Harrison chuckled. She had never done that with him, she always fought the attraction, never gave into it. She had taken his advice and she seemed glad of it, judging from the way she was looking at Dill after.

"All right! Enough of this! For now, we have lost Miss Turner. Not forever, Harrison. We need to get her back and solve this case. To do that, we need to figure out who the hell Mary was passing this information to," he said.

"Well, we have two options as far as I can tell. The Reform Mechanics leader, Bodie Polk, or this new group, The Robotic Patriots. Impossible to know which it was she worked with, but there you go," Mr. Wills said.

"Could be a third party as well," Marcus said.

"Could be, but hard to say. My money's on those two groups," Mr. Wills said.

He glanced at Harrison. He was sitting with his arms crossed, staring at the table. He looked crushed and angry with himself. Mr. Wills sighed. Marcus rested a hand on his shoulder with a small smile. Harrison gave him a grateful smile which Marcus returned. Of all his agents, Marcus was the most stiff. He was ever the gentleman. He excelled at tracking down people, resources, following patterns and working on the cases where someone with class and manners was required. He came from a wealthy family and had the posture and manners to prove it. He and Harrison started out on a difficult foot in the Crow's Nest academy, he was a by the book fellow, Marcus, but they came to be good friends. They all had. Simon was the polished, debonair sort. Always dashing in and falling for some lady. Douglas was the scrapper, he'd get into a fight with anyone who looked at him sideways. He was the muscle. FeFe was the sex appeal, the brilliant woman who kept up with the guys, and Dill was the anchor for them all, even Mr. Wills, because he was steady, loyal. Now Zara was a part of the only real family Mr. Wills had of his own and he had no intention of losing her. She'd be back, he knew it. She just needed some time.

"Well, then. I am going to take these files, all this information to Nathan Cross, head of the Crow's Nest. In the meantime, I need all of you to get to work. Find any connections you can, try to find the link between those bombings if there is one," he said. He stood and rested a hand on Harrison's arm, "All of you."

Harrison nodded, but refrained from comment. Mr. Wills went to Room One, which was just an office like any other, it didn't move around like the rest of the nest. Nate hated that sort of thing. Nathan looked at him and sighed.

"Mary?" he said.

Mr. Wills frowned, "You knew?"

"Suspected. She was always a little too eager for pillow talk from me. Not at first, but lately. She was a little too eager for sex with me, told me I was the only one she was with, that she cared for me. She wanted to sleep over, not that I stopped her, sex all night with a beautiful woman is marvelous and I was flattered she seemed to want my attention. But, she was always asking about Zara, as if she had a hidden agenda. I suspected she was up to something," he said.

"She asked about Zara? What about her?" Mr. Will said sharply.

"About her father and what he did here, about her family. That sort of thing. I never offered her much, just said he was a friend. As I mentioned, I suspected her. I heard Mary was dead, police of Jakarda called me, knew she worked here. It was a courtesy call. I was disappointed, no one gave a blow job quite like Mary," Nate said.

Mr. Wills laughed, "She did excel at that."

"We can find another Mary, no trouble. I have a few girls in mind that would willingly leave a job on the streets for a chance to start over. Us old guys tied to the job need a willing partner in the office to service them," Nate said.

"I disagree. God knows how long Mary was at it. What she learned in these files, we cannot have a repeat like that, Nate. Cannot. Best we look elsewhere and hire someone within to do the job," Mr. Wills said.

Nate sighed, "You're right. It was just damned inconvenient, her turning out to be a double agent. She came to me with all these skills and I won't lie, mentioned what she would do with me for the job. She proceeded to show me and I hired her on the spot it was so good. Mary came in here and we screwed on my desk every day at lunch. I'll miss that."

"We did the same in Room One Hundred a few times a week, not at lunch, when I sent the team out. I will miss it, too. We can always call in a girl and do the same at home or here if need be. Someone with no ties and never the same girl more than a few times, agreed?" he said.

Nate nodded and sat back. He ran a hand over his white hair, "How did Zara take it?"

"Not well. She went to the tinkerer's room," Mr. Wills said.

He winced, "We promised Hal we wouldn't stick her in there, Gilbert."

"I know, I'm hoping it's temporary. She was going to leave! I had to offer it up to keep her here, she's a very good employee. We need her, she's a damn fine agent. Harrison's in love with her," Mr. Wills said.

Nate grinned, looking much younger than his sixty-two years, "Damned good news! Does she know?"

"No. She read in the file how he said she was odd, cold, bitchy, standoffish and a dozen other unflattering things, my nephew runs off at the mouth too often when he is frustrated. You'll see when you get to it. Like the rest of us with Mary, he shared a bit too much," he said, setting the files on Nate's desk with a sigh.

"You said they would make a match. You knew after watching them a week together. Couples do the best for us, agents and tinkerers, hardly matters. We work to the same goal. Protecting Jakarda," he said.

"Yes. I just want them to be happy, Nate," he said.

Nate smiled, his brown eyes full of understanding, "Me, too. Harrison is a good agent and we owe it to Hal. Mary told me what Amanda did to Zara. I didn't think she—"

"Me, either. Amanda was not a bad woman, she just..." he said.

"Lost Hal in more ways than one. He always loved Jessie, carried on the affair with her his entire marriage. Never should have married Amanda, or at least should have divorced her after the affair went on from the beginning. You think Amanda knew about that affair?"

"I have no idea. But if the beatings were as bad as Zara said, I think she may have," Mr. Wills said tiredly, "Read the files, Nate. I have to get back. My nephew needs me. He's heartbroken, worried Zara is lost to him for good."

"Make sure he gets her. This bachelor life seems great to the young fellows, but it's damn lonely," Nate said.

Mr. Wills nodded, "It sure as hell is."

"Try mentioning that to him. He idolizes you, Gilbert," he said.

He left on that sour note, and went to look out for his nephew, determined to see him happy.

CHAPTER SIXTEEN

Zara looked at the strangers in Room Thirty, the tinkerer's room. They were quiet, involved in their work. No one spoke to one another, unless it was to whisper. Seven men and three women, all of whom complimented her on her designs and never spoke to her in the week

that followed her exit of Room One Hundred. Zara was free to work on what she liked. She used to love to work like this, but she couldn't think of a single thing to work on. She sat on her chair and looked around the room. It was the same as the other room she had been in, except the tinkering tables were massive, one for each of them, and lined up in a row. No pastries and coffee either, no morning chit chat and laughter. Just quiet thoughts and self-driven work. She got the desk near the window. She looked out at the street below with a sigh.

It was strange this morning, not seeing Mary at the front desk. Jamie Miller had been chosen to take her place, a plump, serious girl who was all business. She was nice, Zara liked her, but she wasn't as boisterous and cheerful as Mary. She hugged Zara and apologized for her losing her friend though, that was kind of her. But she missed her friend.

Friend.

She didn't feel she had any of those after reading the files. She learned Mr. Mills had hired her in Room One Hundred because he promised her father he would look out for her. He said as much, but when he read about how badly it bothered him to see her sad, it hurt. The worst file she read was Harrison's. She hated that one the most. He thought she was odd. He was relieved she wasn't ugly, but he told Mary he didn't trust any woman who didn't know how to flirt properly and he found her boring. Boring. The file did come around in the end, he grew to like her, they all did. She thought they liked her from the beginning, it bothered her that they didn't. She thought she fit, but she was wrong. She struggled not to cry, wondering if they really did consider her a friend or not.

Before Harrison got home last week, she moved all her things from his house and went back to her apartment. She did her best to fix it up, but it was shabbier and worse than before. More lonely now that she had lived with Harrison for two and a half weeks. Her chest ached with longing for his company, she missed breakfast together the most. She wished she was with him, laughing over dinner and breakfast. Kissing him. She began to feel that burning fire deep within her. She wished she was still kissing him like he had kissed her in the carriage before work and all that following week. He kissed her all the time, hugged her, told her she was pretty. He listened to her talk, cared about what she said. She knew he meant his affection towards her, but she was unsure how to make things better, to let him in after what Mary did. That fire feeling grew to an acute ache between her thighs. She missed him so much. But she was afraid to trust now.

She had seen him a few times in the hallway. Her heart would pound. He always grinned at her, made polite conversation, told her how pretty she looked, mentioned he missed her. He looked at her tenderly, flirted shamelessly. He went out of his way to make her blush. Then he asked her to come back to Room One Hundred. She said no and rushed off. A few times she caught a look of hurt and disappointment on his face. She hated that. She didn't want to hurt him and the fact that she knew she was made it harder for her to stay away.

"Zara?" Kyle Underhill, her supervisor, said.

"Yes?" she asked, smiling at him.

"You've been looking out the window all morning, are you going to tinker?" he said.

"Oh, yes! I had an idea for ah, bats. A robot bat, with sonar, I like to visualize before I build. Is that ok?" she asked.

"That's marvelous! What a great idea, how do you plan to do it?" he said.

"You saw Dill's bird bots, you all make them here. I would like to employ some sort of sonar, I have those ocular cameras I invented. Maybe I can give them some kind of night vision. Most criminals operate at night. Maybe, make a night vision camera," she said.

He grinned excitedly. He was handsome in an understated way. Sandy colored hair, blue eyes. No muscles at all, just tall and thin, unassuming. Just the sort of man she would have gone for before she met Harrison. He cleared his throat, flushing a little.

"Excellent idea! Zara, I was wondering if I could perhaps take you out to lunch today," Kyle said.

"Oh, that's kind of you to ask. I have some errands to run, some other time?" she said.

He nodded, "Of course."

He shuffled off. He would never ask her again, and she preferred it that way. She forced herself to work on the bat. It was an idea she and Dill had tossed around in the other room and since she had only made copies of her past work this week, she was due for a fresh idea. She tinkered till lunch, then decided she simply couldn't give up on the case.

"Have to see it to the end, then I can focus on this room," she muttered.

A few of the others looked at her. She ignored them and checked the clock. The morning had gone by quickly. She left her table to get lunch, throwing her bag over her head. An idea had formed in her mind, one Harrison would be furious with her about, if he found out. She walked out of the office, her head down. She crashed into Simon, who steadied her with a chuckle.

"Zara! How are you?" he said.

"I'm fine! Sorry, I didn't see you," she said.

"Me, either. We're working long hours on the case," he said.

"Any progress?" she said.

"Not since we lost you. You had good insights. For the record, I liked you in the beginning. I did think you were odd, but not for the reasons Mary said. See, when someone I hardly know asks me questions, I don't tell them everything. Hard to know if I can trust them. I liked you, but you were standoffish, hard to get to know and I was reserving judgment. Taking my time to get to know you, just as you did with me. We are friends, Zara. Good friends. And that is why I can say to you, you have to consider coming back to Room One Hundred. We miss you, even FeFe. Poor Harrison is crushed. Chap is wild about you and very unhappy you're not there. He glares at your spot at the tinkering desk," Simon said.

"He does?" she said, her heart hammering.

Simon smiled and kissed her cheek, "Yes. Zara, have you ever told him you love him?"

She turned red and looked around, "No."

He smiled, "You might be surprised if you do."

Her heart was at it again.

She shrugged, "Maybe. I have an appointment. Nice to see you, Simon. Thanks for being so kind."

"That's how friends are. Oh! By the way, if you don't return to Room One Hundred in three weeks, Mr. Wills will be forced to re-place you. Company policy. Then you never can, unless Harrison manages to chase of another tinkerer. I have a feeling he will and the rest of us might help if it comes to that, we want you there, not some hack with less intelligence and far less talent."

Zara laughed, "I'll keep that in mind."

She hugged him tightly, then hurried out the door. Maybe she should consider going back. She loathed her time in the tinkerer's room. It was so dull and tedious. She spotted FeFe and Dill walking down the street. She waved and they returned her wave. She walked over to her motorized bike. She was surprised when FeFe walked over to her with a smile.

"I wish to apologize to you," she said.

"What for?" Zara asked.

FeFe took her hands, "For not being your friend. You see, you are beautiful, in a way that I'm not. I'm sexual and aggressive, smart. I know I'm good looking and it helps me in the field. You're the most intelligent person I ever met, and you have no idea of your beauty. I was also in love with Harrison, and the second he met you, he forgot me completely. I was jealous. I was jealous and now, I realize, I was cruel to you because of that. See, I have always liked Dill, and he liked you, too. Found you beautiful, they all did. I messed up completely with Dill and nearly lost him. I fell in love with him, can you believe that? Me and Dill!"

"Actually, I can. I think people sometimes love those who make us better versions of ourselves," Zara said.

"Like Harrison does for you?" she said gently.

Zara looked away and shrugged, "Yes, I suppose."

"He loves you, too. He hates that you're not in Room One Hundred. We all do, even me. I know we got off on the wrong foot, but, I am your friend, Zara. Maybe not the ideal female friend, I'm no good at that. But I will try to be better. I think we could both benefit from such a friendship. Come back to Room One Hundred, please. We miss you," FeFe said with a smile.

Zara smiled and hugged her tightly. FeFe made an annoyed nose that made Zara laugh. She pulled back and studied her, "I get a discount at my mother's shop. Thirty percent off. If you would like, we could go shopping sometime. I'm a deplorable shopper, maybe you can help me. I hate having to let my mother help me. My clothes are free for life, but my friends can use my discount."

FeFe smiled brightly, "I'd love to!"

Zara nodded and looked at the ground, "Should I really come back to Room One Hundred? I…do you all pity me?"

She looked at FeFe, her eyes awash with tears. FeFe seemed taken aback. She took Zara's hand.

"No one pities you. We quite admire you. I admire you," she said, her gaze level.

Zara nodded, "I'll consider it, then. It's very dull in the tinkerer's room and there are no pastries in the morning."

"Sounds dreary," she giggled.

Zara laughed, "It actually is."

FeFe chuckled and left with a wave. Zara got on her bike, more determined than ever to help her old friends. She rode her motorized bicycle to the street she grew up on. She looked at her mother's old house and shivered. It was a beautiful two story white home with a copper roof and shutters. It looked like a picture with its red flowers and porch swing. She remembered as if it were two places. The first was good, when her papa lived. The second, a hell which she thought she might never escape. She stopped in front of the blue house next door and walked determinedly to the front. She knocked.

Mrs. Gaskill, an older and more plump version then Zara remembered, answered the door.

"Hello, Mrs. Gaskill. How are you?" Zara said with a smile.

"Well! Zara Turner, look at you! I'm fine, just fine! Surprised to see you!" she said.

She proceeded to ask Zara where she was now, how was work, what she was doing. Zara endured the polite conversation for as long as she can and then, cut Mrs. Gaskill short.

"I was actually looking for Mike. Can you tell me where he lives?" she said.

Mrs. Gaskill sent her a knowing look, "You two always did fancy one another! He got an apartment in the city. He lives at Seventh and Front Street, apartment sixteen."

Zara smiled, "Thank you! I plan to pay him a visit. It was lovely to see you!"

"You, too!" she said.

She waved and got back on her bicycle. She started the engine, and zipped back into the city to find Mike and the answers she hoped to get about Mary's murder. She parked her bike outside of a swanky city apartment building, much nicer than the one she lived in. She nodded to the doorman, and went inside. She took the functioning elevator upstairs to apartment sixteen and knocked on the door.

Mike opened it with a grin, his hair standing on end, shirtless. His smile fell, eyes widened.

"Zara?" he said.

She smiled, and spotted a young woman with brown hair and blue eyes. She had on his shirt and nothing else. They seemed to be having some fun. Zara flushed a little. He looked at the girl in alarm.

"Relax. I was just hoping you could arrange a meeting with the gentleman you introduced me to. I have some questions," she said.

"Ah, yes. Yes, I can do that. When?" he asked.

"Today. Send a Courier Bot to the Crow's Nest, and I'll meet him wherever he wishes," Zara said.

"Certainly. Could you, ah, not mention you saw me here with her?" he said.

Zara glanced at the young woman who looked an awful lot like Bodie Polk, now that she noticed. She smiled slowly and sent him a knowing look. He looked panicked then.

"As long as you do as I wish," she said.

He smiled in relief, "How did you know where I lived?"

"I asked your mother. She thinks I fancy you."

"But, you don't?" he asked sadly.

"No. No, I do not, nor would I ever. Not after what you did. Nice apartment," she said.

He smiled a little, "Thanks."

She nodded and walked off. He was playing a dangerous game, sleeping with Bodie's daughter like that. Mike needed to be careful. Zara went back to the Crow's Nest. She spotted Harrison in the hallway and offered him a smile. He grinned back and walked over to her.

"Hi, Zara," he said.

Her heart hammered, "Hi. You…look handsome today."

He gave her a slow smile, "Why, thank you. I should wear red more often, especially if it means you'll smile at me and speak to me. You've ignored me all week, except when I trapped you a few times. I miss you."

"I miss you, too. Miss Room One Hundred, as well."

He studied her, "Thinking of returning?"

She considered, her eyes hungrily searching his face, "Do you really miss me?"

He smiled slowly and took a step closer to her, "Every damn day."

She grinned then, "I miss you, too."

She put her hand on his cheek and kissed him softly. He froze, his eyes boring into hers.

"I have to get back to tinkering. Enjoy the rest of your day, Mr. Lowell," she said and turned to walk away.

"Wait!— Will you have dinner with me?" he said.

"I can't tonight. I have something to attend to," she said, stopping.

"A date?" he asked.

"No, plans with a friend; although I don't know what time yet, or else I would have liked to have dinner with you," she smiled at him.

He looked relieved.

She raised an eyebrow, "I'll see you later?"

"Yes. Yes, you will," he affirmed.

And then he took two strides across the floor to her, held her face between his hands and kissed her right there in the hallway. She melted against him. His hands moved down her neck, one resting above her left breast and the other slowly tracking down her spine. She kissed him eagerly, her tongue seeking his, tangling itself with his. Zara never wanted it to stop.

"Zara, you're late!" Kyle snapped.

She pulled back, taking in air, and grinned at Harrison, "I'm... late, evidently."

He chuckled and rubbed his thumb along the small of her back, "I heard," his voice was gruff, "It was good to see you."

She laughed softly, "You, too. I do love it when you wear red, Mr. Lowell."

"I noticed, Miss Turner."

They looked at one another for a while, then she stepped back. She turned with a wave, grinning at him over her shoulder and walked into the tinkerer's room. He stood rooted in the hallway, watching her hips sway as she walked through the door until it closed behind her. Zara moved across the room and sat at her desk. She started to work on the bat bot, a big smile on her face.

One hour later, she got the message by courier bot. It flew in the open window. She opened the container and read the slip of paper. She was to meet Bodie in one hour at the Tinker-Time Cafe. It was a struggle to focus on the rest of her job at that point, but she managed to finish the work. She feigned illness and left early, then hurried out to her motorized bike. She rode across town to the cafe, and went inside. She waited for fifteen minutes. She was going to leave, sure he wouldn't show, when Bodie walked in. He was dressed in a three piece suit with a top hat on. He looked so different, so like everyone else, that she hardly recognized him. He had a file in his hands. He smiled at her.

"Zara! Lovely to hear from you. I hadn't expected you to contact me again," he said.

"Well, sometimes we must keep our enemies close, Bodie," she said.

He grinned, "Yes, we must. I have something for you, anyway. I planned to meet with you."

They ordered coffee and a doughnut, smiling at one another. Zara liked him in spite of herself.

"Let's discuss what I wish to know first," she said.

"Mary? Yes, she was working for me. That's how I kept tabs on you, on everyone there. She was very good, gathered a lot of data. You see, she was excellent in the bedroom with men. I used to have her and one other girl come on the dirigible when we were in the air for long periods of time. I had my wife, but some of the gents were interested. They would fly with us for two or three days, then we dropped them off. She fell in love with my son, just as she did with Dill, from your office, and I promised her a chance to be with him if she proved she could spy. His attention moved elsewhere, so did hers, and I was left with an asset at the Crow's Nest," he said, adding cream and sugar to his coffee.

"Did you kill her?" she said.

"No, I did not. I am no killer, I keep telling you. Eventually you might believe me. I think Mary got involved with the Robotic Patriots, too. You see, their leader is a woman and she has, ah, particular tastes," he said.

Zara nodded, "She prefers women, then? I went to school with a woman like that, she asked my friend Sara out. Sara liked the gents, like me, and politely declined, there were a few men who liked men, too, I understand. But, Mary liked men."

"Mary liked information and being in dangerous situations more. That's why she loved passing on information to me. She also fell in love easily, with both men and women. Whoever was sweet to her, took her on dates and such. If I had to guess, that women who runs the Robotic Patriots found out what Mary was up to and killed her. I hear rumors, Zara, and she was not the sort of woman to be trifled with," Bodie said.

Zara made a face, "I'm sorry to hear that. Did she like me at all, Mary?"

Bodie's expression softened, "Yes, she came to. At first, she said you were odd. But, she mentioned more than once, she liked teaching you how to be thrifty, about men and flirting, about people in general. She said she admired you because the two of you had a difficult past in common. She came to think of you as a friend. In truth, the reason I roughed you up a little was to remind her to stay in line. It worked, she came forward with all sorts of information. However, I'm not at all certain she didn't do the same with her lady friend at the Robotic Patriots."

Zara nodded, "I thought as much."

He grinned, "You are clever."

Zara laughed and took a bite of her doughnut, sipping her coffee, "Can you tell me what my papa was like as a child?"

He smiled then, "He and I were tinkerers. We built bikes, wagons that moved on their own, flying contraptions. We crashed and caught things on fire often, too. Hal was fun, fearless, but loyal. He and I were the best of friends. I know you have no need to know, but he died saving me, my wife and my youngest daughter, not to mention the rest of my crew. You see, one of the Crow's Nest agents had put a bomb on the dirigible we lived on and Hal couldn't bring himself to kill innocent people. He thought he could stop the bomb, and he did, but he had to die to do it. Hardest day of my life. So that is why I am going to pass on this information to you now," he held up the file. "Because I loved your papa, owed him a great deal. This is only part of what I can give back. Should you need another favor, call me. Only one more, mind you. Then the favors will have to be give and take, since I lost my mole in your organization."

Zara took a deep breath, "I'll consider that last bit."

He chuckled and sipped his coffee, "Ok. I have news and it is shocking. I don't know exactly where to begin, so I'll do my best. Your father loved a woman his whole life and it was not your mother. He cared for Amanda a great deal. Amanda loved him so much. So much, that your fool of a papa thought if he married her, she might be enough. For a time she was. They had your sisters, and they appeared to be happy. He loved his girls, we often talked about it—being parents. I have a son and three daughters. He liked being a father, too. When his third daughter, you, came along, he was far more excited than the other times. I had never seen him so elated, he was beaming. Mary and Mike told me about how your mother was unkind to you."

"I remember," Zara said, glaring at him.

"I did apologize, it will not happen again. I had to test you and send a message to Mary, she was wavering and her information was detrimental to me as you can imagine. At any rate, when I met you, you reminded me of your father so much and of my second daughter, she's the same age as you. You have his spirit and his courage, you even look like him. Oddly, you look nothing at all like Amanda. It got me thinking. So I traced your birth records. Zara, Amanda was not your mother. Your mother's name was Jessica Ventura. Your father had an affair with her. She was a tinkerer, like him. They met in secondary school, dated for years. Jesse was the unconventional type, never wanted to marry. Hal hated it, wanted the white picket fence. He was hurt when she turned down his proposal. So desperate to get what he wanted, he married Amanda. He told me he couldn't end it with Jessie—was having an affair with her. I spoke to her parents, they are still alive. I knew that he planned to leave Amanda, to divorce her to be with you and Jessie. They planned to marry someday, her finally realizing she loved him and didn't want to lose him or have an illegitimate child. But Jessie died giving birth to you, some kind of complication," he said.

Zara's heart was going so fast. She blinked at him in shock, struggling not to cry. He reached over and took her hands, his eyes glassy. Zara just stared at him for a time, trying to figure out what she was supposed to say. Her mother was not her mother?

"Is that why my mama hates me?"

Bodie swallowed hard, holding her hands like a vice, "I believe so. I spoke to the Ventura family, your mother's family, they want to know you. I guess, and this is what I could piece together, your papa admitted to your mother, Amanda, that he had a third daughter and an affair. He begged her to help him raise you, told her he loved her, made a mistake—even though I believe that was a lie—and he wanted a mother for you. Amanda must have loved him so much, she agreed to it. I don't know more than that, but I do know, the Ventura's wanted to see you from the beginning. They truly did and still do. Jessie was their only daughter. Everything I have about them, where they live, who they are is in this file I gathered for you. They tried to contact you a number of times, but in your father's will, he made your mother keep your lineage a secret. I'm sure he thought you'd be protected, loved by Amanda, otherwise he would have never kept you from them. I know it. There is a copy of the will in the file, too. I want you to take it all."

Zara took a deep breath and nodded. She held his hand tightly, "She was so cruel and vicious to me. The things she said and did. I wasn't beaten daily, just every few weeks or so when I got her good and mad. I tried to stay out of the way, most of the time it worked. It makes sense now, how she used to look at me as if she hated me. Especially as I got older. I was a day to day reminder that he loved someone else, that he was unfaithful and she was stuck with me because of his indiscretion and his death."

Bodie winced, "I am sorry."

Zara shrugged pretending it didn't matter, "Thank you for telling me. I'll let that information process and go from there."

Bodie smiled and studied her, finishing his doughnut, "What do you plan to do?"

"I have no idea," she said.

He chuckled and sipped his coffee then stood. He smiled at her, "Two more favors, one for each life he saved."

Zara nodded, "Bodie, I think my papa was right. You are a good man, even if your methods are deplorable. This was a kind thing for you to do for me, a good one. Thank you."

He chuckled, tipping his hat. Then left. Zara laughed when a dozen men and women followed after him. Of course! He was late to be sure she was alone. Zara shook her head and finished her food, then paid the tab. She sat there a moment, looking out at the Tinker's Academy. The campus used to be her favorite place, her home. Now, she realized, home was Room One Hundred and anywhere Harrison was. She was not going to make the same mistake her papa made. She would be with him, no matter how he wanted her or for how long. She loved him, and it was time she told him.

Zara stood with a happy smile and walked out to her bicycle, stuffing the folder in her bag. She stilled. Folders! Of course!

She hurriedly put on her goggles and started the motor. She zipped through the streets of Jakarda City and went straight to Mary's apartment. She knocked on her neighbor, Mrs. Jankowski's door.

"Zara! I'm so glad to see you came to get some of her things, I took some and passed them out to the others on the floor, but, the rest goes to the auction tomorrow, her having no family and all," Mrs. Jankowski said.

"What a shame! I'll see if there's anything I might want," Zara said.

Mrs. Jankowski nodded and unlocked the door for Zara. Heart pounding, Zara looked sadly around the room.

"Do you think I might be alone for a while?" Zara asked.

Mrs. Jankowski nodded sympathetically and left. Shutting the door behind her. Zara raced to the bedroom. Mary liked to keep records so she had to have some files on the Reform Patriots, on that woman she had the affair with. She could have been the one in the fancy dress at the party. If Mary had pictures of all of them in her files—! She might have a photo of that woman. Zara opened her drawers and looked everywhere, careful not to leave a mess, just in case. She reached under the mattress and froze. A journal! She gingerly pulled it from under the mattress and grinned. Sitting on the edge of the bed, she read some, but had to stop after ten minutes, it was so full of sexual encounters.

"Oh, my!" she said, stuffing it in her bag, her face red.

She went to the wall and searched the loose boards. She found another stack of files in the wall beside it and took those. She checked everywhere else, but found nothing. For the purpose of Mrs. Jankowski, and because she really did love her friend, she picked a few doilies, a potted plant and a picture of her and Mary. She looked at it for a while, then walked out, showing the neighbor her finds. She should have looked more closely. If she had, she might have seen two small Spy-ders fold up their webs and trot off. Those Spy-ders were not headed to the Crow's Nest, and they had just seen that Zara had found some things she should not have.

Harrison looked up to see Zara stride into the Crow's Nest, Room One Hundred. His face lit up. She looked damn beautiful in a little black dress with more of those thigh high stockings, these ones sheer and black to match her dress. Her hair was down, windswept and she had on red lipstick. That was a fantastic look for her.

"Zara! What are you doing here?" Mr. Wills said.

"I've returned to Room One Hundred, if you'll have me. I loathe the tinkerer's room, it's dull and there are no pastries," she said. They grinned at her and she smiled back, "I'm sorry I left you all in a lurch. But, the good news is, I have made progress on the case."

Harrison had been grinning, but his smile fell when he heard that, "What?"

"I contacted Mike and met with Bodie an hour or so ago," she said.

"That was who your plans were with?" Harrison snapped.

"Yes! He was quite helpful in more ways than one. Mary was working for him. She passed him information because she had a liaison with his son years ago when she was a lady of the night. She and a friend of hers used to come on the reform Mechanic's dirigible and then they would provide a service for the gents or the ladies, Mary liked both. Mary fell in love with Bodie's son. He told her, that if she got a government job and traded information, she could be with his son. They eventually lost interest in one another, but Mary liked the spy business more than any of us realized. That's how she got the files," she said, sitting at the table.

Harrison sat next to her, his brow furrowed, "Did he kill her?"

"No, he said he didn't and I'm inclined to believe him. This is where it gets a bit sticky. She somehow made friends with the woman in charge of the Reform Patriots. Bodie didn't know much about her, just that she sexually preferred women and Mary didn't mind that, ah, preference, so she provided that, ah, service, for whoever this woman is. It got me to thinking, what if the only folders Mary kept were not about us!" Zara said.

Harrison smiled slowly, "That's clever, honey."

She smiled and kissed him then reached in her bag, Harrison smiled a little because he was normally the one kissing her.

"I found these at Mary's apartment! I had Mrs. Jankowski let me in. I had to take some other things to cover. I know I'll kill this plant. Maybe we can keep it here in Room One Hundred so someone else can keep it alive?" she said.

Harrison laughed and kissed her cheek, "Sure, honey. You're rambling. What else did you find?"

"Oh, right! Sidetracked, sorry! I found her journal. It's, ah, graphic. Sexually graphic, I glanced at it briefly then, well, I was shocked and I'm a lady, so I closed it," Zara said, her face red.

Harrison grinned, "I'll read it."

She laughed and shook her head, "I found these, too. Oh! This one is personal, not from her place. These others though—look!"

She opened the folder with a smile.

Harrison blinked, "Simon, is that the woman we interviewed at the halonite plant? Miss Walkerwall?"

"At the plant? Harrison, we met her at the ball! She was the one we spoke to about halonite, she knew a great deal about it. I asked her all those questions and you kissed my cheek so I'd shut up," Zara said.

Harrison sat back and sighed, "Oh, my god. Simon, she recognized me. She knew who I was, that's why she spilled her guts to us, to throw us off. She said a dark haired woman with blue eyes came to them, she was talking about herself. She's the only link. She's the head of Global Technologies. She made up that whole story to hide the fact that she was the one in charge, and her brother, if that is indeed who he is, went along with it. I bet if we check that warehouse, it's empty."

"It's been shut down for two days at least. I pass it every day on the way to work. I assumed it was closed because halonite is a garbage product."

"But, what is the purpose of all this?" Marcus said in confusion.

"Let's read the files and find out! Is there pastry?" Zara said.

Harrison laughed and kissed her. She kissed him back eagerly. His heart hammered hard.

"Do stop it! We have work to do," FeFe said.

Zara laughed and kissed him a final time, "Someone else read that journal. I'm not sure I want to know the rest of the things in there."

All the men reached for it, even Dill. FeFe and Zara rolled their eyes.

Mr. Wills snatched it up, "I will read it, the rest of you choose a file and do try and be professional."

They grumbled and took a file. Harrison put his arm around Zara and sat back. She leaned against him and read the file on Miss Walkerwall, he had the one on her brother. He scanned the paper.

"Listen to this, the Walkerwall's at one point were wealthy. They invested badly in gorumite, collecting it from the tunnel he and Zara uncovered. Their father thought it was a good product, but it didn't turn out to be. The Reform Mechanics exposed that product as shoddy and unreliable. The shock of losing all their money, their social standing and their home, left them with nothing. Furious, the Walkerwall's decided to use that stuff, package it differently, in a solid form and give it a new name, halonite. They found the Reform Mechanics and their families, and tricked them into investing in the product, buying all their supplies. They wanted to discredit the Mechanics for exposing them, so they mimicked their outfits and made bigger, worse crimes to tarnish their reputation," Harrison said.

"Her file on Miss Walkerwall says basically the same, except she mentions they are not happy with the government, either. Mary was her lover, that's discussed a lot. Funny, Mary was approached by her because she somehow found out Mary was an informant for The Reform Mechanics. What started out as blackmail to get information turned into sex after about a month or so," Zara said.

"Yes, well, Mary was very skilled at seduction, more so than I realized after reading this smut! She liked a large variety of sexual endeavors," Mr. Wills said, mopping his brow.

Harrison burst out laughing, "Your face is red, Mr. Wills."

"Yours would be too if you saw what was in these pages! She does mention all her lovers in here. She talks about a man, Mr. S, formerly of the Reform Mechanics, he seems to be a key player as well," Mr. Wills said.

"I have his file! Hubert Shrinkle, tinkerer who shunned government work and disappeared years ago, hated the mechanics, didn't trust the government. You recognize him?" Marcus asked, holding up a photo.

"Harrison! That's the man who chucked you out of the window! The massive fellow with two different colored eyes who pummelled you!" Zara said.

"Yes, it is. Wouldn't forget him," he said.

"So we have the key players here," Douglas said. He took all the pictures and set them on the table, "I got this gent, Larry Conroy. He's a mastermind, the one who does the deals for Global Technologies. He takes all the calls, arranges the sales and does the marketing. A former agent of the Reform Mechanics, also shunned by the organization because he's a violent bloke and out to get revenge. Must have been really bad for the mechanics to chuck him out. They really angered a lot of people."

"Yes, they did, Harry Jacoby, too. He was a former reform Mechanic," Simon said, indicating a tall, thick man in a top hat.

"Bruce McMillan was one, too. He left the mechanics because he fell for Bodie's youngest daughter, had sex with her, and was kicked out when Bodie found out," FeFe said.

"His youngest daughter really gets around," Zara muttered. Harrison rubbed her back and sent her a curious look. "Never mind. There are others in this group calling themselves the Patriots, there has to be. Mary must have just started her files on them. But, why?"

"She wanted to work in Room One Hundred with her best friend, Zara, and the man she loved, Dill." The room went silent and everyone turned to look at Mr. Wills. He looked up at them and shrugged, "She says so here in the last entry, listen; Zara is my friend. I don't know how it came to be that a fine lady like her befriended a former street walker, but she sure as hell did. I never expected to go and like her so much, but she's such a good, kind person, it's hard not to. She's not as odd as I thought, as we all thought. She's just not been around people much and her mother's abuse and cruelty made her feel as if she were different than other people, when she isn't all that different at all. I hate lying to her, and to my Dill, most of all. I'm playing so many sides these days, I don't even know who I am anymore. All I know, is that I want to be on a good side for once, to be a decent person like Zara. I hate working for the mechanics and even more, I hate working for the Patriots. I never believed in their cause, either of them. I only got involved with Jemma because I noticed how she liked my body. She frightened me with her ruthlessness and better to keep a sick, twisted person like her in your good graces. Being in the business, I know when a man or woman fancies me. She's a skilled lover, I didn't mind servicing her at first, she always returns the favor and she's tender, sweet in the bedroom. Trouble is, I never did fancy the ladies like I do the gents and every time I look at my friends at the Crow's Nest, I feel sick inside. Especially when I see Zara. She's the first real friend I ever had, and if she finds out, I might not have that no more. I can't let that happen. I plan to go to Mr. Wills tomorrow, confess all I know and give him the files on everyone, even if it costs me my life in the end. Zara told me the path to doing what's right is never an easy one, but you do it because otherwise you come to hate yourself. She's right, too. I do hate myself, but I won't after this," he closed the book.

Harrison looked at Zara. She looked stunned, her big blue eyes wide. He kissed her head. She frowned.

"When was that dated?" she asked.

"The day before she died," Mr. Wills said.

"So that entry killed her," Zara said sadly.

Harrison stilled because Zara had no idea what she had just said, "Zara, when you went back to her apartment, did you see anything unusual?"

"No, why?" she said.

"If someone read that, and killed Mary for it, why was it there for you to find?" Harrison asked.

Zara's eyes widened, as if she realized what she said, "Oh, shit! So you think they were trying to find the files and left the diary for me to find?"

"Yes, I sure as hell do," he said.

Zara smacked herself in the forehead, "Like a dummy, I go and do just that!"

"Don't panic. We don't know that for sure," Mr. Wills said.

They looked around at one another. There was an odd noise, a creaking sound. Harrison looked towards the door. There was a boom, then the building shook. The room started to drop then. He was flung to the ceiling, Zara beside him. She screamed. Harrison took her hand. They were all on the roof of Room One Hundred, and falling fast. The tables and desks were bolted down, but the lamps and the chairs and everything on the desks were not. They crashed into the ceiling. Zara covered her head and screamed.

"We have to stop the room from falling!" Zara said.

"I can do it!" Dill said.

He crawled across the ceiling and made his way down the wall. He punched something in the key pad. They slammed to a halt. Harrison landed on top of the round table, Zara and Mr. Wills beside him. He grunted and gasped for air. Zara whimpered.

"Honey, you ok?" he said.

A stapler hit her in the arm, "Ouch! Yes, I'm ok. Are you?"

"Yes. Mr. Wills? Simon, FeFe, Marcus, Douglas?" he said.

They all muttered they were fine and got to their feet. They were banged up, covered in cuts and bruises.

"What happened?" Zara asked.

Harrison wiped at a cut on her cheek and kissed her. FeFe rushed over to Dill, whose head was badly cut and fussed over him, her expression worried.

"Someone blew up the Crow's Nest," Mr. Wills said, looking out the window. Harrison stalked over and looked out. He swore. All the other people in the rooms that managed to keep from falling were peeking out the windows to see what had happened. The building was on fire, at least the lower levels.

"What about the rooms? Did they all fall?" Zara asked.

"That's what the button I hit does. Stops the rooms from falling. We would have heard a bang if one's fell, the lowest ones may have before they hit the buttons, but it is a failsafe. We do need to get out of here. There is no way to get out of Room One Hundred, now. I'm guessing the Patriots had something to do with this. We're close to the top today, best go up," Dill said.

"How do we do that?" Zara asked nervously.

Harrison grinned, "You can do it. There's a hatch."

Zara groaned, "I don't much like heights, my love."

Harrison stopped, "Your love?"

She smiled and nodded, her face and neck very red.

Harrison grinned, "I like that. Come on, honey."

He took her hand. Dill opened the wooden hatch on the ceiling. There were people scaling the walls all over. Inside the massive inner workings of the Crow's Nest, each room moved on four tracks at the bottom, rather like the tracks the home robots moved on, but on a larger scale. There were one hundred rooms at the Nest, always ever changing position. When they reached the safest spot, they stilled. Zara was looking around with this excited look on her face at the steel, copper, silver and gold creation before her eyes. The space was massive, clever, and the best bit of tinkering she had ever seen, no doubt about that.

"My love, focus on climbing. I don't want you to fall," Harrison said.

She beamed at him, sending his heart hammering. They gazed at one another 'til Marcus nudged him with a warm smile. Zara climbed the ladder against the wall, they all did. It was a treacherous climb. Some of the rooms were broken, sparking and Harrison definitely smelled fire and smoke.

"What about the people that can't go up?" Zara asked.

"Some can go down, you have two choices. There are grappling hooks to ride to the nearest buildings, too, safety protocol. See the scaffolding against the back wall, there are two fire exits at the rear," Dill said.

"Grappling hooks? I'm quite glad I didn't have to do that," Zara said.

He chuckled. They climbed for a long time. It took forever to get to the roof. He heard the fire brigade. They piled onto one of the dirigibles with all the others, waiting until they didn't see any more people, then they flew off on the two dirigibles. Harrison looked down at the burning Crow's Nest, angry someone had the nerve to do this. Zara took his hand.

"Harrison, all that information I got is gone, now!" Zara said.

"Not all of it," Mr. Wills said, holding up the diary, "I managed to take this and we know what they look like. Room One Hundred is safe and intact as long as they put out that fire and we can get back to it eventually."

"But, was this my fault?" Zara asked.

"No, honey. This is the Patriot's fault and we are going to stop them now that we know who's behind all of this," he said.

Zara nodded. Douglas was getting his foot bandaged by Dr. West. Yvette was patching up some of the others. Harrison sat on the deck with Zara, one arm held her tightly, the other—her hand. He couldn't stop kissing her head.

"How do we do this with no base of operations?" Zara said.

"We'll manage, Zara. We'll manage," Harrison said.

CHAPTER SEVENTEEN

Zara rubbed her eyes tiredly. She and the others were in the temporary headquarters of the Crow's Nest, the current one having been blown up, but just a little. It had been cleverly reinforced in case that happened and the main lobby and back section full of the larger gadgets the tinkers worked on got the brunt of the blast. Thanks to the magnificent tinkerers, the structure had not crumbled to the ground, it was just full of holes and none of the rooms could come down because the mechanical system had been utterly destroyed, all the rooms were now stuck in limbo. Of the two hundred employees, eighteen were killed, including the new desk receptionist at the front, Jeannine Kyle from the Tinkerer's room and Elizabeth from the geological department. It was a crushing and terrible blow for Jakarda City and its government protection facility.

Four men were seen running with two boxes to the front of the building. They set them down and within moments, there was a series of explosions. They knew exactly where to set the bombs, near the controls hidden in the walls that moved the rooms about. It was obviously their hope that all the rooms would fall and everyone would be killed. They didn't realize there were safety protocols and the agents had been trained on what to do. Their attempt at taking down the Jakardian government had failed, but their attempt had ensued a great deal of chaos. Zara had an idea as how to stop that from ever happening again, she and Dill discussed it. For the time being, all agents were hidden in a plain building across town. It was an abandoned office complex, surrounded by the local Jakarda Police to keep the Government Protection Agency from falling completely. They had been there twenty-four hours, answering questions and telling everyone what they knew. The fact that a new evil, the Robotic Patriots, had formed less than a year ago, infiltrated the Nest via a spy, one of their own no less, blew it up, and no one noticed had them all rattled. There was talk of a more complex system to interview and hire, a review of current employees was going to be done and, more safety protocols were in the works.

Zara looked out the window, hugging her arms tightly to her chest. It was a mess, all of this. She couldn't help but feel she was somehow to blame, that there was something she had missed all this time. She couldn't fathom what it could be, but she felt it in her bones.

"Zara?" Harrison said, jolting her from her thoughts.

She smiled at him, "Yes?"

"We can go home for a while, we have to be back in a few hours," Harrison said.

"Ok," she said, grabbing her bag, the only thing she managed to get from Room One Hundred.

Harrison cleared his throat, "Will you stay with me?"

She reddened and nodded. He grinned and took her hand. They rode in a handsome carriage to his house, looking at one another and smiling the whole way. She felt that longing for Harrison, that pull she always felt towards him. She wanted to touch him, imagined it, but her inexperience made her hesitate, let him take the lead. They reached his front door in seconds, Harrison leading her by the hand in a rush. He locked the door and kissed her. She dropped her bag to the floor and arched her back kissing him, eager, losing herself in that kiss as she always seemed to do with him. Hardly realizing what she did, he deftly unbuttoned her blouse, and unzipped her skirt. She hooked her thumbs through Harrison's belt loops and let him run his hands down her warm flesh and push her undergarments below her knees. She kissed him back eagerly her tongue probing his. They disrobed in a rush, then tumbled to the rug. Harrison kissed her face, her lips, her neck. She did the same to him, her hands in his hair. He ran his hand down her body, caressing her until she was ready for him. Zara was half out of her head. He moved between her legs, his body rippling with muscle as he started to move. She gasped in pleasure, shocked at the feeling he was causing her. His eyes locked with hers. They moved together in perfect sync, in a rhythm Zara never had with another man. She felt the pressure building, swirling inside her, then something happened to Zara that never happened before, she felt an aching need for something, some release. Her body responded, moved more quickly, kissing him frantically, then she cried out with the explosion within her, She called out in sounds she didn't know she could make and arched her back. Harrison swore, his body jerking, his lips seeking out hers. She dug her nails into his backside, pulling him in deeper. He swore again. The last waves of pleasure seemed to ebb away as they finally found that release they both wanted.

Harrison slowed, breathing hard into her neck. She reached up, took hold of the back of his hair, a feeling of contentment, of perfection making her smile.

"Oh. That's what that feels like," she said.

Harrison snorted with laughter, "Pretty good, huh?" He pushed up from her and rolled to one side.

"No wonder Mary went on and on about that!" she said with a grin.

He laughed delightedly and kissed her, "Sorry we had sex in the foyer by my front door. I wanted to take you to the bed, but I couldn't wait."

"I won't complain about that after experiencing my first orgasm. I lost my head completely and I loved it. Can we do it again?" Zara asked.

Harrison grinned, "Yes."

He stood and picked her up, wrapping her legs around his waist, his hands holding her backside. He grinned at her and teased her with his erection.

"Wow, that was fast," Zara said.

"It's been awhile since I had great sex and I have spent two months imagining you naked. It's so much better than I thought," he said carrying her up the steps.

She kissed him and wiggled forward so he was back inside her, then she moved against him slowly. He grinned his eyes dark with desire.

"I imagined it, too, but this is even better than I imagined."

"That was nothing. I got more where that came from," he said.

She giggled and he proceeded to show her just how much more. He was right. She had no idea sex could be so good. Hours later, Zara was lying naked, half on top of Harrison in his bed. She was groggy, her eyes heavy. He was kissing her head softly, his hand rubbing her back under the warm blankets.

"Zara?" he said.

"Hum?"

"I love you," he said.

She looked at him, her eyes meeting his, "I love you."

He smiled and kissed her tenderly. He pushed her onto her back. They kissed sweetly. He moved between her legs and pushed himself inside her gently. He moved slowly together, their bodies intertwined. She felt that now familiar building sensation. She looked into his eyes and kissed him, her hand at his face. She cried out in pleasure, he followed suit. They looked at one another kissing each other softly, holding each other tightly. Zara had never felt so loved before. She looked at him, her face full of wonder.

"That was perfect," she said.

Harrison smiled and stroked her hair, "We made love. I've never done it before."

Zara smiled, "Me, neither."

Harrison kissed her. She snuggled up beside him and fell asleep. In the morning hours, they made love again, then dressed for work. Zara had forgotten a few outfits from when she stayed here, so she pulled one on after sex in the shower, which was incredible, and braided her hair. She got into Harrison's carriage with him. She was going to ask him what they were going to do today, when he reached for her breast and demonstrated to her how to have make love in a moving carriage. She liked that. Twice. She buttoned up, her cheeks pink.

Harrison laughed, "I love it when you blush. It's so cute."

"Well, all my good sense goes out the window with you. My brain actually stops when you kiss me. All I think about is you. These curtains hardly cover anything, I was astride you, someone could have seen!" Zara said.

Harrison laughed and kissed her, tucking in his shirt, "I like that I have that effect on you, you do it to me, too. Honey, you'd be surprised how many people do what we just did in a carriage."

"Not after I read part of Mary's diary, I wouldn't! Last night, I read a bit, it's scandalous!" she said.

"I know! I read some, too, we all did. She had, ah, unusual tastes," he said.

Zara nodded in agreement, but did not elaborate. Zara walked inside the temporary Crow's Nest, her hand in Harrison's. He glanced at her.

"I realize this is sort of fast, considering we just, you know, but, if we got married, would you want me to leave the Crow's Nest?" he said.

She studied him, her heart going fast, "Married? You would want me forever?"

He stopped and pulled her close, his eyes on her face, "Of course. I love you."

"Oh! I didn't know if this was temporary or we would be unmarried and live together or something," she said.

"I cannot live with you and be unmarried, my mother and father will kill me. Besides, they stopped by the other morning because I told my sister Joanne at lunch when she met me, I was in love with you. She blabbed to my whole family, so my parents came over to meet you. My father was concerned I would, ah, are you on birth control?" he said.

"Of course. I have been since I was sixteen. I wasn't that first time, I, ah, with Mike. There was a scare, once will do me!" she said.

"Do you want children?" Harrison asked.

"I never considered it. Possibly, if they were with you. I wouldn't be a very good mother," she said.

He softened, "Sure you would. You never answered my question. I never thought about kids either. We can figure that out down the line. The tangent was my fault this time."

"Oh, right! I'm rubbing off on you. No, I would never make you quit your job, so long as you never asked me to. I love to tinker and I love the job. We're very young, you and I. Would you wish to be married right away?" she said.

"Yes. Yes, I believe I would. Would you?" he said. She flushed and nodded, her heart going faster. Harrison grinned, "Good."

"You two at it again, are you?" FeFe said, walking in with Dill.

"Yes. You two as well?" Zara asked with a grin.

FeFe winked at her, "You bet."

"We got married last night!" Dill said with a smile.

FeFe chuckled and kissed him. She held out her hand, he did the same. She had a beautiful round sapphire with diamonds and a simple silver band that matched Dill's.

"Wow! Just like that?" Zara said.

FeFe nodded, "Funny thing, when Dill went flying, all I could think was I should have married him when I had the shot because I loved him. I didn't realize I loved him before then, but I always have. He's been my friend for ages, and I think I always knew it was more than that, but I was stupid. He had the ring a week ago, I told him I needed to slow down. I didn't need to after all."

She looked at him tenderly, her dark eyes soft. Dill put his hand on her face and kissed her, "I love you, muffin."

She giggled, "I love you, Dilly."

He chuckled. Zara watched them with a smile, "Well! Congratulations and pastry are in order. Well, doughnuts. My mother told me about a place near here. I can run and get some to celebrate! I have money now! Harrison, I forgot to tell you, the two major kitchen stores in Jakarda, Rosen's and The Grove Kitchen decided to carry my coffee pot and little fridge! They love it! And my patent for the bread cooker came through. The retailers feel it will be bigger than the other two! I have gotten two massive checks!"

She grinned at him. Harrison looked at her, his eyes dancing, "Good job, my love."

She kissed him, "I'll be right back."

"Want me to come with you?" he asked.

"No, it's right across the street," she said.

Harrison's lips thinned, "I'm coming. There's too much craziness going on."

Zara shrugged and took his hand, "Ok. There was something else I needed to mention, anyway."

Harrison nodded and they walked outside and crossed the street. It was not as busy here, there were new buildings springing up. This was a smaller area than the busy downtown section of Jakarda, but a nice one a lot of people were moving to now that places within the city were filling up.

"What did you wish to tell me?" he asked.

"Well, Bodie found some information for me. Some information, I'm not sure I wanted. I didn't have a chance to look at it, it's in my bag. You know how my mother was ah, not kind to me," she said.

"Of course," he said his brow furrowed angrily.

"Well, it seems it was because I am not her daughter," Zara said.

Harrison looked at her in disbelief, "How is that possible?"

"It's complicated. We can take a moment and I'll show you what's in this envelope, then bring the doughnuts. I'm not sure, exactly," she said.

They got the coffee and doughnuts in the little yellow shop and sat at a table. Zara sipped her coffee then took out the folder.

"Here is my birth certificate. My papa, Harold Turner, he went by Hal, he's on here, but my mother is listed as Jessica Ventura. She went by Jessie. Then this is a copy of his will. He had it in there that my mother had to provide clothes for her daughters, specifically me, for the duration of my life. I thought it was odd, I have a copy. She's supposed to provide food, too, but she doesn't do that all that well, as you know," Zara said. He nodded and she flipped the page, "I didn't get this page, this page says she is never to tell me that she's not my mother. She's supposed to claim me publicly, or I can sue her for breaking the will, she signed it. Nearest I can figure, she agreed to these terms when he was alive, thinking he could do most of the work and she wouldn't lose him because she loved him so much. Bodie, he told me he married my mother because Jessie was not too keen on marriage. She was a tinkerer, Harrison. She made kitchen gadgets, like me."

Zara smiled at him a little. Harrison grinned and kissed her, "That's amazing you're like her. I bet you're sweet like she was, too. Didn't get that from your mother, or, Amanda, according to this. Did you see the photo of her? Zara, you look just like her. My god!"

Zara looked at the woman in the black and white photo. She had a button nose and pretty lips. Her eyes were wide and she had curly lashes. More than that, she was small framed, on the tall side and delicate looking, like Zara.

"I have my papa's hair and eye color, plus his freckles. I do look like her though, don't I? Wasn't she beautiful, Harrison?" Zara said.

She was staring at her longingly, wondering what it might have been like to have a mother who loved her and tucked her into bed at night, instead of yelling at her and saying horrible things.

"Yeah, honey. She was beautiful, just like you," he said gruffly.

She offered him a sad smile. There was a series of photos of Jessie and Zara's papa together, one of her pregnant. They looked in love, excited, his hands on her belly.

"Bodie said my papa planned to leave Amanda, well, my mama. Do you think I would have been different if he did and she had lived?" Zara asked.

Harrison put his hand under her chin and turned her head to face him, "If it were different, we might not have met. I'm sure as hell, glad we did. I like you just as you are, Zara. There's nothing wrong with you."

"Me too! I'm happy we met, you and I. I love you so. That's an excellent point."

"I love you, too. What's this address?" Harrison asked.

"Oh! It seems I have grandparents who wanted to know me, tried to after their daughter died, and my papa. That's their address. She was an only child. He said they wanted to know me. We should go back," Zara said.

"Ok. Honey, why did Bodie give you all this?" he said.

"Oh! My papa died saving his life and the life of his wife and daughter, and his crew. He said I get three favors from him for each life. This was for one, that's why he answered the questions about Mary who was in fact his informant, as we know. He lumped it all in for me. He said if after I cash in I want to trade favors we can. I wasn't so keen on that," she said.

Harrison gaped at her, "Your papa, did he do that?"

"Yes. I believe Mr. Wills and the rest of his team knew that. We can ask," Zara said.

Harrison nodded and studied her, "I don't want you to do that. He's dangerous; and working with him, after what he did to you, please don't."

"As of right now, I have no intention of doing that. I will most likely cash in on those two freebies. He could help us in our cases in the future," Zara said.

Harrison sighed and nodded. They crossed the street and went to room ten on the bottom floor. It was small, they smashed in, but they had doughnuts and coffee. It was noisier in this building and not at all suited to their needs. Dill looked at Zara.

"I feel odd not being able to tinker as we have our meeting," he said.

"So do I. Here! I brought a bat bot, let's work together," she said.

He nodded and changed seats with FeFe, who reached for another doughnut.

"We need to regroup! Our resources are currently trapped in Room One Hundred. The building is being guarded by the Jakarda police, thankfully, and the tinkerers, repairmen and government officials have been sent in. They estimate that we should be able to go in by dirigible in two days' time. For now, let's go over what Zara brought us," Mr. Wills said.

"How did you get the sonar to work on this?" Dill asked.

"Radio waves, same as on my Spy-ders," she said.

"Clever. We could use the same material you used on the umbrella for these wings. I think they might be too heavy otherwise," he said.

Zara smiled, "Good suggestion. It would make them look more realistic too."

"Yes, it would. What gave you the idea to make that fabric anyway?" he asked.

Zara giggled, "My mother's corsets. I used some of the fabric to shape the umbrella, then brushed it with a combination of, of, oh!"

"What?" Dill asked.

"I used a combination of halonite I melted with a polymer she uses to make bots stand up and stay tall. I added a synthetic compound to another silver nitrate derivative called Holderon, also used in making clothes. Then I brushed the mixture on the inside and the outside of the umbrella. It made a sort of, I don't know, hard coating, a cross hatched pattern. Then I coated it with more of the mixture. We can use some of that halonite and make protective gear for the agents, vests! The rest, it can be used to mix with the synthetic compound in clothing like corsets, boots, to give it shape! I'll have to tinker, but maybe none of those people will lose their money! Except the Walkerwalls, we can send them to prison," Zara said.

Harrison laughed, "So there is a use for halonite after all, huh?"

Zara nodded, "Quite possibly. I still think it might make a handsome paint too, a unique one if marketed properly."

"That's good news! I pitied some of the people I spoke to. One of them had six children, six! I can't imagine that," Marcus said with a shudder.

Douglas laughed, "That's my family, I'm the fourth of eight. My dad jokes he's got potent seed. Makes me very cautious with the ladies."

Zara giggled, "I can imagine."

Douglas winked at her. Simon reached for another doughnut.

"What is on these?" he asked.

"Cinnamon, sugar and lemon rind. I read in the literature, that the lady who opened the shop, her husband was a sailor. She made them doughnuts for their long voyages and the crew liked them so much, he asked his wife to make them at home. She did, and Mrs. Dinkles Doughnuts were born!" Harrison said.

"They're excellent. Not as good as our usual pastries, but excellent," Marcus said.

"I agree. I love apple cheese danish, that's my favorite," Zara said.

Mr. Wills sighed, "Once again, we are off topic. How do we find Miss and Mr. Walkerwall?"

"We could try the halonite factory, I suppose," Zara said.

As if on cue, the door popped open. Nate, the head of the nest popped his head in.

"Someone just blew up the Jakarda City halonite factory, we think it was the same people as before, the Walkerwalls and the Patriots. Ten citizens are dead," he said.

Zara jumped up with the others and raced out. This was getting serious. They didn't care who they hurt, that gave them a very short window in which to stop them. If they saw her take the diary and get the files, they knew she was onto them, that the Crow's Nest was and it was making them desperate. But why were they doing this? It still made no sense.

CHAPTER EIGHTEEN

Zara was rooting through her apartment. She and Harrison, with the help of the others, were gathering her things because the wall in her apartment was missing from the blast at the halonite plant. She could see the factory wreckage from her living room. Her apartment, the one above hers, and the one beside hers seemed to have gotten the main concussion from the blast. She was sure that was no accident. Bits of brick were strewn about the floor, wood beams overhead were cracked and protruding from the plaster and exposed pipes leaked liquid all over. It was not safe to live in. Thankfully, no one in her complex was hurt badly, there were just reports of cuts and bruises; there had been no report of serious injury. There were others at the site trying to salvage what they could, too. The Walkerwalls had sent representatives and were attempting to cash in on their insurance policy, but the Crow's Nest arrested Larry Conroy and Herbert Shrinkle, whom they recognized from Mary's files. They came to the halonite plant, thinking the government didn't know who they were and were arrested on the spot. The pair did not expect to be noticed, they told the Crow's Nest they were from Global Technologies and a swarm of agents hauled them off.

"I packed your clothing and jewelry, Dill helped so it will be wrinkled. I got the bedding off your bed, too," FeFe said interrupting Zara's reverie.

Zara thanked her. Harrison had already loaded Annie and her bots into his car. Zara gathered as many of her tinkering supplies as she could, the pictures of her papa and her, and some of his blueprints and her own. The furniture was basically ruined, it hadn't been all that good to begin with, but she did take her papa's old chair. Simon, Marcus and Douglas emptied her kitchen, her dishes were shattered, but the food was ok, so they boxed it up for her. Zara took the doilies she had gotten from Mary and her satchel. They salvaged what they could. Zara looked at the apartment and sighed.

"Shame this old place went down. I knew it was a hovel, but I liked it," she said.

"I know. Come on, honey. Let's go home," Harrison said.

She smiled, because she really was going home now. Zara locked the apartment door with a chuckle. It was silly to do, but habit. They loaded the last of her things into her carriage. Zara got her motorized bicycle. They strapped it to the roof with her papa's chair. Zara said goodbye to her landlady, she had already paid for the month, but she couldn't come back, now. Harrison was kind enough to offer that she live at his place, insisting she never leave again.

"We can send someone for the bedroom furniture. It's very nice and in good shape, that part of the wall wasn't blown out entirely. We can use it in the one bedroom I never decorated," Harrison said.

"We can?" she said.

He kissed her, "We are going to be married, we should have 'our' stuff. That'll be 'our' bedroom furniture."

"Does your mother know you're getting married?" Mr. Wills asked with a grin.

"No! Don't tell her, for the love of god!" Harrison said.

He chuckled, "Not to worry. Will it be a big affair?"

"No," Zara said firmly.

"My future wife has spoken. Justice of the peace for us, a pretty dress for Zara and a handsome husband for her," Harrison said grinning boyishly.

Zara giggled, "Exactly!"

He kissed her and they got into the carriage. The others piled in with them, since all available cabs had gone. They made room for everyone. Zara sat on Harrison's lap, FeFe on Dill's. Mr. Wills squeezed into a small space between them and the door. It was a tight fit, but they made due. At Harrison's house, they unloaded her things. They settled everything into corners of the dining room and sat down at the table while Bernard went to get food. Zara hooked up Annie who rushed to help Bernard.

"What did they find in the rubble from the factory? I missed that part of the investigation when I saw my home had been blown to bits, then Harrison followed me, and the rest of you came when the team was finished over there," Zara asked.

"Not much left to find," Mr. Wills said helping himself to coffee, "Thank you, Annie."

She patted his shoulder, "You're welcome."

Mr. Wills arched his brows and Zara shrugged, "I made her as humanlike as possible. My family is loathsome."

Harrison winked at her and helped himself to the meat, cheese and cracker tray Bernard set down. Annie set out fruit and nuts along with bread baked fresh in Zara's new machine and a honey-cinnamon butter. Harrison grinned at her and tried it. He groaned.

"Good job, honey," he said.

"It's very good, isn't it?" she said.

The others tried it and complimented her.

"Delicious! Now, we need to figure out how they got out of that plant," Mr. Wills said.

"We should question those men they took into police custody," FeFe replied.

"I bet it was the tunnels. They are familiar with them. FeFe, remember there was a tunnel that ran under the halonite factory?" Simon said.

"Yes! Dumped us out four blocks away near that part of town with all the Farmer's markets," FeFe said.

"Eastern Market. Zara, this is marvelous bread and butter, really," Douglas said, reaching for a second slice.

"Shall I make another loaf, Zara?" Annie asked.

She nodded, "Yes, please!"

Annie rolled off to make more bread. It was done and served warm to the guests in under twenty minutes, thanks to Zara's invention.

"We have to find a way to draw them out. What would draw them?" Simon said.

None of them had an answer. After their meal, they went to the local police station where James Carver was waiting for them. It was a two-story, clean, brownstone building with easy access for citizens. In Jakarda there were only eighty staffed police officers, all of whom were easily identified by their blue vests and jackets with black pants and boots. The badge on James' chest glistened when he saw them. He puffed up his chest and stood up, a smirk on his handsome face.

"Well, well, if it isn't my old ex-friend, his fellow agents, and his fiancée. Oh, wait! You're his tinkerer, aren't you?" he said mockingly.

"Actually," Harrison said coldly, "she happens to be both. If you make her cry like you did when her apartment was robbed, I'll break your damn nose!"

"You really do plan to marry her?" James asked.

"Yes! Why is that so hard for people to believe?" Harrison said.

"Darn. Well, I had hoped you'd have dinner with me, Zara," James said.

Zara looked at him like he was insane, "You were pretty mean to me, calling me an idiot. Why on earth would I go out with you?"

James flushed and looked at her, "Yeah…about that…I wanted to make it up to you. I feel bad about how I treated you. And," he gave her a sly smile, "I think you're pretty."

Zara, unsure of what to say looked at Harrison. He glared at James and grabbed Zara's hand.

"Stay away from her, James. You already slept with the last woman I loved, I think once was enough. I mean it. I love Zara way more than I ever loved Brenda," he said.

James chagrin was palpable, his expression apologetic, "I know. I wish I'd never done that. It was a horrible thing to do to you. It won't happen again. I found this for you, Zara." He pulled out something with a paper attached to it and offered it to Zara with a smile, "I felt bad I made you cry. I found it at a pawn shop, tracked the two thugs who robbed your place. They copped to taking it because it was gold, the shop owner identified them. Someone hired them, I don't know who yet, but I'm working on it. I'm so sorry, I could tell this meant a lot to you."

Zara took the necklace. It had a hammer her papa made for her on it, it was gold, so was the chain. She smiled at him and kissed his cheek.

"Thank you. You're a very good police officer, James Carver," she said.

He smiled at her then and shrugged, "Tell that to your husband to be."

Harrison rolled his eyes, "James, enough. I think you're a good cop, I always thought you would be. Our issue was never a matter of belief in the others abilities. It was a competition, everything was since boyhood. Jobs and school, but it was women that made us stop being friends. It was never because I thought you were a bad cop or a bad man. You were my best friend once. I just thought you were a terrible friend in the end, and you know it because you were. But that's done now. Thanks for getting Zara's necklace back for her. It means a lot to her, so it means a lot to me."

James seemed taken aback. He studied Harrison, his expression apologetic.

He nodded curtly, "Of course. You want to see the detainees?"

They nodded and walked into the back of the building. Zara looked at the two men matching the descriptions they uncovered in the files they found at Mary's apartment. The Robotic Patriots watched them approach curiously. They had on normal suits and ties, Zara expected them to be far more sinister. One of them was familiar, especially to her; one blue eye, one brown, she knew him straight away, Hubert Shrinkle. They finally had a name to put with those two colored eyes of his. He glared at her, as did Larry Conroy, his chum from another file Mary had in her secret notes.

"Oh! So sorry I hit you with the rock twice, then you went in to chuck Harrison from the window. I'm so glad you're not dead!" she said with a smile.

Harrison snorted with laughter. Mr. Wills chuckled and stepped forward, "My name is Gilbert Wills. I'm with the Crow's Nest. Now, normally I don't make deals with thugs, but in exchange for your cooperation, we can discuss your options. If, and only if, Miss Walkerwall, who we know to be the mastermind of the bombings, and her brother, Mr. Walkerwall, are apprehended with your help."

"Go to hell," Hubert said.

"Yeah, straight to hell!" Larry snapped.

"Very well. Officer Carver, as an agent of the Crow's Nest it is my prerogative to see that these men are sent to prison without a trial. See that they never again see the light of day and their families are denied access to them. The bombs they were involved in setting off killed eighteen agents of the government, twenty civilians, three of whom were children along with four police officers, your brothers in arms. See that the guards are made aware of that at the penitentiary and they are punished accordingly," Mr. Wills said.

"I certainly will, Mr. Wills," James said.

Herbert and Larry exchanged panicked glances. They knew Mr. Wills was serious and that he was the sort of man who never made an idle threat.

"Wait!" Larry said.

"I'd like to see my girl, we just had a baby," Herbert said.

"Congratulations!" Zara interjected.

He glared at her. Harrison laughed again, so did James and Mr. Wills. Zara shrugged. She felt bad about conking him over the head like that, twice.

"Then you will tell us where the Walkerwall's are, as well as everyone else who was involved in this. Start at the beginning," Mr. Wills said.

Herbert sighed and sat back, "Halonite is a byproduct of two types of rock and steam. It's in a liquid form. We used to call it—"

"Yes, yes! We know! We know they passed it off as a different product, that the Walkerwall family started it all," Mr. Wills said.

"Yeah, they did. Miss Walkerwall said we would get revenge on Reform Mechanics and the government. She said it was a given. What we ended up doing, was getting revenge on the government and embarrassing the Reform Mechanics, not that that wasn't a very good start. That Miss Walkerwall, she wasn't always called that. She used to be called Jamison. She and her brother, their dad worked for the Crow's Nest," Herbert said.

Mr. Wills grew very still, "Their father was Bertram Jamison?"

"Yes. He was killed in the line of duty," Larry said.

"Yes, he was. He was partnered with your papa, Zara. He was dishonorably discharged from the Crow's Nest, I quite forget what about now. He was paired with me after that. Bertram never married, but he had two illegitimate children, twins. He was dedicated to their mother, if I recall, but he wasn't the sort to marry. I know who they are now. How can we find them?" Mr. Wills said.

"We have a base near that tunnel these two went into. That messed up the operations, whoever tossed all our guns and gas masks into the halonite," Larry said.

"That was me! I gassed you with your own gas too, I thought that was clever of me," Zara said.

They nodded begrudgingly in agreement. Harrison laughed again. Zara smiled sheepishly. Larry looked at her.

"She's after you, Zara Turner. We got your picture from an informant," Larry said.

"Mary McGinty?" Mr. Wills asked.

"Yeah, Mary. The second she found out Zara Turner was working there, she got funny. Her brother too, kept exchanging these looks, not sure why. I'm impressed the government knows more than we give them credit for. Yeah, Mary McGinty was playing both sides. Miss Walkerwall blames Zara for having to kill Mary. She did it herself, see? She, ah, she liked ladies instead of gents," Larry said.

"We suspected as much," Mr. Wills said dryly.

"When you say she blames Zara—-?" Simon began.

"She thought Mary was in love with Zara. Said Zara turned her away from her. Lovers' quarrel. Me and Herbert, we suspected it was more than that, but we dunno if that's true. She was a strange woman, cold," Larry said studying Zara, "You best watch yourself. If Miss Walkerwall wants something done, usually gets done and she's still out there. You been messing up her plans since the moment you started at the Crow's Nest and you took her girl. She ain't the sort to share her things. That's no good for you."

Zara felt a rush of fear. That didn't sound good. Not at all. Harrison took her hand. Mr. Wills sent in Mark Hubburger, the man who took down confessions for the Nest, with them. The pair in jail were spilling their information out, names and everything. They had no loyalty to anyone. They just wanted less time in jail. Mr. Wills sprang into action. He put together a team to go and take down the Walkerwalls and the Patriots. In a matter of three hours, nearly all of them were rounded up, except Miss Walkerwall. She was nowhere to be found and her brother wouldn't talk. It was a mad house in the station, the jail was jam packed with Patriots all shouting their innocence and willing to talk if it would get them out of trouble and that cell. None of them had any loyalty to one another and they were all terrified of Miss Walkerwall.

Zara, in need of a fresh breath of air, stepped outside the police station. She sighed and looked up at the sky. It looked almost purple as she gazed up at it. She found this whole situation rather anticlimactic. All this time, and all that had happened was the police rounded up these men in cars and brought them in. They were not even hiding! Most of them were in their homes with their families or friends, some were even at their jobs. She expected it to be more, well, exciting. She had been through so much to get here. It hardly seemed fair that this was all that had taken place. Harrison told her most of the time it was like this, a joint effort between local police and the government and the bad guys turned one another in. He told her she'd done well, they all did, insisting they couldn't have done it without her. Zara supposed she'd seen too many picture shows of the bad guys hauled away in cuffs after a dramatic encounter. She rubbed her head.

She heard an odd noise, a clang.

Zara turned and looked down the alley near the police station. She spotted a kitten, a real one. She smiled, wondering if Harrison liked cats. She wanted to get one badly, the cat-bot was the first bot she ever made as a little girl. Her mother wouldn't let her have one, even though both her sisters got a kitten which they soon tied off and booted from the house. Zara had tended them in the back yard, 'til her mama found out and called the pound, Zara had cried and cried while Annie comforted her. Zara walked towards the tiny grey mewling creature with a smile.

"Here, kitty, kitty!" she said.

A rag closed over her nose and lips as a strong arm grabbed her from behind. That spicy smell of ether stung her nose, eyes and lungs. Zara struggled, dropping her leather satchel on the ground in the process, sending its contents all over. She elbowed her assailant hard in the ribs, but they held firm. Her eyes rolled back in her head. At the last second, Zara regretted her wish for excitement.

Harrison looked around the crowded police station. He had been conducting interviews for over an hour. His head hurt, so did his neck. He looked at James Carver, his brow furrowed.

"James, have you seen Zara?" he asked.

James glanced at him, "Ah, about an hour ago now, I'd say. She stepped out for air, promised to bring me coffee. I got busy, forgot. Figured she most likely got side tracked. She seems to do that. Sort of adorable. She goes off on these tangents."

"I know, I love it," Harrison muttered.

He looked in all the offices and asked everyone if they knew where she was. FeFe noticed his distress and walked over to him.

"What is it?" she asked.

"Have you seen Zara?" he asked.

"Not for a while, she went out for air, said she had a headache," she said.

He nodded and rushed from the police station. He looked up and down the street, "Zara! Honey!"

"Zara!" FeFe called.

Harrison looked all over, but she was gone. His heart thumped hard, his hands shook.

"Harrison! Her bag! Oh, god!" FeFe said.

Harrison ran into the alley, fear making his head throb painfully with every heartbeat. Her things were strewn about the sidewalk. FeFe cleaned them up, scooping them into her massive satchel. Harrison just stood there in a panic, his heart thumping hard. FeFe froze, then slowly bent to pick up a rag. She held it up and sniffed it from an arm's length away.

"Ether. Oh, god! That lunatic Miss Walkerwall is still out there. Do you think she took Zara?" FeFe said.

"I don't know. We have to find her. Come on, we need help," Harrison replied.

FeFe ran into the police station, Zara's bag clutched in her hand, her eyes wide. Harrison let her tell the others. He sat down shakily and looked at her bag. He stared down at her tin of marshmallows and fought the urge to cry, fear like he'd never known made it hard for him to breathe. He couldn't lose her. He just couldn't.

Zara opened her eyes with a moan. She was tied to a chair, her arms behind her back. Her vision was out of focus. She looked around, struggling to see. She was in some sort of room, no, it was a cave. The same cave she and Harrison were in weeks ago. She noticed the smashed pipes and hardened barrels of halonite, guns sticking out of them, a gas mask too. Zara struggled to move her head.

"A tinkerer. A little tinkerer, new to the government took down my whole operation and stole the love of my life. Nearly all of my men are inside, spilling their guts. That's what you get with rejects from other organizations, no loyalty," a female voice said.

Zara blinked and looked over at a woman sitting nearby. She was handsome, more than pretty, with dark hair and eyes, and a nice smile. Zara had seen her before, at the ball. Miss Walkerwell. Zara groaned and tried to shake the fogginess from her mind. Miss Walkerwall chuckled.

"Ether does take some time to shake off, apologies. I was at the building, ready to blow it up and everyone in it, including my stupid brother, when I spotted you. Zara Turner, the blonde-haired, freckled beauty who took Mary from me," she said.

"Mary liked men and women. I only like men. She was only, ever my friend, " Zara said.

Miss Walkerwall nodded, "I know. I read her diary. I left it for you to find and I saw it with those handy Spy-ders you invented. I didn't, however, count on you finding the folders I had no idea Mary kept. I thought you would stay there, cry and I could come and kill you like I did with her. I read her diary one night after we made love, and in it, she talked about how she came to hate me, hated herself for being a bad friend to you. Mentioned she only ever slept with me because I frightened her. She pinpointed that moment she wanted to change her life, she said it was the day she met you. She loved you as a sister, a friend, trusted you as she never trusted me. I know that now. But she loved you more than she loved me, just in a different way. Here, I finally found a woman who was useful to me, desired me, and I found out it was all an act. You can imagine how it crushed me. I truly loved her."

"I'm sorry," Zara said.

She studied Zara, "You are very beautiful. Those big blue eyes and the blonde hair. So lovely, and the freckles are oddly attractive on you. You're intelligent too. Mary told me about all your inventions, well done."

"Thank you," she said.

Miss Walkerwall stood. She had on a three piece suit, she dressed like a man, but her hair was long and curled. She looked nice in the outfit. It oddly suited her. She studied Zara.

"It's not the true reason I hate you, lovers do come and go and I'm not all that shallow. It was just the icing on the cake, so to speak. Our fathers were partners at the Crow's Nest, did you know?" she said.

"I just learned that, yes," Zara said.

She smiled of course, "Did you know it was your father who got mine fired?"

Zara realized then, that this was what it was about. This was the true reason she hated Zara, she blamed her for taking everything that mattered to her, "No. I had no idea."

She nodded, "I thought not. See, when I learned you were working for the organization that ultimately destroyed my father because of Mary, I thought, marvelous! How marvelous, I can take down the daughter of the man who destroyed mine. Do you want to know what happened?"

"Ok," Zara said.

"They were on a case. My father, he had the opportunity to send a man to jail but, shall we say, tweaking a bit of evidence. Your father caught him and turned him in. All his other cases were reviewed, he lost his job, his self-esteem, then he died by suicide. The Crow's Nest, said he died on the job, kept what he'd done a secret because what they discovered was that this was the first and only time he ever tampered with evidence. it was to put a man bringing drugs into Jakarda City away. A drug dealer! But your father, with all his perfect morals, friends with a known leader of the Reform Mechanics, he was too good to do a thing like that. He was a hypocrite! He had the nerve to show up at the funeral, knowing full well it was he that killed him in the end!" she snarled.

Zara refrained from comment. She watched as the other woman paced the floor, her eyes wild. She looked livid, full of hate and mentally disturbed.

"I'm sorry," she said.

"Sorry? You're sorry your father killed mine? That you ruined my plans? Took the woman I loved from me? Sorry? You're a fool if you think that matters at all to me. I have no intention of going to jail. I'm going to kill us both. You shouldn't be allowed to live. Not after you took everything from me," she said bitterly.

Zara felt a rush of horror. She could tell she meant it. She had to stall, get out of this and she needed time to think of what exactly to do. This was a woman ready to die for her cause and willing to take her along the way. Zara looked around. She spotted a large amount of explosives behind her. Shit! She needed to stall before they both went up. If only she could reach her pockets.

"Can I ask you something?" Zara said.

She smiled prettily and nodded, "Why not? We have a bit of time before we die. Let's share things. Get to know one another since we're going to die together."

"O-Ok. Was this ever about the Reform Mechanics?" Zara said.

She grinned, "You are clever! Mary said so! Never about the Mechanics, not a bit. They were a clever way for me to get away with blowing things up! The bombs I set off, each of them were places so that someone who discredited my family died. The lawyers at his trial, the judge who banished him from the Nest. A retired head of the Nest's Family, that was fun, she was an old woman. I pretended to be a maid, poisoned her and everyone thought she died of old age. The wealthy families we robbed, that was for fun, just to take from them. I need the maps they had for the tunnels, not all the branches were on them and that was how I ran my operation, kept it unnoticed by the Crow's Nest. They got us all over Jakarda City without being detected. The tunnels were key to outer operation. The halonite was needed just so I had the money to destroy everyone who tore apart my family. I found some fools to invest in it, desperate folks eager to make money. It wasn't hard. Then my brother and I did the same to cover our true plan. Made it look like we were investors. It was always about revenge. You see, I loved my papa. He gave his life to the Crow's Nest, then, he killed himself and they hushed it up. I found him with a bullet in his temple, you see. I was shipped off to some other family with my twin brother. I was responsible for the explosions around the city this past year. I killed forty people. Killer, they called me, but among the dead were the people who hurt him and us, friends who turned on us, shunned us. We were punished because of that investigation, all of us. We had to change our names, hide. None of our friends would speak to us because of what the papers said about my father, and it was all because of the Crow's Nest. It took me years to plan all this. I was nearly there, when you showed up at the Nest and ruined it all. Meddlesome like your blasted father, so bent on the so called right thing. I killed all the people involved with bombs, pinned it on the Reform Mechanics, made piles of cash from the halonite, killed some people at the Crow's Nest. Then we were caught because of what you did to Mary. You are terribly clever. To clever, Zara, and Mary was not going to be your friend! That was an insult to me, your friendship. I hated the fondness in her eyes when she talked about her dear friend, Zara. She had to die."

Zara winced, "Oh. Well, I never meant to mess up your plans. I had no idea about your father, or that my papa had anything to do with yours. Blaming me for what he did, it won't bring your father back, and Mary did not need to die, you're mistaken about that. It seems to me you don't want anyone to be happy since you're so bent on revenge. My papa died working for the Crow's Nest too, Miss Walkerwall, did you know?"

"Call me Jemma, Zara. How did he die? Mary was supposed to ask, but she could never get it from you," She said, looking happier than she should have about the suffering of a fellow human being.

Zara managed to get to the tracker she kept in her back pocket with her hands tied. She pushed the button, praying they would find her. It was an invention Dill made in the tinkerer's room. She pressed the button, hoping Dill would realize and get to her. Zara looked her in the eye.

"He was a tinkerer like me, as well you know. He was on a Reform Mechanics dirigible, there was a bomb set to blow up and there were families on board. He tried to stop the bomb, it didn't work for him. He was killed, trying to do what was right. Our fathers were perhaps the same," Zara said.

She softened a little, "I'm sorry. It's hard to lose a parent."

"It is. Since we're confessing, I found out recently my mother, who was physically abusive to me, was not my mother after all. My papa had an affair, and I was the byproduct. Which is why the woman who hated me so much and beat the tar out of me, did the things she did to punish me. I'm relieved that evil woman is not my mother. How was your mother?" Zara asked.

Jemma smiled, "Kind, but weak. What happened destroyed her. I was the one who took care of my brother."

"I understand. I took care of myself and learned to tinker because I knew I needed a way out. Thank god I was smart. Now I'm going to die here because I, unlike you, wanted to emulate my papa's career with the Crow's Nest. Funny we have something in common, isn't it?" Zara said.

"Yes. I suppose it is. Was my brother in jail?" she asked.

"Yes," she said.

"Did he turn on me like the others?" she asked.

Zara winced and nodded, "I'm sorry."

Jemma sighed and sat down. Zara fidgeted. She managed to get the little laser knife from her pocket. Che clicked the button and sliced through the rope at her wrist. Jemma was looking down at the ground. Zara held the knife in one hand, the rope in the other. She would have her moment if she played her role carefully, as Harrison taught her. He was right. Theatrics were important to this job, very important.

"Me, too. My brother was weak, he never wanted to do any of this. He wanted to run the halonite scam and take the cash," she said.

"That's a garbage product," Zara said.

Jemma laughed delightedly, "Spoken like a true tinkerer. It certainly is!"

If she could just get her close, she could injure her, get her legs free. She studied Jemma.

"I can see why Mary liked you. You're smart and I think she liked people who were powerful," Zara said.

Jemma's dark eyes met hers. She smiled and studied Zara.

"I can see why she liked you, too," she said.

Zara smiled and looked around, "I suppose there are worse ways to die then with a brilliant criminal mastermind."

"Or with a brilliant tinkerer," Jemma said.

Zara chuckled. Jemma stood and walked slowly over to her. Zara watched her approach with a little smile. She licked her lips and Jemma reacted as she hoped she would. She leaned down, her lips inches from Zara's, desire in her eyes. She opened her mouth to say something. Zara jabbed her in the face with the hot laser. She screamed in pain. She dropped to the floor, clutching her face, writhing in agony. Zara cut her legs free of the ropes and took off at a run down the tunnel. Zara grabbed the detonator from Jemma's chair on the way.

"You bitch!" Jemma screamed.

Zara ran faster and pressed the button before that psychotic witch could come after her. She heard her scream of pain, and the boom of the explosive. It shook the ground and erupted into flame, knocking her from her feet. Zara jumped up and ran. She was nearly there, to the opening she saw on the map, as long as her memory was correct, that is. She heard another boom as more charges went off, a chain of therm. She went as fast as she could, her lungs burning, fear and adrenaline driving every step. Almost, almost. She saw a flash of light behind her, running at top speed down the tunnel. Zara grasped the ladder to the left, it was well lit from the fires. She shimmied up as fast as she was able. When she reached the cage at the top, she shoved it hard. It moved a few inches. She shoved it again, then forced her way through the small opening she created. She yelped when her legs and part of her hair got singed. She rolled out of the way just as the flames shot up the tunnel, banging on her smoking hair. She screamed, and crawled backwards on all fours when the flames got taller. The ground shook under her backside and a few spots caved in.

She swore and hopped up taking off at a run. The ground beneath her feet felt unstable, wobbly. She quickened her pace. She had nearly made it when she fell into a hole and landed at the bottom in a heap, rocks, grass and dirt pelting her. Then, it stopped. Zara laid there panting for a while. She felt around her body, hoping to god she wasn't mortally injured or disfigured in some way, but she felt fine.

"Oh, my god!" Someone yelled, "Zara!"

Zara laid on the ground, stunned, looking at the night sky, painting. She was ok! How was she ok?

"Zara!" they yelled again.

Was that Harrison? She heard sobbing, broken, male sobbing. Zara coughed and waved at the puffs of dirt flying about her. She crawled slowly out of the hole she had fallen into up the rocky, sunken angle that led to the top, grunting and breathing hard. She was covered in cuts and bruises, but that was not so bad. She pulled herself up, vowing to work on her upper body strength in the future and laid on the grass a moment, breathing hard. She spotted the team with Harrison, who was sitting on the ground, crying while Mr. Wills comforted him. A dozen police officers had come with them, all of them looked stricken. Zara got shakily to her feet and limped towards them. She may have sprained her ankle in the fall. Harrison looked at the pile of rubble that was once the cave. He was on his knees, his face streaked with tears.

"She's gone. My Zara's gone," he said hollowly.

"No, I'm not. I'm ok, my love," Zara called.

His eyes shot to her. He jumped up and ran over to her, crushing her in a hug.

"Ahh! Careful, I fell in that hole over there. It hurt a little. I think I sprained my ankle," she said.

He kissed her lips, her face, then her lips again, "I love you. I love you so much. What happened?"

The others rushed up and hugged her, grinning in relief.

"Jemma got me, ether again. She explained how and why she did it, revenge. I outsmarted her, I was nearly cooked. I think my hair got a bit singed, my legs, too," Zara said.

Harrison winced, "You might have to cut off a few inches of your hair."

"That's ok. It will grow back. Here I was wishing this was a more exciting ending at the police station. I regret that now. It was stupid. I set myself up for catastrophe," Zara said.

Harrison laughed and kissed her.

"Miss Turner, tell us what happened, everyone, in the carriages," he said.

Zara retold all the things she learned. Mr. Wills looked horrified, "Her father was your papa's partner before I was. I hadn't realized. All Hal ever said was he had a partner before me and he died because of something he'd done, mentioned it was the right thing to do, but never said any more. Oh, my god! Then she realized who you were and because of Mary, wanted you to die to."

"Yes. I think I became a symbol of how she could right what happened to her father somehow," Zara said.

"You tried to seduce her to get her close?" Harrison said.

"No, I just smiled at her in the way all you gents told me was appealing and never looked away. Then, thanks to FeFe, I licked my lips and she came right over, giving me the opportunity to jab her in the face with my newest invention, portable laser. She was sort of sad, so desperate for someone to like her, I thought it might work. It did and I ran into a secret tunnel I recognized from the map nearby and set off the bomb. Didn't realize she had so many wired, did it take out the whole system?" she asked.

"We think so, police are checking on that now. Most of the area is unstable and collapsed on itself. We will recover her body to be sure she's dead," Mr. Wills said.

"I can show you where I left her," Zara said.

Zara sat painfully back. They were in one of the police wagons. She was exhausted. They were talking about where to go from here, but Zara drifted off, her head on Harrison's shoulder. He took her home to his townhouse after that. She took a shower, then Annie cut off her damaged hair; it was just past her shoulders. Harrison patched her up while Annie worked, tending to her burns and cuts. Harrison smiled when she finished.

"I love it. You look beautiful," he said.

She smiled, "Thank you. I'm exhausted."

"We should go to bed," he said.

She yawned audibly. They crawled into bed together and snuggled tightly. Zara fell asleep with Harrison's protective arms around her.

CHAPTER NINETEEN

Harrison made love to her in the morning, kissing her and telling her he loved her over and over. Nearly losing her scared him, but she was clever, his Zara. She was so damn clever. She was strong and perfect, a fighter and a damn good agent. They reached orgasm together, kissing frantically when Annie barged in the room.

"Go away!" Harrison said, kissing Zara, his body shaking, "Shit, honey. That feels so damn good."

Zara was breathing hard, her hands on his butt. He loved when she did that, pulled him inside her even more.

"Harrison, three times?" she said.

He grinned and flopped beside her, "I can do better. Want to go again?"

She nodded eagerly and reached for him, stroking him with a smile. He grinned and kissed her.

"Sorry to interrupt your love making, but Harrison your family has come for breakfast. They are in the dining room," Annie said.

"What?" he said, jerking away from Zara.

He jumped out of bed and slammed the door, yanking on his clothes. Annie handed Zara a simple dress which she pulled on. She brushed her hair and teeth in his bathroom. She looked at herself and winced.

"Every time I see your parents I am so banged up!" she said.

He kissed her, "You look pretty, honey. I like your hair down."

He took her hand and they rushed down the steps. Harrison heard the noisy clatter in the dining room and winced.

"Oh, for shits sake! They've all come," he muttered.

Zara laughed. She looked nervous. He kissed her hand and led her into the dining room with a smile.

"Morning! What brings all of you here?" Harrison said.

His mother rushed forward and Mr. Wills, or Uncle Gilbert as he was called at home, winced apologetically.

"Gilbert told us what happened! Terrifying. Zara, we're so glad you're all right," his mother said, hugging Zara.

She flushed, "Thanks."

"You cut your hair!" she said

"I burned it off last night. It will grow back," Zara said with a shrug.

Harrison offered her a half smile, "Zara Turner, I would like you to meet my family. You know my mom and dad and Mr. Wills, Uncle Gilbert here. This is my sister Joanne, my other sister Emily and her son Miles, my sister Beth and her husband Rick, their two children David and Parker, my Uncle Albert and his wife Ginnifer, my cousin Hank and his wife Mia and lastly, my Uncle David and his wife Clary. They are my dad's brother and his wife. The non-agents of the family, like my sisters. This is Zara Turner. I, um, I love her. We're getting married."

There was a collective cheer. Zara took a step closer to him. She sent him a nervous look. Harrison kissed her. It occurred to him, she had no idea what a family like this was like. He wondered if she wanted to meet her grandparents, her real ones. He planned to ask her after this.

He led her to the table. She sat down next to his mother. He sat on her other side, beside Joanne who studied her as she answered their questions and nervously talked about her background. She was trying not to ramble, bless her heart. She was hardly eating all the scrambled eggs, bacon, sausage, fresh bread and fruit Bernard and Annie brought with juice and coffee.

"She's smart," Joanne said quietly.

"She's brilliant actually. Top tinkerer to graduate at the Academy ever. She's, Jo, she's incredible. She's so clever and sweet. I love her so much," Harrison said with a small smile.

Joanne grinned at him, "I'm glad, Harrison. I really am. She's very beautiful, so lady like and freckled."

"Oh, god. I love the freckles," he said.

She laughed delightedly and kissed his cheek. Miles was toddling around, trying to catch Zara's cat bot. Zara watched him giggling. Harrison watched her, his eyes soft. Unbeknownst to him, his family watched him and exchanged knowing glances because they could see he was besotted with her. Mr. Wills sat back, satisfied, and thought he had made a perfect match. He knew she'd be good for his nephew from the beginning. Perhaps he would make a match for all his agents someday?

After they had gone, Harrison kissed Zara. He had his hand on her breast and he was planning to have her hold the desk while he showed her a new position when someone knocked on the door. Harrison swore and pulled back.

"Who the hell is that?" he said.

Zara ran to answer the drawer, adjusting the front of her dress, "Oh! Officer Carter, how are you?"

"I'm fine. Can I come in?" he asked.

Harrison strode over and smiled at his old chum, shaking his hand. They were trying a new thing where they didn't say rude things to one another. It was like walking a tightrope. Rude things were on the very tip of Harrison's tongue at every turn and vice versa. He gestured to the sitting room.

"Have a seat! You want something to drink?"

"No thanks. I'm here on official business," he said sitting on the sofa and looking around, "Nice place. I always liked it when your grandpa lived here, too."

"Thanks. It was a mess when I got it, he had all my grandma's old things," Harrison said.

James laughed, "Pink!"

"All over the damn place," Harrison said with a snort.

James chuckled and looked at Zara. Harrison tensed. He'd known James a long time. He was stalling, he didn't want to tell her whatever it was he had to say. Zara smiled at him, looking beautiful and crossed her ankles. Her cat bot hopped into her lap. She stroked his metal body.

"Zara, I traced that robbery of yours. I, ah, well, the thing is, the necklace I found for you, you have it on! That's nice," he said.

Zara's hand wandered to her neck. She smiled and nodded, "Thanks again, James. I'll be forever grateful."

Harrison took her hand and sent him a look like, out with it James. James nodded and winced.

"It was sold by a woman who took great pains to conceal her appearance, but the person who bought it recognized her because she's known to everyone in the land of Jakarda. The thing is, well, you see, it was your mother," he said gently.

Zara froze. Harrison watched as she struggled to process the information, "My mother? What? H-how can that be?"

Harrison felt like his heart wedged in his throat. Zara was so pale, so stricken that her face filled with the hurt. He put his arm around her.

"You're sure, James?" he said.

James nodded, his expression apologetic, "I'm afraid so. I did some checking and she hired three men to go into your apartment, smash specific things and steal that necklace, twice. It bothered me, the way it was all done, no forced entry. She gave them the keys and told them exactly what she wanted them to do. I'm not sure why she did it the second time—"

"Because I never reacted," Zara said in a quiet voice. "I didn't mention it to her and my mother was angry with me. I'm sure she thought I was too happy, that I needed to crawl back to her like I've had to in the past. She's happiest when I'm miserable. When I am indebted to her."

"Jesus," Harrison said.

James winced, "I, ah, the thing is, she gave them the keys, so technically, there was no breaking and entering because she has a set. I can arrest her for the theft and sale of the necklace and hiring those men, and for destruction of property, but she is your mother. I wasn't sure what you wanted me to do."

Harrison studied Zara. She looked furious. Harrison rubbed her shoulder.

"I'm going to speak to her. Thank you James, for being so kind about this. I really appreciate it. Can you keep a record of this, and should she ever do something of this nature again, maybe you could arrest her?" Zara said.

He nodded, "Of course. I'm sorry she…was insane."

Zara laughed mirthlessly, "It's ok. You're a very good man, James Carver. I appreciate your kindness and all your hard work."

He stood, looking proud of himself as he tugged on his blue uniform. Harrison walked him out and shook his hand. James turned to leave, but Harrison stopped him.

"James, Zara and I are getting married this weekend, my family has stopped by for a visit and now they know we live together and we wanted to be married anyway, so we're going to the justice of the peace. We're having a small party here at my house at five. I hope you'll come. Be nice to have my childhood friend here," Harrison said.

"Sure, Harrison. Be nice to see your family again, and get to know my old friend," James said.

Harrison clasped him on the shoulder. He left with a wave. Harrison turned to Zara. She was putting on a pretty brown coat. She looked livid, her blue eyes flashing.

"I'm coming too," Harrison said.

"I'm going to have to give her a piece of my mind! I see her all the time, do as my papa asked! She disregarded his wishes, Harrison, and she lied to me!" Zara said.

Harrison was quiet a moment, "Zara, do you think it's wise to speak with her at all any longer? She's not your mother, Zara. She raised you, I understand that, but she's very cruel. Why speak to her at all?"

Zara hesitated, her expression vulnerable, "I feel indebted to her. She did take me in, even when I wasn't hers."

"Honey, she took you in, but at what cost? She was so cruel to you. With your birth mother's family, a family that wanted you, you would have known kindness and love. You may have had a happy life with your mother's family, just imagine it."

"I don't want to! I feel very sad when I think of it!" Zara said, her eyes watering.

Harrison took her cheeks in his hands, stroking them gently with his thumbs, his eyes holding hers, "I know that, my love. That's why I think it's time to break contact with your mother, and with your sisters. It's time, Zara. I'm your family now, not them, and you are way past giving her a piece of your mind."

Zara studied his handsome face a moment. She nodded hesitantly, "It seems I must be very firm and make a clean break. You're right."

They strode out to the carriage hand in hand. Zara sat there, her foot hopping angrily as the carriage drove along, a strange mixture of anxiety and anger on her face. The more she thought about how her mother acted, the more angry she looked to Harrison. Zara had spent years wondering why she was treated with such disdain when her sisters were lavished upon, treated so well.

"Harrison, I cried so hard as a child, worked twice as hard as my sisters to mend what was broken between me and my mother and sisters, but to no avail. You're right! It is far past time to stand up for myself and a clean break is exactly what I need—what we need, to start our new life together," Zara said.

Harrison felt a rush of relief, "Good! I'm happy to hear that. You can do this."

"Of course I can do this! I am furious! She ruined my food! I was hungry all the time! She stole from me just to make me suffer! I was already struggling, I did not need her help to make it harder!" Zara said.

"I know," Harrison said while stroking her hand, taken aback by her rage, her ire.

They pulled up to a massive white house with a copper roof. It was a palace, modern and beautiful, lavish in comparison to Zara's humble apartment. It was such a contradiction to the home Zara lived in, that it made him feel sick. Zara stomped up to the door, Harrison at her heels. She pounded on the door vigorously with her fist then put her hands on her hips. Her sister Cait, the one with the massive head, answered the door. She spotted Harrison and batted her eyes. Harrison took Zara's hand and held it tightly, not bothering to hide his look of disgust. She reddened and gestured inside.

"Might as well come in," Cait said.

"Mother! I need to speak to you. Cait, you and Tempie should go," Zara said.

Mrs. Turner walked into the foyer and rolled her eyes, "You have no right to send them away."

Zara glared sternly at her and spoke in a level tone, "Jessica Ventura and robbery say I have every right."

Mrs. Turner's eyes widened slightly. She paled, her hand fluttering to her chest, the panic in her face evident. Harrison fought the urge to smile. It was nice to see her squirm. She deserved more than that as far as he was concerned.

"Girls, go to your rooms. We have a ball to attend tonight. Have your maid bots help you get ready, you know it takes all day to look your best," she said with a cold smile.

Zara's sisters exchanged surprised glances, but did as their mother asked. Zara strode purposefully into the parlor and sat on the edge of a finely upholstered divan. Harrison sat beside Zara. Mrs. Turner at least had the grace to look upset, but not apologetic as far as he could tell.

"You know the truth about who your mother is, then?" Mrs. Turner said.

"I do. I would have preferred to have heard it from you. Why all the lies? Why did you smash the things that meant something to me? I had so little. Wasn't it enough that you beat me? Treated me like vermin, hated me? My life was hell in this house and when I find such a small bit of happiness, you need to take it from me?" Zara said.

Mrs. Turner sniffed and looked at Harrison, as if she didn't want to speak with him present.

He glared at her, "She told me what a heartless bitch you are, don't hold back on my account, but do watch your words. I love her. You will not belittle her in my presence."

Mrs. Turner flushed, then looked at Zara raising her chin. "Very well…I hate you. I hate you Zara, because Hal loved you more than he ever loved me or your half-sisters. I was the one who supported him on his low salary as a government employee. I encouraged him in that blasted job he loved because it made him so happy. I loved him so much, so damn much, I would have done anything he asked of me. And, I did. So—He strayed and I forgave him and took you in after your mother died in childbirth, pretended you were my own because I never could say no to him. He told me he loved me, that he had made a mistake. Later I learned he made that mistake through-out our entire marriage, that he had started making that mistake from day one. I didn't know that until he died of course, but it was a horrible realization for me, I was so head over heels in love with him. When I agreed to take you in, I thought he had strayed just the one time. Lots of men stray! All my friends' husbands do, and I could live with once. I was willing to pass you off as my own, especially with your mother dead. We called you a surprise, said you came early and no one was the wiser. I had put on weight at the time, with all the stress of expanding the business the way I did, so everyone thought it was that. I lost the weight and that was that. Things were good for a while. I resented you, but I had him, so it was worth it. Then what happens? He dies in the line of duty and leaves me with you! The lit-tle girl who has had his heart and his attention from the second she crossed the threshold of my house! You took him from me!"

"I was a child! That was your choice to take him back! You could have said no, considered your own worth! You could have told him there was no way you would be with him. If you felt you deserved more, then you should have had the guts to stand up for yourself instead of agreeing to be with a man who never loved you! Deep down, you had to know he didn't if he strayed. You picked this life, then you were too weak to handle me being in your house. You beat me and yelled at me, made me feel useless and made me think I was ugly while you walked around telling your homely daughters how marvelous they were. How my father ever liked you I will never know. No wonder he looked elsewhere! You're ugly, inside and out, cold, heartless and cruel!" Zara said, her chest heaving.

"How dare you, you I ungrateful little bitch! I took you in, I—" Mrs. Turner gripped the arms of the chair.

Harrison stood angrily, "Careful, Mrs. Turner. You see, we know what you did and we work for the government. Your attacks on her were sloppy, stupid, and easy to trace. We have a record of it with the local police and the only thing standing between you and prison, is Zara and I. I know what you did, and our friends at the police department know. You say one more ugly thing to her, do anything at all. If I so much as catch a whiff of you plotting, I'll discredit you, I'll see you bankrupt and in jail, then I'll see those hideous daughter of yours, the ones you claim are beautiful, whoring themselves out at the docks. You see, you don't get to hurt her anymore. She's not alone, she has me and all her friends at the Crow's Nest. And there is the matter of the will. If you say anything about her parentage, well, the legal trouble you'll incur will send you to prison too. I also know a lot of judges, Mrs. Turner. Comes with the government job. I might not have been honest about what it is I do at the Nest. In short, stick to the original agreement with Hal. Send piles of clothes, not the plain ones either, dress her splendidly, or we'll be displeased. I want sexy night gowns too, I like those. I'm not the sort of man to do things by small measures, I think you know that. I love her, you don't get to hurt her ever again, or I will hurt you worse than you can imagine."

Mrs. Turner looked terrified. She swallowed hard, her pinched face pale. Zara kissed his cheek, her expression tender.

"I love you, Harrison," she said.

He kissed her and winked, "I know, honey."

Mrs. Turner looked like she sucked a lemon, "What else?"

Zara took a deep breath, and for a moment, Harrison wasn't sure if she could cut things off. She was kind, so kind, and she wasn't the sort to be cruel, not after all she endured. When she was spoke her words were quiet, he could barely hear her.

"I don't wish to have those monthly dinners with you anymore. Not ever again. Or my sisters. It's a shame, they are my sisters, but…"

She paused, taking a shaky breath, her eyes watery, "You made them hate me because you were too weak to handle what happened to you. We could have been friends, my sisters and I, instead, Annie tucked me in at night, then you sent someone to smash and take only thing I loved growing up because I had a robot my papa made as my only company. You're the worst person I have ever known. My papa would be ashamed of you, hated you for what you did to me. You have to know that. He trusted you with me, the person you yourself said he loved more than anyone and you were so selfish, you treated me like a dog you got stuck with. I know why my papa picked you. he must have seen goodness in you once. Maybe he thought your love for him would transcend to me. He was like that, wasn't he? Saw the best in people when there was none. You must live with that hate and what the man you claim to love would have thought of you for the way you treated me from now on, but you stay away from me."

Mrs. Turner looked pale, upset, as if she never realized what Hal would think of her. She was struggling not to cry. It never occurred to her that he trusted her with his most precious love because he thought she was the right person for the job. He assumed she would treat Zara as she had their daughter because of her love for him, and she let him down, Zara was right. Mrs. Turner's lip wobbled. She blinked back tears. She cleared her throat, for the first time, her face full of regret. Harrison found he had no pity for that selfish, stupid woman. She deserved to spend the rest of her life feeling badly for what she'd done.

Harrison kissed Zara's head, "You're doing good."

Zara took a shaky breath, "Can you tell me about my real family?"

"Of course. Your grandparents, they live in the Green Isle. They tried to meet you every year, several times a year after the death of your father, monthly at first. You saw them a few times, asked who they were, and I told you they were selling something. They wanted you to live with them. I had promised your papa I'd keep you, but I considered it. In the end, I did what he wished of me for his sake, certainly not your yours as it should have been. They run a grocery store in the Green Isle, a very nice one," she said.

Zara nodded and studied her mother, who, to her credit was trying to be kind. Too little, much too late, but she was trying. Harrison took Zara's trembling hand in his.

"In the future, if I contact you or need you for anything, you'll come. No complaining. No more disparaging me or my future husband. No more telling me how ugly I am, how useless. We both know that's a lie, because of all your daughters, I'm the only one with an education, a future and good looks. My sisters are nitwits, because you made them that way. Shame, you're quite intelligent, they could have been more if you didn't make them so silly. Keep your comments to yourself from now on," Zara said.

"And I mean it about prison. Snap of my fingers, Mrs. Turner. Never hurt her again and do as she asks," Harrison said.

"Yes. I believe I understand, Mr. Lowell. When are you getting married?" Mrs. Turner asked.

"This weekend," Zara said.

"Do you need a dress?" she asked.

"Yes," Zara said.

"I'll get it to you today. What time? Your sisters and I—"

"You're not coming. I don't want you there. For a long time, I hoped we could patch things up, but it was stupid. It's too late. I can't forgive you for what you did to me or for all the lies. Just send the dress, please and the clothes as my papa asked you to," Zara said in a rush.

"But your sisters will want to come," Mrs. Turner said.

"Why? So they can tell me how ugly I am and ruin the best day of my life? They and you have ruined enough days to suit me. No. You tell them, it's your fault they're not invited because you were to cruel to me for too long for me to forgive you and I'm no longer a part of your lives. It's the truth," Zara said.

Mrs. Turner studied Zara, her eyes watery and nodded, "Very well. Zara, I know this is too late. I am sorry."

Zara stood and studied her, "There are some things that word cannot cover, Mrs. Turner. Good day."

Mrs. Turner did cry then. She looked away, silent tears of regret falling down her cheeks. Harrison took Zara hand. She was struggling not to cry, shaking a bit as if her resolve might crumble at any minute if he didn't get her out of there. He offered her a half smile.

"Let's go home and be happy," Harrison said.

Zara took a shaky breath, offering him a dazzling smile, "Yes, let's! We have a new life to live together, you and I."

"Yes, we do, my love," he said, kissing her softly.

Harrison led her out of that house. She kissed him on the drive home and he held her tightly. She smiled at him.

"We're a family now, aren't we?" she said.

He grinned, "Yes, we are."

"Can we get a real cat?" she said.

He laughed, "What?"

"I've always wanted one. My mother let my sisters get one, but she wouldn't let me," Zara said.

He softened, "Of course we can."

"I think living with you will be much better than living with her."

He laughed delightedly, "I sure as hell hope so."

Harrison hated cats, but he was never going to tell her that. He'd give her whatever she wanted. Zara studied him and realized she would love him forever. Her past didn't matter. She had him for the future. Harrison was thinking the same thing. She cuddled up to him, and they went home to happy.

ACKNOWLEDGMENTS

First and foremost, many thanks to Kaylie Sorenson, who took the time to read my book before anyone else, warts and all. I cannot tell you how much that means to me! Thanks to Deb Gehle for doing the same, and offering support on all my writing adventures and disasters. You always have something nice to say to me about my work, and I am grateful to you for that.

Thank you to my husband Ben, for putting up with my stress, inability to make a decision when it comes to my books, and for helping me design a pretty good book cover. You're the best! Thanks for listening to me yammer on and on about character profiles, edits, things that work, things that don't, and all the useless things I come across on the internet while you are at your real nine to five job. Because of you, I do what I love. Your endless support and belief in me is humbling and appreciated, as is your enthusiasm, and willingness to take a crack at whatever I throw at you when it comes to the publishing process.

Thank you to Karen Cunnien for helping me make this book better with you editing suggestions and in depth spelling and grammar knowledge. We missed a lot of deadlines, but we got there in the end!

Many, many, thanks to Rob Siders at 52 Novels for formatting my book so it looks superb for my readers and for me, since I have no idea how to go about doing anything formatting related. You do a great job, and it shows in the finished product.

And lastly, thanks to my dog, Indy, for dragging my butt outside, away from my computer every single day, insisting I come to play. Walks are important, and so are you, my four legged friend.